Once Bitten, Twice Dead

Once Bitten, Twice Dead

BIANCA D'ARC

BRAVA

KENSINGTON PUBLISHING CORP.

www.kensingtonbooks.com

ISBN-13: 978-0-7582-4729-2
ISBN-10: 0-7582-4729-X

First Kensington Trade Paperback Printing: March 2010

10 9 8 7 6 5 4 3 2 1

Printed in the United States of America

Prologue

Somewhere near Stony Brook, Long Island, New York

"Unit Twelve." The dispatcher's voice crackled over the radio.

Sarah perked up. That was her. She listened as the report rolled over the radio. A disturbance in a vacant building out on Wheeler Road, near the big medical center. Probably kids, she thought, responding to Dispatch and turning her patrol car around.

Since the budget cuts, she rolled alone. She hadn't had a partner in a long time, but she was good at her job and confident in her abilities. She could handle a couple of kids messing around in an empty building.

Sarah stepped into the gloomy concrete interior of the building. The metal door hung off its hinges and old boards covered the windows. Broken glass littered the floor and graffiti decorated the walls.

The latest decorators had probably been junkies and kids looking for a secret place to either get high or drink beer where no one could see. As the early Autumn weather grew colder, places like this became more popular. There didn't appear to be anyone home at the moment. They'd probably cleared out in a hurry when they'd seen Sarah's cruiser pull up outside. Still, she had to check the place.

Nightstick in one hand, flashlight in the other, Sarah made her way into the gloom of the building. Electricity was a thing of the past in this place. Light fixtures dangled brokenly from the remnants of a dropped ceiling.

As Sarah advanced into the dark interior, she heard a scurrying sound that could have been footsteps or could have been rodents. Either way, her heart rate sped up.

"Police," she said, identifying herself in a loud, firm voice. "Show yourself."

She directed the flashlight into the corners of the room as she crept inside. The place had a vast outer warehouse-type area with halls and doors leading farther inside the big structure. She didn't really want to go in there but saw no alternative. She decided to advance slowly at first, then zip through the rest of the building, hoping no one got behind her to cut off her retreat.

She had her sidearm, but she'd rather not have to shoot anyone today. Especially not some kids out for a lark. They liked to test their limits and hers. She'd been up against more than one teenage bully who thought because she was a woman, she'd be a pushover. They'd learned the hard way not to mess with Sarah Petit.

She heard that sort of brushing sound again. Her heart raced as adrenaline surged. She'd learned to channel fear into something more useful. Fear became strength if you knew how to use it.

"This is the police," she repeated. "Step into the light."

More shuffling. It sounded like it was coming from down a corridor on the left. Sarah approached, her nightstick at the ready. The flashlight illuminated the corner of the opening, not showing her much. The sounds were growing louder. There was definitely someone—or something—there. Perhaps waiting to ambush her, down that dark hallway.

She wouldn't fall for that. Sarah approached from a good ten feet out, maneuvering so that her flashlight could penetrate farther down the black hall. With each step, more of the corridor became visible to her.

Squinting to see better, Sarah stepped fully in front of the opening to the long hallway. There. Near the end. There was a person standing.

"I'm a police officer. Come out of there immediately." Her voice was firm and as loud as she could project it. The figure at the end of the hallway didn't respond. She couldn't even tell if it was male or female.

It sort of swayed as it tried to move. Maybe a junkie so high he or she was completely out of it? Sarah wasn't sure. She edged closer.

"Are you all right?"

She heard a weird moaning sound. It didn't sound human, but the shape at the end of the long hall was definitely standing on two feet with two arms braced against the wall as if for balance. The inhuman moan came again. It was definitely coming from that shadowy person.

Sarah stepped cautiously closer to the mouth of the hallway. It was about four feet across. Not a lot of room to maneuver in.

She didn't like this setup, but she had to see if that person needed help. Sarah grabbed the radio mic clipped to her shoulder.

"This is Unit Twelve. I'm at the location. There appears to be a person in distress in the interior of the building."

"What kind of distress, Unit Twelve?"

"Uncertain. Subject seems unable to speak. I'm going to get closer to see if I can give you more information."

"Should we dispatch an ambulance?"

Sarah thought about it for a half a second. No matter what, this person would need a medical check. Worst-case scenario, it was a junkie in the throes of a really bad trip.

"Affirmative. Dispatch medical to this location. I'm going to see if I can get the subject to come out, but I may need some backup."

"Dispatching paramedics and another unit to your location. ETA ten minutes on the backup, fifteen on the paramedics."

"Roger that."

With backup and medical help on the way, Sarah felt a little better about taking the next step. She walked even closer to the corridor's mouth. The person was still there, still mostly unrecognizable in the harsh light of the flashlight beam.

"Help is coming," she called to the figure. From its height, she thought it was probably a male. He moved a little closer. Wild hair hung in limp, greasy clumps around his face. It was longer than most men's, but junkies weren't known for their grooming and personal hygiene.

"That's it," she coaxed as the man shuffled forward on unsteady feet. "Come on out of there. Help is on the way. No one's going to hurt you."

Sarah stepped farther into the corridor, just a few feet, hoping to coax the man forward. He was definitely out of it. He made small noises. Sort of grunting, moaning sounds that weren't intelligible. It gave her the creeps, as did the way the man moved. He shuffled like Frankenstein's assistant in those old horror movies, keeping his head down.

This dude had to be on one hell of a bender. Sarah lowered the flashlight beam off his head as he moved closer, trying to get a better look at the rest of him. His clothes were so shredded it looked like he'd been in a fight with a bear—or something else with sharp claws. His shirt hung off him in strips of fabric and his pants weren't much better.

Sarah grew more concerned. He had to be in really bad shape from the look of the blood that had been spilled. She wondered if that was all his blood or if there was another victim lying around here somewhere in even worse shape.

His head was still down as he approached, and Sarah backed up a step. Only as he drew closer did she realize his hair wasn't matted with oil and dirt. It was stuck together by dried blood.

Then he looked up.

Sarah stifled a scream. Half his face was . . . gone. Just gone. It looked like something had gnawed on his flesh. Blank eyes stared out at her from a ruined face. The tip of his nose was missing, as were his lips and the flesh of one side of his jaw and cheek.

Sarah gasped and turned to run, but something came up behind her and tripped her. She fell backward with a resounding *thud*, cracking her skull on the hard cement floor.

She fought against the hands that tried to grab her, but they were too strong, and her head spun from the concussion she'd no doubt just received. She felt sick to her stomach. The adrenaline of fear pushed her to keep going. Keep moving. Get away. Survive until her backup arrived.

Thank God she'd already called for backup.

Not one, but two men—if she could call them that—were holding her down. The one with the ruined face had her feet and the other had hold of her arms, even as she struggled against him.

She looked into the first one's eyes and saw . . . nothing. They were blank. No emotion. No feeling. No nothing.

Fear clutched her heart in its icy grip. Her flashlight had rolled to the side but was still on, lancing into the darkness of the building's interior nearby. Faint light shone on her two assailants. The second man looked wild.

They both looked like something out of a horror movie. The one from the hallway was by far the more gruesome of the two, but the one who wrestled with her arms was frightening, too. His skin was cold to the touch and it looked almost gray, though she couldn't be sure in the uncertain light. Neither spoke, but both made those inhuman moaning sounds.

As she kicked and struggled she felt teeth rip into her thigh. Sarah screamed for all she was worth as the first man broke through her skin and blood welled. The second man dove onto her prone form, knocking her flat and bashing her head on the concrete a second time. Stunned, she was still aware when his teeth sank into her shoulder.

She was going to die here. Eaten alive by these cannibals.

Something inside Sarah rebelled at the thought. No way in hell was she going down like this.

Help was on the way. All she had to do was hold on until her backup arrived. She could do that. She *had* to do that.

Channeling the adrenaline, Sarah ignored the pain and kicked the man off her legs. She bucked like a crazy woman, dislodging the first man.

Once her legs were free, she used them to leverage her upper body at an angle, forcing the second man to move. The slight change in position freed one of her hands. She grasped around for anything on the floor next to her and came up with a hard, cylindrical object. Her nightstick.

Praise the Lord.

Putting all her remaining strength behind it, she aimed for the man's head, raining blows down on him with the stick. When that didn't work, she changed targets, whacking at his body with the hard wood of the stick. She heard a few of the bones in his hand crack at one point, but this guy was tough. Nothing seemed to faze him.

Finally, she used the pointy end of the stick to push at his neck. That seemed to get some results and he shifted away. He moved enough for her to use the rest of her body for leverage to crawl out from under him.

His friend was up and coming back as she crab-walked away on her hands and feet, toward the door and the sunshine beyond.

The two men followed her, moving as if they had all the time in the world. Their pace was steady and measured as she crawled as fast as she could. It didn't make any sense. They could have easily overtaken her, but they kept to their slow, walking pace.

Sarah hit the door and practically threw herself over the threshold. She had to get out in the open where her backup would see her right away. She was losing blood fast and her vision was dancing, tunneling down to a single dim spot. She was going to pass out any second. She had to do all she could to save herself before that happened.

Backup was coming. That thought kept her going. They'd be here any second. She just had to hold on.

She crawled into the sunlight, near her cruiser. Leaning against the side of her car, she tried for her radio, but the mic was long gone—probably a victim of the struggle with those two men. They were coming for her. They had to be.

But when she looked up, she saw them hesitate at the doorway to the building. The second man stepped through, but the first stayed behind, cowering in the darkness. He looked like some kind of walking corpse, with grisly brown stains of dried blood all around his mouth and on his clothes. Some of it was bright red. That was *her* blood—from where the sick bastard had bitten her.

The man walked calmly forward, under the trees that shaded the walkway to the old building. Sarah had parked on the street, out in open sun. She watched in dread as the man walked steadily toward her, death in his flat gaze.

Then something odd happened. He stopped where the tree cover ended. He seemed reluctant to step into the sun.

Sarah blinked, refocusing, but there wasn't any other explanation for his hesitation she could think of. Then she heard the sound of an approaching vehicle. Her backup.

With salvation in sight, she finally passed out.

USSOCOM Commander's Office,
MacDill Air Force Base, Tampa, Florida
The next day

"Commander Sykes, reporting as ordered." Matt stood at crisp attention waiting for the admiral to acknowledge his presence.

"At ease, Commander. Have a seat." The busy admiral pointed to a chair in front of his giant mahogany desk and pulled a red folder from a stack on his desk. It sailed through the air toward Matt and he grabbed it in a purely reflex action. "Read that while I finish signing these orders. Note the security level. It's eyes only, Commander. Understand?"

"Yes, sir."

Whatever this was, it couldn't be good. Matt had met with this terse admiral only once before, when he'd been called down to MacDill unexpectedly to interface with some Army Special Forces officers. Admiral Nealy was the current head of the unified Special Operations Command that got involved whenever the special ops groups from different branches of the armed forces needed to work together.

Matt was still working on the mission this man had tasked him with at their first meeting. Matt's normal duty station was Quantico, Virginia, but lately he'd been spending most of his time in Fayetteville, North Carolina. He'd been at Fort Bragg for the past week, helping some Army Rangers deal with an unexpected problem he'd seen before. Everything had been going reasonably well until this morning when he'd been rousted out of bed at 0-dark-thirty and pushed onto a cargo plane heading south. It had spit him out here at MacDill where an attaché was waiting at the airstrip to escort him directly to the admiral's office. No waiting in line. No appointment necessary.

This couldn't be good, he thought again. A feeling of foreboding invaded his mind.

Matt opened the folder and scanned the single sheet of paper it contained. Oddly enough, it was a police report from Suffolk County, New York. A report that sounded all too familiar.

No, not good at all.

"What do you make of it?" The admiral had finished with his paperwork and was looking at Matt expectantly when he finished reading.

"Sir, I think we have another flare-up on our hands."

The admiral's expression turned even grimmer. "That's what I thought, too. You'll have to send someone to check it out. Who can you spare?"

Nobody, Matt thought. They needed every single soul they had to fight the problem in North Carolina. They were spread too thin as it was. But this couldn't go uninvestigated. He had to find someone. . . .

"Captain Beauvoir is probably our best bet. He has enough rank and experience to run an op with little supervision, and he's learned fast since being released from the hospital. I'd say he's our man to look into this potential problem."

"All right." The admiral scrawled Beauvoir's name into the empty space on the set of orders he'd been signing when Matt arrived. "I want you to keep track of both operations. Beauvoir will report directly to you. He can pick a small team from among those who've been briefed but not rated to work in the field. If this really is another outbreak, I want this contained quietly. Impress that upon the captain."

"Aye-aye, sir."

"Now, while I have you here, give me a sitrep on the situation at Bragg."

Matt spent the next half hour talking with an admiral he never would have known, if not for the colossal screwup at Quantico a few months ago. His life had taken a turn for the decidedly strange, and his career was going places he'd never expected because of it.

Being at the wrong place at the right time had given an otherwise normal career a boost. He now had expertise on something so top secret only a few people in the world knew about it. And Matt was rubbing elbows in the stratosphere of not just the navy brass but the marine corps and now the army as well. Not to mention the political aspects. He'd been given his initial orders directly from the president herself.

Nothing had been normal since the first outbreak. Matt had thought it was all over, then he'd gotten the call about Fort Bragg. Now this.

Matt was truly worried. It seemed more and more like this nightmare was only just beginning.

Chapter One

Sarah woke with a pounding headache. Little jackhammers were beating against the inside of her skull, and her eyes didn't want to open. The fog in her brain lifted all at once and she gasped. Was she safe?

She forced her eyes open and a beeping sound interrupted her panic. She was lying in a hospital bed, and the beeping came from a machine to her right. The pace of the sound had increased as her heart rate began to spike higher and adrenaline hit her system.

She was safe. No need to panic.

A doctor moved hurriedly into the room. "You're awake," he said.

Sarah had to wonder why he sounded so surprised.

"Did they get them?" Her voice was a croak of sound that made her headache even worse, but she had to know.

The doctor looked confused. "Did who get who?" He didn't wait for her to answer. Instead he moved closer and took her hand. "Can you squeeze my fingers?"

Of course she could squeeze his damn fingers. She proved it, making him wince. What she really wanted to know was if they'd gotten the . . . creatures, or whatever they were, who'd done this to her.

"Good." The man slipped his hand out of hers. "How are you feeling?"

"Concussion, right?"

Again, he seemed surprised. "As a matter of fact, yes. I assume your head hurts. How about the rest of you?"

The rest of her? What was he getting at? Sarah assumed the doctor would be more interested in the condition of her skull than anything else. Apparently, she was wrong.

"Aches and pains. Nothing major. Can you give me anything for the headache?" She squinted against the bright hospital lighting. "And can you shut off some of the lights?"

The doctor seemed to consider her for a moment, then walked over to the wall where there was a dimmer switch. He lowered the light level, sending blessed relief straight into her brain.

"Thanks." She sighed as the pain diminished.

"Now, can you tell me more about your condition? Where else do you have pain other than your head?"

He was looking at her like she was a bug under a microscope. Sarah didn't like the feeling at all, and the dude gave her the creeps.

"I ache all over. Everything hurts. Sort of a generalized pain." She didn't know what this guy wanted from her. "How long was I out? Did they catch the kids?"

"Kids?" His eyebrows rose.

"Had to be. I mean, what else could it have been but a couple of kids in Halloween makeup?"

"You saw them?" The doctor seemed a little too interested in her response.

"Yeah, but not well. It was dark inside and I lost hold of my flashlight pretty early on," she hedged. Some instinct for self-preservation was telling her to tread lightly where this guy was concerned. He made her uneasy, but she couldn't figure out why.

She looked him over, committing his image to memory. Something about this guy wasn't on the level. Trapped in a hospital bed with all kinds of wires stuck to her body, she wasn't in any position to do much about it, but she'd remember his face at least. If and when the time came, she'd be able to give a good description of him.

He seemed to bristle under her scrutiny. His hands clenched and unclenched in a staccato rhythm, a sure sign of nervousness.

"I need to draw some blood for more testing." He came closer, pulling a needle from the big front pocket on his white lab coat.

Sarah tried to sit up but was still too weak to go that far. "Why? It's just a concussion. I'm not sick."

"Nevertheless"—the man was now hovering over her— "you need a few tests in case of infection. That building they found you in couldn't have been very clean."

Now she knew this guy was full of it. If he'd been at all familiar with her case, he'd know she'd been found outside, near her patrol car, not inside the building. She didn't see any reason for blood tests and she didn't like the idea of this man poking needles into her. Who knew what he could be injecting her with? There was no way she could tell if there was already liquid in the chamber of the syringe. For all she knew, he could be trying to drug her . . . or worse.

"Doctor, I really do have to object. I got a bump on the head, not malaria." She tried to make a joke of it but he wasn't laughing. Neither was she as she backed as far away from the menacing man as she could.

Movement at the door. A nurse walked in carrying a clipboard. She was wearing a face mask and looked at the man in surprise over the edge of the cloth that hid her nose and mouth.

"I'm sorry, Doctor. This room has been put under quarantine. Didn't you see the sign? You'll have to leave." Her voice was both firm and puzzled.

"By whose authority? This is ridiculous! I'm going to have a few words with the chief of staff."

The doctor—if he really was a doctor—seemed to want to bluff his way out. Sarah wasn't buying it, but the nurse hesitated, her expression uncertain. That was all the opening the man needed to get himself out of the room. He pocketed the syringe and swept past the flustered nurse, muttering about incompetence and putting her on report.

The nurse dropped her clipboard into a slot at the foot of Sarah's bed and looked at her. "I'm sorry about that. It's good to see you're finally awake. We called Dr. Singh the moment we noticed you stir. I don't know why that other doctor was in here. The army ordered the quarantine and things have been crazy since they showed up. How are you feeling? Headache?"

The woman could certainly babble with the best of them, Sarah thought. At least she was asking the right questions as she pulled a penlight out of her pocket and checked Sarah's pupils. But why was the army involved? What in the world was going on here?

First things first. Sarah submitted to the woman's fussing, answering her questions.

"Bad headache," Sarah reported. It felt a lot worse after being stabbed with the beam from the nurse's penlight.

"That's to be expected. You were out for quite a while. Dr. Singh is our top neurologist. He's been concerned that you were unconscious so long, but the others seemed to think it was to be expected."

"What others? I have more than one doctor?" Sarah had a hard time following the nurse's chatter. "How long was I out?"

The woman stopped moving to look at her. "Almost a week, dear. You were brought in last Tuesday. Today is Monday."

"You're kidding." It felt like she had blacked out just a few minutes ago, although there had to have been time to get her from the scene to the hospital. She'd expected the nurse to say an hour or two, but almost a week? It didn't seem possible.

"Sorry. It really has been almost a week. I guess it probably feels like a lot less to you, huh?" The woman looked kindly at her. The door opened and a dark-haired man in a white coat and face mask entered. "Here's Dr. Singh now. He can tell you more."

The nurse moved aside to let the doctor examine her.

"Hello. I am Dr. Singh, head of neurology." He used his

own penlight to check her pupils, then looked at the readouts on the machines at her bedside before turning back to her.

Sarah didn't have time to acknowledge him as he bustled about. The introduction seemed a mere formality to him, to which he didn't expect a reply.

"You're doing well. How are you feeling?" The man was abrupt, with a thick accent. Sarah liked his no-nonsense approach.

"My head hurts. Muscles ache a bit. I won't be running a marathon anytime soon, but I'm okay."

"Good."

While he'd been talking, a few more white-coated people had entered the room. They formed a line near the wall, and she realized then that she was in a single room that seemed a lot larger than the average hospital cell. Everyone wore masks and at least one of the men in back wore camouflage fatigues under an oversized lab coat that wasn't buttoned, with a distinctive bulge under one shoulder. He was armed. Now, wasn't that interesting.

What the hell had she stumbled into?

"Who was the other guy? I take it he wasn't with you." She looked pointedly around the room, making eye contact with the armed man as he stepped forward. Concern was written clearly on his face.

"What other guy?" His voice rolled over her, smooth and faintly accented.

"The doctor who came in when I first woke." She looked over at the nurse. "She saw him."

The nurse looked flustered. "I didn't recognize him and he wasn't wearing containment gear. He left right before you arrived."

"Seal the ward," the man in the camo pants ordered, and two men scurried out of the room to fulfill his command. "Nurse . . ." He seemed to search for her name tag.

"Aspen. Hillary Aspen, R.N.," she supplied.

"Nurse Aspen"—he seemed to make an effort to charm the

woman, or maybe it just came naturally to him—"I'd like you to go with Sam over there and tell him what this other doctor looked like. If you see the doctor in the corridor, I want you to tell Sam and no one else. Okay?"

The nurse visibly gulped. "All right."

She allowed herself to be ushered out of the room with Sam, who'd been among the people standing in back. They were down to three now: the man who seemed to be in charge, another man who wore what looked like a perpetual frown, and a woman who just looked frightened.

Dr. Singh examined her skull with his fingers, then reached for her chart to make a notation. He took a moment to study a few pages in the chart before turning back to her.

"You should progress well from here. I was concerned that you remained unconscious so long, but my colleagues seem to think that might have been caused by other factors. Regardless, your head appears to be coming along nicely."

The man's thick accent made it hard to follow his rapid speech, but from the satisfied look on his face she gathered that she was doing okay. He dropped the chart back into the holder and abruptly left the room.

Dr. Singh didn't have the greatest bedside manner. That was for sure.

The man in charge—the one in camo—moved closer. His eyes were a whiskey shade of brown and focused on her as if she were the most fascinating thing in the world. Sarah knew she looked like hell. Such a shame, when she was faced with such a handsome specimen of manhood. Even with the mask obscuring his face and the shapeless lab coat hiding his true form, she could tell there was something special about this man.

He nearly crackled with power. He had a presence about him. She had no doubt he was used to being in command.

"Who are you?" The question slipped out before she could censor herself.

"Captain Xavier Beauvoir, U.S. Army, at your service, ma'am." He took off the face mask, much to the surprise of the others in the room. It looped over his ears, and the significance of the Green Beret attached to his belt, visible through the open front of his lab coat, wasn't lost on her. This guy was Special Forces. What in the world had she stumbled into? She wondered again.

"Aren't you afraid I'm contagious?" She looked pointedly at the others who still wore their masks.

"Darlin', there's not much in this world I'm afraid of. What's a few little germs among fellow defenders of the innocent?"

"Defenders of the innocent"? Was he flirting with her? The sparkle in those whiskey eyes, the warmth in his tone and the teasing lilt of his words made it seem like he was. Was the guy nuts?

"You're a cop. I'm a soldier. We protect and serve. Each in our own way."

She thought about it for a moment and had to concede his point.

"So what brings a U.S. Army Green Beret to my hospital room with a team of doctors?"

His expression closed up. Like a door slamming shut. "Why don't we let the docs do their thing, and then I'll tell you everything I can. I also want to hear your take on what happened to you. Deal?"

Grimacing as her head began to pound again, Sarah nodded. "All right."

"Just one more thing. Did that first doctor try anything? What did he say to you?"

"He seemed more interested in the rest of me than my poor, aching head. He asked repeatedly how I felt aside from the headache. And he wanted a blood sample."

"Did he get it?" The question snapped from him like a whip.

"No. Nurse Aspen arrived in the nick of time. I asked him why he wanted a blood sample for a concussion, and his answer was vague and not very convincing."

The soldier's lips thinned to a compressed line. He was annoyed and pensive. Her instincts had been on the money. That first doctor wasn't supposed to have been in here. Though why the army was so interested in her case, she had yet to understand.

"Can you describe him?"

"Caucasian, five ten, clean-cut, black hair, dark brown eyes. White lab coat, white dress shirt with a button-down collar, khaki pants, worn-in dark brown boat shoes and manicured hands."

The soldier looked impressed. "That's the nice part about working with a police officer. You're way more observant than a civilian. I'll have some photos to show you later. I assume you'd recognize his face?"

"Of course."

"Good." He moved back. "I'll get out of here so the doctors can do their thing. See you later, Officer Petit." He winked at her and left the room.

She hadn't been winked at since she was a little girl, but somehow this guy got away with it. She had to stifle a smile as he walked out of the room. The sexy soldier had a really nice smile and his accent was drool-worthy, not to mention his chiseled features. He was definitely too sexy for his shirt. Problem was, he knew it.

Sarah had dated a guy like that once. He'd been a fellow officer, back when she was a rookie. Good-looking and charming, Rob had spent a lot of time admiring his own muscles as he worked out each morning in the gym. She'd fallen for his practiced lines and killer smile, and had the scars on her heart to prove it. Since then, she'd stayed away from the handsome brutes who populated the gym and attracted aerobics groupies like flies on dung. Give her a normal guy who didn't spend more time on his appearance than she did, and she was happy.

Of course, even those kinds of guys were growing thinner on the ground the older she grew. Sarah hadn't dated much in the past year and she hadn't been really serious about anyone in longer than that. She was devoted to her work and her small garden. She had a quiet life staked out for herself, although she missed having a man in her life, and the social activities that went along with dating. She didn't get out much.

The handsome soldier whose voice dripped with sinful invitation could save his winks and flirtatious banter for someone who was interested. Yes, sir. Sarah didn't want any part of him. Of course, it couldn't hurt to look. And he did have a really nice, tight butt.

Sarah spent the next forty-five minutes being examined by two of the doctors. These legitimate doctors had extensive paperwork on her already, in addition to that in her chart on the clipboard at the foot of her bed. These doctors tested each and every one of her joints, checking her reflexes, and asked detailed questions about specific items.

They also told her details about her progress. They let her know what had been done to her over the time she'd been out of it. The only thing they didn't talk about was her head, but she assumed the concussion was Dr. Singh's specialty, and he was long gone.

About the time she was starting to get annoyed with the medical jargon and all the poking and prodding, the door opened and Studly the Soldier came strolling back in. He hadn't replaced his mask and the lab coat was gone. Hubba-hubba. He certainly filled out those camo fatigues of his. She admired his physique even as she caught him giving her bare legs a thorough once-over while the doctors finished examining her calves, ankles and feet.

When they covered her again with the blanket, Xavier's gaze roamed upward to meet hers. A hint of a grin lifted one side of his sensuous mouth. He knew damn well she'd caught him ogling her, and his expression said he didn't much care. Yeah, he was definitely a scoundrel. She'd have to watch herself around him.

"So what about the bite?" Sarah refocused her attention on the doctors. They'd talked about every bruise and contusion on her body but hadn't mentioned the bite yet.

The doctors drew back and looked at each other, then at

Xavier. Neither of the medical personnel said anything for a long moment.

"It's all right." Xavier stepped up to her bedside as he spoke. "I'll take it from here. Why don't you two go back down to the lab?"

The two doctors followed the soldier's orders without further comment and left the room.

"Alone at last," Xavier joked as the door shut behind the doctors.

"I'm waiting for answers, Captain Beauvoir."

"Straight to business, eh? Okay, I guess we can do that. You've been out for a week. You've earned some straight talk. But let me ask you one question first." He leaned against the side of her bed, cocking one hip in an unconsciously sexy pose. "How much do you remember of the incident?"

"All of it," she answered without hesitation. "I remember the guy down the hall and his buddy who snuck up behind me."

His eyes narrowed. "There were two of them?"

"Definitely." His surprise told her they hadn't caught the guys.

"Maybe you'd better tell me what happened in that building before your backup arrived."

"I'll tell you, but then I want some answers, Captain. I don't understand why the army is involved in this, unless the perps were yours somehow." She was willing to play his game . . . to a point.

"You'll have your answers, Officer Petit." Oddly enough, she believed him. "First, I'd like to hear exactly what happened out there."

She told him the sequence of events with as much detail as she could put in without editorializing. She didn't talk about the way the perps had looked. She'd tell him if he asked, but she chalked up her impressions of gruesome monsters to an overactive imagination paired with makeup and special effects. Why the perps had been wearing it, she still couldn't fathom.

"What about their appearance?" Xavier asked. His gaze

told her nothing. When he wanted, he could be as stone-faced as any seasoned law officer.

She had to tell him, even though it would sound strange. She sighed heavily before replying, dreading his reaction.

"They had to have been wearing makeup. Special effects of some kind. The first one looked as if half his face had been gnawed off. The second one wasn't so bad, but his skin was gray."

"Give me details on the first one, if you can. What parts of his face were missing?"

He was humoring her. Either that or he was dead serious about wanting her to describe the makeup. But why would he bother to take notes on makeup when something like that could change with the swipe of a towel?

"Like I said, I only saw the first perp from a distance. By the time he was on top of me, the second one had me down on the ground and I lost the flashlight. It still gave off a dim glow, but it didn't shine directly on them." She suppressed a shudder, thinking back on how they'd looked and how it had felt to be helpless against them, her head swimming in pain, adrenaline spiking her fear and the weak flashlight beam making their theatrics seem all too real. The darkness made her unsure of what she'd really seen.

"Describe what you can of his wounds."

"He was made up to look like the tip of his nose and lips were gone. One side of his face was hollowed out, as if his cheek were missing, and there were what looked like teeth marks all around the wounds. There were also brown stains on the edges of skin and on his clothes like dried blood. And he stank like rotting flesh."

"But the second man had none of the disfigurement?" Xavier seemed very interested, almost clinical in his questioning.

"The second guy looked okay. All his features were intact, but he also had the brown stains around his mouth and down the front of his shirt. Like I said, his skin was gray, and it had a powdery sheen and he smelled as bad as the first guy. I don't think either of them had bathed in weeks, but it was more than that. They must've augmented their natural stink with something else. It stank of death."

"Which one bit you?"

"Both, actually. The first one had my feet and he chomped on my thigh. The second perp held my arms and bit me on the shoulder." She raised the arm that wasn't hooked to the IV and gestured toward her opposite shoulder.

She couldn't see it, but she assumed there was a small bandage there, unless in the week she'd been out the bite had healed sufficiently for them to forego covering it. It didn't feel sore when she moved, so maybe the bite hadn't been as bad as she'd thought. She didn't feel the tug of a bulky bandage, but it could be a small one she wouldn't necessarily feel. The doctors had looked closely at her thigh, blocking her view as they unwrapped the dressing, then rewrapped it with a little less gauze. It didn't really hurt.

In fact, she was starting to feel better the more she talked. The longer she was awake and alert, the more her head ceased to pound. That was weird. She would've expected the exact opposite, but she wasn't a doctor, so what did she know?

"Now that I've given you what you wanted, how about telling me what this is all about?" She didn't want to think about those men . . . creatures . . . anymore. She wanted some answers. "Were those jokers yours?"

"Yes and no." He flipped his little notebook closed and stowed it in a pocket along with his pen. "First of all, you need to know that everything you saw was real. That wasn't makeup or special effects."

He paused, probably to let those startling words sink in.

"You're kidding, right? No way was that real. I mean, it had me fooled at the time, but with a little perspective I can't believe any of that was legit."

"You should." His eyes narrowed. "You are one of only a handful of people to have survived being infected with a contagion inadvertently developed by a team of military scientists. They were trying to do something good—creating a biological substance that would induce rapid healing of battlefield injuries—but something went wrong. Really wrong. The dead marines they were testing the substance on became reanimated and started attacking others. The brass thought they'd handled the problem and disbanded the team of scientists, but in the months since that first incident, there have been two known flare-ups. One at the army base where I was stationed until last week and here, on Long Island."

"No way." She had to stifle a giggle. He was nuts if he thought she was buying any of his bull.

The captain straightened and rested his hands on his utility belt. "We've traced the outbreaks to members of the scientific team. They apparently broke their agreement with the government to drop this line of research and have been working independently. The creatures you saw were very real, Officer Petit, and very deadly. Like you, I survived being bitten. The substance actually did what it was supposed to and gave me quick healing abilities. I'm here to contain this outbreak and eradicate the threat."

Yeah, right. Next he'd be telling her martians were about to land on the hospital roof. She stared him down, waiting for the truth.

Chapter Two

"What?" He didn't like the way she was staring at him. "I'm trying to figure out which one of the X-Men you think you are."

He couldn't believe it. This woman refused to take anything he said seriously.

"I mean, the one with superhealing ability is supposed to be the guy with the blades in his hands, but the Cajun-accent guy is the hottie with the playing cards. And then you said your name is Xavier, and I figure you're the head honcho. So which is it?"

He gave her a long, disgusted sigh. This woman was a hard case. "None of the above. Like I said, I'm Captain Xavier Beauvoir, with the U.S. Army Green Berets. I was sent up here to check on reports of a possible zombie problem."

She burst out laughing, clearly mocking him.

"Are you one of those science fiction guys from the university? I know I gave some of your conventioneers a hard time last year, but they really were disturbing the peace. Lightsaber battles on Main Street at four a.m. aren't something we ignore around here."

"For the last time, this is no joke. You were bitten—do you know what that means?" His voice rose along with his anger.

"What? Did the guys have rabies?"

Her smart mouth was just begging to be kissed.

Now, where the hell did that thought come from? Xavier pushed it aside. He had to stop thinking about how gorgeous she was and concentrate on how annoying she was.

"Not rabies." He ran his hands through his hair in frustration. "A contagion designed and developed under auspices of the U.S. Navy. It was meant to boost natural healing, but in ninety-nine percent of those who've been infected, the test agent is lethal. You're one of the very lucky few to have survived, Officer Petit. If you hadn't had natural immunity working for you, you'd have died. Then your corpse would have been reanimated by the contagion. You'd have been just like that poor soul who attacked you."

"So, worse than rabies."

Clearly she still didn't believe him.

"What will it take to convince you I'm on the level?"

She pretended to think. "I doubt there's anything you can say that will make me believe some cockamamie story about zombies running around on Long Island."

"How about the fact that if the contagion did what it was supposed to do in your system, you will heal just as fast as me?" He rolled up the sleeve of his camo shirt and pulled a knife out of his boot. She scooted back in the bed, her eyes wide.

"What the hell are you doing?"

"Watch and learn, sweetheart." He didn't even flinch as he ran the tip of the sharp blade over his forearm. Blood welled in the shallow cut, but then something miraculous happened. His skin started to knit together right before her eyes.

"Holy cow," she breathed, looking from the healing cut to his face and back again. In a matter of seconds, the shallow cut was only a thin red line. He used one big thumb to wipe away some of the blood and she saw even the red line begin to fade.

"Seeing is believing, isn't it?"

She wasn't prepared to go that far just yet. "Was that some

kind of trick? You got a latex prop on your arm or something? Special effects?"

"Sorry, darling. Just my flesh and bones. No titanium on my skeleton, either, in case you were wondering."

He winked at her and she caught the teasing reference to her earlier crack about the X-Men.

"Let me see your arm, then," she dared him. But he moved closer, holding out his arm for her inspection.

"Careful of the blood. I'm clean as a whistle—the docs monitor me closely since the bite—but it's still frowned on nowadays to be touching other people's blood without a mask and gloves."

She studied his arm, not touching the blood, but she'd be damned if she could see any kind of trickery. Her stomach felt hollow as his words began to take hold. Maybe he wasn't crazy after all.

"Did they put my things in the closet?"

He seemed surprised by her question but went to check, opening the door to the small closet opposite her bed. She saw that some of her clothes and gear had been put in there, minus her firearms, of course.

"Would you mind bringing my utility belt over here?"

He didn't say anything as he picked up the heavy black leather belt and brought it to her. It was still loaded with most of her gear. She sought and found what she was looking for— a small box cutter.

"Hey now . . ." He seemed ready to try to stop her.

"I'm testing your theory. If what you say is true, the same thing will happen to me, right?"

He seemed cautious. "It should. As I told you, there are only a handful of people who've survived to tell the tale after being infected. So far, all have the speed-healing thing. It's likely you will, too."

He folded his arms and leaned one hip against her bedside, down by her feet. He stood back, and his body language said he was prepared to let her do what she wanted. She liked that. He wasn't trying to pressure her either way.

Holding her breath, she ran the sharp blade over her forearm. The cut was even shallower than the one he'd made. She didn't want to do any real damage in case this guy really was a fruitcake. A thin line of blood welled in the shallow cut, then healed over. She wiped at the blood to find the cut, but it didn't exist.

Damn. She tried again, making a shorter, deeper incision. It hurt like hell, but only for a moment. Then the healing began.

"It feels warm and kind of tingly," she said aloud, cataloging the sensations.

Xavier nodded. "Does that for me, too. You want to take a look at your shoulder? There's no bite mark up there. That's why we didn't realize you'd been attacked by two of them." He opened the drawer in the bedside table and took out a small mirror. She took it with wide eyes.

He was on the level. She'd been attacked by . . . zombies. He'd called them *zombies*. Damn.

She tugged at the collar of her hospital gown, exposing her shoulder, then held up the mirror in her free hand. The other hand was attached to the IV and immobilized. Looking at her reflection, she was shocked to find her neck and shoulder were blemish free. Nothing marred her skin, not even a red mark. She lowered the mirror to her lap and reached to touch her shoulder, examining her skin with her fingers.

Nothing. Not a raised bump. Not a depression where a scar had formed. Nothing. It was as if she'd never been harmed, never been bitten.

"He sank his teeth into me right here." She rubbed the spot absently. "I thought they were trying to eat me. The other one—" She broke off, remembering the pain in her thigh. Her gaze shot to the army captain. "The other one took a bite out of my leg, didn't he?"

Gravely, Xavier nodded. "It's repairing itself, but he got a piece of you. The docs are watching it closely. The skin and muscle are growing back at a really fast rate."

Sarah felt queasy. Just the idea that someone—some*thing*,

really—had eaten her flesh made her want to barf. She took deep breaths, trying to calm her racing heart and uncertain stomach. Only one thing really mattered now.

"Did you catch them?"

Xavier straightened, all business once more. "Not yet. For one thing, until you woke up, we could only guess at what went on in that building. We assumed only one assailant. Now we know that one is making others."

"Making others?" The thought sent shivers down her spine.

"The first man you saw. The one with the disfigured face. That's a classic sign of someone who's been attacked by one of these creatures. The victim is infected with the contagion and dies. A few hours later, his corpse rises and starts attacking others. For whatever reason, these creatures like to bite and infect more people, though they don't seem capable of speech or other higher brain functions."

"What's with the claws?" Both of the perps had abnormally long, sharp, yellow fingernails that had scratched her skin.

"Something about the way they die and regenerate on a cellular level. The science team explained it better than I can. From what I recall, inert cells like those in fingernails and toenails respond differently to the contagion. Hair, too. All the zombies I've seen had hair that was at least a few inches longer than when they'd died. The nails seem to lengthen by at least an inch as well. They get thicker and turn yellow. Those things can do some serious damage to unprotected skin." His face tightened as if in painful memory. "After being exposed to the contagion, they're not human anymore."

"The perps made a sort of moaning sound," she said, remembering. "It sounded like a sick cat or some kind of wild animal. It didn't sound human at all."

"I've heard it. Chills you to your bones, doesn't it?"

They shared a moment of commiseration until she got back on track, out of the fog of frightening memory.

"So what now? How do we catch them?"

Xavier eyed her strangely for a moment, then relaxed. "Ordinarily, I'd tell you that your part is done and I'd handle it from here." She was about to object when he held up his hand, palm outward to forestall her. "That's ordinarily. But as you can imagine, this situation is far from ordinary. For one thing, you are now the only one, outside of a few military personnel, who has been proven immune to the contagion. In fact, I'm the only one they could spare to investigate this incident. Now that we have confirmation it's a zombie infestation, I've been assigned to solve the problem as I see fit. I think you can be instrumental in helping me fulfill my mission. For another thing, you're a highly trained officer of the law. You know how to shoot and how to be cool under pressure. I've seen your file and your fitness reports. Your superiors speak highly of you and your abilities. I'm inclined to believe them."

He gave her a little nod of guarded respect. She interpreted it to mean he was willing to give her the benefit of the doubt, within reason.

"And since you're immune, that, more than anything, makes you qualified to go after these guys. Are you willing to help?"

"Willing?" She couldn't believe he was asking. "Of course I'm willing."

"Hold on a minute there and think about your answer. It would mean facing a bunch of zombies, more than likely, with the full knowledge of what they are and what they can do. If they manage to trap you, they'll eat you, and because of your immunity, you won't have the mercy of dying quick."

The queasiness in her stomach returned at his words, but he wouldn't scare her off that easily. If she was one of the few people who could hunt these creatures without fear of turning into one of them, she had to help. It was her duty.

"I'm in." She managed a tight nod.

Xavier gave her a sexy grin. "I was hoping you'd say that. As soon as they spring you from this joint, we'll go back to the building where you were attacked. I'll want you to walk me through what happened. We'll start there. Sound good?"

"Sounds like a plan. I assume you'll square all this with my chain of command?"

"Already done."

That lopsided smile of his threatened to make her mouth water. He was altogether too appealing for her peace of mind.

"You were that sure of my answer?" She couldn't help but be amused by his overconfidence.

"In my experience, lady warriors are often fiercer than some of their male counterparts. I know what your fellow officers think of you. I would have been disappointed if you'd shied away from this challenge." He winked and sauntered toward the door, turning to speak as he grasped the doorknob in one hand. "I'll be back in the morning. The docs will want to keep you for study, but it's more important to stop the creatures before the contagion spreads. Innocent people will die unless we go out and end this as quickly as possible."

"You'll get no argument from me."

"Good. I'll see you around 0700. Rest up." He paused as if remembering something. "Your friend Terry came to visit but we couldn't let her in. Likewise, your dad and brothers have been asked to leave you be for now. You can call them if you like, but you're not to give them any specifics about your condition or what happened to you. If they ask—and I'm sure they will—just tell them it's a matter of national security."

"Oh, they're going to love that." Her tone was sarcastic enough to make him smile.

"I talked to Terry. She said she was looking after your place and had a key to your house. I asked her to bring a clean uniform and some other stuff. It's in the closet. I hope that's okay with you. Even though you'll be working on my team, it's better if you're outfitted in your official gear for now."

"I prefer it, actually. Thanks for thinking ahead." She was touched by both his words and his tone. He seemed more human in that moment, displaying a capacity for thoughtfulness she wouldn't have expected.

He gave her a sketchy salute. "It's part of my job, Sarah. I'll be back in a few hours. Get some sleep."

He left without further words, and only then did she look out the window and realize it was nighttime. There was a clock on the table next to her bed. Its glowing numerals told her it was close to midnight. He must've been waiting for her to wake. Who knew how long he'd kept vigil in the halls of the hospital. The thought gave her pause and caused a warm glow to begin somewhere in the region of her heart.

She'd been alone a long time. Oh, she had her family, but her dad and brothers tried to smother her at times and disapproved of her choice of profession. Her mother had died a long time ago, so Sarah had almost always been the odd woman out in a house full of overbearing males. She placed the inevitable phone call to her dad and spent a good part of the next hour reassuring him that she was all right.

As she had predicted, her dad didn't take well to the national security argument, but as a retired New York City police detective, he understood when some things had to be kept under wraps. He wasn't happy by any stretch of the imagination, and he kept asking subtle questions to get her to give him more details. He was a skilled interrogator, but his daughter had picked up a few things from him over the years. She didn't reveal any more than she had to.

After the challenging phone call to her dad, she made another quick call to Terry. Her best friend and neighbor was a lot like her. Terry worked long hours at her research job, and they got together a few times a month to share dinner or go out shopping together. That was the extent of Sarah's social life at the moment. It was kind of pitiful, actually, but it was her life.

Sarah sat awake in her bed, thinking for a while, but eventually she drifted off to sleep. Seven o'clock came early and she wanted to be ready.

At seven sharp, Xavier tapped on Sarah's door. He wasn't surprised to hear her chipper voice telling him to enter. As he'd expected, she was already awake, dressed in her uniform and ready to go. All he had to do now was get her past the phalanx of doctors who no doubt wanted to keep her under their microscopes.

Xavier wouldn't allow that to happen. A set of doctors had tried to make him a prisoner of their medical ward, too, but had been overruled by his superior's need for him to be out in the field, fighting the monsters some of their colleagues had created. No way was he going to become a human pincushion, being stuck by needles every five minutes, his life lived at the pleasure of a bunch of pencil-necked geeks in white lab coats.

He didn't want that for Sarah, either. She was too good at her job. Everyone he'd talked to about her had the same high opinion of her skills, personality and dedication to her duty. She couldn't help being bitten by a nightmare creature any more than he could have. She didn't deserve to have her life turned upside down by a medical community that was as guilty as sin, as far as Xavier was concerned. They'd created this menace.

His brother Special Forces soldiers had ended it once before. Now the damn scientists had moved on and were taking their terror with them, unleashing it on an unsuspecting populace. Even though they'd been prohibited by the government and had sworn all kinds of vows to drop this line of research under penalty of death. Despite all that, the greedy bastards were pursuing something they knew was dangerous. As far as Xavier was concerned, that went beyond stupidity into downright insane hubris. The original project had used an experimental viral agent to try to make soldiers more resistant to disease. An expected byproduct had been the speed healing, that he and Sarah had experienced firsthand. The experimental substance—the contagion—actually worked on them the way it had been designed. But they were rare. In the vast majority of people, the contagion killed them quickly, and then reanimated their corpses with truly evil results.

Maybe the scientists thought they could contain their creations. Or maybe they didn't care how many innocent lives were lost. Xavier would bet the latter. The medical researchers hadn't seen him as a person when he'd miraculously survived the zombie attack. They'd treated him like a guinea pig or a lab rat. They barely even spoke directly to him, speaking *over* him instead. Nothing pissed him off faster than that. He hadn't lasted more than a day in the hospital after waking before he'd checked himself out.

He'd walked bare-assed out of that ward but for a thin hospital gown and never looked back. Anyone who tried to stand in his way was forcefully, but politely, moved aside. After the first few orderlies and doctors hit the floor, the rest let him pass without making even the slightest objection.

Xavier's first stop had been his quarters. He'd needed clothes. After dressing, his next stop was his commanding officer's office. He'd never forget the look on his new CO's face when he had marched in. His Green Beret unit had been decimated by the zombies. Xavier was the only one left. The loss of his comrades had hit Xavier hard. Then he'd been reassigned to a former Navy SEAL who headed up the team tasked to stop the zombies.

Matt Sykes was that navy commander and former SEAL. There was always a little good natured army-navy rivalry, but the Special Forces brotherhood bonded them. More than that, Sykes had proven himself in that moment when Xavier showed up in his office. Xavier owed his release from the scientists' clutches to Matt Sykes. The navy man had gone to bat for Xavier, declaring him vital to the mission and unable to be spared for more testing.

Sykes had the balls, and the authority, to stop the science geeks in their tracks. As the zombie plague spread, the brass had become convinced that only a very few specialists—people like Xavier who were immune to the contagion—could safely get this situation under control. They'd put Sykes in charge of the whole ball of wax and given him absolute authority. And now here Xavier was, in charge of this ancillary cleanup-and-containment operation with a lady cop as his only comrade-in-arms. There were others in support positions, but only the two on the mission who had been proven immune would be risked in direct confrontation with the creatures.

"You ready?" he asked Sarah as she buckled her gun belt. She didn't have her sidearm, but he'd take care of that shortly.

"I'll be glad to see the outside. I hate hospitals."

"Me, too." Before they could make good their escape, Dr. Singh walked in with his two colleagues. "Damn. Almost made it." Xavier leaned against the wall, watching the expressions of consternation cross the doctors' faces. They weren't wearing masks today, and, sure enough, they looked like they had expected Sarah to meekly lie in bed while they studied her.

"What's going on here?" Dr. Singh's accent was much thicker when he was agitated, that was for sure.

"I'm leaving." Sarah's answer made the doctor's eyes bug out.

Xavier had to stifle a laugh at Singh's reaction.

"But you can't," the female doctor objected. "We have to study you."

"You can study my blood all you want, but I have a job to do."

Xavier liked the way Sarah stood firm.

"You can't go out there like this. You have a concussion, right, Dr. Singh?" The woman was clearly grasping at straws, looking for a way to keep Sarah in the hospital.

"Actually, her skull is repaired and her scans are normal," Singh reported. "I hypothesize that whatever agent caused her rapid healing also accelerated recovery from the concussion."

"Great." Sarah finished buckling her utility belt and faced the three doctors. "I'm going. By force if necessary." Her intent was clear. Nobody would mess with her plans.

The female doctor sighed and gave in. "I'll get an orderly to take you down."

"Is that really necessary? I'm perfectly capable of walking."

"Hospital rules," Singh replied, crossing his arms over his clipboard.

"All right. But I won't wait long."

The female doctor was out the door like a shot. Xavier raised one eyebrow at her abrupt departure and sent a glance Sarah's way. She was eyeballing the doctors, making them fidget. Man, that woman had real presence when she chose to use it. He recognized that ability as part of what went into making her such an effective cop. She might be petite, but she was mighty.

The orderly was there in record time. Sarah rolled her eyes as she sat in the wheelchair but allowed the man to wheel her out of the room and into the elevator. Xavier was at her side throughout. He grinned at the doctors right before the elevator doors closed them out. Round one to the lady in the uniform.

Xavier had left his ride in the drive. It was an official vehicle, and he hadn't planned to be there long. As he'd expected, he'd been upstairs less than ten minutes, and the vehicle was still there, waiting for them when the orderly let Sarah off at the curb.

She stood at Xavier's side, barely coming up to his shoulder. Something inside him wanted to see her smile. Or, if not smile, then laugh, even if it was at his expense.

"You certainly live up to your last name, don't you, *ma petite?*"

"It's pronounced 'Petit.' Like 'pet it.' "

He couldn't resist a little risqué humor. It was, after all, his specialty. "Oh, *ma belle*, I'd love to pet yours. Thought you'd never ask."

She laughed. Bingo. Mission accomplished.

"I bet you would, you French perv."

"Cajun, actually. There's a difference."

"Really? Aside from the obvious geographical distinctions, what's the difference?"

"We Cajuns are much better lovers. Smarter, too. We don't waste time on manicures and fifty-dollar haircuts. We have all the finesse of the French, tempered by the machismo of being true-blue American."

"Don't forget all that humility," she scoffed, and he laughed right along with her.

The guy had a sense of humor and a giant-sized ego that could take a hit. Despite herself, she was beginning to like him. He had a government vehicle waiting for him. Not the usual black town car. This thing was a behemoth camouflage Humvee. This was no dressed-up civilian version with shiny trim. This was the real deal.

A gentleman with apparently excellent manners when he chose to use them, Xavier opened the door for her. She grabbed the door frame for leverage, jumping up into the high seat. He secured the door after her. Scooting around to the driver's side, Xavier climbed in and started the vehicle. The engine purred like a rhinoceros—or something equally big and mean.

Despite the bad gas mileage and impracticality of driving something this huge on the crowded streets of Long Island, Sarah had to admit to a little thrill at being in one of the real military vehicles. Deep inside, where her inner child lived, she thought these tanklike cars were just cool. Not that she'd ever admit it out loud.

He maneuvered the wide vehicle deftly out of the parking area and onto the road without incident. Unerringly, Xavier headed in the direction of the old building where Sarah's odyssey had begun a week ago.

"I thought we'd retrace your steps at the scene first, unless you'd rather start somewhere else." He looked at her questioningly.

"No, retracing the incident is as good a place as any to start. Maybe we can find something at the scene to tell us where the perps might've gone."

"One more thing . . ." Xavier reached over and popped open a compartment built into the dash in front of her. There was a pistol inside. "This is for you."

Sarah took hold of the pistol and carefully removed it from the protective covering to look at it. It wasn't a run-of-the-mill weapon. Instead of bullets, it was loaded with some kind of dart.

"A dart gun?" She was puzzled by the lack of firepower. "Wouldn't hollow points be more effective?"

"Bullets don't work on the dead, Sarah. We can't kill them twice. They don't even feel pain. Direct hits with conventional ammo from close range don't even slow them down." He paused while she digested that information.

"What's in these? Not tranqs, right?" She gestured toward the pistol in her lap.

"The darts contain a toxin developed specifically to deal with these guys. It interferes with the bonds that hold them together on a cellular level. It breaks those bonds, and the creatures . . . dissolve, for lack of a better word. Once the toxin takes effect, there isn't much left. Use extreme caution when you handle the dart rounds. I'm authorizing you to carry and use them on this mission, but otherwise, the ammo is to be kept under lock and key at all times. It's a highly controlled substance."

Sarah could easily understand how something as dangerous as what he'd just described needed to be carefully controlled. Who knew what could happen if such a substance fell into the wrong hands.

Xavier drove with competent skill. The more she was around him, the more she realized he did everything with an air of confidence most men couldn't quite pull off. He didn't need directions, which surprised her. She knew darn well he wasn't from around here.

"Have you spent much time on Long Island?" she asked, curious.

"This is my first time here. I was called in last Thursday, after news of your attack made it down the chain of command. They pulled me off the detail I was working on at another base and flew me up here with a small squad to check things out. We had to determine if what happened to you was related to our mission."

"I guess you needed me to wake up for confirmation."

"I had confirmation from your blood tests on Thursday night. What I didn't know was the exact circumstances of the attack until you woke up and told me. I've been keeping my superiors up-to-date and am authorized at the highest levels to do whatever is necessary to contain this outbreak. After your disclosures yesterday, we all realized the problem was even larger than we'd feared."

She thought about that for a moment as he continued on to the scene of her attack.

"You checked the site already?" He wouldn't have known exactly where to go if he hadn't.

"I went in and took a quick look, but I didn't want to disturb the scene until you were available to walk me through the sequence of events."

She understood his reasoning but, suddenly, going back to the scene made her feel odd. They pulled up in front of the abandoned building, and Sarah fought against a pang of anxiety. It was a short-lived burst, but it was strong.

Xavier's big hand covered hers, drawing her attention.

"You okay?"

She read real concern in his expression, tempered with understanding. It gave her strength.

"I'm fine." She took a deep breath and tried to focus her thoughts.

"I remember my first time back on duty after a sniper almost took my arm off. Hit me from the side. An inch either way and it would've been a really bad day for me. As it was, I was out of commission for a couple of months. When I finally got back to my unit, it was hard to get out into the real world again. We were still deployed in the same hellhole of a country, in the same area where the sniper had taken potshots at me. He hadn't been caught or killed to our knowledge. I kept wondering if he was still out there, still gunning for me from the invisibility of distance. My head was on a swivel those first few hours, but eventually I got back into the swing of things. Give yourself time, Sarah. It's understandable to be a little jumpy after what you've been through."

"I'm not jumpy. I'm scared shitless." She figured he'd earned a bit of honesty with the sympathetic story, even if it was just a story. She didn't think he'd lie about being injured, but she wouldn't put it past him to exaggerate the true level of his postinjury anxiety in order to make her feel better. Come to think of it, that was a nice quality. One of many she was discovering he had.

Better not to go there. They had a job to do, and she had a quiet life to get back to once the horror-show portion of the festivities was over.

Xavier laughed outright at her statement and she joined him. The mere action of laughing helped her nerves settle. She turned her hand over under his and gripped his fingers for a quick squeeze.

"Thanks, Captain. I'm good to go now."

"You're a trouper, Officer Petit."

He winked at her—there was that charm again—and let go of her hand. He opened his door and slid out of the high vehicle while she jumped down from her side.

"So let's start this from the beginning. When you rolled up, where did you park?"

He towered over her, but she didn't mind. His height and size made her feel safe in an odd way. There was no doubt he was one of the good guys, even if he was wearing camo fatigues instead of a policeman's uniform. They were definitely on the same side here, and she could use an ally with knowledge of the enemy if she was really going to face those creatures again.

"I parked right along here. Maybe three yards forward from where you just parked the Humvee."

He dutifully walked three yards forward. "So your driver's-side door was about here, right?" He walked to the spot and she shadowed his movements. "Making this your approach angle." He pointed, using his arm to indicate the line he thought she had walked along. "Get in front of me and show me your path as closely as you can remember. Go slow and stop at the entrance. We'll go in together."

She was impressed by his all-business attitude. The laconic teasing had ceased the moment they got to work. She liked that. His charm was nice, but his sharp-eyed intellect was even more attractive.

Dangerous ground, she chastised herself again. They were here to solve a problem. That's all. Of course, it couldn't hurt to admit—in the privacy of her own mind—that she found him dangerously attractive. The more she saw of him, the more she liked the sexy Southern boy.

She did as he asked, walking slowly along the path she'd taken the week before. He paused a few times to study the ground but didn't say much. She wondered what he could possibly be learning from the broken concrete and dirt, but didn't ask him. He looked too pensive to interrupt, and they hadn't even really gotten started yet. The fun part would be inside.

She shuddered, not enjoying the anticipation of reliving those horrific moments when she thought she'd die in that abandoned building, at the mercy of two nightmare creatures. Her life hadn't exactly flashed before her eyes, but she'd had a revelation or two in those panicked moments. She didn't want to die. Not like that. Not so young, without having ever done anything really worthwhile with her life. Sure, she was a respected police officer, but other than her work, her life was empty.

She wanted to change that. She wasn't really sure how she'd go about it, but she was determined to do something different in the future. As soon as this nightmare was over. She'd see these creatures finished first. It was a vow she'd made to herself last night as memories of those terrifying moments returned.

Sarah stopped at the door to the building. It still hung askew, the rusted steel no barrier to the gloomy interior. She peered inside cautiously, reaching for the flashlight on her utility belt. Xavier had given her a small, high-powered one to replace the big one she'd lost when she'd been attacked. He'd also given her a nice holster for the dart pistol, which she'd put on gratefully. It felt good to be armed again. Especially now that she knew what was really out there, lurking in the dark.

A bright light shone over her shoulder before she could even get her own flashlight free of its holster. She looked upward, unsurprised to see the high-beam light in Xavier's big hand. He moved beside her, shouldering her aside with polite movements.

"I'll go first for now. I checked this place out already and believe they've moved on, but I don't like to take chances."

Sarah wasn't about to argue. If there was the slightest chance of coming face-to-face with one of those creatures again, she'd rather approach it on her own terms, not be surprised by it in the dark. Not like she had been when they had almost killed her.

She still had the pain in her thigh to remind her of what kind of damage they could do, even if the contaminant in their bite wouldn't kill her outright. The more disgusting of the two creatures had taken a chunk out of her thigh. Her body was growing new muscle and skin to replace what had been removed, but the area was still tight and painful even though it was healing at record pace. She was good to go with only a thick bandage. She'd have to change the dressing later, but for now, it didn't slow her down physically. No, it only made her pause mentally to evaluate the threat level, but caution was a good thing.

"It's clear." Xavier turned back to her. "Now, show me the path you took. What did you see, hear, smell, et cetera. Don't leave anything out."

She retraced her steps as best she could recall, giving him the information he wanted and answering questions as he came up with new ones. When she got to the place where she'd been laid out on the ground, cracking her skull and giving those creatures the opportunity to bite her, her voice shook with memory and returning horror.

A strong arm came around her shoulders, silently shoring up her defenses. She gulped, swallowing the tears of frustrated terror that returned briefly as she recalled the moment when she knew she was going to die.

"They had me pinned and my head was swimming from banging on the concrete floor," she recalled. She took a deep breath to steady her voice but it didn't help much. "The first one had my legs, the second one—the one that snuck up on me—had my arms. He bit me here." She touched the spot between her neck and shoulder where the second perp had broken skin. Not even a scar marred the spot now, of course. The contagion in their saliva had done that to her, though it would've killed almost anyone else, according to Xavier.

"The first one bit you on the thigh, right?" he asked in a gentle voice. "I saw the medical reports. Is it healed yet?"

"Not completely. It's still got a big scab and hurts when I overdo it or move in a strange way. They tell me the chunk of muscle and flesh that was taken out is still growing back in."

"The healing effects of being immune to the contagion are

pretty powerful. Too bad it comes at such a high price and only works on a miniscule percent of the population." The irony in his tone wasn't lost on her.

"I can almost understand why the researchers wouldn't want to give up on this avenue of research. Almost. But, as you said, the price is too high."

She shuddered and he drew her into his arms, wrapping her in his warmth. It felt good to be comforted by this mountain of a man. He was so much bigger than she was, so much stronger physically. It felt good to lean on that strength for just a minute.

"Much too high," he agreed with her, tucking her head under his chin. "We'd both be dead if it weren't for a quirk of our body chemistry. I don't know about you, but I'm much too young and pretty to die."

She laughed, as he'd no doubt intended. "The only thing pretty about you is your way with words, captain." She leaned back and looked up into his mysterious dark eyes. The moment dragged as their gazes met and held.

"Don't you think you should call me Xavier, considering we're fellow survivors?" His eyes darkened with intent. "And especially considering the way you fit in my arms?" He pulled her closer, angling his lips downward to meet hers.

She saw the kiss coming a mile away but was powerless to resist. She'd been through so much in the past week. She'd come face-to-face with death and had spent a few hours reconsidering the direction of her life's path. One of the things she most regretted was turning away from opportunities when they presented themselves.

Well, here was an opportunity of the sexiest kind. What woman wouldn't want to know this handsome Cajun's kiss? It was just a kiss, after all. She knew she'd regret it the rest of her life—however long or short that may be—if she turned down this opportunity to experience Xavier's kiss.

For all she knew, it might be disappointing. He might not be a good kisser. He might be all talk and no substance. But then again . . .

He just might be the real deal. She wanted to know. She wanted like never before to find out if he lived up to his sexy advertising. Could a man who looked that scrumptious on the outside be as good at love play as he looked?

Sarah was about to find out.

Chapter Three

She met his kiss halfway, leaning up on her tiptoes to cut down on the difference in their heights as much as she could. Xavier's arms tightened around her waist and back, supporting her. She'd never felt safer in her life.

When his lips touched hers, Sarah felt a sharp tingling, like an electric jolt where their skin touched. She'd heard about sparks flying but had never experienced it herself. If this first tentative touch was any indication, she was in for a rare treat.

Sarah moved closer to him, pressing herself against his wide, muscular chest. The feel of him was maddening in the best possible way. He was beyond fit—tall and lithe, with strong muscles that made her want to stroke him all over . . . for hours. She'd love to take her time discovering all the sensitive places on his hard body.

But she was getting ahead of herself. This was just a kiss, after all. And it hadn't even really started yet.

She yielded to him as he molded her body to his. Her breasts pressed against his chest as his lips took possession of hers in a more definite sweep. He was in command of not only the kiss but of her response as well. She felt as if he'd taken control of her free will and her pleasure. He held both in the palm of his hand, and, most disturbingly, she trusted him with it all. She trusted that he wouldn't push her too far, wouldn't take her beyond her boundaries, though he would test them.

Xavier's tongue plunged deep, playing with hers as one of his hands roamed lower to cup the curve of her butt. He squeezed, drawing her closer to his lower body. She could feel the buckles and straps of his utility belt against her, but there was also a delectable ridge of hardness running up the front of his trousers that made her want to touch and tease. He was hard for her. Just like that.

Sarah felt a little thrill of feminine power at being able to affect him in such a blatant way. He made her feel desirable and powerful. He also made her hotter than she'd ever been.

Xavier backed off little by little. He pressed her lower body against his hardness one last time before letting up on the pressure. He moved his hand off her ass, holding her waist instead. When she would've pressed herself against him, he held her off.

Thank goodness he was thinking for both of them. At this point, Sarah was almost too far gone to care that they were both still on duty and had a job to do.

He lifted his lips from hers, keeping his arms loose around her midsection. Those soft brown eyes looked down into hers, the hint of humor in the crinkles at the corners making the moment more intimate somehow. He watched her closely, seeming to gauge her reaction.

Sarah felt boneless. Her knees were wobbly and her pulse raced. All that from just a simple kiss.

"Wow." Damn, she hadn't meant to say that out loud. It had just slipped out. Xavier smiled down at her, the devilish quirk of his lips making her insides squirm. The man was potent. Sanity began to return as she straightened in his hold. "That shouldn't have happened."

"Why not?" His gaze hardened and dared her to come up with a reason.

For the life of her, she couldn't. Not a good reason, anyway. She finally settled for one of her weaker excuses as she stepped away from him and brushed off her clothing, removing imaginary lint. Too bad she couldn't remove the feel of his hard body against hers as easily.

"It's unprofessional."

Xavier laughed outright. "I'm not buying it. You're not in my chain of command. We're not even coworkers."

"We're working together now," she argued.

"I'm army. You're a cop. We're working together on this, but only because of some very unusual circumstances. There's nothing unprofessional about giving in to the very real attraction we have for one another."

"Speak for yourself, lover boy." She tried to push her way past him, but he slipped one big hand around her upper arm, gently halting her progress.

"I didn't figure you for a coward, Sarah. In fact, I know you're not a coward. So don't run from this." His voice dropped as he whispered into her ear. "Don't run from me."

Sarah suppressed a shiver as he let go of her arm and let her proceed. Her senses were in an uproar and her mind was in a state of utter confusion. She'd never felt like this before. It seemed only this annoying Green Beret could drag this response out of her. She didn't like it. Not one bit.

But to be honest, she had enjoyed his kiss. A little too much. She hadn't responded to a man like this in a long time . . . if ever. She doubted she'd ever gotten so hot from just a kiss. As it was, Sarah had felt desire for him right down to her bones. He'd lit her on fire with the tender brushes of his tongue and the demanding power of his kiss. It had been totally unexpected and had caught her completely unawares.

She'd learned something. She would have to be on guard around Xavier from now on. Her life was screwed up enough right now as it was. She didn't need to get mixed up with a sexy Cajun soldier who would be around only for a short while. She didn't want to lose her heart to him, only to have him leave.

Sarah knew that about herself. She couldn't love 'em and

leave 'em. She wasn't that kind of girl. If she got involved with a guy, she got *involved*. Xavier could easily break her heart, if she allowed herself to get closer to him than she already was. They had to work together. She could do that. Anything more? She'd have to forget about.

She headed for the hallway where she first saw the perp, trying to refocus the situation. Business. They had to stick to business from here on out.

Sarah pulled the flashlight from her utility belt. She'd done this before. Only this time, she had company. The zombies were gone and an even more dangerous male was guarding her back. Fear wanted to sneak up on her, but it didn't stand a chance with Xavier in the room.

"I heard something over here." She cleared her throat, well aware that she'd croaked like a frog on her first try. "So I identified myself and approached cautiously. I saw something at the end of the hall. It looked like a person. I asked him to come out but got no response. After about a minute, he began to shuffle forward, toward me. I moved a little closer, expecting it to be a junkie or a drunk. I thought maybe he might need medical help."

"Oh, yeah," Xavier whispered, checking out the hallway with his more powerful flashlight as he stood close over her shoulder. "He needed medical help all right, but it was already too late."

"Yeah," she agreed, a lump in her throat as she remembered the unnatural gait of the creature as it had approached her. "I called for backup and an ambulance, then went closer to check out the perp. He was moving closer, but not quickly, and he was making that sort of moaning sound."

"The inhuman groan that sends shivers right down your spine."

She looked up at him, but Xavier was concentrating on his inspection of the walls and floor. His expression was tight, though. He understood better than anyone that horrible sound.

She cleared her throat again, trying to push the memory of

that sound from her mind. "When the perp got close enough that I could see his face—well, what was left of his face—I tried to run."

"Smart move."

"Not really. I didn't hear the second perp come up behind me. He had me before I even knew he was there." She was still kicking herself for that rookie mistake.

"I imagine you were pretty surprised after what you'd just seen."

His gentle tone made her look over at him sharply. "Don't make excuses for me. I know it was a stupid mistake. Nothing should've rattled me so badly that I didn't even notice the second perp sneaking up on me. I'm better than that."

"Under normal circumstances, I bet you are, Officer Petit. You're an exemplary officer of the law." He gave her a solemn nod. "But I think we can both agree, this was far from normal."

"Look, it could have been a couple of kids in Halloween masks. Those same kids could have been armed. They could have shot me or sexually assaulted me just as easily."

He turned to face her. "But these weren't kids in masks. These were zombies. The real deal."

The moment stretched while in her mind she went over the recriminations that had been playing nearly nonstop since she woke. Then her sense of humor reasserted itself.

"I can't believe you really call them that. Every time I hear the word I want to giggle. It makes it sound like we're on the set of some low-budget horror movie." A smile quirked her lips.

Xavier joined her in a faint grin. "Only thing is, this is real. No cameras. And it's my job to keep it that way. 'Reanimated corpses' is what they are. 'Zombies' for short." He winked at her before heading down the hall, inspecting every square inch of the floor, walls and ceiling.

She watched him for a moment before following behind, doing her own inspection. That zombie had to have come from somewhere.

"I went over this space after I was sent up here. I didn't

know where to concentrate, so I checked everything, hoping you'd wake up and be able to point me in the right direction." Xavier paused, drawing his knife to pry at something in a crack on the floor. "Bingo."

"What?" He was crouching, blocking her view of whatever it was he'd found on the floor. She moved to look over his shoulder.

"Step back." He shifted on the balls of his feet, crowding her backward. A second later, she realized why as he opened up a trapdoor in front of them.

He looked back at her for just a moment to signal for silence. She didn't have to be told twice. If anyone was still down there, the element of surprise might still be on their side.

Before she could ask what he meant to do, he jumped, avoiding the steps on the ladder that ran down the opening, holding on to the rails on either side. He slid into the darkness, zipping downward at breakneck speed.

Sarah wasn't sure he wanted her to follow, but she'd be damned if she was going to be left up here standing watch. If there was danger to be found, it was down there, not up here in an empty building.

She took the slower way down, using the rungs of the ladder, though she went as fast as she could. The floor wasn't far below. She found herself about twelve feet belowground, in an area with a concrete floor.

As her eyes adjusted, she saw the flicker of light ahead. It was Xavier. He was using a smaller light now, creeping around corners using his stealth skills.

He was impressive in action. The man had skills. No doubt about that. And she didn't mean just as an operative. He had kissed the daylights out of her, and though she'd tried to put it from her mind and concentrate on the mission, her senses were still reeling. Xavier Beauvoir certainly knew how to kiss.

She shouldn't have been surprised. The man was walking, talking, sex on a stick. From the lazy roll of his hips as he walked, to the velvety accent of his words, he was temptation with a capital *T*. Sarah had to gird herself against him. He'd be here only until this problem was cleared up. He no doubt had led a very different life, far from here. He'd leave and never look back once his mission was over.

She couldn't really blame him. That was the nature of his profession.

Musing about Xavier when she should have been paying more attention to her surroundings almost cost her dearly. Sarah spun around, hearing a noise in the darkness behind her. She didn't know what it was and couldn't see anything beyond the beam of her flashlight, but the tiny hairs at the back of her neck stood on end. She'd been in trouble once before in this building. As far as she was concerned, once was enough.

"Xavier?" Her voice came out calmer than she'd expected. Score one for her acting ability. Her knees were shaking with fear, but hopefully the big soldier wouldn't be able to hear the rising panic in her voice.

"What?" His voice floated to her out of the darkness, closer now, but still some distance away.

"I heard something over here. That direction." She pointed with her flashlight, but it wasn't powerful enough to cut through the deep, inky darkness, and so did diddly-squat to help her pinpoint whatever was making those furtive sounds.

Xavier appeared next to her like a ghost. The man was unnervingly silent on his feet.

"You stay here, by the ladder where I can see you. I'll go check it out." He kept his voice low, his breath whispering across the sensitive whorls of her ear as he leaned close. She suppressed a shiver of pure, feminine awareness. Damn, the man was truly potent. "Now would be a good time to draw your weapon and release the safety. Just don't shoot me."

His flat words shocked her gaze up to his and she read the graveyard humor there. A little curl of forbidden attraction wound through her abdomen.

"I only shoot the bad guys," she promised with a solemn nod, and was gratified by a short moment of camaraderie as she followed his instructions.

She'd shared many such moments with fellow officers in her years on the force, but none had ever felt this intimate. There was something about this soldier—this Special Forces warrior—that made each moment special in some indefinable way.

Maybe it was just that he was the real deal. Many of her fellow officers had some military background, and she respected them for their service. But none of them had made the grade to join one of the elite Special Forces. There was a lot of respect among her colleagues for those select few.

Xavier was gone in a heartbeat. One minute he was there, standing next to her, the next he was gone, swallowed by the shadows. Damn, he was good.

She heard more movement and stepped a little closer to the ladder. Her eyes had adjusted to the dark, and even the small amount of light that came down from the unlit building above seemed like a lot of illumination compared to the complete absence of light in the underground space. The ladder was her lifeline. Her only route of escape. She was no coward, but after what she'd been through, she admitted to feeling a little apprehensive about encountering one of those creatures again. She'd keep the ladder in sight.

A grunt followed a scuffling sound in the darkness. Then she heard the distinctive sound of darts being fired. It wasn't the loud, percussive bang of bullets. Rather, it was a *whoosh* and *zing* as a slim dart left the weapon at high velocity.

Xavier wouldn't have fired unless he was certain there was one of the creatures in the basement with them.

"He's heading your way, Sarah." Xavier's loud call was the only warning she got before a hideous-looking man, dressed in filthy rags that had once been a T-shirt and jeans, stumbled into her line of sight.

His face was a mess, covered in blood and ripped to shreds along one side. One of his arms was dislocated and looked as if giant rats had been gnawing on it. For weeks. There was little flesh left and the sickly white of bone showed in several places.

Sarah felt bile rise in her throat as her last meal threatened to make a reappearance, but she breathed lightly, trying to block out the stench of rotting flesh as the creature drew nearer. She firmed her spine and took aim with her pistol. She knew what she had to do.

"Fire in the hole. Stay clear, Xavier," she called as she let loose with two shots in rapid succession. She hit her targets cleanly. One dart landed in the middle of the man's chest, the other in his left thigh. Yet, he still shuffled forward, directly toward her.

Sarah backed up, her back connecting with the ladder behind her. The zombie showed no signs of slowing down. The darts hadn't even fazed him. They bobbed up and down, embedded in his skin, unnoticed as he stalked toward her, unrelenting in his determination to reach her.

"He's not going down," she yelled to Xavier. "I hit him twice, but he's not stopping."

"I hit him in the back. Give it time. He should be imploding any second now. Are you in the clear?"

"He's coming right for me." Panic threaded its way through her voice regardless of her attempt to maintain a little dignity. The truth was, she was scared shitless. Xavier had to realize it, too, just from the tremor of her higher-than-normal pitch voice.

She reached for the ladder and started scrambling upward as fast as she could. Too late.

The zombie grabbed her booted foot and pulled. Hard. The guy was stronger than he looked, even though he could use only one arm. Sarah was stuck. No matter how hard she pulled, his strong, single-handed grip kept her from getting away.

She tugged and tugged, to no avail. Then she saw his brown-stained teeth bearing down on her leg and she really began to panic. She still hadn't healed from the last time one of these guys started chomping on her leg.

A beefy fist came out of the dark to knock the zombie's grip loose from her leg. Xavier moved like lightning, spinning the creature away from her. She went a few more rungs up the ladder, out of range of anyone on the floor, then turned to shine her light down from above, illuminating the scene in a halo of light that extended only a few feet in a hazy, circular pattern.

It was enough. She could see Xavier squaring off against the zombie. They circled each other like prizefighters sizing one another up.

"Why is it taking so long? We both hit him, so shouldn't he be gone by now?" she asked worriedly, watching Xavier stay out of arm's reach. If he was touching the creature with bare skin when it imploded, there was the possibility of some of the toxin making its way into Xavier's body. Since the toxin was so incredibly deadly, that was to be avoided at all costs.

"Sometimes it takes a while to work through their systems," Xavier finally answered her, but she could see the furrow in his brow. He was concerned, too, though he wouldn't speak of it.

She didn't want to argue with him. Not while he was facing off against something out of a nightmare. Later, they'd have time to talk through what was going on. In the debrief. Right now, they had a job to do to make sure they both made it to the debrief.

The zombie lunged at Xavier, scraping those inch-long claws the zombies all seemed to have, too close for comfort. He barely missed Xavier's midsection as Sarah watched helplessly from above. She could see Xavier's darts sticking out of the man's back as they circled. The guy had been shot with four doses of toxin. Xavier had told her it usually took only two doses to end one of these creatures. Had he been disastrously wrong?

Sarah was afraid they were about to find out.

"Dammit, stop this," she prayed aloud, watching the action intently. The zombie looked up at her and something flickered through his dead eyes. A look, almost of uncertainty, passed over his ruined features.

Could it be he understood what she'd said?

"Stop!" she said again, louder this time, directly to him, putting all the authority she could muster into the command.

The creature hesitated. His mouth opened. He seemed to be struggling to speak, though Xavier had said these creatures were incapable of forming words. Still, it looked like this one was trying to do just that.

"*M-mst—*"

Dammit, he really was trying to speak.

Just then, his body disintegrated. It flowed like sand . . . or runny Jell-O . . . right down to the floor. The toxin had done its job. If she understood it correctly, the man had been reduced to a gooey puddle of biological material. The bonds between his cells had been dissolved on a molecular level.

"Holy shit." She'd never expected anything like what she'd just seen, even though Xavier had warned her what would happen.

"You're not kidding." Xavier stepped into the circle of light emitted by her flashlight. "That son of a bitch was trying to talk to you. Could you make out what he was trying to say?"

Sarah stared blankly at him for a short moment. She really needed some time to regroup, but she knew it was impossible. They still had the rest of this basement to search. That one might not have been alone down here.

"Hard to say." She started back down the ladder, joining Xavier on the concrete floor. "It sounded like *mst*—must. Or it could've been 'mast' or maybe 'mist.' *M-S-T* something."

Xavier pulled a small device from one of his many pockets and twisted it between his fingers. A small LED light began to blink. He dropped the blinking object on the pile of old clothes and goo that had once been the zombie and picked up his more powerful flashlight, doing a sweep of the area.

"Tracker," he explained as she looked at the softly blinking electronic device. "For the cleanup team. We label all kills with these so the nerds know exactly where we dropped the tangos. They come in after us and sanitize the place."

He'd alluded to that before, but in all the tumult she was having a hard time recalling exactly what he'd told her about his process in the field. Hearing about it and actually doing it were two very different things.

Dammit, she was better than this. Maybe the blow to the head really had scrambled her brains. She was a professional. An officer of the law. No matter how bizarre the situation, she should at least be able to remember what she'd been told, and how to perform her duty.

Instead, fear was choking her and the insanity of this entire ordeal was making her weak. She wasn't pulling her weight on this team and they both knew it. Xavier was babying her, ushering her along like some feeble-minded responsibility rather than an equal partner.

She'd do better from here on out. She could handle this. She *had* handled this—all on her own—just a week ago. She needed to find her reserves of courage and pluck to get back on her feet and back to the competent officer she used to be.

They went through the rest of the underground area together. Sarah got a handle on herself and managed to participate in checking and clearing each room. Once they were sure the place was empty aside from the two of them, they commenced a cursory search.

"We'll go through it as best we can right now. The geeks will bring in lighting and do a more thorough job after they clean up the kill site," Xavier said offhandedly as he walked through what looked like an office with her.

He flashed his light around the empty room. All that was left were a wooden desk and some other furniture. A rolling chair. An empty filing cabinet.

Sarah took her time, looking closely at each joint of the wooden desk. Her persistence paid off when she saw a glint of something metallic.

"There's something wedged in here."

Xavier was at her side in an instant. "It's a wire. Look, it shows under the desk for an inch before disappearing under the carpet." He shined the light downward, following the path of the wire. "Why leave this when everything else in the place had been stripped?"

"Let's see what it leads to." Sarah bent down to examine the carpet. "We're in luck. They used commercial carpet tiles in here." With the tip of her utility knife she lifted the edges of the squares covering the thin silver wire as she spoke. Sure enough, the wire made its way from the desk, directly toward the wall. "This is weird." The wire ended at the wall, disappearing behind it.

"Can I borrow your nightstick?" She handed it over to him without comment. "Stand back and hold the light for me," Xavier directed, and Sarah followed his lead. He took a swing at the sheetrock with the business end of the stick, breaking through the thick gypsum board as if it were paper.

When the dust settled, he shined his light inside the wall, following the wire's path upward toward a small grate at the top. The grate was no more than five inches square. Using his own, much larger knife, Xavier pried off the plate and reached inside.

"Camera. Video feed must've gone to whatever equipment was on the desk. Most likely a computer. I wonder why they'd wire the office? We should check for surveillance equipment like this in the rest of the place. Could be the former residents were a touch paranoid."

Once they knew what to look for, it was easy to spot similar view ports in all the other rooms on the subterranean level. In the fifth room they searched, they caught a break.

"Looks like someone missed a DVD in the shuffle to get out of Dodge," Sarah observed, picking up a shiny silver disc that had fallen behind a piece of furniture. "I wonder what this will tell us?"

"Secure it for now. We'll check it out after we finish here."

"Yes, sir." She gave him a mock salute along with a grin that he answered ruefully. Command came easy to the man, it was plain to see. She didn't take offense but wanted to remind him gently that she wasn't one of his soldiers. The nod of his head told her without words that her message had been received.

They finished up with the lower floor. They hadn't found a lot belowground except for the disc and the camera. Sarah hoped that would give them a good solid lead. They needed one about now.

Although she'd encountered two of the creatures on the premises and now they'd faced a third belowground, they hadn't found anything to tell them why or how the zombies had gotten there. Whether it was just dumb luck that the creatures were attracted to the building or whether they'd been stationed there on purpose was still unclear. The basement rooms were suspicious, but whoever had cleaned them out had done a thorough job. It was hard to tell what the rooms had been used for. Only a few pieces of ubiquitous office equipment had been left behind.

The disc was their only hope to somehow connect the building with the creatures and whoever might have unleashed them.

"I'm guessing whatever was here last week cleared out after you were attacked upstairs," Xavier said, breaking into her musings as they headed back toward the ladder. "They probably left that one behind to guard whoever might come after. Or maybe he was just a mistake. Whichever is the case, I think the premises are clear now and are likely to stay that way."

"And that's important why?" She sensed he was leading up to something.

"You saw some of my men that first day in the hospital. They're not immune, but they know what we're up against. They've been assigned to support roles on this mission and this is the perfect opportunity to do their thing. I'm going to turn investigation of this site over to them."

"What about the local authorities?"

"We have authorization from the highest levels. The president, the head of the CDC, the surgeon general, chairman of the Joint Chiefs and on down the line."

"Wow."

"Desperate times call for desperate measures. They want to nip this in the bud before the general population finds out about the mess they let develop on their watch."

"No doubt."

"But we'll keep the locals in, as much as we can. In fact, you're the local tie for this mission. You're authorized to report, within certain parameters, to your chief. I'm sorry, but I'll have to clear all your written reports and be present at any in-person debriefings. He can know certain things. The cover story is close to the truth—a terrorist bioweapon that's a national security risk and needs to be kept top secret. Nobody else is supposed to learn about the creatures if we can possibly avoid it."

"I guess I can understand that. You don't want to cause a panic." She scratched her chin as they entered the area with the ladder.

"Not only that, but this technology could be sold, Sarah."

"Sold? You're kidding. Who'd want to make zombies?" Even as she said it, she realized there were a lot of unscrupulous people out there who'd like this kind of weapon. It was a terrorist's dream come true and a hostile nation's doomsday device. No matter what, this information needed to be contained. "My God."

"Yeah." Xavier caught her eye, nodding as a moment of understanding passed between them. They made it to the ladder and Xavier motioned for her to go first.

Stepping gingerly around the pile of goo and ratty fabric that had once been a human being, Sarah started up the ladder. Now that the action was over, her leg began to stiffen up. She sort of half-hopped upward, doing the best she could on her injured leg. Xavier followed right behind, and she had the embarrassing sensation that he was staring at her butt on her way up.

She waited for him at the top, and, sure enough, he had that lazy, devilish grin on his face when his head popped up through the trapdoor.

"Lovely view," he commented, looking around with mock innocence.

"I bet." She had to suppress a chuckle. The man was a rogue through and through. "Next time, you go first."

"Anytime, sweetheart. You can ogle my ass all you want."

He didn't give her a chance to come up with a snappy comeback. As it was, she sputtered a bit as he marched down the hall toward the exit of the building and the sunshine outside.

He'd pulled a radio from his utility belt and was already talking to someone on the other end as she followed behind, taking two steps to every one of his. The man was tall and long-limbed. His steps were giant-sized in comparison with hers, so she had to scramble to catch up when he decided to move at full speed.

He was at the Humvee when she emerged from the building, still talking on the radio. When he saw her, he ended his conversation and turned a bright smile on her.

"This is one of those times when you can be of great assistance, Officer Petit. This building is soon to become an army work area, which means we'll be shutting off access through this road, if at all possible. Since you know the area, not to mention your boss, your government would be grateful if you could run interference and help coordinate some roadblocks. What do you say?"

When he poured on the charm, she doubted many females ever said no to him. He was right in this instance, though. She was best suited to coordinating the local effort, since she knew all the players personally and they knew she'd been seconded to this high-level, hush-hush operation.

She knew the cover story, such as it was. Vague innuendo about a terrorist bioweapon and an army intelligence officer run amok. National security secrets at stake. Her chain of command had been told that she'd stumbled onto a major terrorist operation in the abandoned building and could personally identify the bad guys. She'd been put under federal protection, partnered with an army escort authorized in this one instance to *consult* on U.S. soil because one of their men was involved.

It was flimsy, but with all the official seals and political heavyweights backing it up, her chief believed it and was willing to work with the feds. Too much had happened in the New York Metro area since September 11, 2001, to allow local cops the luxury of territorialism when it came to federal operations on their turf.

The turf wars were over. Or, at least, put on hold. For now.

"You got police band on that fancy radio of yours?" She grinned at him.

Chapter Four

"In the truck." He grinned back at her, seeming truly happy that she was onboard with his plans. "It's hardwired into the battery, so just flip the switch for power. It's the unit closest to the passenger side. I installed it there just for you."

She wasn't sure if she bought that, but it was nice to know he'd at least thought ahead to have the equipment she'd need put into his ride. Sarah walked over to the passenger-side door, trying her best not to limp. Her injured leg was making itself known. It was a relief to hop up into the big vehicle and plant her butt in a sitting position, taking weight off her leg. The muscles were still reforming, knitting at an amazing speed, but they still had a way to go.

She found the radio and switched it on. First, though, she'd place a call to her chief. Using her cell phone, she reached him with little difficulty. His secretary had apparently been instructed to put her calls right through. He asked how she was doing, politely inquiring about her injuries. She answered noncommittally and got down to business.

Within moments, she had authorization for two roadblocks and whatever other support, within reason, the feds needed. Her chief was only too happy to let her coordinate everything, since she was embedded with the feds. Less work for him. Less hassle for her and Xavier. It was a good plan all the way around.

She ended the call with her commanding officer, then hopped on the radio to coordinate with Dispatch for the units they'd need. Two roadblocks would suffice. One on either end of this sparsely traveled lane. There weren't any other structures on this stretch of road, just a wooded lot across the street. The big medical center could be seen over the roof of this building, but it was to the rear of this abandoned property, on the main thoroughfare. The police units would be at the intersections on each end of the block, far enough away that they couldn't really see what was going on in the building, which was a plus.

While she was on the radio, Xavier came around to her side of the vehicle and listened in. He looked well satisfied with the arrangements when she signed off.

"They'll be here in about fifteen minutes."

"Perfect." Xavier looked at his watch. "My guys will be here in ten. I'll give them the grand tour and get them started. If you wouldn't mind interfacing with your people up top first, then running through events just one more time with Sam— that's Lieutenant Sam Archer—my XO on this. He's in charge of the B Team."

"Does that make us the A Team?" She had to laugh.

"As a matter of fact, we are. Only those who have been proven immune to the contagion are being utilized in direct combat with the creatures. We've lost too many good men to this menace already. Sam's willing to go up against them again if he has to, but I don't want him, or anyone who isn't immune, anywhere near these creatures if at all possible. We're the only ones I'm authorizing to go head-to-head with them. Hence, the A Team."

"Suddenly I'm hearing that old TV show theme song in my head. I wonder if Mr. T will start building a tank out of tractor parts for us or something?"

They had a good laugh, cut short by the arrival of another camo Humvee and a few nondescript cargo vans. Some of the vans were white, a few black, and none had windows in the rear.

"Ah, the cavalry is here." Xavier turned toward the new arrivals. "You rest here a few minutes more until your friends show up. Get them set, then join us in the building, okay?"

Dammit. He was babying her. He'd seen her limping and was giving her *rest* time. She didn't like it. She always hated being babied. But she'd admit, to herself at least, that her leg needed the breather. Playing tug-o-war with the zombie over her foot on that ladder had not helped her hurt leg. Every tug had been agony. Only the adrenaline of the moment had deadened the pain. She hadn't really noticed it at the time.

She'd felt it afterward, though. Bad. Real bad.

Resenting that leg with every passing minute, Sarah waited for her fellow officers to show up while watching men scurry from the vans. A couple of big bruisers piled out of the second Humvee. They all wore green berets on their heads, and even from a distance, they crackled with highly focused energy. Sarah watched the way they deferred to Xavier, saluting him when he walked over to speak with them, only falling at ease at his order.

What her chief wouldn't give to command obedience like that, she thought with an inward chuckle. Though her police brethren took their jobs very seriously, there wasn't that same level of military crispness. At least not all the time. Every once in a while they trotted out the formality for special occasions, but it definitely wasn't an everyday occurrence. Things tended to be more laid-back and friendly at the precinct.

Sarah saw the first patrol car arrive at the end of the street a few minutes later. She hopped out of the Humvee, very aware that several sets of male eyes were on her, following her progress. She paid them no mind. She'd just spent a good five minutes studying them, after all. She figured turnabout was fair play.

She did her best not to limp as she walked down the street and greeted Fred Cummings, a veteran cop who'd seen a lot in his years on the force. He was a good officer who had helped her from time to time as she made her way up through the ranks. He'd always been ready to offer advice and encouragement when she was a rookie, and they'd even rolled together once or twice back before the budget cuts had dictated only one officer per cruiser.

"Quite a party you have over there," Fred observed as he got out of the car. He'd positioned it across the road, blocking access. "Nice of the feds to invite us. How you feeling, Sarah?"

"Getting there. Glad they sent you, Fred. I'm not sure how long they're going to be over in that building, but it's important to keep any civilian traffic out of the area."

"Roger that, Sarah. Nobody in or out unless the feds clear it. The chief mentioned something about national security when he said you'd been lent out."

He seemed curious, but she knew he wouldn't push.

"Yeah. I stumbled into a real hornet's nest." She walked with Fred toward the rear of his car. He opened the trunk as they talked. "It's been an interesting couple of days."

"So you're okay with the feds? They're treating you right?"

"No complaints. In fact, they've been respectful and forthcoming so far." She read the relief on the veteran cop's face, and was glad to know he'd been truly concerned for her.

"That's good. I remember a time when cooperation wasn't as easy among different organizations. Things have changed since 9/11 for the better, as far as that goes. I mean, we're all on the same side, right?" He straightened, hooking his thumbs into his utility belt as he drew his gaze away from the swarm of activity in the middle of the block and looked back at her.

"You got that right, Fred. I have no complaints," she replied easily.

"Glad to hear it. You know, everyone was concerned when we heard the 'officer down' call." That was as close as the old cop would come to expressing emotion. She'd learned to read the guys she worked with over the past few years, so she understood what he was getting at.

"Thanks. It's all good now, but it was a hairy situation there for a few minutes." They fell into small talk as Fred scooped some wooden pieces out of his trunk.

She helped him set up two saw horses, then lit and set a couple of traffic flares. He seemed interested about her leg injury. Apparently, everyone on the force had heard she'd been attacked. He told her that they'd sent flowers, but that the hospital insisted they be sent on to her home rather than to her hospital room, for some reason. Fred seemed to wait for her to explain that oddity, but she declined, making a fast getaway when she saw the second patrol car pull up at the other end of the street.

She said a hasty good-bye to Fred and walked through the gauntlet of federal employees to the other end of the block. Xavier and his army brothers were nowhere in sight. They were most likely already in the building. And the guys from the vans were busy setting up lighting rigs, then transporting the self-contained lighting arrays into the building. Sarah thought it would be lit up like a ball field in no time, judging by the hardware these guys had brought with them.

She repeated the greetings with the other officer, Pete Simmons. She had a good opinion of him, having worked with him a time or two on parade duty and other special events. He was still a rookie, but seasoned enough to be on friendly terms with most of the other officers.

She also helped him with his saw horses and flares, then made her way back to the building. The van guys were mostly inside now. She could see the glow from within as she neared the dilapidated door.

As she entered, she realized everyone was standing silent, listening to someone speak. It was Xavier, commanding their attention. Funny, she hadn't seen him in *commander* mode yet. Despite herself, she was impressed. He definitely had a way about him. It wasn't obnoxious or flamboyant. It was more a steady presence that made people want to listen to him and do what he asked. No wonder he was in charge. He had the gift of a born leader.

"I want this place searched from top to bottom, piece by piece. Tear it apart and put it back together again if you have to." Xavier eyed everyone in the room. Even Sarah felt the deadly seriousness of his words. "This is a crime scene as well as a national security–threat site. We need to find any additional evidence that may be hiding in here. We also have to decontaminate anything that could be hazardous. Reno"—he pointed to one of the Green Berets who stood with a group of the guys from the vans—"I want you to coordinate the teams. One of our guys with each decontamination team. Decon first, then go in and search, room by room." Xavier spied Sarah in the doorway and motioned her forward. "Sam, Lewis, I'll want you to come with Officer Petit and me to go over the trail. Everyone else, set up your gear. Reno, clear the north wall first and use it as a staging area. Got it?"

A chorus of affirmatives answered him as Sarah walked through the clustered groups of men. She reached his side as activity resumed, one team of van guys heading over to work on the north side of the building. She saw them donning protective gear that included eye and respiratory protection. Then she watched as they hefted big cylinders that looked like they held compressed gas of some kind with hoses coming out of one end. She assumed the cylinders held whatever substance they were using for decontamination. She quickened her step.

"Is that stuff safe?" she asked Xavier in a low voice as she stepped close to his side.

He looked up, following her gaze to the decon team. "We're far enough away here. Besides, it's not harmful to humans unless you're exposed to massive amounts over a long period of time. The masks and goggles are just a precaution because these guys have been using the stuff for a while now."

"Good to know." She turned back to find two other men had joined their small group. One was a giant blond who must've had Viking roots, and the other had a wiry build with brown hair, brown eyes, and a gorgeous tan.

"Officer Petit, this is Lieutenant Sam Archer, my second-in-command for this mission," he said, motioning to the blond, "and Private Lewis Kauffman, the unit's bloodhound." Xavier's slow grin invited her to join in their little joke.

"Bloodhound, huh? I didn't know there was a rank for that in the army." She reached forward to shake hands with both men.

"I'm a good tracker, ma'am," Lewis said as he shook her hand. "Learned the skill first from my grandfather, then Uncle Sam helped me add to my skills."

"There isn't a thing in the woods Lew can't find," Xavier added. "This urban jungle might prove a little more difficult, but we can definitely use his skills outside. I want you to go over the attack just one more time with Sam and Lew so they'll know where to concentrate. Then I'll show them the lower level and we can leave them to it." Unspoken went the reason he wanted to leave—the disc they had yet to check out.

Each time Sarah went through the events of the attack it got easier. She was almost dispassionate this time as she described what had happened and where. It was comparatively easy to walk the two soldiers through the building in a repeat of what she'd done earlier with Xavier. She was glad now that he'd done a rehearsal with her. She was much more composed this time.

Sarah wondered if he'd done it on purpose, to help her. She wouldn't put it past him. He was a nice guy, no matter how much he tried to pretend otherwise. It would be like him to try to put her at ease privately before subjecting her to this dog and pony show.

Her leg was throbbing by the time they came to the end of her tour, and they'd gathered a small crowd. A few soldiers had begun to follow along when they'd emerged from the hallway. When they reached the main area all the Green Berets surrounded her as she described her fight with the two zombies. Xavier seemed content to let them listen in, so she didn't object. Sam asked a few pertinent questions, and she thought she read approval in some of their eyes when she looked up from the place where she'd fallen over a week before.

She described the mad scramble away from the creatures and the way she'd headed for the door, calling for backup. She tried to keep her voice composed and thought she'd succeeded, but she still caught a few emotion-filled looks from the men gathered around her. Some of their expressions held pity, others admiration or a mix of the two. When she met Xavier's gaze, all she read there was pride.

He was proud of her? What a strange thought, but that's what she saw in his whiskey-colored gaze. It puzzled her, but it also made her feel warm in the secret heart of her that craved his approval like a teenager with her first big crush. Damn. The man had affected her in ways she hadn't even realized. He'd slipped right under her defenses and turned her into a silly schoolgirl. She should really be annoyed with him, but she was too busy falling under his spell to grumble too much.

"Thanks, Officer Petit." He ended the retelling of her nightmare encounter once they were outside and she'd gotten to the point where she'd passed out. He sent his guys back inside, then stepped over to Sarah. "Why don't you get off that leg? I'll show them around downstairs, then pop back up here so we can check out the disc together. All right?"

She hated to admit to weakness but knew the value of truth. "I'd be grateful not to have to climb up and down that ladder again today," she admitted, earning a nod of understanding from Xavier. "I'll wait in the Humvee."

Xavier stilled her as she moved away by placing one big hand over her forearm. "You heal fast now, but you still have to take time with serious injuries like the one you suffered. It's not weakness to admit when you need to take it easy. It's just common sense."

She was touched by what he was trying to say. "Thanks, Xavier. I hear you."

She limped away, her leg too painful to hide.

Xavier joined her in the vehicle about fifteen minutes later.

"I think we should head over to the precinct," Sarah said without preamble as he seated himself in the driver's seat.

"Why's that?"

"The chief wants to meet you. He called a few minutes ago. Seems he began to rethink things after we hung up before. Plus, I have a fast computer with good virus protection on my desk at work. I'd rather not chance destroying my home computer with an unknown disc."

"Good point," he conceded, starting the powerful engine. "The precinct it is."

When they arrived at the station, her fellow officers greeted Sarah with genuine happiness. It was clear she was well liked and respected among her coworkers. Most expressed their concern over her injuries and mentioned that they'd tried to visit her in the hospital, but had been turned away.

They eyed Xavier with varying levels of inquiry, concern and even a little distrust. That was only to be expected, he figured. He'd swooped in and denied them the right to visit their fellow officer in the hospital, then had taken over her work schedule and had her reassigned to his top-secret little project. He wasn't surprised by the way they eyed him, taking his measure as Sarah introduced him around.

He was taking their measure, too, though they probably didn't realize it. He wanted to meet the people Sarah worked with so that he could observe their reactions to her injury. Their reactions to his presence were just as interesting. He didn't expect to learn anything troubling, but it was better to take a look just to be sure. He couldn't leave a stone unturned in this investigation. The stakes were just too high.

Not that he suspected anyone on the local police force of having dealings with the people he was after. Still, it didn't hurt to gauge their expressions. If, by some odd chance, one of them started acting suspiciously, Xavier could have Sam and the rest of the team do a little digging. So far, though, he wasn't seeing anything other than a group of people who were genuinely concerned about their coworker and curious about the Green Beret at her side. All in all, that was totally acceptable and understandable.

"One more introduction before we can get to our mystery disc," Sarah said in a low voice as they approached a big office in back. She knocked perfunctorily before opening the door. A big man with wavy salt-and-pepper hair sat behind a cluttered desk. He had his shirtsleeves rolled up and appeared to be laboring away, pecking at keys on his computer keyboard with a scowl on his face.

"Chief O'Hara, this is Captain Beauvoir." She made the introductions as the older man rose from behind his desk. He stuck out a hand and Xavier returned the gesture.

"Have a seat," the police chief invited, gesturing toward two empty chairs as he reseated himself and cleared a space in front of him on the blotter. "It's good to see you up and around, Sarah." He gave her a rusty smile. "I was with you at the hospital when the feds arrived. They quarantined everything, and a day later, this guy showed up but didn't do me the courtesy of an introduction." The sarcasm in his tone was pointed and not easily missed.

"I'm here to rectify that now, Chief O'Hara." Xavier did his best to soothe the chief's very obviously ruffled feathers. "Things have been moving rapidly since Officer Petit woke up."

"So I gathered, given the roadblocks you requested and all the activity my officers are reporting out on Wheeler Road."

"Sir, I believe you've been briefed on the national security aspects of this incident. I can't tell you much more than what you've heard already, except to say Officer Petit is vital to the ongoing investigation and a credit to your department."

O'Hara stared him down for a long moment. Finally, the old man nodded and leaned back in his padded leather office chair.

"Special Forces, eh?" The chief nodded toward the row of ribbons pinned to Xavier's chest with knowing eyes. "I was in Nam—82nd Airborne. So I have a great deal of respect for the uniform, son, but I don't know you. I'm willing to give you a lot of leeway based on Uncle Sam's recognition of your skills and honor. Don't abuse my trust."

"You have my word, sir." Xavier read knowledge in the older man's eyes. He wasn't surprised to hear that the chief of police was a vet who had seen action abroad. The old guy seemed as tough as they came. No doubt he'd learned those people skills during his time in the service.

O'Hara held Xavier's gaze for a moment longer, his jaw like

iron. He nodded once and turned to Sarah. "Anything you need, Officer Petit, you just call. We're on the federal dime, so we can afford all kinds of overtime to assist you, if necessary. More than that, you know I'd never leave one of my officers out in the cold. You may be on loan to the feds, but you still work for me. You need anything, you let me know."

"Will do, sir. Thanks."

They left the chief of police after only a little more small talk, and headed back to Sarah's desk. She was a patrol officer, so she shared a workstation. A guy named Officer Riley, according to the plaque on the desk, who, Sarah informed him, was out on patrol. He wouldn't be back for hours, so they had the desk and the small area around it all to themselves for the time being.

There were only a few other people in the office at this hour. Most of the other officers were out on patrol or going about their various clerical tasks for the day. After a few greetings and introductions, they left Sarah and Xavier alone to work.

He understood her caution about slipping this potentially dangerous disc into her home system, but he didn't like doing his investigation in public. Still, a police station was about as secure as you could get in the civilian world.

He could've just booted up the disc in his laptop, but he'd wanted to see where Sarah worked. He also wanted her to feel like she was contributing to the mission. She was a vital player on the team he'd put together for this. The only woman. He'd never had a female on his team before in the field. It was a novel experience.

Not only that, but Sarah herself was a special lady. Skilled and brave, she'd proven her mettle. She was going through a rough patch right now. It was up to Xavier to help her through it so that she could continue the career she so obviously loved. He needed her help on this, and she needed a helping hand through the aftereffects of the attack and the changes it had made in her life.

He'd been there. He knew something about how she felt. A

combat veteran, he'd been better prepared to deal with the emotional storm after his own first rude introduction to the nightmare creatures. The zombie attack had shaken him to his core. He could only imagine what a police officer who normally didn't see anything worse than the occasional drug-related shooting would feel when faced with being savaged by two zombies and left for dead.

Sarah booted up the computer while he snagged a chair and brought it around to sit next to her.

Her shared desk was toward the back of the large room, which suited Xavier fine. He had a good view of the others and none of them could easily see what might come up on the computer screen. After getting her permission to make a cursory inspection of the system, he was satisfied that it had good encryption and other protections. He handed over the disc and Sarah stuck it into the drive. Both of them leaned forward, watching the screen eagerly as the disc spun up.

Xavier reached for the keyboard, then pulled back. "Sorry. Do you mind if I do it?"

Sarah handed him the keyboard. "Go for it."

Typing in a few commands, Xavier quickly searched the directory of the disc. "There are some video files on here in addition to text files. I can't see a lot of coherence. This could be a partial backup of something."

"Play one of the videos. Let's see what they are."

"Here's an interesting date. The day you were attacked." He brought up the video file. The picture was dark at first, but he figured it out quick enough. "It's a surveillance camera. See the angle from above this doorway?" He pointed to the screen. "Do you recognize anything about the setting?"

"There's not much to see. Just a door. Could be anywhere." A little frown line appeared between her eyebrows as she concentrated. Xavier had to force himself to focus on the screen rather than watch her. She really was the most distracting little thing. Cute as a button and tough, too.

She'd probably deck him—or at least try to—if he ever told her she was cute. In his experience, officers of the law didn't appreciate that sort of description. But she was. Cute, sexy and very distracting. It was a potent mix.

"Wait." She touched his forearm where it rested on the desk between them, her eyes focused on the computer screen. "That's me."

Xavier paused the playback, going back a few frames. Sure enough, that was Sarah, entering a doorway.

"This has got to be the building on Wheeler Road. Surveillance caught you going in."

"Play the rest of it. Let's see what else they thought important enough to back up to disc."

Her eyes narrowed and he could tell she was angry now. Good. That was a healthy reaction to realizing she'd been spied upon and observed by use of hidden cameras. He hit the button to let the video resume.

The camera angle switched. It showed her walking into a new frame, somewhere within the old building. Her small flashlight was a flare of brilliance on an otherwise dim scene.

"They were using infrared. There's the heat signature of your flashlight. There's you in red, orange and yellow. See this green and blue shape in the corner?" He kept his voice low and pointed to a human-shaped object that was stationary in the far corner. "This is probably the guy who came up behind you. The creatures don't register as hot to an infrared, but they do hold some warmth. The science team explained it's the kinetic energy of the cells which make up their bodies. They don't live like you and me anymore. They've been reanimated on a cellular level. That requires some energy and that's what you're seeing on the infrared. It's cold compared to us, but it's not ice-cold."

"Son of a . . ." She was focused on the screen as the creature began to move up behind her. It was shadowing her movements as the camera angles switched again and showed her walking down the hall toward another blue-green being.

Xavier covered her hand with his as they watched the blue-green shapes converge on her glowing form. The attack played out before their very eyes. Xavier saw firsthand how she'd fought back, how she had tried her damnedest. That initial blow to the head had been her undoing.

She fought like a wildcat. The action caught by the infrared surveillance footage revealed the scenario just as she had described it. Even with her police training, she hadn't stood a chance against the creatures in the darkness that was their domain.

In the end, she had succeeded in saving herself. Xavier had to hand it to her. She had grit and skills to back it up. She'd gotten herself out of the situation, badly injured and in serious need of help, but she definitely had rescued herself.

The surveillance cameras followed her out into the sunshine, zooming in on her, using regular film once there was enough light. Xavier saw the pain on her face, the disoriented focus of her eyes, the blood pouring from her wounds. She held out until the last possible moment, propping her battered body against the tire of her patrol car. A minute later, a second patrol car pulled up and her fellow officer called the rest of the cavalry.

Xavier stopped the replay. She was breathing hard, her free hand fisted on her thigh, the hand he held gripping his tightly. She stared at her image on the screen and swallowed hard, anger and dismay warring on her lovely, pale face.

"I know that was hard to watch," he said in a soft voice. He bent close to her ear, wanting to offer comfort. They were in her office, with others about, or he would have dragged her into his arms for a hug. She looked like she really needed a hug.

"You have no idea."

She took a deep breath and straightened her spine. Damn, the girl was a trouper.

"Did you see the way the cameras were zooming in and out?" she asked him. "Someone was watching this live. They were controlling the cameras, following my progress."

He had noticed it and was pleased she had, too. The woman was smart, brave and intelligent. A lethal combination.

"You acquitted yourself well, Sarah. That initial fall scrambled your brains, but you fought back and managed to save yourself. You deserve a lot of credit."

"For letting that bastard shadow me all over the damn building? I should've realized I wasn't alone. I should've known someone was following me. That was a rookie mistake. I let him catch me from behind."

"Sarah, these things are better at stealth than anything I've ever seen before. They don't breathe. They don't make a sound until you confront them. I'm not surprised you didn't know it was there. You were expecting living, breathing human beings. Not them. You did better than most would have in such a situation. You have nothing to be ashamed of."

"Thanks for being nice, but I expect better of myself." She squeezed his hand and let go, turning back to the computer.

"Nice, eh? Can't say anyone's ever called me that before." He felt the moment needed a little levity. He wanted to see her smile. "My unit would laugh their asses off if they heard anyone call me 'nice.' They'd say I was slipping."

She laughed, and he felt a small victory at seeing the light of humor in her eyes. She was tough on herself, but then, she probably hadn't gotten where she was by going easy. She was a fighter and she demanded a lot of herself. He actually liked that about her.

"Your secret is safe with me, Captain. You're nice and there's little you can do to convince me otherwise."

"Just you wait, Sarah." He gave her a sly look filled with sensual promise. The more he got to know her, the more he wanted to really *know* her.

He wanted her. He wanted to be inside her and drink in her light. He wanted to hear her scream his name as she came. And he wanted to come inside her sexy body, claiming her as his own.

Chapter Five

As they looked through the rest of the disc a disturbing picture emerged. Since the attack, someone had been compiling information about Sarah. They had some of her medical records, her work history, even some of her school records. It was a blatant invasion of privacy that went above and beyond any normal background investigation.

"This is bad." Sarah sat back in her chair and stared at the screen.

Xavier looked like he wanted to say something, but he reached out and blanked the screen as a uniformed courier made his way toward Sarah's desk. He had a thick envelope in one hand.

"Captain Beauvoir? Your team said I could find you here. I have a special delivery from the commander."

The guy looked skeptical and Sarah just watched as Xavier stood and produced ID, which the courier checked carefully.

"Thank you, sir. You'll have to sign." The courier proffered a clipboard bearing official insignias.

Xavier signed and the man saluted before leaving. He had to be army, though he wasn't dressed in anything remotely official looking. He looked more like a postman or special messenger than a military courier, but Sarah supposed that was the idea.

The file was marked TOP SECRET in red letters. Despite herself, Sarah was impressed. This was the real thing, not some prop in a movie.

"I was waiting for this," Xavier said as he sat again, pulling a file from the envelope. "I'm willing to bet one of these guys . . ." On the desk in front of her, he arranged a few ID photos that had been blown up to 8 x 10s. "One of them is probably the mysterious doctor who was in your hospital room when you woke up. Do you recognize any of them?"

Sarah took a look at the photos. There he was. The third one down. Bingo.

"This one. He was the one all hyper about getting a blood sample from me before the nurse showed up." Sarah lifted up the photo and handed it to Xavier.

"Sellars." He said the name contemplatively. "Makes sense. He was one of the senior scientists on the initial project. Looks like he's started up his own illicit project right here on Long Island, despite the prohibitions against pursuing this research any further." Xavier paged through the file until he came to a sheet with the name Sellars at the top. "Last known place of employment is the university medical center here in Stony Brook. This is our guy."

"Do you want to put out an APB or handle this some other way?"

"No APBs. We'll do this quietly for now. That's proven to be the best way."

"So this has happened before?"

Xavier looked uncomfortable as he stowed the remaining pictures back in the envelope. "I'll fill you in, but not here."

She could accept that. No matter that this was a police station, there were still too many potential eavesdroppers in the office. She began to shut down the computer, popping the disc out of the drive. She handed it to Xavier, and he put it into the large envelope with the photos and some other papers.

"Come on, I'll drive you home."

Xavier waited for her to precede him out of the office. He helped her into the Humvee, then slid behind the wheel, stowing the big envelope in a secure pocket behind his seat.

When they got to her house, Xavier parked the Humvee in her driveway. He grabbed a duffel bag out of the back of the huge vehicle and followed her up the walk to her front door.

"What's this?" She looked from him to the big gear bag and back. She'd thought he was just going to drop her off, but it sure looked like he thought he was staying.

"I'm with you for the duration, Sarah. After what we learned tonight, coupled with the visit Sellars paid you in the hospital, you've got to realize you're a target. He wants to talk to you. He wants to observe you. Study you. Maybe even abduct you. If we can catch him, we can end this a lot sooner. So I'm moving in."

"Just like that?" She leaned back against her doorjamb, bone weary . . . and unwilling to concede his very valid points.

"Just like that," he agreed. "Come on, you have to see it. If I'm miles away at a hotel with the cleanup team, I can't help you if Sellars finds out where you live. Hell, even if I'm parked outside on a stakeout of your house, I'd be of little use while you're behind closed doors. I'd have to sweep through your yard every few minutes to be sure nobody has gained entry from the back and I'd never sleep. Do you want that?" He gave her his most hangdog look, and despite herself, she was charmed. "It'll be easier for all of us if I'm camped out on your couch. It'll also save time when we're ready to work. I have an expense account and will gladly pay for any expense having me around might incur. Scout's honor."

Damn, he really was charming when he tried. He also had made some good points, and she was now willing to admit it. It didn't make sense for him to run back and forth to the hotel— miles away—every day. She also knew it would take manpower her department didn't have to put a watch on her house on the off chance that Sellars would come here. Xavier didn't have that kind of manpower at his disposal, either. Despite the army's support in sending him here to solve the zombie problem, they'd sent only him and a small team of techs to clean up the kill sites, and a few other Green Berets.

So far, Xavier had seemed unwilling to put the other soldiers in direct contact with the zombies. They weren't immune like he and Sarah were. So their roles were more in a support capacity, running interference with the locals and keeping the work sites secure. They couldn't be spared to babysit her.

Sellars didn't appear to have her address or phone number. Both were unlisted and protected since she was an officer of the law. Still, there were ways he might be able to find out. She felt safe enough to stay in her home for now, but she admitted to herself that she'd feel a lot safer with backup on the premises.

The fact that she wanted to jump Xavier's bones didn't help her internal debate, though. Having him in her house would be a huge temptation. Of course, they were both adults and capable of refraining from acting on their impulses.

She hoped.

"You can have the guest room," she relented reluctantly. "It isn't much, and you'll have to clean up after yourself. I'm not the maid."

"I promise to be the perfect houseguest." He solemnly crossed his heart, a twinkle of devilry in his eyes.

She pushed open the front door, muttering, "I know I'm going to regret this."

She entered and he followed obediently behind. The obedience was all an act, she knew, but she didn't really fear him. He wouldn't try to push too far beyond her boundaries. Having worked with him over the past day, she'd already made up her mind that she liked him. More than that, she trusted him.

It wasn't normal for her to trust someone on such short acquaintance, but there was something about Xavier that invited that kind of confidence. He was so sure of every move he made, so nonchalantly observant of everything around him, so careful of her—both physically and emotionally.

He'd been a rock of support when she'd had to face the scene where she'd been attacked. He'd prepared her to go over the details with his team, never letting on how he was rehearsing her to deaden the pain of having to relive those horrific moments. He'd also been a solid pillar of strength when they'd faced that creature in the basement. She had faced the enemy with him now and knew he could be counted on to back her up as well as let her do her job.

A lot of her fellow cops tried to protect her from the hazards of their line of work because she was female. They didn't even do it consciously. It was an instinct in them to protect the female, but they had to overcome it if they wanted to work with her. Normally, she avoided those guys who couldn't overcome their chivalrous instincts to make life easier for both herself and for them. She couldn't fault them for being gentlemen. It was actually kind of nice—when they weren't on duty.

She preferred to work with the guys who could put that aside and see her only as a fellow officer. Because they mostly patrolled alone, it usually wasn't an issue. Only once in a while, when they had to work a special detail, did they have to team up. When that happened, the chief knew her preferences and understood her reasoning. He was a great boss, willing to play to his officers' strengths.

Xavier didn't crowd her, but she definitely felt his company in her tiny house. He filled it almost to overflowing as she showed him the guest room. He dropped his bag inside and followed her back out into the hallway.

"This is the kitchen." She felt him close behind as she gave him the nickel tour. "Help yourself to anything in the fridge or cabinets. If there's something special you want, add it to the shopping list on the freezer. I usually go grocery shopping on Saturday morning . . ." She trailed off uncertainly. Her whole life was upside down for the time being.

"We can still go shopping on Saturday morning," Xavier said softly from behind her.

She turned to face him, touched by the understanding concern in his expression.

"Or we can go sooner, if you like. Maybe tomorrow, on our way home."

His words struck her as odd. It was weird to hear him talk about her little house—her haven—as home. Weird in a forbidden-fruit kind of way. She'd almost given up hope of ever finding that one special man she could share her life with, and her home. Having Xavier here was like playacting. A fiendish dress rehearsal for something she wasn't certain would ever really happen.

She was convinced Xavier wasn't the settling-down type. Sure, he was probably willing to shack up with her for as long as his mission lasted, but he wasn't the staying kind. No, he had "love 'em and leave 'em" written all over his bad-boy persona.

"The bathroom's down the hall from the guest room and my room is on the other side." She refused to give in to the gentle magic that flowed between them whenever their eyes met. Sarah moved away, toward the short hallway. "Living room is on the other side of the kitchen. I've got a big-screen TV in there with surround sound. Make yourself at home. I'm going to shower and change before dinner."

"I'll cook something," he volunteered, leaning one hip against the counter in an unconsciously provocative way. Every move the man made was sexy, whether he was trying or not.

"You don't have to." She backed toward the hallway—and escape—even as she protested.

"It would be my pleasure. Don't worry. I know my way around a kitchen. Dinner will be ready by the time you're out of the shower."

She paused to give him a thankful smile. She hadn't been home in over a week and realized only now, surrounded by her belongings, that she'd missed her little nest. She needed a moment alone to reacquaint herself with the secure home she had built for herself over the years. Xavier's expression was filled with understanding and a gentle sort of compassion that was nearly her undoing. She nodded once at him before fleeing for the comparative safety of her bedroom.

Sarah took a long, hot shower, her skin turning prunish before she was willing to give up the luxury of the hot water beating down on her. All the stress of the day melted away under its influence and she began to feel a lot more confident. She was relaxed, too, though still unsure about facing the giant Green Beret who was clanging pot lids in her kitchen.

Whatever he was cooking in there smelled wonderful. As her stomach growled, Sarah threw on her fluffy terrycloth robe. The wound on her leg was pretty much gone, so she left it uncovered. It was just a little red, but judging by how rapidly she'd been healing, even that would be gone shortly. She didn't want to take the time to dither over clothes. She hadn't eaten much of her lunch and was feeling ravenous. The terrycloth robe was thick and full-length. It covered her from neck to ankles. It was more than decent.

Feeling a little wicked, she entered her kitchen a bit uncertainly. Xavier was at the stove, just turning off the heat and lifting the last pot off the burner. His bulky utility belt was nowhere to be seen and he'd stripped off his long-sleeved camo shirt. Only a soft-looking, army-green T-shirt hugged the rippling muscles of his upper body. He still wore the camo pants, but the combat boots had been exchanged for flip-flops, of all things. She hid a smile as she took in the incongruous footwear.

"Just in time." He turned to face her, stirring what looked like homemade spaghetti sauce.

A big serving dish of pasta was already waiting, steaming, on the table. Two place settings had been laid out, complete with tall glasses of ice water. They had stopped for lunch earlier in the day at a neighborhood deli. He'd probably seen then that she preferred water with her meals, and he'd remembered. His thoughtfulness, even over such a small thing, touched her deeply. It had been far too long since anyone had given thought to her preferences.

"I hope you like Italian cuisine." He poured the sauce into a serving bowl and set it on the table.

"Love it." She shot him a suspicious look. "As long as you're not one of those guys who puts hot peppers in everything they eat."

He pulled out her chair and seated her with courtly manners before sitting next to her at the small round kitchen table. "Hot peppers have their place"—he stated emphatically—"but they don't belong in every dish. Certainly not in Italian-style marinara sauce."

"Thank goodness we agree on that." She laughed as she spread a napkin on her lap. It seemed strange to sit at a formal place setting in her robe and nothing else, but Xavier had a way of making the strangest situations seem commonplace. She'd already followed him into battle against a zombie. By contrast, being half-dressed at dinner was nothing at all to blink at.

"I bet you're hungry." Xavier served her a generous portion of pasta before serving himself. "I remember how it was when I woke up after the bite. I was sort of sick to my stomach at first, then my metabolism kicked into high gear. I noticed you didn't eat much of your sandwich at lunch." One eyebrow rose in question as she spooned just the right amount of sauce over her pasta.

"You're right. I wasn't very hungry. Everything tasted kind of bland and made me nauseous. Now, though, I'm starved." She grabbed the shaker of Parmesan cheese and went to town. The sharp bite of the grated cheese was a flavor she couldn't get enough of at the best of times. With hunger riding her, she doubled her usual allotment of the salty cheese.

"I figured as much. That's why I made carbs. Fill up on pasta and your body will have enough energy to satisfy the craving. Then you'll crash and sleep solid for the rest of the night. By tomorrow, you'll be almost back to normal. That's how it worked for me, at least."

She rolled a wad of spaghetti on her fork, eyeing it hungrily. "Let's hope you're right."

They ate in silence for a while. Sarah couldn't get the food shoveled in fast enough and Xavier seemed not to mind her display of gluttony. After the initial rush to quell her hunger, she began thinking of the day's events. She winced as she remembered her reaction when faced with that horrific creature in the basement.

She'd acted like a fool. An untrained idiot. And Xavier hadn't said a word to correct her. Lord knows, her fellow cops wouldn't have wasted a beat in correcting her behavior. Xavier, however, was letting her come to her own conclusions about her performance, and those conclusions were troubling, indeed.

She looked at him, stunned by the patient compassion in his expression. This man was one in a million and, no doubt, a gifted leader of men.

"I owe you an apology." It wasn't easy for her to say the words. She couldn't look him in the eye after that initial contact, focusing instead on her plate. "I was no help at all in that basement. In fact, you would have been better off without me, much to my embarrassment. I'll do better next time."

"I know you will."

His softly spoken words made her look up. The confidence in his tone was reflected in his eyes. His faith in her made her feel a lot better, though she still didn't think it was deserved.

Before she could speak, he covered her left hand where it rested on the tabletop. His gaze sought and held hers as he leaned closer.

"You did really well, despite what you perceive as your failures, Sarah. In fact, you did a lot better than I did the first time I saw one of those creatures."

"It wasn't my first time. I should have been better prepared to face them again."

"That may be," he conceded, tilting his head consideringly. "But even knowing what to expect, it's hard to come face-to-face with something like that. I've done it enough now that I can still function, but the first few times it really threw me."

"You're just being nice." She seriously doubted anything could throw this Special Forces soldier off his game for long.

Xavier laughed out loud. "There's that word again." He shook his head.

"What word?"

He'd captured her attention, as he'd hoped. "Nice. You called me *nice* again. Jeez, woman, you're going to ruin my rep at this rate."

She shared his grin. "Well, you *are* being nice. At the very least, you're making allowances for me, either because I'm a woman or because I'm a cop, not a soldier. Either way, I should probably be insulted, but I can't fault you. I did drop the ball today. For whatever reason."

"How about being human?" His low voice was kind. "While I admit to being as chauvinistic as my granddaddy in certain ways, I don't think less of your abilities either because of your sex or the fact that you're a cop. We both serve justice in our way. You're just used to playing by more civilized rules than I am." He sat back, releasing her hand, though his eyes followed her every movement.

"Maybe, but I still feel I need to do better next time." She conceded the point as she finished the last bite of pasta.

"Seeking to improve with every day is something I think we both have in common."

His gracious words were spoken in a low, respectful voice that struck a chord deep within her. There were depths to this man she hadn't expected. He wasn't just the laid-back Cajun bad boy she'd expected. No, he had more than a little of the philosopher in him.

It was a tantalizing combination. An all-too-attractive combination for her peace of mind.

Sarah stood and collected the plates, heading for the sink to rinse them before placing them in the dishwasher. She shooed Xavier away when he tried to help.

"You cooked. The least I can do is load the dishwasher," she protested.

"Fair enough."

He appeared to give in but continued to bustle around her, putting the unused cheese back in the refrigerator and tidying up everything but the dishes she had claimed. He even opened the dishwasher door for her, much to her amusement, and loaded the detergent dispenser—as if it was his house, not hers.

He was all around her, his masculine presence crowding her even though her kitchen wasn't tiny by any means. It was cozy but not snug. Normally, she had plenty of room, even when she had guests over.

Xavier changed all that. His tall, broad body took up all the space. After a while she got the idea he was doing it on purpose. All the little brushes of his body against hers as he passed her on his way to the fridge, all the innocent, teasing touches of his hands as he moved in and out of her personal space. He didn't give her a chance to object. He was on the sneak attack and winning every minute skirmish until she was totally disarmed and quivering, waiting for his next foray.

Then the innocent game turned not so innocent. Xavier took her by the waist and turned her to face him squarely, backing her into the kitchen counter. She read intent in his gaze just before his mouth dropped to hers and his lips claimed hers with a passion she'd only glimpsed before.

He wasn't kidding around this time and she doubted he'd be the one to call a halt. If she wanted to stop this delicious madness, she'd have to do it herself this time.

And she would . . . in a minute. Or two.

Xavier loved the feel of soft, willing woman in his arms. Especially when the woman in question was the lovely Sarah Petit, hellcat in the field, pussycat in bed—or so he hoped to discover. He wanted her like he'd never wanted another woman. And he would have her. He had no doubt about that.

Whether it was today or some other time, he had made up his mind almost from the first moment he'd met her. She'd impressed him with her determination, humor, quick wit and grit, but she'd wowed him with her courage, compassion and beauty. She was a force to be reckoned with, both as a police officer and as a woman. He wanted to get to know her better, in the most intimate sense.

Beyond that, he wasn't sure where the road they were on would lead them. For now, they rode together. After this mission was over, he wasn't sure what would happen, but he couldn't see himself wanting to give her up once he'd had her. Not for the foreseeable future. If she was willing, he'd even give a long-distance relationship a try, if he had to.

That would work itself out when the time came, though. For now, he wanted to enjoy every sigh, every little catch of her breath as he touched her. His hands ached to get to know the soft curves of her naked body and his cock wanted to find its home between her lithe thighs.

Her small hands went around his shoulders as he pressed her back against the kitchen counter. She was so petite, he was almost afraid of hurting her with his ardor. She gave as good as she got, though, making her own demands in that ultrafeminine way of hers. Little moans and tugs at his clothing drove him wild while the scent, taste and feel of her drugged his every sense.

She was as sublime in her passion, as he'd dreamed. And he had dreamed—since first meeting her, he'd thought often about how she would respond to him. Their first tempestuous kiss earlier had only whetted his appetite for more. More of her. More of their combined passion.

It was like setting spark to tinder. He was hard and wanting with her slightest touch.

"Baby," he whispered against her cheek, drawing back slightly to breathe. They were both gasping for air. "You're sweet to kiss, Officer Petit."

She looked at him, her eyes dilated with pleasure and not quite coherent. He loved that he'd put that look on her face. He'd kissed her silly . . . and he'd only just begun.

He dove for the soft skin of her throat, nudging aside the damp terrycloth of her robe with his chin and teeth as he worked his way downward. She didn't object when he bared her breasts. In fact, she encouraged him, dropping her head back and pulling her shoulders back, offering herself up to him like a pagan goddess of bounty.

Her breasts were perfect. Round and heavy with pointed nipples that begged for his attention. Frustrated by the differences in their height, he bent, placing his hands under her lovely round ass, and lifted her onto the kitchen counter. Her thighs spread to admit him between as if it were the most natural thing in the world.

And it was. For them. It was as if they'd been made to fit together like two puzzle pieces.

He pressed his advantage, leaning in to kiss her once more, rubbing his T-shirt-covered chest over her luscious tits. He felt her nipples stabbing into him, exciting them both as he dragged against her in a sensuous circle.

He had to taste her. Ending the kiss, he leaned back, forcing his hips into the cradle of her thighs while his gaze roamed down her body, visible in the open V of her robe. The belt still held on for dear life while the upper parts of the robe had come away to reveal her breasts. The lower halves had parted when she spread her legs for him. He had a clear view—and feel—of her pussy.

She was neatly trimmed, with shaved edges that made his mouth water. He'd like to do the honors next time. Such an intimate act required the utmost in trust. He'd like to earn that kind of trust from her. But that was for later. For now, he wanted—no, *needed*—to taste her.

Xavier lowered his head, one goal in mind. Well, two, actually—they were soft and round and begging for his touch. His hands framed her breasts, cupping them, stroking with his thumbs just beneath the pointed nipples as her breathing hitched. He licked his way down her throat, following the beating pulse at the side of her neck, then lower, to the soft skin that had tantalized him even under the stiff cotton of her uniform shirt.

She'd been braless of necessity in the hospital, and he'd gotten a good long look at the shape of her under that thin hospital gown. The form revealed by her uniform hadn't disappointed at all. She was fit and firm, soft and feminine in all the right places.

But he hadn't really expected the bounty before him now. She filled his palms and then some, the pinkish tan of her nipples calling out to him. He couldn't resist any longer.

Teasing one excited nipple with his fingers, he dipped his head to capture the other one in his mouth.

Good Lord in heaven, what that man could do with his mouth. Sarah gasped as Xavier made her body dance to his tune. She'd never had so much pleasure from such a simple act.

She'd also never been so decadent as to allow a comparative stranger to feel her up on her kitchen counter before. She'd never look at this room the same way again. She just knew it.

Then again, Xavier and she were closer than they would normally have been on such short acquaintance. Facing danger—and a zombie—together had that effect. He knew just how to touch her, just the right pressure to apply, to make her want to whimper with pleasure. To make her want more.

Her robe was wide-open up top and gaping around her legs. The studly Captain Beauvoir had wasted no time in claiming a place between her thighs. It was all she could do not to rub her aching core against the hard ridge in his pants. In fact, she resisted the urge with everything that was in her, even as she begged for his tongue to continue working its magic on her breast.

He switched sides, pausing to blow a stream of air over her wet nipple. Oh, man! He really knew how to make her squirm.

"Xavier, unh . . ." She was reduced to incoherence when he used his teeth on her. He was gentle, but she felt the masked force of his nibbles. They quaked through her tummy like ripples of something that closely resembled orgasm. If he really tried, she bet he could make her come just like this. Forget about fucking her. All he had to do was fondle her breasts and she was putty in his hands. The man was dangerous.

"What, *cherie*? Do you want more?" His accent grew thicker when he was aroused. It made her hotter as well.

"More. Yeah." She would agree to anything if he'd just keep touching her exactly like that. One hand continued to tease her breast while his lips worked their magic on the other one. His other hand drifted down to her waist, working on the knot that held her robe together. She didn't care. She wanted it gone, too. She didn't want any barriers between him and her skin.

In fact, she moved to help. Between them, they wrestled the knot free and he shoved the robe out of the way. It pooled around her as she shrugged out of only one of the sleeves. She was too busy attacking the button at the waist of his pants to drop the other sleeve.

"Whoa, darlin'." Xavier intercepted, freeing the button himself and disposing of the others just as easily. Her hand slipped inside, down past the soft cotton of his briefs and within to touch the long, hard length of him.

He shuddered as she gripped him, his eyes closing as he felt the impact of her touching him. Then he reclaimed her mouth with his, kissing the daylights out of her while she fondled his cock and he played with her breasts.

The ringing phone sent an unpleasant shock between them. Xavier drew back.

"I'd better get that," Sarah whispered.

She tried to pull her hand out from his shorts, but he stayed her, one large hand gripping hers, pressing her into him for one long, torturous moment while he held her gaze. The intimacy wasn't lost on her. He was staking some sort of claim, even as he started to let her go. He held her hand as it emerged from his pants, taking a short moment to kiss her palm before letting her go completely.

He stepped away, his gaze lingering on her body, especially

between her spread thighs. She blushed, clapping her legs together and hopping down off the kitchen counter. Grabbing her robe as she went, she reached for the kitchen phone, hanging on the wall near the back door.

It was her friend Terry, calling to see how she was feeling. Sarah shrugged into her robe and retied it as she reassured her best friend that she was on the mend. Terry wanted to come over but Sarah put her off. All the while, she felt Xavier's eyes on her, as if burning into her skin. She refused to acknowledge his attention. For one thing, if she looked at him, she'd no doubt begin to babble to her friend. For another, she wasn't sure yet how she felt about what had almost just happened.

She should probably be appalled by her behavior, but she couldn't work up enough energy for it. The delicious hum of arousal still rode her hard—as hard as she imagined he'd have ridden her if she'd let him stay between her thighs just a little bit longer.

They'd been on the verge of having sex. She wasn't usually so easy, but there was something about this soldier that blew down all her defenses. She'd wanted to have sex with him. More than anything.

Saner heads prevailed now that she was free from his seductive spell. He was potent at close range. She'd remember that for the next time.

She had no doubt there would be a next time. With a man as highly sexual as Xavier, it would be a miracle if he didn't try something—or if she didn't—before they finally parted ways. It would be up to her to remain strong against his charm because she'd be the one who ended up with a broken heart when he went on his way.

Sarah ended the conversation with Terry after a few minutes more and hung up the phone. When she turned, Xavier was gone from the kitchen. He'd moved so silently, she hadn't even been aware of his leaving. Perhaps it was for the best. She didn't think she could face him right now.

As she made her cowardly way down the hall, she heard him moving around in the guest room. He'd retreated for now and she was grateful. She would use this night to shore up her defenses. The first skirmish was his. It would be up to her to regroup to fight another day.

Chapter Six

After spending what remained of the night tossing and turning, she finally fell into a deep sleep. Sarah rose late to find Xavier sitting at her kitchen table. He had papers spread out before him, his phone on the table within easy reach, and half a pot of coffee left on the burner. It looked like he'd been hard at work while she'd slept late.

The awkwardness she had feared after what had transpired between them the night before had dissipated. Seeing him working focused her like nothing else. They had a job to do. It was critical that they work together to solve this problem before anyone else died.

"Why didn't you wake me?" She made a beeline for the coffeepot and poured herself a cup. An infusion of caffeine was welcome, considering she felt like she'd been through the wringer and it wasn't even noon yet. The one bright spot was that her leg felt worlds better.

"Within the next day or so we're going to have to switch to night patrols. I figured you could ease into it if you slept late today and went to sleep later tonight." Xavier rubbed one hand over his face and reached for his cup of coffee. Come to think of it, he probably didn't look like he'd slept much better than she had. "You just got out of the hospital, after all. You still need your rest to complete your healing."

That he would think of her comfort and health was extremely appealing. It had been a long time since anyone put her needs first. So long, in fact, that it felt distinctly strange. Strange and wonderful at the same time.

"Why nights?" Sarah took a seat next to him at the table.

"The creatures prefer darkness. They didn't follow you into the sunlight during your first confrontation, remember? That seems to be a common trait among them all, even if this batch has one or two modifications."

"Modifications? You mean how that last guy tried to talk?" She sipped her coffee, welcoming the rush of energy it gave her.

"Exactly. That was totally new. I spent some time this morning discussing our observations with my superior officer and a few others who've had a little more experience with zombies than me. No one has ever seen them try to talk before."

"So what does it mean?" She grew concerned, troubled by the frown wrinkling his brow.

"Who knows? It could be nothing—just an anomaly of that particular creature. Or it could be something much more significant. Like maybe that Dr. Sellars has improved on the original experiment. I know for certain the zombie in that basement didn't go down as quickly or quietly as he was supposed to. I've ended them before. That took way longer than I've ever seen."

"So what can we do?"

Xavier breathed a heavy sigh. "Just keep doing what we're doing, for now. The toxin did work, it just took longer than expected. The zombie tried to talk. Okay. So next time we'll see if the others do the same. If so, we deal with the situation as it presents itself. We'll have to think on our feet. Improvise, if necessary. Don't worry. I do it all the time."

She tried to be as confident as he appeared, but she wasn't feeling it. Not yet, at any rate. Oh, she was certain of Xavier's abilities and skills. It was her own that she worried about.

"I've been making a lot of other calls this morning. One of my guys already checked out Sellars. We've got his file, which includes most of his employment history as well as his current place of employment. Seems he was recently hired by the university medical center in their microbiology department. He even got his own private lab out of the deal. I had Sam swing by there on recon, but it looks like Sellars cleared out. Still, we can go by there today and see if there's anything we can learn."

"Sounds like a plan." She finished her coffee and put the dirty cup in the sink. "I'll just get my stuff."

He caught her arm as she turned to leave the kitchen, forestalling her departure. "I'd like to take your patrol car today. It's a little less obvious than the Humvee."

"Good idea." She had to grin. She'd liked riding around in the big military vehicle, but it was really impractical for suburban streets, not to mention parking lots. "We can drop the Hummer at the station and pick up a patrol car. I'm sure the chief won't mind. I would have been on patrol today, anyway, and they haven't changed the schedule, so my unit should be free."

Sarah felt a lot more comfortable once they were ensconced in the patrol car. She wondered if maybe Xavier had realized how out of her element she'd felt before and had made this concession to help her readjust to "life after the attack," as she was coming to think of it. It felt like everything she'd done before was the prelude to what she was experiencing now.

Apparently, she now had superhuman healing powers and was one of the rare few who were immune to the contagion that killed everyone else it infected. Her life had changed permanently. She feared this mission with Xavier was just the tip of the iceberg. The officers she served with looked at her strangely now. They didn't know exactly what had happened to her, but they sure knew she'd been singled out to work with the military on something top secret.

It marked her as different from the rest of the cops she worked with. That might fade in time, but she'd never be able to talk about her recent experiences with anyone other than the few men on Xavier's elite team.

* * *

The university medical center was located on a sprawling campus. It took some time and maneuvering to find the right building and parking lot but being in an official vehicle helped considerably. Sarah parked her cruiser in an official spot, notifying Dispatch of her location and intent to leave the vehicle. Now that she was back in her official role, she had to do things by the book. She wasn't on patrol, but she had to follow police procedure. If there was an emergency, they had to know where to find her.

Xavier watched everything she did, saying nothing. She liked the fact that he hadn't tried to interfere in any way. He hadn't tried to give her directions, suggestions, or any other kind of pointers now that he had been relegated to the passenger seat. He also truly didn't seem to mind that she was driving instead of him.

Having grown up in a family of men who rarely let their female relatives behind the wheel, she had half-expected some sort of commentary. Lord knew, she'd heard it often enough from her father and four brothers whenever they couldn't avoid letting her drive.

"You're quiet today," Xavier observed as they headed from the car toward the entrance to the building.

"Just enjoying the sunshine and being back behind the wheel." She decided to bait him a little and see if he really was as good as he seemed with letting her drive. "You don't mind that, do you?"

"Mind what? You're the cop. It's only right you drive the cop car." His grin said he knew what she was trying to do. The wink he sent her clinched it.

"What if it was my Mustang? Would you still be content to let me drive?" She watched his response carefully as they neared the row of doors leading inside the office building.

"Somebody give you a hard time, darlin'?"

He opened the door for her, motioning for her to precede him inside. She had to pass close to his tall, hard body. She felt the heat of him as he crowded her on purpose, that devilish grin fixed on her as she passed.

"Because I'd let you take me anywhere. Anytime."

Somehow she knew they weren't talking about driving a car anymore. And she'd be damned if her body didn't respond to the sinful invitation in his velvety voice. Her pulse leapt, her tummy clenched, and she could feel a sudden slipperiness between her thighs as she walked toward the bank of elevators.

"I'll remember that," she promised him in a teasing voice. He trailed behind her and she could almost feel his eyes following the sway of her hips as she walked. It was enough to make a girl self-conscious, but there was little she could do but keep walking. If she stopped, he'd no doubt take it as an invitation. The scoundrel.

Why his outrageous flirting made her want to laugh defied logic. She should be upset with his insistence on treating her like they were on some kind of extended—admittedly weird—date. His playfulness was contagious, and she couldn't help being attracted to him. A woman would have to be dead not to be ensnared by his honest charm.

Besides, what could it hurt to be friendly? He'd already proved he could be as serious as a heart attack when they were in a combat situation. He was good at his job, and when they'd faced that zombie together he'd picked up the slack caused by her hesitation. As long as he continued to perform at that high a level when it really counted, a little friendly banter during downtime couldn't really hurt anything. Cops did it all the time.

Of course, none of her brother officers ever flirted with her. Not like this. Fraternization among male and female officers was strictly prohibited. Xavier, though, was a law unto himself. He wasn't in her chain of command. He wasn't even in law enforcement, per se.

They rode up five floors in the elevator, surrounded by a few people in white lab coats and members of the general public. Sarah's uniform didn't raise any eyebrows. There were police officers coming and going from the medical center all the time. But Xavier's army fatigues drew more than one curious glance.

His hot bod also drew its fair share of feminine attention. A little spike of jealousy wound through her as she watched the other women ogling Xavier. It made her uncomfortable, which was unreasonable. She didn't have any claim on the man, and to his credit, he seemed totally unaware of the women who watched with slack jaws and silly smiles as he passed.

"So how are we getting into Sellars's office and private lab?" Sarah asked as they passed a row of locked doors, all with nameplates on them belonging to different doctors.

"Already taken care of. Sam got a national security warrant and presented it to the proper authorities yesterday. Apparently, Sellars hasn't been seen in a week. Sam did the initial sweep of the place, looking for Sellars. When he turned up nothing of use, he reported back. Here's where I'm hoping your investigative skills are better than his . . . or mine." Xavier stopped in front of a door that had Sellars's name on it.

"I haven't made detective yet," she hedged. "But I'll do my best."

"Our talents run to the snatch and grab. I think your training in the old search and find might be well beyond what we've been exposed to."

She liked the way he was looking at her, as if he truly respected her training and skills. How many times had she been underestimated in her life? She'd lost count. But Xavier . . . He seemed to expect only the best of her. Perhaps that was his leadership style—expecting the best of your people often prompted them to deliver it. Whatever it was, she enjoyed the change and almost basked in the confidence he exuded.

Xavier opened the door as she reached into her utility belt. She always kept a couple of pairs of rubber gloves in one of the pockets in case she had to deal with evidence or blood. She noted Xavier donning a pair he'd taken from his own pocket. They could touch things in the lab now without worrying about leaving fingerprints behind.

"I assume a fingerprinting crew will be coming along behind us, right?" She looked at him over her shoulder as she swept past, into the office.

"As soon as we leave, they're going to go over this place with a fine-toothed comb searching for microscopic evidence. We'll want to know who else has been in this office since Sellars moved in. It'll probably take the techs a few days to sort out all the stray fingerprints and trace evidence that must be in here, but this mission is too important to leave any stone unturned." He shut the door behind them and pulled the shade. He didn't want to be seen searching the office if anyone happened to walk by in the hall.

Late-morning sunlight came in through the blinds on the windows, bathing everything in stripes of light and shadow. Sarah did her best to ignore the distracting play of light as she searched the obvious places first—the desk, file cabinets and credenza—while Xavier booted up the computer and set to work tapping keys.

"Sam did a quick search of the hard drive, but I have a little more geek in me than he does."

The comment startled a laugh out of her and she looked up from a file she'd been leafing through to meet his gaze. "There's nothing remotely geeky about you, Xavier."

"I'm glad you think so." His smile was pure seduction. "But I do have a couple of certifications from Uncle Sam as well as a degree in comp sci from MIT."

"MIT? The Massachusetts Institute of Technology? That MIT?" She was shocked by the idea. Xavier was about as far from a geeky engineering student as she could imagine.

"The very same." He didn't seem insulted by her patent disbelief, but she realized her tone was insulting.

"I'm sorry. I just can't picture you as a college student."

"I didn't hatch fully grown, you know." He continued to grin and she hoped he wasn't offended.

"So how'd you get from MIT to Green Beret? I assume you got the degree before enlisting."

He shrugged, still tapping keys at lightning speed. His voice was pitched low when he finally answered. "The terrorist attacks of 9/11 changed a lot of lives, Sarah. I was engaged to a girl who worked in the World Trade Center. She died and I signed up. I wanted payback, I guess. My family understood even though my original plan had been to join the family business after I finished grad school."

"Oh, Xavier, I'm so sorry." She didn't know what else to say. A native New Yorker, Sarah knew firsthand about the tragedy. She'd lost friends that day, too.

He seemed to shake off the sad memories before replying. "Well, the good news is, Dad still runs the firm and I definitely have a job to go to after I retire from the army."

"What kind of company is it?" She tried to keep the conversation going in less volatile and depressing directions.

"Have you heard of XB computer chips?"

"Who hasn't? They're in everything from coin dispensers to my laptop. They revolutionized the microprocessor when they were introduced—or so everyone says."

"XB stands for 'Xavier Beauvoir'... Senior. My dad invented the whole thing and marketed it from our garage."

"You're kidding." She knew her jaw was hanging slack in amazement. She must look like a fool, but Xavier wasn't laughing at her. He was concentrating on the computer screen as if it held the secrets of the universe. She realized then that he was sharing something with her he didn't tell many people. He was opening up. Trying to impress her? Or maybe just being honest with her out of respect ... and hope that they might be building toward something here.

She tried not to get her hopes up. Of course, there was an undeniable chemistry between them. She'd had her hand in his pants in the middle of her kitchen, for cripe sake. She didn't get in that kind of situation with every man she met. Hell, she'd never done that before—never behaved so brazenly with someone she'd just met.

It was Xavier. He had some kind of magic pull over her. All he had to do was breathe to make her hot. And when she was aroused by him, all her inhibitions seemed to fly right out the window. It was a phenomenon she'd never encountered before. Xavier was a law unto himself.

"You were in grad school when the towers fell?" She tried

desperately to get the conversation back on track, away from dangerous waters. "You have a master's degree from MIT?"

Xavier looked up at her, a sort of sheepish smile on his face. "Actually, it's a doctorate. I warned you I was a geek. I skipped a lot of grades and was one of the youngest in my graduating class. I've been around computers all my life. I helped my dad build and program systems when I was a kid. I could've taught most of the lower-level classes. I didn't really start learning anything until I hit the doctoral level."

"Good Lord. You're some kind of computer genius and you're risking your life as a special ops soldier? And I thought *I* was crazy." She went back to searching the files, even though her mind was racing. Not only was Xavier out of her league as far as men went. He was, after all, an Adonis in camo. He was also some kind of millionaire heir to a giant corporation and brilliant to boot. It was like something out of a movie. No way did people like him exist in real life. And never in her experience. Everyone she knew was solidly middle class. They worked hard for a living, and if they risked their lives on the job it was because they had a deep sense of honor, duty and justice.

That thought stopped her short. Xavier had all of those things as well. So maybe there wasn't as much difference between him and the men she knew as she'd thought.

"I like the army. I like what I do." He shrugged. "I made a commitment to my country and myself. I mean to see it through."

She understood that kind of philosophy. It was a code she tried to live up to every day she put on the uniform. Though they were different uniforms, the ethic was the same.

She paused in her search to look at him. "You're a good man, Xavier Beauvoir." Their gazes met and held for a timeless moment. Then he smiled at her.

"I'm glad you think so." He returned to tapping at the keys. "So what made you become a cop?"

"Come on. You've read my file. You probably know all about me."

"Humor me." He stretched his fingers before returning to the keyboard with new zeal. "I know the dry facts but reading them in a report and hearing it from you are two very different things."

"My father was a cop. He was a detective with NYPD. My brothers followed in his footsteps, mostly. The oldest, Bryan, just made detective, though he did a stint in the marines to earn money for college. The twins, Jesse and Jimmy, are both still in the Corps. They love being marines and I doubt they'll leave until somebody gets wise and kicks them out. The youngest, John, was also a marine, but he got recruited away by a government agency."

"The CIA, right?"

She shot him a teasing look. "That's on a need-to-know basis, Captain."

"Hey, I needed to know," he protested with mocking innocence. "So I got dossiers on your family from my chain of command. It's amazing how much of John Petit's file was redacted for reasons of national security. Even I was impressed."

She laughed at his blatant teasing but knew there was probably more than a hint of truth in his claims. Johnny was a risk taker and she worried every time he mentioned offhandedly that he was leaving the country. He'd taken to not telling her much about his travels until after he got back. It didn't help. She still worried about him.

"Bingo." Xavier's focus was on the screen in front of him.

"What?" He'd no doubt found something.

"I've got an address, and it's not the one Sellars listed on his employment contract." Xavier took out his pad and pen, writing furiously. "He thought he'd deleted this e-mail, but it was stuck in the cache. Someone arranged a little hideaway for Dr. Sellars as some kind of perk. I'm forwarding this to my team. They can trace the metadata while we visit the scene and clear it."

Xavier spent a few more minutes at the desk while Sarah completed her survey of the room itself.

"Nothing very useful in here," she concluded, putting her hands on her hips as she faced him.

"All right, let's tackle the attached lab. It's not big, but there might be something in there." Xavier shut down the computer and headed for the doorway to the private lab.

"So why did you major in chemistry in college?" Xavier asked her as they went through the lab together. It was small but fully equipped.

"I had some idea about going into forensics," she replied absently.

"The thought of your own patrol car lure you away?" he teased, standing back and letting her do the initial search.

She stopped to look at him. "You know darn well why I decided to be a cop instead."

"Your friend Terry." His voice dropped to a compassionate pitch and she read understanding in his eyes.

"When she was attacked . . ." It was hard to talk about this, even now, all these years later. "When I found her after the rape, I realized the importance of being a first responder. I knew I could help more people that way than if I locked myself in a lab. The first officer on the scene was a rookie who didn't have a clue. I practically led him through the steps to secure evidence. If I hadn't been there, Terry's attacker might've gotten away for lack of evidence."

"You're a good friend, Sarah, and a great cop. I've read your file. I've seen the letters from people you've helped. In just the few short years you've been wearing the uniform, you've already made quite a difference. I bet your family is proud."

A warm glow filled her at his words, but the last bit drew a troubled frown. "Proud? Actually, I don't think they understand my motivations at all. The Petit men . . . well, they're what you might call a bunch of macho chauvinist pigs." She chuckled at her own description. "Don't get me wrong, I love my family, but they don't understand me at all. They'd be much happier if I gave up police work and did needlepoint for the rest of my life."

"That would be a supreme waste of talent, Sarah. Take it from me. I evaluate soldiers and make recommendations for their places within the unit. I know a leader when I see one."

Again that feeling of warmth suffused her being. She'd never been praised like this by any man. Not this openly or this honestly. If it was all some ploy to get in her pants, he had to know he didn't need to flatter her. She'd already proven to be despicably easy where he was concerned and they both knew it. So the praise had to be real.

Wow.

She let that sink in for a moment, basking in the feeling.

"Thanks, Xavier."

She reached up and gave him a totally inappropriate peck on the cheek. When she would have pulled away, he caught her around the waist and went way beyond inappropriate. He went straight into sinful territory as he captured her lips with his and kissed her like there was no tomorrow.

They were alone. Locked inside a private lab where nobody could see them. Sarah couldn't think of one good reason to object other than the fact that they were both still on duty. Of course, her duty nowadays was to work with Xavier. She didn't have any other place she had to be.

And the man could kiss. He'd already proven it twice over and it looked like he was going for the trifecta. He backed her up against the edge of the slate lab table. It hit her in the back, but she didn't care. All she cared about was the warmth of his long, lean body in front of her, caging her in and making her crazy with need.

His hands dipped, riding over the curves of her ass, then lifting her straight up, onto the lab table. The tabletop was cold through the cotton of her uniform pants, but it barely registered. Not with Xavier's hard body spreading her legs and stepping between.

He was a tall man and the height of the counter put her in the perfect position for him. He pushed against the crotch of her pants, the ridge of aroused flesh unmistakable even with two sets of clothing between them. He was hard and heavenly rubbing against her. She hadn't felt this needy since she was a teen. Xavier had the ability to make her want him with just a few kisses.

He leaned into her, surrounding her, making her feel small

and feminine. His warm body touched her just right. Her passion spiraled out of control. And then he stopped.

His kiss went on, only it lowered in magnitude. He moved back slightly and she tried to follow, but he wouldn't allow it. She wanted to pout, to cry, to throw something at him.

She also wanted to moan at the sweet turn the kiss had taken. He cherished her lips, his body a warm presence in front of her that no longer drove her to near madness. Now it seduced her. It drew her in. It made her want to be his lover, his woman, his slave.

Xavier kissed her for what seemed hours. To be honest, she lost all track of time while he teased her with his mouth, his tongue, his looming presence. She wanted it all and she didn't want it to end. Ever.

He drew back farther.

"Now that's what I've been missing all morning." Xavier left her lips with obvious reluctance as he gazed into her eyes.

"Wh-what?" Great. She was really out of it.

"My good-morning kiss. The day isn't complete without it." He was altogether too chipper for her frame of mind. How could he tease after rocking her world like that?

Now that he'd brought up the subject, so to speak, she had a thing or two to say to him about what was going on between them. He probably wouldn't like it, but she wanted to set a few things straight before this went any further. She lifted her arms from around his shoulders and sat back on the table, seeking space so she could think more clearly. She was the next best thing to incoherent when he had his arms around her. A frown creased his brow as she pulled away.

"Look, Xavier . . . about last night. And just now. We can't do this."

"Seems to me like we did just fine."

"You know what I mean." She shot him a disgusted look when he only grinned at her. "I'm happy to work with you on this case, but I feel anything else would be a mistake."

"You're calling what we did last night a mistake? It felt pretty good to me—up to the point where we got interrupted."

At the time she had cursed the interruption, but after putting some distance between them and giving herself time to cool down, she realized it was for the best. She couldn't let this go any further.

"Come on, Xavier. Be realistic. You're leaving and I'm not the kind of girl who can jump in and out of bed with different men every week."

"I never thought you were." He looked shocked by her words. Shocked and on the verge of anger, if she read him right. Now, that was confusing. He wasn't responding at all the way she had anticipated.

He stepped away from the table, pacing in what looked like annoyance as she jumped down from her perch. She felt more stable on her feet, even when he was so much taller.

"I don't want to get involved, all right?" She turned away, wringing her hands. She was being downright rude, but she didn't see any other way to get through to him.

"No."

"What?" She spun around, meeting his gaze.

"You heard me. You may not want to *get involved*"—he emphasized the words with a sneer—"but I have news for you, sugar, we are already involved. At least I am. More than I've been with any woman in recent memory."

He looked *this* close to losing his temper. Xavier took a step back along with a deep breath, seeming to regroup.

"I didn't look for this. I didn't expect it when I came here, but I can't deny it and neither can you. Am I right? I know you're attracted to me."

"You've got one hell of an ego, Beauvoir," she muttered darkly.

"Good thing or I might just start to think you don't like me." His self-deprecating chuckle invited her to join in.

"Xavier . . ." The man exasperated her.

"Sarah." Her name was a mere rumble as he moved in front of her, taking her hands in both of his. "Give me a chance. Give us a chance. I've never been this attracted to any woman in my life. I want to see where this could lead."

Oddly, she believed him. The honesty in his voice and sincerity in his expression—for once open and laid bare for her to see—was her undoing.

"I know you're not easy. Hell, I probably wouldn't be half as attracted to you if you were. You're the kind of girl a guy is proud to bring home to meet his mama. I'm not messing around here. I hope you're not, either, because I'm not that kind of boy." The last was said in a teasing voice that made her smile despite herself.

"I'll just bet you aren't. You've probably left a string of broken hearts through every bayou in Louisiana." Was she melting under his concentrated charm offensive? Damn, she thought maybe she was.

"I'll admit, I did sow my share of wild oats." He nodded sagely, his tone at odds with the sheer devilry in his eyes. "That's all over now. I've seen the light." He paused, his expression clearing as he freed one hand so he could cup her cheek. "It was the light in your eyes, Sarah. The moment you woke up and started sassing me, I knew I wanted to get to know you better."

Son of a gun. She thought he just might be serious after all. No way would a man use a line like that if he was really up to no good. Not when he knew the woman in question carried a gun and knew how to use it. She was beginning to think he was sincere.

"You're serious?"

"As I've ever been." He moved his other hand, still grasping hers, to cover his heart. She felt the steady beat against her palm. It was reassuring. "We have an opportunity here that I don't want to waste. I want to see where this attraction leads—to the end of this mission and beyond if that's what's in the cards for us. Between you and me, I think it is, Sarah. I think there's voodoo in the air when we touch like I've never felt before. Do you feel it?" His words dipped low, rumbling through her very being. "Tell me you do."

"Xavier." She shook her head, trying to clear herself of the spell he'd woven around them. "I don't know what this is. I'm afraid . . ." She tried to think how best to end that sentence and realized there were too many things to list. "I'm just afraid."

"Don't be, *ma petite.*" He tugged her into his arms, cradling her close. "I'm a soldier and you're a cop. Together, there's nothing we can't handle. You watch my back and it will be my utmost pleasure to watch yours, sweetheart."

But who would protect her from the broken heart she was sure was coming? Who would protect her from *him*?

Sarah extracted herself from his arms after a long moment spent worrying and wondering if she was about to make an even bigger fool out of herself than she already had. In the end, it didn't matter. Nothing mattered other than the intense attraction she felt for him, and the promise in his eyes.

He seemed sincere. She thought she was a good judge of people. She'd honed her instincts over her years on the force. She wanted to believe Xavier was on the level—that he wasn't just trying to get into her pants while he was in town, intending even now to leave her high and dry when his mission was over. She was afraid of a *wham, bam, thank you ma'am*, but after the way he'd just opened up and hinted at a possible future, she was beginning to believe he wouldn't do that to her.

Would he leave? Indeed he would. He wouldn't have a choice. Once his mission was over, he'd be reassigned. Would he dump her? She was starting to believe he wouldn't. If—and this was a very big *if*—they discovered something lasting, something loving, in their time together, she believed he would try to find a way for them to be together.

He was holding out the hope for a possible future. He wasn't just trying to con her into being his bedmate for the duration of his mission, as she had feared. No, there was more to it than that. More than just the moment and the mission. There was hope for something more. Something lasting. Something that could even prove to be permanent.

Instead of answering in words, she reached up and pulled him down for a long, slow, lingering kiss. The room spun, time stood still, and two heartbeats stuttered, then began beating in rhythm as Xavier answered her passion with his own.

"Mmm," he growled when he finally let her up for air long minutes later. "A fellow could get used to that."

"You think so?" She dared to flirt now that she'd decided to trust him.

"Does this mean you're willing to give it a go? To take a risk? Take a walk on the wild side?" He teased right back, his hands roaming down from her waist to cup her butt cheeks, giving them a naughty squeeze.

"I'm willing to see where this leads. For now. And only when we're not on duty. The case comes first. What happens after hours is strictly between us." She patted his chest and freed herself from his loose hold. He let her go without complaint, a wide grin on his handsome face. He'd won and he knew it.

"Yes, ma'am," he drawled, his eyes sparkling with warmth. "I can live by those rules." He caught her hand when she would have turned away, his expression clearing when he had her attention. "Thanks, Sarah."

His naked honesty impressed her. She squeezed his hand and nodded, not knowing what else to say. She was taking a big chance on him. A chance of a broken heart.

Chapter Seven

They decided to press on with their search of locations Sellars had been known to use. The lab was empty of anything helpful at first glance. The techs would have a field day looking for trace evidence over the next few days. If they found anything helpful, Xavier would be the first to know.

He'd won a victory in that snug laboratory. Sarah had agreed to give him a chance. He felt like shouting his triumph to the sky, but thought better of it. He had a reputation to maintain and he doubted Sarah would take well to such behavior on his part. She was skittish enough as it was. He had to tread lightly, lest she change her mind and leave him out in the cold.

He wanted her to the point of madness. And he would have her. He would have kept hammering away at her defenses until she agreed, if she'd shot him down today. Luckily, he didn't have to go through that agony. She'd agreed to let him court her. Oh, he hadn't used those exact words, but that's what he intended to do. The Beauvoir men were known for their charm. Xavier had every intention of bowling her over with his, then capturing her heart and never letting her go.

Whoa. He had to slow himself down. Those thoughts sounded awfully permanent, and awfully scary to a man who'd never contemplated such a thing before. Tying himself to one woman wasn't something he'd ever wanted to do, but Sarah was making him think of all sorts of crazy things. She'd had a potent effect on him since the first time he saw her lying in that hospital bed.

She'd looked so helpless and fragile. He'd wanted to protect her from the very first. But he knew she was a police officer, well capable of taking care of herself. She'd fought off two zombies and lived to tell the tale, for heaven's sake. She was a trouper and didn't need him acting like a caveman. Still, there it was—the need to be with her, to be beside her, sharing the danger of her job and shielding her from whatever he could.

She'd probably throw a fit if he ever said anything like that to her out loud. He had to chuckle inwardly. Sarah was feisty, feminine and utterly adorable. He'd watch over her and trust in her to watch his back, just like he'd said. They were partners in this mission, unlikely as he'd thought that just a few days before.

Now he needed something to get his mind off what had happened in the lab. He decided to discuss the mission as they walked toward her patrol car. "I think we should hit the apartment listed on Sellars's employment records first this afternoon and save the other address for later."

"Why? I thought the address you found on the computer would be a hotter property than the apartment."

"It is, which is why I want to wait until later, around dusk. If the creatures are there, they'll be active when night starts to fall. If we go in too early, we run the risk of having them flank us. If we wait for them to be active, we'll see them head-on."

She unlocked the patrol car and he opened her door for her, waiting for her to get in before going around to the passenger side. She seemed surprised by the courtesy. He made a mental note to step up the chivalry. She'd get used to his respectful ways, given time, and he'd enjoy surprising her and treating her like the princess she was.

Sellars's apartment had an empty feel to it. The man had probably lived there at some point but appeared to be long gone.

A few articles of clothing hung in the closet and the pantry was stuffed with food. It was fully furnished, and newspapers and magazines littered the coffee table. The utilities, phone and cable TV appeared to be in good working order.

"He left in a hurry," Xavier observed, noting the place where a desktop computer system had been installed. The cabling and peripherals were still there. Only the tower case containing the heart of the CPU was gone.

Sarah was in the living area of the small apartment, doing a detailed search according to her police training while Xavier took a look in the other rooms. Xavier continued to be impressed by her skills and abilities. She did everything by the book and knew how to handle this kind of work way better than he did. It had been a wise decision to include her on the team.

"I found something," she called out.

Xavier stuck his head through the doorway, curious as to what could put that note of triumph in her voice.

She held up a small rectangular object. It was no more than three inches in length and about a half inch wide. He knew what that baby was. A grin stole across his face as he moved into the room.

"A USB flash drive. Nice," he commented as she handed him the small black stick. There could be a wealth of information on this device, or it could contain nothing. They'd have to plug it into a computer to find out. "Where was it?"

"Stuck in the couch. It probably fell out of somebody's pocket and slipped down in between the cushions. I almost missed it. It was wedged in there real good."

He grew suspicious of their continued good fortune. "Does this feel a little 'Hansel and Gretel' to you?"

"You mean like a trail of bread crumbs? You think they're leaving these things around for us to find on purpose?"

"Could be. It's a little convenient, wouldn't you say?"

Her enthusiasm seemed to deflate before his eyes. "Yeah. I guess you're right."

"It's worth looking at, though. Right now, it's our only clue, regardless of how we got it. We'll have to follow where it leads—if it leads anywhere."

"Even into a trap?" Her expression grew calculating.

"Even into a trap," he agreed, nodding. "Forewarned is forearmed. We'll be on the lookout. If it is a trap, maybe we can turn the tables."

"All right, then." She seemed to regain some of her attitude. "You want to go back to the station to check this out on my computer?"

Xavier felt a little chagrined. It was time to come clean. "We don't really have to do that. I have a secure machine we can use."

"You have a computer stashed somewhere?" He nodded and she continued. "So why didn't we use it before?"

"I was curious. Sorry. I wanted to see your workplace and what kind of interest your injury and reassignment had sparked among your fellow officers. I was doing a little recon, you might say."

"Recon."

She seemed insulted and a little angry from the way her brows drew together. That was to be expected, but he still felt guilty about it.

"In the police station?"

"Yeah. It had to be done, but in retrospect, I probably should have told you what I was up to. In my own defense, I thought if you didn't know, you couldn't give me away by acting abnormally among your coworkers, just in case."

She looked like she was considering his words. He was unprepared for how important her acceptance was to him.

"I guess I can see your reasoning. So." She slapped her thigh, dusting off one hand. "Did you notice anything odd at the station?"

"Did you?" He couldn't resist teasing her, even though he was on uncertain ground with her at the moment.

"I asked first." The hint of amusement on her lips reassured him.

"Indeed you did." He tilted his head, giving her a lazy smile. He sensed her forgiveness, which mattered way more than it probably should. "To answer your question, no, I didn't see anything to arouse suspicion at your station. I'm satisfied, between my observations and the detailed reports I had commissioned, that there's nothing funny going on there."

"Well, that's a relief." She didn't sound relieved. "Of course you could have just asked me. I've only known those guys for years." The sarcasm was thick in her tone, but he refused to rise to the bait. He didn't want to argue with her. Especially about something so inconsequential.

"Next time, I will," he promised.

She eyed him suspiciously. "Are you humoring me?"

"Not at all, *chère.*" He made an X across his heart as he grinned at her.

She seemed to consider his words, then shrugged, letting the matter drop. "So where's your computer and how soon can we check this memory card?"

"Are you finished searching here?"

"Yeah, I'm done. There's nothing else I can find. Maybe the techs will have better luck with trace evidence." She looked around the room, her eyes lighting here and there on the areas she'd searched.

"I'm hungry." He rubbed his stomach as he stretched tight muscles in his neck, shoulders and back. "You about ready for lunch?"

"I could eat," she answered simply, following him toward the door.

"Then we'll check out your find over lunch. I noticed a little bistro down the block that had a free Wi-Fi sign in the window."

He let her precede him out the door and shut it carefully behind them.

They paused for a late lunch at the small café he'd seen. It did indeed have Internet access, which might come in helpful. Xavier pulled a small notebook computer out of the knapsack he'd brought in with him. He fired it up and spent a few moments connecting the USB stick Sarah had found.

"Well, well, well. Would you look at that?"

"What have you got?"

"*We've* got a bonanza of evidence." His eyes narrowed as he read the damning information contained on the memory stick. "Looks like the good doctor is considering selling his research to the highest bidder. More than considering, actually. He's taking bids and accepting perks from at least two foreign governments and agents, that, I can only assume are either other foreign powers or arms dealers." Xavier tapped more keys, getting to the heart of the information on the chip. "He must've lost this thing about two weeks ago."

"How can you tell?"

"That's when the last file was accessed. No activity since." He tapped keys as he spoke, scanning the contents of the flash drive.

"Do you still think it was planted?" Her tone was low, almost worried.

"I'm not sure. I'm leaning toward thinking it was truly lost. Sellars would've had to plan ahead or just happen to have a drive he hadn't accessed in two weeks. He also would've had to be willing to give up all this information. I don't know, but considering how he's behaved to date, he probably wouldn't have wanted us to have all this. If it were a setup, there probably would've been only one or two carrots dangled in front of us. Not all this."

"Unless he's willing to sacrifice that much to get what he really wants," she countered.

"Which is?"

"Beats the heck out of me. That's all I've got." She sat back and gestured with her palms held outward as if in surrender.

"You may have a valid point. Still, I'm going to send this up the line to see what the others can make of these names. If they're real contacts, this could help break the investigation of the paper trail wide-open."

"Then there are more people involved in this than just you and me in the field and your support team?"

"A lot more. Each carefully selected for their expertise or, as in my case, because they were in the wrong place at the wrong time and learned about the threat the hard way." He shook his head slightly. "Those who were chosen to participate after the fact have been carefully screened and have top-level security clearance. People are added as needed, and those in charge are trying to keep the total number who are aware of this problem to a minimum, of course. They may need to get some spooks in on this soon, though. Especially considering what's on this chip. If there's a foreign connection, the CIA will most likely become more involved. From what I was told, they were acting in an advisory role because somebody up the chain of command was already worried about foreign powers getting involved."

"This is bad, Xavier." She frowned, her face serious with worry.

"And getting worse if this information is correct. But that's for the spooks and my superiors to worry about. Our immediate assignment is to stop this outbreak by any means necessary. So, if this chip was last accessed two weeks ago . . ."

"That means we can say Sellars—or somebody with access to sensitive information about his operation—was at his apartment two weeks ago."

"I doubt he'd give that kind of information to just anyone. I'm willing to bet this chip was his."

She'd already dusted the outer plastic case of the little drive using the fingerprint kit from the trunk of her patrol car. "There were no prints on it. I guess rubbing against the couch cushions repeatedly wiped it clean."

"Sounds about right." He looked up from the laptop.

"I've already begun reconstructing his movements from known data." She pulled out her notepad and turned to a page toward the back. "I started a rough timeline. I haven't got much on it yet, but each piece of information we find helps me fill it in a little." She made a notation as he watched, putting a little hash mark on the date of the last file access. "It might amount to nothing, but you never know. It could help us find a pattern or something."

"That's good work, Sarah. Every little bit helps."

He refocused on his computer and spent the next few minutes uploading the information from the chip, sending it to Commander Sykes. He could figure out what to do from there, Xavier was certain.

Sending information over a public Wi-Fi system was tricky, but Xavier had top-level encryption. The data itself consisted of names, addresses, calendar notes and other identifying information. It wasn't scientific in nature. It certainly wasn't the secret to creating the zombie formula. If Xavier had seen anything like that, he wouldn't have chanced sending it to Sykes over any network—not even with his personal encryption.

As it was, this set of data was relatively harmless. Although it could prove to be Sellars's downfall if they were able to make connections and draw conclusions that led them to him. It could also incriminate a good number of foreign powers, operatives and arms dealers. Yes, sir, the spooks would have a field day with what he'd found on the chip, if it turned out to be good information and not some kind of planted ploy.

Sarah was turning out to be quite an asset to his mission. Their training was similar in some ways but as different as night and day in others. She was trained to investigate, while he was more of the "destroy first and ask questions later" mindset. Having her along was making him rethink his instinctive actions, which in this case wasn't a bad thing.

"Where are we heading next?" She had finished her meal while he'd been busy typing and uploading.

"I think we'll stick with our original plan to hit the next address."

"Clouds are moving in. Could get dark early tonight." She nodded toward the floor-to-ceiling windows that fronted the café. Indeed, it was getting dark as the sun was covered by pale gray clouds.

"Let me finish this and we'll get moving." He finished his sandwich while he shut down the laptop.

When he was done, they headed over to the address Xavier had found on the disc from the office. It was late in the day. Clouds now completely covered the horizon and night was falling fast.

If any zombies were on the premises, they'd be active shortly, if they weren't already. Xavier had learned the hard way not to let any of the creatures get behind him. Better to face them head-on than to try to sneak up on something that was even better at stealth than he was.

The address turned out to be a big house on a wooded lot. There had to be an acre or more of woods around the home along with a huge, seven-foot wall that provided a lot of privacy in the upscale residential neighborhood.

"What do you think a property like this goes for around here?" he wondered idly.

"The land alone is worth over half a mil in this neighborhood," Sarah said. "With a house of that size and its pretty looks, I'd say this place probably listed at well over a million, easy."

Xavier whistled low. They had parked out on the county road and walked the rest of the way, just in case. Sarah's gray uniform blended well with the twilight and Xavier's camo was even harder to discern among the trees along the side of the road. They'd paused at the edge of the property to get the lay of the land before approaching any closer.

The woods were dense leading up to the house. The only direct route to it seemed to be the long, straight, narrow driveway. Xavier didn't like the look of it. To his battle-trained senses it looked too much like a trap. No doubt there was some kind of security system in place. Cameras at the very least. Perhaps motion or heat sensors as well.

"I'd rather go through the woods to get to the house than up that driveway." He nodded toward the one open path and kept his voice low.

These residences were huge and set well back from the road and they were still under cover of the trees at the side of the road. Still, someone might see them from a window, or hear them if they spoke too loudly.

"I'm game for a hike if you are."

He liked her sense of adventure. Even in this potentially dangerous situation, she could laugh and joke with him. His fellow soldiers were like that for the most part. He just hadn't expected it in a civilian. He had to keep reminding himself she wasn't really a civilian. She was a cop. They shared a sense of duty and an oath to protect. He shouldn't have been surprised by her easy humor in dangerous situations. Cops probably faced danger even more often than regular soldiers did.

They approached the house at an oblique angle from the woods. The first few yards in, everything looked okay. Xavier led, stopping every few feet to check for anything obvious— sensors or booby traps—but there wasn't anything he could detect.

Then he began to notice footprints in the loamy soil beneath the trees. They were dragging footsteps. The hairs on the back of his neck began to prickle in awareness. He pointed to the footprints, making Sarah aware of them. She'd noticed but her shrugging reply to him said she hadn't made a connection between the pattern of the print and the way the bad guys walked, sort of dragging their feet behind them.

"Zombies." He whispered the word so only she could hear, still pointing to the drag marks. Sarah's eyes widened. Xavier drew his weapon. The one that was loaded with toxic darts. Sarah did the same.

The prints proved the creatures had been here in the past. The recent past, if he was reading the freshness of the prints correctly. They might've left, but he wouldn't bet on it.

God, he hated putting Sarah in the path of danger. She did have training to deal with rough situations, though. That was some consolation. It helped, too, that she'd faced these guys on her own before and lived to tell the tale.

This time, they would face the zombies together. Nothing really bad would happen to her if he had anything to say about it. He also felt good knowing that she was impervious to the contagion that would kill almost anyone else. He had to end the danger. He and the very few others like him who were immune had to shoulder the burden for the rest of humanity.

It was his calling to protect, just like it was Sarah's. As a cop, she was sworn to protect and serve. Well, she was about to get her wish. Xavier saw movement in the woods ahead.

He gestured and she nodded. Good. She saw it, too. She probably had never had to do much sneaking around in her line of work, but she was a quick study and light of foot. Her petite size helped her when it came to moving silently through the trees. That was good. So far, it looked like the zombies had no idea he and Sarah were there. He'd like to keep it that way as long as possible.

Xavier positioned them along the side of the property about twenty yards from the house. The area was filled with trees, only a ten-foot clearing between the woods and the structure.

Xavier caught sight of one of the creatures as it came around the corner of the house. He dragged his feet in a sloppy imitation of a march step, his eyes empty, his expression slack. Xavier spared a second to glance at Sarah. Her eyes were wide with recognition. This, then, was most likely one of the creatures that had attacked her.

He was a big son of a bitch. And he'd died young. The kid was no more than twenty-two or so, if Xavier was any judge. His face was also suspiciously free of bite marks. He'd been one of those made by the experiment, then, and not one made by an attack. His blond hair was riddled with filth, but the empty blue eyes and the leeched skin that still retained a pale tan made Xavier think this kid had spent a lot of time at the beach. Hell, he was probably a surfer. Poor kid. He was dead now, and in a few minutes there'd be nothing left of him at all but a pile of goo.

Not after Xavier got through doing his job. He had to put the surfer kid out of his misery, but first he had to see if there were more of the creatures in the area. It wouldn't do to launch an attack, only to be surrounded by dozens of the bastards. More reconnaissance was in order.

Xavier began to move, mentally tagging the surfer's location for the moment he launched his offensive. It wouldn't be long now.

Moving carefully, Xavier circled the house, trying to cover as much of the woods as possible, Sarah his silent shadow. He didn't see any other zombies, though he noticed a lot of tracks. Dragging feet of different sizes meant several different creatures had been through here in the recent past. Where were they now? In the house? Or waiting in the woods? Or have they been let loose on an unsuspecting population?

He hoped to hell they were still here, even though that would make his job more dangerous. The more of them he had to take out at one time, the more potential for problems. Of course, he had his trusty sidekick with him. That meant double the firepower. Maybe they could swing this after all.

Xavier motioned Sarah to hang back while he went around the corner of the house first. She nodded agreement and he moved stealthily forward.

He rounded the corner and . . . damn. There was another one, not five yards from him. It looked up.

Xavier let loose with two darts, hitting the target cleanly as it advanced slowly on his position.

"Xavier?" Sarah's voice came from behind him.

"One up here," he reported swiftly. "He saw me. I darted him twice but he's still advancing."

"Xavier . . ." She sounded breathless. "There are more behind us."

He glanced over his shoulder.

"Shit!" Four more were coming at them through the woods from different angles. They were nearly surrounded. How the *hell* did that happen? "Open fire. Take the two on your left. I've got the other two." They were both moving and firing before he'd even finished speaking.

They put two solid hits in each target. The four in the woods continued to stalk forward, their slow and steady motion unchanged.

He heard that moaning sound that set his teeth on edge as he looked for the first one he'd darted. Damn. The guy was still standing, closer now, even though Xavier and Sarah had darted through the only gap in the line of creatures, out into the deeper woods in back of the house.

"Are any of those one of the ones that attacked you before?" Xavier was trying to keep a mental tally of the monsters. There were too damn many of them.

"No. Just the one we spotted first. He's the one that snuck up behind me."

"Son of a—" Xavier spun around, checking the dense woods. Sure enough, there was the surfer, trying to perform the same maneuver. They'd been neatly trapped. He'd ponder the implications of that bit of news later. If they survived.

Xavier let loose at the surfer with two rounds but one ended up stuck in a tree. Sarah had a better angle and she took it, hitting the surfer solidly in the thigh.

"They're all around us. They're closing in!" Sarah's voice held a trace of panic, though she seemed to be holding it together pretty well. Xavier knew their situation wasn't good.

"They're not disintegrating, either. We shot each of them twice. They should be gone by now."

"Should we hit them again?"

"Yeah. Two more pops each. Try to spread out your shots." He suited his words to his action and they both started firing, standing back to back. They were at the center of a very deadly circle. Only a few yards separated them from the ring of monsters, their slicing claws and sharp teeth.

Sarah could see the deformed, blood-stained faces as they neared. Bite marks showed where they had been savaged, and bits of dead flesh hung off their skulls in places like something out of a Halloween horror show. Except makeup could never look as bad as this. Or smell as bad.

Sarah wanted to gag but did her best to keep her professional demeanor. She wouldn't let Xavier down again. She wouldn't let herself down again. She could handle this without falling to pieces.

"They're getting closer, Xavier."

"The toxin should take effect any moment now. Damn. Come on, darts, do that toxic thing."

Despite the nearly desperate situation, she was amused. "I don't think talking to the darts is going to help."

"Couldn't hurt." Xavier's back touched hers. She felt his warmth, his strength and his quivering alertness. His body was on edge, but not with nerves. No, it was more eager anticipation of action. "You okay, Sarah?"

"Just peachy." She watched the creatures advance, her heart racing. They were closer now, just a few feet away.

"Bingo." Xavier's soft exclamation alerted her.

She turned just in time to see the first one he'd shot take a step, then sort of implode right before her eyes.

"Quick! That way."

Xavier pushed her ahead of him, out of the tightening circle. She jumped over the pile of old clothes and organic goo, Xavier right behind her as the zombies changed course. The two of them could outrun the zombies, as long as the creatures weren't setting another trap.

Damn. They'd actually set a trap. She didn't think they were supposed to be capable of that kind of organized thought.

"Xavier, do these guys seem a lot smarter than the other ones you've faced?"

He looked at her sharply before returning his attention to the woods around them and the zombies on their trail. "Yeah. And they're harder to kill. Takes more of the toxin and more time."

As he said that, the others started imploding behind them. One by one, they went down in the order they'd been shot. Only the one who'd snuck up behind her in the abandoned building remained.

"Surfer boy will go in another minute," Xavier said quietly as they kept alert for more of the creatures while watching the one they'd shot. "He's the one who bit your shoulder, right?"

"Yeah. Sneaking up behind people seems to be his thing."

"Not for long." Xavier's head swiveled as he searched the grounds, then returned to focus on the remaining zombie. "Ah. There he goes."

As they watched, the creature sank in on himself, dissolving in seconds into a steaming pile of organic debris and old clothes on the ground. Sarah felt an immense sense of relief knowing that one of her attackers was no more. She also felt sorry for the young man who'd been cut down in the prime of life. Somewhere, someone would grieve for his loss, if they were ever able to identify who he'd been. Otherwise, his loved ones would never know how or why he'd disappeared.

"So that leaves at least one more. Probably more than that, actually, based on their current multiplication rate." Xavier was moving again, his head turning from side to side as he scanned the woods. Sarah did the same, even as she asked questions. There was no need for silence any longer, though she kept her voice low. After that last little confrontation, anyone else on the grounds had to know they were here by now.

"What multiplication rate?"

"They like to bite. They seem driven to do it. One can become many in a few days. Judging by how many we just took out and the fact that only surfer boy looked like one of the original models, these things have been multiplying for a while. There are bound to be more in addition to the one who messed up your leg." He shot her a concerned look. "How's the leg holding up?"

"I'm good," she rushed to assure him. She wasn't about to let on how the uneven ground was causing more than a little discomfort to her thigh, despite the rapidly growing muscle and skin. "The woods look clear," she said, trying to take the focus off her condition. Xavier gave her a suspicious look but allowed the change of subject.

"I agree. I think we can check out the house now, but be careful. There may be more hiding inside. I noticed there was only one viable entry. The back door was boarded shut."

"Yeah, I saw that, too. It's not unusual for empty places around here to be boarded up to keep kids and vandals out."

They skirted the edge of the wooded area, approaching the front entryway at an oblique angle. There was a larger clearing in the front of the house where the long driveway led to a parking area. There were no cars in any of the parking spots and no sign that anyone was home.

"The house looks deserted," she observed.

"Looks can be deceiving. Stay sharp."

Xavier made his move, covering the distance between the trees and the front door in a hustling sort of crouched jog. Sarah followed behind as best she could on her gimpy leg. The twilight had turned to full dark as they finished searching the woods around the house. No lights shone from within.

Sarah's eyes had adjusted to the dark. It wasn't a pitch-black night. There was thin cloud cover and a bright moon that had risen before dark. Its light reflected off the clouds, bathing the world in an eerie glow. Creepy, but useful.

Xavier went to the door, warning her first and counting down before he kicked it open. It made the most horrendous noise. He reached one hand in, looking for a light switch in the dark interior.

The light went on inside, casting a warm glow over the threshold.

"Looks clear. I'll go first. I want you right behind me, then shut the door. We'll hear it if anyone comes in after us."

She understood. The door squeaked like the dickens. If anyone opened it after them, they'd definitely hear it. There was no way around it.

Xavier entered and she followed close behind, shutting the door after her. When she turned around, Xavier was already across the large, open great room and in a short hall. He was at the door to a side room and reached in to find the light switch.

"Fuck!" he swore, pulling his hand back. It was bloody. Long furrows marred his tanned skin from wrist to elbow. They were deep and painful looking. "There's one in there. Bastard scratched me."

The lights were still off in the room and no sound came from within.

"Hang on. I'll shine my light inside."

"Do it from back there." He indicated a spot about three feet away. "I may need room to maneuver."

Sarah backed off three paces while she reached for her flashlight. On Xavier's nod, she flicked it on and aimed the widely dispersed beam into the small room.

She saw the creature right away, huddled in the corner. It was female.

The poor girl was young. Maybe twenty or so, with what had been long blond hair, now matted with blood and filth. Her face had no doubt once been pretty but was now a ruined mess. She shied away from the light as Xavier walked into the room. He took aim as the pathetic creature looked up at him.

"Mas-ter?"

The girl seemed to be addressing Xavier. She'd clearly called him "master."

"What the hell?" Xavier seemed completely taken aback.

So was Sarah, if truth be told. The creatures weren't supposed to be able to speak, according to Xavier.

"That's right," Xavier temporized. "Be a good little zombie and stand up for your master. Stand up, girl."

Astonishingly, the girl got to her feet. Sarah could see the fresh, bright-red blood on the talons of her left hand. That was Xavier's blood.

"What's your name?" Sarah asked from the hallway.

The girl looked past Xavier to stare blankly in Sarah's direction.

Xavier shot Sarah a questioning look. She shrugged. "It was worth a try. If we knew who she was, we might be able to learn where Sellars is getting his victims. It would also help to be able to notify next of kin when this is all over. Knowing who she is would probably close a missing person's case. Somebody is bound to be looking for her."

Xavier looked impressed by her reasoning. Suddenly the

girl started to move toward him. Her claws rent the air as she advanced on him. There was no doubt about it. The girl was out for blood.

He took aim and fired three rounds into the girl at point-blank range, backing off as she continued to move forward. He added a fourth dart for good measure as he crossed the great room, Sarah preceding him toward the door. The girl followed behind, her left leg lurching at a funny angle. It was broken near the ankle, but still she kept walking on it. The very image of it made Sarah want to retch.

"I suppose that's why she wasn't outside as part of the welcoming committee," Xavier observed, watching the girl's halting progress carefully. "Probably why she was left behind, too. She can't move fast on that."

"This is so sad." Sarah felt awful for the ruined creature that had probably once been a beautiful young woman in the prime of her life.

Xavier looked at Sarah with understanding in his eyes. "It is, but what we're doing is a good thing. We're putting them to rest, giving their souls peace."

"You truly believe that?"

"I have to."

He backed off farther, almost to the door as the girl came nearer.

As she drew close to the door, she disintegrated right before their eyes. Xavier turned to check the rest of the house. He did it quickly and efficiently, circling back to Sarah a few minutes later.

"The house is clear. Stay here and poke around while I make sure we got all of the ones in the woods and mark the debris piles." Xavier opened a pouch on his thigh and clicked a locator transmitter to life, dropping it on the pile of goo just inside the door. She knew he had to do the same to all the others they'd taken down tonight, so the cleanup team could find them and decontaminate the area.

Xavier surprised her, cupping her neck in one strong hand

and pulling her into a searing kiss that rocked her world. No warning. No mercy. Just an all-out assault that made her body hum with want and need. Then it was over and he stepped back.

"Be careful, Sarah."

The look in his eyes said much more than his simple words, warming her down to her soul. Could it be that the big, strong soldier cared? Something led her to believe he just might.

Sarah edged into the house. It had a simple layout for such a large place. It looked almost unfinished inside. There was one massive great room that was open clear up to the ceiling. There was no second floor—just high cathedral ceilings in every room—and very little furniture. Someone had either moved out in a hurry or nobody had ever moved in to begin with.

She began a methodical search of the premises, snapping latex gloves on her hands before she started. It wouldn't do to contaminate a possible crime scene or any evidence she might have to handle. There wasn't anything of immediate interest in the great room, so she moved on to the smaller rooms. The kitchen held a few bottles of chemicals the techs might be able to make something of, but Sarah continued her exploration. A bathroom held nothing of interest that she could see.

It was when she hit the corner bedroom that she felt a chill run down her spine. Taped to the wall, just inside the door, where she'd be certain to see it, was an envelope. It was one of those square jobs with a clear plastic cutout in the center to showcase a computer disc. The shiny silver disc had a name scribbled across its face in bold capital letters. It simply read SARAH.

With numb fingers, she reached for the envelope, examining it carefully before removing it from the wall. Thankfully, it wasn't booby-trapped.

"Sarah, I'm coming in," Xavier called out as he reentered the house.

"I'm back here," she yelled back. "You'd better see this."

"What have you got?" He moved quickly to her side.

"Somebody left this taped to the wall." She pointed to where the tape hung from the sheetrock, then held up the envelope so he could read the writing.

"Damn." His lips compressed into a thin, angry line. "Did you find anything else?"

"Not yet. There's only one room left to check, right next door."

He led the way to the next room and they quickly discovered it was as empty as the rest of the house. All they'd found on initial inspection was the disc addressed to Sarah. What it might mean, she had no idea, but somebody was definitely playing games with them.

"Another bread crumb?" Sarah asked as they contemplated the disc.

"I have no idea if the other two were left deliberately, but this one sure as hell was. Take anything on there with a grain of salt and an extra ammo clip."

She smiled at his soldier humor. "So what now?"

"We need to know what's on the disc." He shouldered his weapon. "We also need to restock and reload. We used more ammo than I expected. By the time we do that, it'll be too close to dawn and our quarry will be going to ground for the day. We might as well go back to base."

"Base?" She shot him an amused glance.

"Your place," he clarified with a grin. "Our base of operations for now, right?"

"Right." She smiled back as she headed toward the door.

Chapter Eight

They backtracked off the property. Luckily, there were no more surprises waiting for them. Sarah didn't think she could take dealing with any more of the creatures just then. Although she'd acquitted herself well and hadn't lost her nerve, she would be glad to have this portion of the evening over.

And that disc was eating away at her last nerve. She wanted to know what was on it and who had left it so blatantly for her. Until those mysteries were solved, she wasn't going to be able to rest.

"Do you want to use my computer at the station to check out the DVD?"

Xavier didn't seem in the mood to answer questions and she was too tired to pry it out of him. Maybe, though, that was it. Maybe he was too tired to deal with the curious stares and questioning looks they'd received in the station the night before. Heaven knew she was just as glad to not have to spend any longer there than the time it took to return the patrol car and climb into Xavier's Hummer. They'd had a bizarre and scary night. They'd done battle. It wasn't something Sarah was used to.

Most of her shifts were spent rather uneventfully. There might be a traffic accident or maybe a break-in, sure. A report of disorderly conduct or a domestic incident. All that she could handle. Battling zombies and turning them into piles of goo while they tried their best to surround you so they could eat your face off was something way more difficult to deal with.

They arrived back at Sarah's home in the wee hours of the morning. They still had some time until dawn, but Sarah was tired. Xavier had been giving her time to acclimate to the nighttime schedule, but she wasn't quite there yet, as her bone-popping yawns testified.

Xavier fetched the ultrathin laptop from his vehicle and set it up on the coffee table while she started making a pot of coffee. By the time she got back to the living room, he was ready to begin.

She sat next to Xavier on the couch as the boot menu of the DVD came up.

"He customized this," Xavier observed, pointing to the screen.

"Tells me that he or someone working with him has some technical knowledge."

The screen displayed a menu that had two selections. The first read simply "Watch Me" and the second was titled "Maps."

"So do we follow his instructions and watch the video first?"

"I'll play his game . . . to a point. Let's see what this clown wants to show us." Xavier clicked on the video option.

After the disc whirred up, a picture came into view. A man stood in shadow in a stark room full of angles and planes of light. She could make out his shape but not his face. Then, over the tiny speakers in the laptop he began to speak.

"Forgive me for not showing my face, but I have altered my appearance since visiting you in the hospital and there's no sense in giving my new identity away." Sellars's voice was smug and condescending. "I have a proposition for you, Officer Petit. Or perhaps I should call you Sarah. After all, I hope to be working closely with you in the near future."

"Fat chance," she scoffed under her breath. Xavier put a hand over hers, offering silent support.

"Since you're watching this, I surmise you got past my little greeting party. Did you enjoy your time with them, Sarah? Did your military escort notice how much improved they are over the initial versions? My new experiments are capable of working as a group when given specific instruction and are more impervious to the toxin we developed at the military's insistence—before those sanctimonious bastards shut down the project and kicked us all to the curb. They'll regret banishing me and you can tell that to your military friends with my blessing."

"He doesn't know who you are, Xavier. He's just assuming I'll have military protection."

"I noticed." Xavier nodded. "Unless he's playing more games. This guy is loony tunes."

"My proposition is this, Sarah," the oily voice continued. "I want you to come to me. I promise you will come to no harm, though you will be forcibly detained. I need samples, you see. I need to know how and why your body is immune to my experiment. Without that vital bit of information, my work is incomplete and the weapon cannot be used."

"Weapon?" Sarah was aghast. The crazy son of a bitch intended to sell the contagion as a weapon. With the knowledge of how to inoculate people against it, any rogue power or terrorist group could unleash it on the world and keep themselves safe from its effects.

"I'll be in touch shortly for your answer, Sarah," Sellars went on. "Oh, and one more thing. You might be asking yourself why in the world would you voluntarily turn yourself over to my care? The answer is simple. If you don't, I'll unleash my creations on the university campus. There are lots of secluded, wooded areas on that campus and lots of stupid young coeds." He chuckled darkly. "In fact, I may have already lost track of one of my little friends over there. Silly me."

"Good Lord." Sarah sat back in her chair, appalled by the idea.

Xavier hit the button to stop the recording. "If anyone on

the campus has been infected, they won't come out into the open before nightfall. It's too late for us to do anything over there tonight."

"With all the buildings and dorms over there, we couldn't do much good even if we did a room-to-room search," she added. "We'd only alarm everyone."

"Not a good idea if we want to keep this thing top secret."

"Do you think we'll be able to? I mean, if Sellars lets those things loose on the campus, the cat will be out of the bag."

"Which is why we have to stop the sick bastard before we get to that point."

She looked at him with shock. "You want me to—"

He stopped her, tugging her into his arms and tucking her head under his chin. "No, Sarah. I'd never turn you over to that psycho. Never."

She felt the strength in his embrace and the power of his conviction. It calmed her and soothed her shattered nerves.

"Then what are we going to do?" She didn't want to move out of his arms yet. It felt too good to be held, just for a little while.

"We'll think of something." One of Xavier's hands rubbed over her back with soothing motions, while the other circled her waist. His grip tightened, drawing her closer as his lips descended to nuzzle the crown of her head.

"Xavier . . ." Her words trailed off as his head dipped lower.

He kissed her, capturing her lips in a caress that was gentle at first, exploring her mouth with his own and discovering a passion that matched and mingled in exciting ways. He deepened the kiss and she went with him, eager for more. Her fingers caressed the hard muscle of his arms, shoulders and chest as his hands pulled her closer. He leaned back on the couch, allowing her to lie against him slightly, fitting her body to his.

Suddenly, her desire flamed to vibrant life. She wanted him, and it was becoming pretty clear he wanted her just as badly. The hard bar in the front of his pants pressed into her, making her yearn. She wanted that thick rod inside her, making her come.

Sarah didn't want to wait. She tugged at the buttons of his shirt, fighting with them at times until they all came loose. Tugging the tails of the shirt out of his pants, she swept it off over his shoulders as he did the same to her.

Their arms tangled, but never did they let go of each other or break the kiss that grew hotter and bolder the more they touched. Sarah felt the slightly chill air of the room brush over her back as Xavier succeeded in pushing off her uniform blouse. All she wore beneath was a lacy white bra. Xavier tugged her closer, his fingers finding and releasing the catch at her back with deft movements. He lowered the straps and she let the bra fall forward as he ended their kiss so he could look at the bounty he'd revealed.

An appreciative growl rumbled in his throat as he reached out to cup her breasts in his hands. In that moment, Sarah felt like the most desirable woman in the world. The look on his face spoke of fascination and true appreciation. It turned her on.

Never before had she felt so in tune with the wants and needs of her body or with the man who would soon be her lover. She wasn't sure where this was going but the time for dithering was over. She was beyond rational thought. Her body had taken the lead and it wanted Xavier and all he could give her.

She wanted his hard body, his big, capable hands and his uninterrupted attention. At least for the next few hours. After that, she might—just might—be willing to let him go.

If he lived up to her expectations. From the feel of his hands taking their time caressing her nipples with just the right amount of pressure, he was already exceeding any expectations that may have formed in her mind about Xavier as a lover.

He pinched the tips of her breasts again, making her squeak in appreciation. His concentration on the task was near total.

She liked the way he looked at her, the way he touched her. Hell, she liked everything about him so far. From the way he handled his weapon to the way he handled her. Now, she'd learn if he handled the weapon in his trousers as well as he did everything else. She didn't think she'd be disappointed.

But he still had that darn olive-drab T-shirt on. It molded every sexy ripple of his abdomen and chest, but she wanted to see him naked. She didn't want any barrier between her questing hands and his skin. Sarah tugged at the hem of the T-shirt, wanting the offending garment gone.

Xavier took pity on her and pulled the shirt off with one arm. She watched in awe as his torso was exposed, all that tanned flesh and hard muscles with just a smattering of silky brown hair across his pecs and in a tight arrow down to his belt buckle. The belt had to go. That's all there was to it. She wanted to see where that intriguing trail of hair led. She wanted to see what she had only felt before—the hard cock that she wanted so desperately to feel inside her.

Just the thought made her mouth water in anticipation as Xavier's light, musky aroma made her insides clench. He smelled delicious. Good enough to eat. They'd barely done more than kiss and she was already wet and wanting, squirming in her perch on the couch.

"Xavier, I don't want to wait."

"You're sure about this, Sarah? Once I have you, there's no going back for either of us. I'll want you again and I'll do my best to keep you under me as often as possible while we're not on duty." His voice dropped as he touched his forehead to hers, holding her gaze. "I'm a starving man, desperate for you, Sarah."

The harshness of his tone touched a chord deep inside her. She felt the reverberations right through her midsection and down into the part of her that wanted to feel his possession so desperately.

"I want you, Xavier. And if you live up to your advertising"—she felt confident enough to tease him—"I'll be happy to go along with those plans. Eager, even."

She smiled at him and he grinned back. They'd come to an

understanding. Xavier reached for her, flipping her over and laying her down on the wide, overstuffed couch. He stripped off her pants and panties. She'd kicked off her shoes when they'd entered her home, so they weren't a hindrance, unlike his boots, which would take a few minutes to unlace enough to get off. Precious minutes she didn't want to waste.

When she was naked, he spread her legs, lifting one to the back of the couch with her full cooperation. Her other foot was planted on the floor in front of the couch, giving her a little leverage. He paused at the sight of the big gauze bandage on her thigh. The muscle had almost finished regenerating, but the skin was still tight.

"Does it hurt?" he asked in a gentle voice.

"Not much. It's almost healed. Just a little scab left."

He traced the edges of the bandage with light fingers. "I'll be careful, Sarah, but let me know if I hurt you. I don't ever want to hurt you."

Their eyes met and she saw tenderness in his gaze she hadn't really expected. Throat tight with emotion, she nodded and he seemed satisfied. The heat flared in his gaze as his attention turned to the object of his desire.

Xavier's fingers toyed with her exposed flesh as he looked his fill. He had talented fingers that really knew their way around a woman's body. When he parted the soft curls at the juncture of her thighs, she gasped.

"You're wet, Sarah." He smiled with satisfaction as her gaze met his. "I'm flattered."

"Don't make me wait, Xavier. I need . . ." She trailed off with a gasp as one of his thick, strong fingers slid up her channel with little warning. Oh, yeah, that's what she needed. More of that.

"You're tight, sweetheart. It's been a while for you, hasn't it." The question was spoken as a statement and he didn't wait for an answer. Instead, he started moving that finger of his in a methodical, maddening motion, thrusting into her and withdrawing only to thrust higher and more forcefully. "Don't worry, Sarah. I'll take care of you. I'll always take care of you."

The light in his eyes was beautiful to behold as he learned her body, playing it like a master. She was reduced to incoherent moans as he drove her pleasure even higher. She'd thought she was ready before. Now he was driving her to the edge of madness and he hadn't even unzipped his pants yet. She wanted cock. Not his finger. No matter how good he was with his hands, she wanted the real deal and she wanted it now.

Sarah reached out to cup him through his pants. He was hard as a rock and ready, if she was any judge. He was also huge. She remembered that from their earlier encounter. She'd tossed and turned thinking about the width and length of him in her hand. She wanted that cock inside her. She'd wanted it from almost the first time she'd seen him and now was her moment. She didn't want to wait.

"Please, Xavier," she gasped, squeezing him through the fabric separating them.

He paused, seeming to deliberate. Then he withdrew that finger from her, only to come back with two. Stretching her, he drove her crazy with the almost painful penetration.

"You're wet, but I'm too big for you, Sarah." He nearly cringed as he said it, rotating his fingers inside her.

"No. I felt you. I want you, Xavier. I want you now."

He seemed uncertain but a teasing light entered his eyes. "Not that I don't love hearing you beg for my cock, but I want to make this first time as easy as possible for you, *chère*. Give me *un moment*."

His sexy accent seemed to grow thicker, and she reacted with a little tingle in her tummy as his fingers worked their magic in her pussy. Xavier bent low over her body, using his free hand to cup one breast, capturing the other breast in his mouth.

She tensed as her body tightened in a small release. The warmth of his mouth tugging insistently on her nipple and his hands working their magic on her skin and inside her body sent shockwaves of sensation throughout her being. She'd never been this hot for any of her past lovers, few as they had been. She'd never felt this needy, this excited, and still he pushed her higher.

Xavier demanded more and, somehow, she gave it to him. He switched to suck her other breast, using his teeth this time, gently showing her the exciting feel of putting herself utterly at his mercy. It shocked her to realize how fully she trusted Xavier Beauvoir after knowing him only a few days. She'd already trusted him with her life. It was only a short leap to trust him with her body . . . and with her pleasure.

She cried out as another small climax hit her, this one higher than the one before. Already, he'd shown her more pleasure than she'd felt in a long time. And he wasn't done yet.

She hoped she lived through it.

He drew away from her breasts, trailing his lips up her neck to hover over her cheek.

"You're nice and slick for me now, *chère*. I like the way you respond to me, Sarah. You make me want to fuck you long and slow, but I have a feeling this first time is going to be hard and fast. You okay with that, sweetheart?"

"Yes, Xavier. Yes."

"That's what I like to hear."

She could feel the upturn of his mouth against her skin. His hands left her body, and a moment later she heard the rasp of his zipper. He moved back for a minute and she opened her eyes to see him ripping open a foil wrapper with his teeth. He rolled a condom over the biggest erection she'd ever had the good fortune to behold, then moved over her, settling between her thighs.

"After the first few strokes, it's going to be hard and fast, *chère*. Get ready."

She felt the tip of him at her entrance and wanted to scream when he took his time, despite the ominous warning he'd just issued. He slid into her an inch at a time, watching her as if waiting for her to object.

But objections were the farthest thing from her mind at the moment. She wrapped her hands around his waist, holding on, urging him deeper as he slid forward another inch. Little by little, he claimed her body, filling her by slow degrees.

Her body welcomed him, slicking the way as he began shallow thrusts to help his cause. He'd been right. She hadn't had sex in a while. And she'd never had such a well-endowed partner. The consideration he showed in making sure she was ready was touching, and if she'd been in a more patient frame of mind, she would have appreciated it more. As it was, she was desperate for him and didn't want to wait another second for the pleasure she was sure lay in store.

Xavier was long and thick. The slowness of his entry made her gasp, and the final few inches had to be achieved by a combination of short thrusts and the application of his skilled fingers. One hand reached between them, coaxing her clitoris to increase her excitement even more. She was gasping for air by the time he achieved full penetration, ready and willing to take anything else he could dish out.

He groaned, then stilled as if savoring the moment. Sarah was savoring it, too. She'd never been so filled. She felt conquered. Possessed utterly. It was a heady feeling.

"*Mon ange*, you feel so good."

Xavier's breath flowed over her senses in a warm wave as he drew closer. Everything about him felt right. From the width of his broad shoulders to the length of his massive cock, now claiming her in the most basic way. He was magnificent.

"You too," she whispered as he bent low for a quick kiss.

He drew away, resting above her, propped up on his hands as he maintained his position inside her. Claiming her. Owning her body.

"Now we begin," he stated, holding her gaze as he began to move.

He started out slow and steady, gauging her reactions by watching her face. Soon, though, the steady, measured pace increased to something wilder and more intense. Hard and fast, indeed.

She was ready. More than ready, if truth be told, and met him stroke for stroke as he rocketed them both toward a climax that lay just out of reach. For now.

Xavier was a force of nature, propelling them ever higher, ever closer to the pinnacle. His gaze grew hot and demanding as his lower body began harsh thrusts against her, into her, grinding them together in a way that lit her up like fireworks on the Fourth of July.

"Come, Sarah. Come for me now," he whispered, holding her gaze as she followed his orders, sliding right over the edge of the cliff and into oblivion as he pounded into her body below. She cried out, calling his name as she went straight into the most intense orgasm of her life.

Her fingers racked down his back. She wrapped her leg around his waist, urging him on as her body convulsed under his. A few seconds later, she felt him join her. His body went rigid as his eyes shut against the strain. They savored the moment together as their bodies quaked with climax, fusing them as one.

It was a long time before either of them moved. It was Xavier who came to his senses first. He'd dropped his weight mostly on top of her, though he'd tried to angle himself at the last moment so as not to smother her. She'd appreciated the effort. The man was huge and darn heavy, but she liked the feel of him too much to complain.

He nuzzled her face and neck, placing little biting kisses on her skin before finally drawing away and pulling out of her protesting body. She'd no doubt be sore later, but it had been worth every second of discomfort for that blindingly bright climax. Never before had she reached so high.

She watched indulgently as he removed the condom, holding it in one hand while he stood and tugged his pants up around his hips with his free hand. He'd never gotten around to untying those damn boots and stripping off those sexy camouflage pants. He tossed the condom into the trash, then came back over to the couch, looking down at her with an indulgent smile.

"You okay?"

"Never better." She smiled at him, still hazy from the delightful orgasm he'd given her.

"Never?" he teased, with an utterly male grin. "I like that."

She grabbed one of the small throw pillows that had fallen

to the floor in front of the couch and halfheartedly threw it at him. He caught it with a laugh and set it aside. Then he turned to her and lifted her into his arms.

"What are you doing?"

"Isn't it obvious? I'm carrying you to bed." He leaned in to steal a kiss as he walked down the hallway with her held tight against his chest.

He paused only to shoulder-open the door to her bedroom, then stopped. She tried to read his expression as he saw her bedroom for the first time. She kept this place just for herself. It was her oasis of peace in an otherwise hectic life.

The room was done in soft pastel blues, greens and purples with gauzy window treatments and a romantic flair. It was the one room in the house where she'd let her feminine side run wild. Yet the colors were peaceful. Tranquil.

"What?" she prompted when he'd been silent a little too long.

He refocused his attention on her, understanding in his eyes. "I like it, Sarah. The colors in here are very soothing and the swaths of silk all over the place are giving me ideas." He waggled his eyebrows, making her laugh as he walked straight to the bed and deposited her in the middle of it.

Good thing she'd opted for the king size. Xavier was too large to fit in most other beds, she was sure. Very deliberately, he reached into one of the many pockets on his fatigue pants and pulled out a handful of condoms, placing them on her night table beside the bed.

"Ambitious, aren't you?" She nodded toward the half dozen foil-wrapped packets.

"I'm just getting started, darlin'. If we run out, I can always get more."

She almost giggled at his audacious wink. She loved the playfulness about him. He was both strong and funny—an incredibly hot combination she wouldn't have expected.

Xavier sat on the edge of the bed, making short work of the laces on his boots. He dropped the heavy footwear neatly next to the night table, then stood, meeting her gaze once more. His belt and the top button of his pants were still undone, his magnificent chest bare.

"Allow me." Sarah rose to her knees, facing him as his eyes smoldered.

Reaching out, she lowered the zipper on his pants, unsurprised to find his cock already stirring. Xavier didn't disappoint. He was already coming back to life, ready for more. She'd just give him a little incentive. . . .

Sarah pushed the pants and briefs down his muscular legs. Sitting back, she got her first real look at Xavier unclothed.

Damn. It was enough to make a girl want to jump him on the spot. Good thing they were already in her bedroom.

Xavier was solidly built, sexily muscular and devilishly handsome. He was also spectacularly well endowed, as she'd learned in their previous encounter. Seeing him stir under her avid gaze made her mouth water as she reached out for her prize.

She took him in her hand, reveling in the way he hardened to full size under her fingertips. Leaning forward, she teased him with her tongue. She held his heated gaze as she licked the tip, sliding her tongue around the head.

"Do it, *chère*. Take me in your mouth." His low-voiced commands stirred her blood, daring her to follow his orders. Luckily, they were right in line with what she had planned.

Leaning even closer, she closed her lips around him, taking him deep. She hadn't done this often, but for Xavier, she'd pull out all the stops. He'd already given her more pleasure than she'd ever known. It was only right she do her best to rock his world, too.

From the way he looked, she was doing a good job so far. She did her best to tease and tantalize. The task that had started as a way to drive him wild soon had another effect. It made her want more.

She liked everything about Xavier. His taste was surprisingly attractive and his scent deliciously masculine. His body was hard and fit in ways most men never achieved, and it was clear he took good care of himself. His body was another of the weapons in his arsenal. In this case, it was utterly devastating to the opposite sex, and Sarah felt good to be the woman causing the slight tremor in his limbs as she sucked him hard.

His hands delved into her hair, holding her lightly, but she didn't feel controlled or threatened as she had a few times before when she'd tried this with other men. No, Xavier made her feel safe. His touch brought excitement, not worry, and his responses made her squirm with her own arousal.

When she drew away to admire her handiwork, Xavier surprised her by sinking down onto the bed and taking her in his arms. He kissed her deeply, as if he needed her like his next breath. He overwhelmed her, drowning her senses in the scent, taste and feel of him. When one of his hands roamed downward to slide between her legs, she knew he would find her wet and wanting, ready and willing.

He ended the kiss, holding her gaze as his hand took possession of the area between her legs, cupping her, warming her, making her want him even more. She wanted to turn the tables. He'd overwhelmed her on the couch. This time, she wanted a chance to do something more than just lie there and take it— although that had been a glorious experience. This time, she wanted to give as good as she got.

A little demon of mischief riding her shoulder, Sarah caught his attention with what she hoped was a sultry smile.

"If I recall correctly, you said the silk hangings were giving you ideas. Did you mean . . . ?" She licked her lips. "Were you thinking about tying me up?"

She felt the flame leap in his pulse and knew she'd hit the nail on the head.

"Would you like that?" His voice was gravely and pitched low, almost coaxing. Just the sound of it made her abdomen clench.

"You know, they say turnabout is fair play." She wondered if she could get him to agree to her daring plan. He looked willing to humor her.

"You want to tie me up?" He sounded surprised.

"I'm a cop, Xavier. I have a pair of shiny handcuffs on my belt that I've always wondered about."

"You're kidding." He didn't sound appalled by the idea, much to her delight.

She'd fantasized about using her cuffs on a lover since the day they'd been issued but had never found the right man to approach with her secret fantasy. Something told her Xavier was bold enough, and confident enough in himself, to let her explore some of the forbidden things that had crossed her mind from time to time.

"I'll even leave the key within reach, just in case. The question is, are you willing to put yourself at my mercy?"

His answer was all-important. Did he trust her enough to let her do this? Was he willing to give over control to her? More than anything, the next moments would tell her if he was willing to be a true partner, willing to share control with her once in a while. That was the kind of relationship she'd searched for all her life and had never found.

Until now? She'd know the answer soon enough.

Instead of giving his answer in words, Xavier rolled to his back on the bed and held his arms out in front of him, hands fisted, wrists side by side.

"Do your worst, Officer Petit."

His gaze held humor, adventure and something much more tender that touched her heart. She went to get the cuffs.

He wasn't sure why he was doing this. Never before had he been with a woman he was willing to make himself helpless for, but Sarah Petit was breaking all sorts of new ground with him. He saw deeper into her psyche. He knew her background and all about her family. He also knew the kind of person she was—driven to succeed in a family and a profession that had been dominated by men.

She needed to know he was willing to let her drive more than just the car. He had to pass this little test of loyalty and trust or they'd go no further. It was clear to him, though she probably didn't even realize what she was doing herself. He could see her need for his respect and trust.

Maybe it was because he knew more about her, thanks to

the mission and his need to read the investigative report on her background. The result was that he knew her better than any woman he'd ever had. Even the woman he'd thought had been the love of his life. In reality, he hadn't understood what made Heather take the job in Manhattan that kept them so far apart so much of the time.

He still didn't understand it. No more than he understood why she'd had to die in such a senseless act of aggression.

Sarah came back to him, a sexy little grin on her face. Damn, she was beautiful. Strong yet vulnerable, confident in her abilities, yet unsure of herself as a woman in so many ways. She was a fascinating dichotomy. A complex woman, a puzzle he wanted to figure out.

Sarah Petit was definitely getting under his skin in a big way.

"Are you okay with this?" She came up beside him, taking one of his wrists in her hands. She was so petite, the contrast of her small, feminine hands to his big paws brought home to him what she was asking. She wanted him to give over control. It was something she'd probably never be able to wrest from him by force. It was a gift he had to bestow.

He drew her hand to his lips for a gentle kiss. "I'm sure, *mon ange*. Be gentle with me. It's my first time."

She laughed, as he'd hoped. "Your virginity is safe with me, sweet cheeks." She expertly trapped one of his wrists in the mechanical silver cuff.

"I sense you've done this before."

"Used the cuffs?" She paused to meet his gaze. "Plenty of times on criminals. Never on a lover. So you're my first, too, in a sense."

"But you've been thinking about it."

"Once in a while. I mean, come on, they're handcuffs. There are all kinds of jokes about handcuffs and sex."

"I wouldn't have pegged you for a BDSM kind of girl."

She tilted her head as she stretched his arms over his head, taking hold of his other wrist before wrapping the smooth metal around it. She was thinking hard, which surprised him.

"I never thought of it that way. I'm not into pain, but I will admit to a fascination with these darn silver cuffs."

"It's the idea of power that turns you on." She looked at him sharply. "That's not a bad thing, *chère*. Being in control is something I can totally understand."

The look of relief on her face was enough to tell him he'd said the right thing. He was willing to give it a try if she wanted it and he could tell she did. When those locks had snicked home, they'd both gotten a little thrill, he'd felt it.

"Keep your hands up there. Grab on to the poles in the headboard if you need to."

"Yes, mistress." He winked at her, liking the way she jumped a little at the strange title. Then she smiled at him. Damn, she was gorgeous.

"Be a good soldier and let me rock your world, Captain." She straddled him, dragging her breasts over his chest, following with her lips.

She teased him, taunted him, and made him hotter than hell in the process. Her lips were everywhere, sucking and placing little nibbles on his skin, his nipples, his belly button and, ultimately, his aching cock.

He loved what she was doing. He'd never had a woman concentrate on him so completely. Usually, he was the one running the show when he made love to a woman. This was entirely new to him. Lying back like some sultan in a harem, being pleasured by his woman. Well, only if the sultan was tied up and the harem consisted of only one, very special female.

It was enough. *She* was enough. Sarah was more woman than he'd thought. He'd underestimated her passion for life, her willingness to take risks. From reading her file he'd thought he'd known what made her tick, but those cold psychological analyses and performance reports hadn't told him everything. No, there was a whole mysterious side to Sarah that was proving delectably fascinating.

If anyone had told him yesterday that today he'd be handcuffed and at Sarah's mercy, he wouldn't have believed it possible. At this point, with her lips wrapped around his cock again and her hands exploring every inch of his body, he was oh so glad life could still surprise him.

"Watch out there, *chère*, or you'll get more than you bargained for," he warned as she sucked him. He was getting too excited. He needed to cool down a bit or there'd be nothing left for her.

She took the warning, coming up for air with a devious smile. "Can't have that," she chastised him. "I'm having too much fun for this to be over so soon."

"Me, too, *mon ange*. Me, too."

"Good."

She covered him like a blanket, rubbing all over him with that luscious, curvy body of hers. Damn, she felt good.

"I don't want to be the only one having fun here."

"No chance of that, Sarah. You're a born seductress."

"You think so?" She gave him a sideways look.

"Oh, I know so."

"I'm not doing anything wrong? Anything you don't like?" She was teasing him with her little questions, but he enjoyed the playful banter.

"I like it all, sweetheart. You know I do."

"You know what? So do I." She rubbed her pussy right over his straining cock and he nearly exploded right there. "Screw this. I can't wait any longer." She reached over to the supply of condoms he'd deposited on the nightstand and grabbed one. A quick trip downward on his body and she had him in her hands again as she sheathed his cock in the thin layer of latex.

He grunted when she positioned herself over him and slid down, ramming his cock up inside her deep, fast and hard. He hadn't expected that at all. It was really different letting her control the speed, depth and force of penetration. Sure, he'd had women ride him many times before, but he'd never been chained up while they did it. That took his indulgence to a whole new level. Always before, he'd been subtly guiding the woman, and he'd known he could flip her over in a second and be right back in charge again. Not so this time.

"I really wanted to take this slow," she panted as she strained over him, riding him in a powerful rhythm. She increased her pace steadily, making little feminine sounds in the back of her throat as her passion rose higher and higher. "I wanted to savor this experience since I doubt I'll ever get another chance."

"I wouldn't be too sure of that, *mon ange*." He was close to exploding. Her movements over him and the sight of her breasts bouncing merrily as she increased her pace again made his mouth water, but he was powerless. He held on for dear life to the rails of the headboard, the clank of the small chain between the handcuffs sounding in counterpoint to her rhythm.

Damn. He never would have thought something like this could turn him on so fast and so powerfully. He'd been all prepared to be the sacrificial lamb, doing what she wanted for her sake. He hadn't thought he'd enjoy it this much. Sarah was teaching him things about himself.

"Xavier . . ." His name was a keening cry ripped from her lips as she tumbled over the edge.

The contractions of her tight pussy set him off, too. He shuddered and came, his vision fading to black for a second as a powerful orgasm hit him broadside.

His breathing ragged as he came back to earth a long time later, Xavier savored the feel of Sarah's lithe body draped over him like a warm, living blanket. He was still cuffed, still unable to caress her the way he wanted, but she was with him, shivering in the aftermath of something bigger than themselves.

She reached up after a while and uncuffed his wrists, taking them to her mouth for a tender kiss as she rubbed gently at the faint red marks the metal had made. When she released his wrists, his arms went immediately around her, holding her close.

If he wasn't much mistaken, their relationship had just taken a turn. He didn't know what it meant, but he was willing to go with the flow for now. Sarah was getting under his skin in a big way, and oddly enough, he didn't really mind. He'd searched all his life for a woman like her.

Whether they could make a go of this relationship after the mission was over, he still didn't know, but he was thinking more and more about giving it a try. One thing was certain . . . Sarah had just rocked his world and he wanted more. As much as she would give him for as long as it lasted.

"Thank you, Xavier," she whispered against his chest as he tucked her head under his chin.

"No, *mon ange*, thank you for teaching me something about myself I never knew."

"Really? What's that?"

"That with the right woman, it's very rewarding to give up control." He kissed the crown of her head, his voice pitched low.

As the sun rose higher in the eastern sky, they fell asleep in each other's arms.

Chapter Nine

A distinctive electronic ring sounded in the room. Sarah blinked awake, disturbed by the strange noise. It was coming from the floor.

Xavier reached over the side of the bed and fumbled with his discarded pants. When he resurfaced, he held a small phone in his hand that must have been in one of his pockets.

"Beauvoir," he answered in a throaty growl as he lay back on the bed.

Sarah heard his end of the conversation, which consisted mainly of grunts of agreement with a few grunts that sounded negative in nature. She grew more curious the longer the monosyllabic conversation continued. Finally, some more actual words were introduced back into the discourse.

"Yeah, it's time."

That sounded ominous. She leaned up on one elbow to watch him and he shot her a heated glance.

"Set it up. We'll meet you there after your shift. Bring dinner." His gaze held hers. "Officer Petit needs to be brought up to speed."

She felt mesmerized by the heat in his eyes, the sleepy growl in his voice. Having sex with this man had been a transformative event in her life. She could feel it even now, after just a couple of hours. She might regret falling for him later, after he'd gone, but for right now, she was going to bask in the decadence and thrill of being with him.

She knew without a doubt that she had fallen for him in a big way. Sarah wasn't the type to sleep around. She had to have some emotional connection to the man she gave her body to. It had always been that way, from her earliest experiences with the opposite sex.

Her heart was involved now. When she'd first met Xavier, just a few days ago, she'd already begun to admire him. He was drop-dead sexy and had a core of iron-hard will that ran through his being, despite his relaxed appearance. He took concepts like duty, honor and loyalty very seriously, which was something she truly admired in a man.

The more she was around him, the more she found to like about him. His compassion, his skill. The way he looked after her. His protective instincts and his willingness to let her do her job and fight beside him. Everything about him made her want him, so it was no surprise they'd ended up here, in her bed.

Xavier ended the conversation, flipped the phone closed and let it fall back to the floor. All the while, his gaze held hers, making her pulse leap in response to the heated message smoldering in his eyes. She'd thought he was done after that last bout of lovemaking. Apparently, he was only just getting started.

"What's our plan for today?" Sarah asked, wanting to learn about his conversation before she got any more distracted.

Xavier cupped her cheek in a tender caress. He moved closer, capturing her lips with his for a long moment before he drew back just far enough to look into her eyes.

"First on the agenda, is making love to you again. Then maybe we'll catch some more sleep. We have a meeting with the day shift before we go out again tonight. I've had them doing recon for us. They've been following leads both from the team's preliminary investigation and from the evidence we've found since you joined the effort. It's time we all got together in one place to compare notes and see what we've come up with."

"Sounds like a good idea. What about the campus?" Never before had she discussed a case under such intimate circumstances. How either of them could concentrate when his hand moved south to cover her breast, she didn't know.

"We'll check it out tonight. If Sellars let the contagion loose over there, the creatures will come out to feed once night falls." His words brought her out of the sensual haze for a moment.

"Do you think he's really capable of doing something like that to a bunch of college kids?" Sarah placed her palm over his chest, seeking comfort from the steady rhythm of his heart. He was so solid, so warm. He made her feel safe, no matter how dire the situation.

"Right now I wouldn't put anything past him. We need to check it out, even though we'll most likely be walking into a trap."

"A trap meant for me, you mean." Her voice was low, echoing the fear she kept locked inside, under wraps. "You think he might be luring us to the campus so he and his men can make a grab for me, right?"

"It's a possibility we need to prepare for. The thing is, if the contagion is present on the campus, I can't risk sending anyone but you and me to face it. I'm torn between wanting to keep you away from the campus tonight—or anyplace where you might be at risk of being abducted by Sellars's people—and knowing there's no one else who would be safe to send in your place. My only consolation is that you're highly trained and managed to free yourself from the zombies once before. This time, I'll be right there with you. To get to you, they'll have to go through me first."

She kissed him, seeing the worry coupled with resolve on his handsome face. It touched her to know he cared about placing her in possible danger. She didn't think there was much chance of having problems with Sellars, or anyone who might be working for him on campus. Aside from a few wooded areas, most of the campus was brightly lit and patrolled by the university's own private security force.

While the security guards wouldn't be much help against zombies, they could certainly raise a ruckus if they thought someone was being abducted right under their noses. Sarah could scream with the best of them and she was armed, too. She wouldn't make it easy for anyone who tried to take her.

And then there was Xavier. She doubted anyone who meant to do her harm would make it past him. Even if they hadn't just crossed the line from coworkers to lovers, Xavier was the kind of man who took his job very seriously. The minute she had accepted the position on his team for this mission, she had become part of his job. Keeping her safe was no doubt something he took very seriously—just as he took the safety of his men seriously.

She continued to be impressed by the fact that he wouldn't put them directly in harm's way against the zombies. The three men she'd met were skilled Special Forces operatives, but no one knew whether they were immune to the contagion. Unlike she and Xavier, who had been bitten and lived to tell the tale. A bite, or perhaps a mere scratch, could kill them. What was worse, they would then rise from the dead as mindless drones, only to become the enemy.

Xavier refused to take that chance with his men, keeping all the action and possible confrontation with the creatures for himself. And Sarah. She was his partner now. She had his back. They'd face the horror together.

"Thank you, Xavier," she whispered as she broke their kiss. "I want you to know that if anything does happen to me—"

"Nothing will," he interrupted.

She placed a finger over his lips to silence his words. "If it does, I want you to know that I value the time we've had together and I trust you to do your level best to protect me as I protect you. We're a team, Xavier. And working with you on this mission has been . . ." She paused to think of just the right words. "It's been one of the strangest, most challenging, off the wall"—she moved her hand to caress his cheek, and then brushed back his hair in a tender gesture—"and magical times of my life."

He gazed into her eyes. Words were unnecessary between them. In that moment, the looks on their faces said it all. Promises were made and accepted. Vows were understood.

Xavier dipped his head for another kiss, this one more tempestuous than what had come before. When he pulled back, her senses were adrift in the pleasure he brought her. She was under his spell, a willing slave to whatever he wanted. Funny thing was, she didn't feel threatened by knowledge. Their relationship had been fast and furious but also one of the deepest and truest she had ever shared with any man. They were more than colleagues, more than lovers. They had a deeper connection, forged in the fire of their experiences and the danger they'd faced together.

It was an unnatural way to develop a relationship, to be sure, but it worked for them. For now. Whether it would stand the test of time, she didn't know. While it lasted, though, it was a beautiful thing.

"I believe you said something about turnabout being fair play?" His mouth curved in a devilish grin.

"Well, yes, indeed. I believe I did." She squirmed under him, already tingling at the idea of him handcuffing her.

His gaze shot to the curtains. They were long silk drapes, closed now but usually held back by wide strips of matching silk that had loops at either end. The loops slid easily over a hook that protruded slightly from the wall, making the ties easy to remove for washing and other maintenance.

"I told you all the soft fabric in this room was giving me ideas." He refocused on her, still grinning. "That's how this all started, isn't it?"

Mutely, she nodded, wondering what he might do. He rose and removed the curtain tie closest to the bed.

"Generally speaking, we don't carry metal cuffs. If we need to restrain someone, we use zip ties. They're too rough for your tender skin, *chérie*." He grasped her wrists, kissing each one before stretching her arms above her head. The silk slipped around her wrists like a whisper. Before she knew it, she was tied.

The feeling of helplessness was outweighed by the naughty notion that Xavier was in charge now. She was at his mercy. She trusted him enough to give him control, as he'd given her control in their last round of lovemaking. Tit for tat. She almost laughed at the phrase, seeing the discreet Special Forces tattoo high up on his shoulder.

The red marks around his wrists from the handcuffs had already faded. She wondered if the soft silk around her wrists would leave any trace of its presence after this session was over. Knowing they had a meeting to go to later with his men, she wasn't certain she wanted them to know what had happened between her and their commanding officer.

For a split second, she worried about how they would hide their new intimacy. Then such trivial concerns no longer mattered. Xavier spread her legs, climbing between as if he belonged there. After what they'd done over the past tempestuous hours, she knew he did. Already her body craved him. It wanted him there, between her thighs, for more than just a few short encounters. Her body wanted him to own it, to be the man making her come for the rest of her life.

But it just wasn't possible. Sarah had to be a realist about this whole situation. He was here for a short time. The length of a mission. She had that long to store up memories to hold against the future.

Loving memories and daydreams of something that could never be.

She vowed not to ruin today with worries about tomorrow. Lying back as Xavier staked his ownership claim over her body, she tried her best to live in the moment, enjoying every second of his attention.

He didn't disappoint. As thorough as she'd been in exploring his body, he was just as attentive to her now that the tables were turned. Those big hands swept over her body, teasing, tickling, tormenting in the most delicious way. His hands were rough, calloused in places, and the slight abrasion against her softest skin caused goose bumps to appear all up and down her arms.

When he teased her nipples with his fingers and tongue, she tried to bite back the whimpers of excitement, but they escaped anyway. He growled in satisfaction, his mouth on her breast and she felt it vibrate through her skin all the way to her toes.

He worked his way down her body until he came to the juncture of her thighs. Then he began to lick her tender folds, focusing on her clit. She was glad she'd taken the time a little earlier to slip from the bed and wash up.

She about rocketed off the bed when he used his teeth on her. It didn't hurt, but it certainly made her want to sit up and take notice. No man had ever taken such time and exquisite care with her body or her pleasure.

"Xavier . . ." She was breathing heavily, excited by his amazing touch and skill as a lover. When his tongue rammed up into her, she cried out and came, just like that. No warning. No long buildup. He rode her through the spasms, his big hands easily holding her in whatever position he wanted.

She began to come down from the peak, and he lifted his head from between her thighs to meet her gaze.

"Good girl," he praised her. "That's one."

"What do you mean?" Her mind was foggy with pleasure.

"I'm counting here, *mon ange*. I want you to come at least once more before I join you. Are you up for it?"

"Up for it?" She flopped back on the bed. "You just might be the death of me, Xavier Beauvoir."

He chuckled and reapplied himself to her body, trailing his lips down her leg. He positioned her like a rag doll, making her feel almost dainty the way he was able to move her around as if she weighed nothing at all.

Her knee was bent and Xavier shocked her by nibbling on her toes. He met her gaze as he sucked one of her toes into his mouth. Just like that, her body was primed again, ready for him, her temperature rising along with her excitement.

She could honestly say she was shocked. No man had ever sucked her toes before. She'd never thought that kind of thing could be sexy, but the handsome devil currently doing his level best to seduce her senses was proving her very much mistaken. About so many things.

Sarah held on to the rails in the headboard. Those small handholds were the only things keeping her grounded. They were her only point of control in this whole magical situation. Her only connection to the solidness of the earth. Otherwise, Xavier was in charge. He was the king of her pleasure, the master of her body, the only man to whom she'd ever been able to surrender so completely.

"Ah, you like that," he purred, dropping her foot to the bed as he crawled closer. One hand swept up her leg to the juncture of her thighs. "Do you want something, baby? Do you want to be filled?"

"Yes!" The word erupted from her mouth as his fingers delved between her legs, sinking deep within. It was good, but soon it wasn't enough. "Xavier, please . . ."

"What, *mon ange?* Do you need more? Tell me what you want."

"I want you, Xavier. I want you inside me." She felt heat rush to her cheeks as she said the words. She'd never been one to engage in explicit talk in bed, but Xavier was opening up all sorts of new avenues for her sexually.

"Will you be a good girl and come for me if I give you what you want?"

The teasing of his fingers and the sexy look on his face was driving her wild.

She nodded, knowing it wouldn't take much to set her off again.

"Then I know exactly what this greedy pussy needs." Xavier covered her with his muscular body as he reached for a condom from the supply he'd put on the nightstand.

Maybe he hadn't been as optimistic as she'd thought when he'd placed a neat pile of the foil wrappers there. The supply was dwindling faster than she would have believed possible only a day ago. There was something to be said for Xavier's stamina and sex drive. She wondered idly if that was a Cajun thing or a Green Beret thing. Either way, she was happily reaping the benefits.

He drew back and ripped open the wrapper with his teeth

while holding her gaze. The move was so blatantly sexy, she gasped. He made short work of rolling the condom over his massive erection, then he paused.

"Is this what you want?" He pushed just the tip of his cock into her and waited.

"You're killing me, Xavier." She tried to squirm downward on the bed to take more of him.

He shocked her, slapping her clit with a light tap that made her yelp in surprise. Surprise and . . . arousal? It hadn't hurt. The little blow had shocked her as much as the resulting clenching of her inner muscles.

"Be still," he admonished. "I'll give you what you want but you must answer my questions. Full sentences, if you please."

Damn, he was going all commander on her. His dominant streak made her even wetter.

"Do you want my cock?"

"Yes," she whispered.

"Say it then, Sarah. What do you want? You have to tell me." His gaze narrowed, pinning her to the bed as surely as the silk binding held her hands immobile. He was serious. He'd wait until she gave him what he wanted. Oh, man.

She gave in. "I want your cock, Xavier. Please."

"That was good, *ma belle*." He praised her, but he didn't move.

She was ready to scream in frustration, needing more . . . needing him.

"One more question before I give you your prize." His devilish grin made her tummy clench. "Did you like it when I spanked your clit? Be honest now. I think you did."

"I told you I wasn't into pain." She was gasping now, needing to feel him claim her fully.

"Did it hurt?" His expression held true concern.

"No. You didn't hit that hard. But it surprised me."

"Surprised in a good way?" His smile was confident as he awaited her answer.

She couldn't lie to him. "Yeah, Xavier. In a really good way."

"That's what I thought." A satisfied grin covered his face as he leaned forward, sliding into her. He sat upright between her splayed thighs, watching the progress as he claimed her eager channel. "Now, I believe you owe me a climax."

He held himself still within her, strain evident on his face. She watched him, amazed by the masterful way he played her body as well as his magnificent control. She'd never been with a man as skilled and creative as this one. He lowered one hand to rest on her thigh. A second later, his fingers began to toy with her clit as she began to squirm again.

It was too much. She cried out when the exploration turned to a firm tapping, right on that little button that set her off like a skyrocket. A ragged sound tore from her throat as she came for him, just as he'd wanted. The look on his face was one of triumph mixed with dominance and an iron-hard will.

Something else was iron-hard, too, and she nearly cried when he pulled it out. Then he flipped her. Those big hands positioned her to his liking, coaxing her up to rest on her elbows, her hands still bound in front of her, her ass in the air as he knelt behind her.

He didn't wait for her to come down from her climax, he simply slid into her contracting channel, still quaking with desire, and pushed her higher. He began a pounding rhythm that sparked renewed interest in her greedy body. The next minutes became a blur of continual pleasure unlike anything she'd ever known. She wouldn't have believed it if she hadn't lived it. Xavier drew out her climax and pushed her higher still.

His rhythm was hard and fast, unrelenting and uncompromising. She pushed back against him as he used her body, giving and taking in equal measure. She screamed as she hit another peak, even higher than the last. She may have blacked out for a second, she wasn't sure, but the orgasm seemed to go on and on.

She could feel him spasming inside her, his harsh breathing music to her ears as they reached that amazing pinnacle together. His hands tightened on her hips as they were swept away together on a tidal wave of pleasure.

Long moments later, after the delicious rigor began to dissipate, Xavier lifted away from her, disengaging gently from her swollen, well-loved body. He stretched her out on her side as he released the silk binding from her tender wrists. Without a word, he spooned her in his arms and drew the sheet over them.

The reassuring beat of his heart as it began to slow matched rhythm with hers. She felt him kiss the top of her head as she drifted away in his arms.

The next time Sarah woke up, the sun was riding low in the sky. The lovely smell of fried bacon wafted through her house and Xavier was gone from her bed. She stood and surveyed the room. The bed was a wreck, but that was to be expected. Xavier's clothes were missing, along with his boots.

She tore the sheets off the bed and quickly remade it with fresh linens from her closet before heading to the shower. Her body was sore in places it hadn't been sore in ages. She hugged a secret smile to herself, remembering just how they'd achieved that spectacular level of utter satiation.

She took a quick shower, already starting to feel better as she moved around. The hot water had helped a lot. No doubt her new healing abilities had also kicked in to make walking a whole heck of a lot more comfortable after the sexual calisthenics of the past few hours.

Sarah dressed in a clean uniform and sought out Xavier. She found him in the kitchen, flipping an omelet. He grinned when he caught sight of her.

"Breakfast is being served. Take a seat, mademoiselle."

"Breakfast at four o'clock in the afternoon?" She stopped to give him a peck on the cheek before taking her place at the table.

Toast and jam had already been set out, along with a plate of cooked bacon and condiments. He'd also set two places, complete with filled juice glasses and silverware. He'd really gone all out.

"For us, it's the start of our day and I've always felt breakfast food is good anytime. It's also easy to make." He put the finishing touches on the omelet and cut the huge thing in half with the spatula as he approached the table. He expertly slid one half of the cheesy egg concoction onto her plate and took the other for himself.

"This is fantastic. It all looks and smells so good." She was just happy with life at the moment.

She'd spent a decadent couple of hours making love with Xavier, and at the moment, all was right with her world. The zombie threat and all the other stuff were on the back burner, to be considered after they'd broken their fast. For now, she was taking a minute to bask in the changes in her life. So much had happened in such a short time. It was overwhelming in a whirlwind sort of way, but if the end result was Xavier in her bed and in her home, she couldn't complain too much. She wouldn't trade this special time with him for anything.

"Dig in. We've got to meet up with the guys in about an hour."

"I thought I heard you tell your XO to bring dinner to the meeting." Sarah cut a piece of the omelet and took a nibble. It was delicious. Perfectly cooked, with a hint of the spices he'd used to make it wafting to her nose and bursting on her tongue.

"I did, but Sam's idea of dinner is probably a couple of pizzas. That's not enough to keep us going all night. I figured we'd be better off with a good protein boost now."

"Good thinking. Xavier, this is spectacular. What did you put in this thing?" She used her fork to point toward the omelet as she took another big bite.

"Cheese, onions, peppers and a few other things I found in your fridge and pantry. Hope you don't mind I went foraging."

"Mind? When this is the end result? Forage away, I say." He seemed amused by her answer and they ate in silence for a while.

"So, how long have you and your team been together?" she asked after the silence had stretched a bit.

"I've known Sam, my XO, since Ranger School. We were assigned to the same unit for a while early on and became good friends. The other guys I knew by reputation and from having worked with them in passing over the years." His expression closed up. "The unit I belonged to until very recently was decimated by the first go-round with the zombies on base. I was the only survivor of those who'd been bitten or gouged. After they realized I was immune"—he paused to take a drink of juice—"I was asked to pick my own small group when the first reports of the attack on you filtered through."

"I'm sorry, Xavier. I didn't mean to bring up bad memories." She felt awful. The look on his face was so tight, so controlled. It was obvious to her that he was trying to tamp down the pain that still afflicted him when he thought of those friends, those comrades he had lost.

"It's all right." He finished eating and stood, taking his plate to the sink for a quick rinse.

She could tell he wanted to change the subject and she was fine with that. He'd lost friends and it had happened recently. Perhaps too recently to talk about. She could understand that and she wouldn't push.

She stood, too, and began clearing the table. When she turned toward the sink with an armful of dishes, Xavier surprised her by taking them out of her hands. He placed them behind him on the counter and turned back to her. He just looked at her, staring downward into her eyes for a long moment. There was emotion there, simmering beneath the surface.

Xavier pulled her into his arms, hugging her loosely while he rested his head over hers. She heard the reassuring beat of his heart under her ear and felt his hands stroking her hair and back.

"I miss them, but I'm not ready to talk about it yet."

The pain in his voice touched her deeply. "I understand, Xavier," she whispered. "Just know that I'm here for you if you ever want to talk."

"Thank you, Sarah. That means more than I can tell you."

He held her close for a few minutes more, while she offered silent comfort. Even if he couldn't talk about it yet, she sensed this helped. She could feel the tension in him ease little by little until he had himself back under control, and she was glad she could be there to help him even in this small way.

He cleared his throat as he let her go. "We'd better get a move on. The guys are expecting us soon."

"Let me grab my utility belt and we can hit the road."

She exited the kitchen, leaving the rest of the cleanup to him, if he felt like doing it. Right now, she didn't care. A dirty dish left standing on the counter wasn't the end of the world. She thought again about the losses he'd suffered. The lives that had already been lost to these mad scientists. They had to be stopped. That was her first—her only—priority at the moment. Everything else could wait til later.

As Xavier had foretold, a stack of pizza boxes greeted them when they entered the hotel suite. The B Team had commandeered a set of rooms and done some furniture rearranging. Where the couch had been in a central seating area, there were now two sturdy, collapsible eight-foot tables pushed together, surrounded by folding chairs. Sarah could tell from the fresh dents in the plush carpet that the guys hadn't left a single piece of furniture where it had been originally. She wondered if they'd put it back when they were through or if the army was going to be fielding complaints from an angry hotel staff.

Paper plates with multiple slices of pizza and cans of soda populated the area in front of each man seated around the table. She recognized Sam, Lewis and Reno from their previous meeting, but there was another uniformed man present as well. Xavier stiffened when he caught sight of the man who wore navy insignia. He was a commander if she was reading his rank properly.

Her brothers were marines. They'd talked about things like protocol and rank from time to time. Some of it had rubbed off. If she remembered correctly, a commander in the navy was equal to something like a lieutenant colonel in the Corps or regular army. This guy was pretty high on the totem pole. And he had combat ribbons on his chest. He wasn't what they laughingly referred to as a "Chairborne Ranger." This man had seen action.

He was handsome, too. Tall and broad shouldered, with

golden streaks in his light brown hair, as if he spent a lot of time in the sun. He had a rich tan and little attractive creases around his eyes, either from laughing or squinting against the sun. She could easily imagine him at the helm of a ship. The guy could have doubled for half the pirates on romance novel covers. He was that yummy.

It was highly unprofessional of her to notice, of course, but every one of the men in the room was so far out of the norm, she'd have to be dead not to notice them. Each of them was built like a Greek god from hours of training and hard physical work. They were also among the best and brightest the armed forces had to offer. She knew that simply by the fact that they had made it through all kinds of Special Forces training to become the warriors they were today.

She knew from her brothers that a lot of men tried to become Green Berets or SEALs, but few made it through the rigorous testing. They had to be both superb physical specimens and outstandingly sharp mentally. All of these men had special skills and a drive to succeed.

The navy man stood and came over to greet Xavier and her, a serious expression on his handsome face as he held out his hand to Xavier. The only thing that really distinguished him from the other guys, aside from his superior rank, was the fact that he was in the navy and the others were most definitely army.

"Commander, it's good to see you, sir." Xavier turned to introduce her. "This is Officer Sarah Petit. Sarah, this is Commander Matt Sykes, U.S. Navy. He's overseeing this operation."

"I've heard a lot about you, Officer Petit." The man had a killer smile, which he flashed full force. He turned on the charm, but Sarah was still pleasantly sated from her encounters with Xavier. Her Green Beret was more than man enough for her.

"Please, call me Sarah." She smiled politely at Sykes but stuck close to Xavier as they moved farther into the room.

"Since we're mixing chains of command with abandon here," Sykes said with a friendly expression, "please call me Matt."

When she reached the table, all the men around it stood. It

took her a minute to realize they were waiting for her to be seated. They certainly taught good manners in the army. She hadn't had this kind of treatment in a long time, if ever. Everyone seemed to want to get her something to drink or eat and she found herself declining politely, until finally Xavier stepped in.

"Guys, I'm certain Officer Petit will let us know if she wants anything." He rolled his eyes at the men until they settled down. It was kind of comical, but then, she assumed these Special Forces types weren't all that accustomed to working with women.

"Since we're all here," Matt Sykes began. "I'd like to start this session by thanking Officer Petit for joining our team. I'm sorry I haven't had a chance to talk to you before this, ma'am. I've just been cleared to brief you on things we weren't sure you'd need to know before. The powers that be finally consider it important for you to have all the available information, which, for the record, I was always in favor of. I don't like sending anyone into the field with only part of the story."

Sarah was surprised by his vehemence and his words. What more was there to know? Could it be any worse than learning there were actual zombies in the world and their mad scientist creator was after her? She was almost afraid to listen.

"You're probably wondering why a navy commander is involved in what appears to be strictly an army mission. The short answer is that the problem started on my base. The first victims of this contagion were marines stationed at Quantico, my current duty station. We thought we'd eradicated the problem with the help of a Navy SEAL—someone like you, who was immune to the contagion. The science team that inadvertently created the problem was disbanded and sworn to drop the research. Most of them found other jobs and we thought the problem was solved for good."

Sykes's expression darkened as he sat back in his chair.

"Since then, we've discovered that some rogue members of the scientific team have started up the research again. Specifically, there have been two known flare-ups—the one here and one earlier at Fort Bragg that wasn't discovered until most of Captain Beauvoir's team was gone. He survived and I was called in to lend assistance once they realized what was going on. That problem is still ongoing and we have a team in the field working to destroy the remaining creatures as we speak. We're spread thin because of the need to send Captain Beauvoir up here to settle this problem. Which is why your help is invaluable, Sarah. We literally don't have enough qualified people to deal with two outbreaks at once."

"Is it getting any better back on base?" Xavier asked, concern lacing his voice.

"Marginally. We still haven't tracked down the source of the problem. Which is why we need to tie up this outbreak as soon as possible." Sykes turned his attention back to Sarah. "Captain Beauvoir is a very rare commodity—as are you, Sarah. You're both immune. We don't want to send any more men to their deaths. Only those who are immune are being sent into the kill zone. They're the only ones who stand a chance against the creatures when a scratch or bite can be fatal."

"Xavier explained all that to me," Sarah said, nodding. "I just didn't realize there was another outbreak other than here on Long Island. I guess I assumed Xavier had been bitten during some initial action that was now over."

"Unfortunately not." Sykes leaned forward again. "I'm only here for this meeting. I came to get a sitrep from your team before I head back to North Carolina and the problems waiting for me there. I'm hoping that something you've uncovered might help shake loose the sticking points in my own investigation."

"Well, we know for sure the scientist behind this outbreak is Dr. Sellars," Sarah told him. "He tried unsuccessfully to get blood from me in the hospital," she put in. "He also left a DVD addressed to me with an invitation to give myself up so he could study why I survived the bites. Xavier and I found it at the last location we searched, along with a phalanx of zombies, which we darted and marked."

Xavier tossed the disc in question onto the table, in front of Sykes. "You can have the original. I downloaded the files and my team already has them."

Sykes placed the DVD in his briefcase. "Lieutenant Archer played the video for me right before you arrived." His expression darkened. "I want you to be careful, Sarah. Under no circumstances do we want anyone who survived the contagion to be captured or even sampled by the enemy. We don't want them figuring out a way to make just a select few people immune. From what I saw on that video, Sellars doesn't appear to be completely sane. You have to know he's probably going to make a grab for you."

"Captain Beauvoir and I have discussed that possibility." She nodded toward Xavier. "We're going to check out the campus tonight. We figure it's a trap, but I don't see any other choice. I either go to the campus and stop the creatures before they kill other innocent kids or I stay home and let the contagion spread. The latter option is totally unacceptable, of course."

"Of course," Sykes agreed, respect clear in his expression. "So what are you going to do?"

"I'll take my chances," Sarah replied. "I'm armed. I have some skills. And Xavier has my back. It'll have to be good enough."

Sykes sat back, watching her with renewed respect. In fact, all the men at the table seemed to be greeting her words with varying shades of surprise and admiration.

"I have heard nothing but good things about you, Sarah, since the moment I started looking into your case," Sykes said at last. "I'm glad to see it was all true. However, I don't like the idea of you and Beauvoir walking knowingly into a trap."

"Me, neither." Sam Archer spoke for the first time since the meeting had come to order. "Isn't there any way we can back you up, sir?" He directed his appeal to Xavier, his expression stern. It looked to her like they'd had this argument before.

"No." Sam had been talking to Xavier, but it was Sarah who answered. "If there are zombies there waiting for us— and after what we've dealt with the past two nights, I believe there will be—Xavier and I are the only ones who can deal with them safely. These things don't go down easily. It's taking four shots apiece and the toxin takes a while to work. Too long to risk anyone who isn't immune."

"Is this true?" Sykes looked to Xavier for confirmation.

"Yeah. It's in my report. Sellars has been improving on his earlier work. These creatures are much harder to dissolve. They also work together—at least a little. A group of them surrounded us at the house we visited last night. The group acted as a distraction while another snuck up from behind. It was the same one that snuck up behind Sarah in that abandoned building. It could have been coincidence, but I had the feeling it was planned. At least on a rudimentary level. I think Sellars can give them instructions and they follow their *master*. One of them actually used that word before she imploded."

"It spoke?" Sykes was incredulous.

Reno looked really concerned. If she remembered correctly, he had some sort of science background and had interfaced with the cleanup teams at the first site. The others just looked grim.

"She did," Sarah answered. "It was a young girl, maybe in her early twenties. Which is what leads me to believe Sellars has already been dipping into the population of the local university." She reached for a can of soda from the stack on the coffee table behind her. "I fully expect there will be more waiting for us when we hit the campus this evening."

They let that sink in for a minute. It was Xavier who refocused the meeting.

"I think we should hear what you've come up with on your end of the investigation, Sam."

Sam Archer sat up a little straighter and gathered his thoughts before proceeding. He had a very deliberate, calm way about him that inspired confidence.

"Only one other member of the original science team took a job here on Long Island. Dr. Sandra McCormick is now working at Cold Spring Harbor Laboratory as a research assistant to one of their Nobel laureates, a Dr. Caruthers. He has no military ties at all and his research is considered purely humanitarian in nature. Nothing that could be weaponized in any way. We did a preliminary investigation into Dr. McCormick's communications and discovered she has been receiving e-mail from Dr. Sellars and some of the other members of the original science team. None of the e-mail appeared suspicious on the surface, but Sellars in particular seemed anxious to meet with her. As a result, we've had Dr. McCormick under discreet surveillance. So far, we haven't seen anything to indicate that she might be working with Sellars or that she has had any contact with him beyond the e-mail."

"As long as the situation remains at this level, I want you to continue surveillance on her," Sykes ordered. "Everything points back to the members of the original research team. I've dispatched orders through channels to track down and keep an eye on the rest of them. The FBI is helping with surveillance, though the individual agents haven't been read into the mission. Their orders are to track and identify the scientists, then observe them from a safe distance. Ideally, there will be physical observations of the scientists' daily activities and especially electronic surveillance of their computer and phone communications. Since you're already in position and there's a potential tie-in with Sellars and your ongoing investigation, I want you to stay with McCormick."

Sam and Xavier both nodded in agreement.

"I think it would also be wise for you to meet with Dr. McCormick, Sam," Sykes surprised them by saying. "Let her know we're aware of her and see what she does. If she's on the level, she may turn into a valuable resource for us. If she's dirty, she could panic and lead us to Sellars."

"I'll arrange an intercept for tomorrow," Sam agreed.

The rest of the meeting went as expected. Sarah was asked detailed questions about her experiences with the creatures, and Xavier reported on their activities since the last time they'd all been together, going over the initial scene in that abandoned building. Was that only a day or two ago? It felt like a lifetime. So much had happened since then. And her internal clock was all turned around. They'd switched to night shift, and now everything was blending together into a mélange of too little sleep and too much action. She rarely registered what time it was anymore.

When the meeting finally ended right before dusk, Sykes cornered Sarah, making small talk about her experiences as a police officer. Sykes was an interesting man, and he didn't have the superior attitude she'd half-expected from such a highly ranked officer. He was a couple of years older than Xavier. Maybe in his late thirties or possibly early forties. She had no doubt he was a career navy man who'd earned his rank over time. Xavier had wandered off to talk with his men, and she was comfortable enough with the group that she didn't mind being left to her own devices for a few minutes.

Xavier and she had been nearly inseparable from the moment he'd sprung her from the hospital. It was nice to have a little breathing room, though he stood only a few yards away, across the room. She liked being with him, but the level of intensity was not what she was used to in a relationship. Never mind that it had been a really long time since she'd been in one of those.

"How are you getting along with Captain Beauvoir?" Sykes asked.

Had he somehow read her mind?

She realized belatedly he might have been reading her expression. Her eyes had strayed to Xavier, who was talking with Sam. Neither man looked happy, and she wondered what could have put that look of consternation on both their faces.

"He's a fine soldier, as I think you know," she answered finally. She wasn't really sure what to say, so she settled for commenting on his professional abilities.

"But how is he doing with you? What I mean to say is, I doubt he's ever been on a combat mission with a woman before. Is he giving you any grief?"

Sykes's friendly smile invited confidences. Sarah wasn't going to fall for that. She assumed Sykes had only her best interests at heart, but she'd never say anything that could damage either Xavier's reputation or his career.

"He's been the perfect gentleman and the perfect coworker. He gives me space and he's taught me a lot about how to operate in the field. He says I've been able to show him a lot about crime scene investigation, so it seems to be a good match." It felt a little boastful to say that last bit. Sarah was never one to toot her own horn, but the situation seemed to call for it.

"It goes without saying that most of these men are trained as soldiers, not necessarily as investigators. It's yet another reason why I'm glad to have you on the team." Sykes seemed genuine enough, if a bit overly friendly. It seemed like he was trying too hard. For the life of her, she couldn't figure out why.

Sarah hated beating around the bush. She had the well-earned reputation of being a straight shooter. People were rarely allowed to get away with subterfuge in their relations with her, both in business and in her personal life. Being surrounded by cops and marines at home had done that to her. She liked having things out in the open.

"Commander—"

"Call me Matt." He interrupted before she could finish her thought.

"Matt." She tried again. "Why is it so important to you that I'm on the team?"

He looked at her oddly for a moment before visibly relaxing and giving a gusty sigh. "That obvious, am I?"

The chagrined smile he gave her invited commiseration. This time, she followed where he led. Now, she thought, she was seeing the real Matt Sykes, not the public relations wannabe he'd tried at before.

"What's the deal, *Matt*?" She put a slight emphasis on his first name, drawing his grin out even more.

"I've been ordered to make sure you stay on the team. Whatever you want, I've been told to provide. It comes down from the highest levels. We need you, Sarah. Badly. They want to make certain you're going to stick with the mission until it's completed." She read pure honesty in his eyes. Now, finally, she was getting the truth behind his odd behavior.

"Whatever I want, eh?" She felt confident enough to tease him. Luckily, he realized she was teasing. She saw the humor reflected in his eyes.

"Yes, indeed. You hold all the cards, ma'am." He nodded, visibly suppressing a chuckle.

"Hmm. I think I like the sound of that." She let him dangle for a moment longer, then relented. "Your superiors should have known just from reading my file that I wouldn't leave this mission in the lurch. I took an oath to protect and serve. Right now, I can do that best from within your little group. Don't worry. Xavier won't run me off. He's been the perfect partner, in fact. I really am learning a lot from him."

"I'm glad." Sykes looked relieved. "I didn't know him that well before this all started, but I've gained a deep respect for Captain Beauvoir."

"Me too." She smiled softly.

"Good." Sykes straightened, some of the stiffness returning to his posture. "If you have any problems, Sarah, I hope you know you can come to me. Anytime. This mission is perhaps the most important I've ever been tasked with and I'll do anything I can to make sure it ends in success. Just say the word if you need me." He reached into his pocket and pulled out a card and a pen. He took a moment to write something on the back before handing the card to her. "This is my office number. My cell phone number is scribbled on the back. Feel free to make use of it if necessary."

She pocketed the card, touched that he'd make the offer. "Thanks, Commander."

"I thought you were going to call me Matt?"

She chuckled. "I'll try."

"See that you do." He laughed along with her. "So besides personnel issues, how is the mission itself treating you? I suspect the Police Academy didn't prepare you for facing marauding zombies in the woods."

A chuckle escaped, and a few of the men turned to look at her before she tamped down the urge to laugh.

"Sorry." She shook her head, still amused. "Yeah, I must have missed Zombie Day at the academy." Reflecting on what she'd been through the past couple of days, Sarah revised her answer. "Actually, I think I'm starting to get used to it, though I'll be the first to admit I wasn't much help to Xavier the first time we faced them together. I'd like to think I've acquitted myself better since then." Thinking about that encounter in the basement of the abandoned building still smarted. She'd been the next best thing to useless. Sarah wasn't used to performing so poorly on duty.

"Sarah." His tone lowered, became gentler somehow. "I've seen the surveillance video they made of your initial encounter with two of the creatures. Aside from being appalled that someone sat there and watched while you fought for your life, I have to say I was impressed by the way you fought back, as injured as you were. You saved yourself. You can be proud of the way you reacted."

She searched his eyes, touched by his concern. "Thanks." Never comfortable with praise, Sarah felt like a change of subject was in order. "I know you've all said that being immune is rare, but I'm curious. How rare is it, really? I mean, are you immune? Is that why they tapped you to head up this case?"

"Unfortunately not. If I were, I'd be out there in the field with you. As it stands, we have too few operatives who can face these things without fear of the contagion. You are part of a very select group, Sarah. Which is why we really need you on this."

"Well, you've got me. I know where my duty lies. Even if the zombies give me the creeps, I'll do what I have to do to help stop them." She shivered jokingly, though the zombies really did creep her out.

"To answer your question, I ended up running this show because the first infestation occurred on my base. After losing a lot of good marines to the contagion, we finally hit on how to neutralize the creatures. We had one immune soldier. Lucky for us, he was a SEAL. He went into the woods surrounding the base and solved our little problem in a few weeks. I honestly thought that would be the end of it. Then I got summoned to MacDill in the middle of the night to meet the commander of all joint Special Forces operations. USSOCOM, which is short for U.S. Special Operations Command. Never did I expect to meet, let alone work for that particular admiral."

Sykes shook his head at the memory. "I was told there'd been another outbreak. Due to my prior experience, I was asked to head up the operation. USSOCOM got involved because the scope had expanded beyond my base and now the army special ops guys were involved. Anytime the spec ops units from different branches have to work together, SOCOM coordinates it. That's how a navy guy ended up in charge of a bunch of Green Berets." He gestured to the men around the room. "Then we got reports about your attack, which earned me another trip to MacDill, and the mission expanded in scope. I hope to God it ends there, but I'm bracing for the worst."

"Probably a wise precaution," she agreed. "From what I gather, Sellars wasn't the only scientist on the initial project. Where there's one bad apple, more could follow."

Sykes looked grim. "So you appreciate the gravity of our problem. The fact that Sellars tried to get your blood while you were in the hospital was actually a lucky break for us. You were able to identify him and we can reasonably assume he's the source of the outbreak. We aren't quite that lucky with the outbreak at Fort Bragg. We're still trying to figure out the source of the creature that started the problem."

"That's awful," Sarah commiserated, thinking hard about how she might be able to help. Not knowing enough about the situation, she couldn't offer much in the way of practical suggestions.

"I'm hopeful your investigation will turn up some leads for us to follow."

"I'll certainly keep that in mind. If I see any potential tie-ins as we go along, I'll be sure to let you know," she promised.

"Excellent."

Sykes offered his hand and she took it, pleased by his firm, no-nonsense shake. She'd often thought you could tell a lot about a man by the way he shook your hand. She liked Sykes. He was a strong man who seemed to earn respect by his actions rather than by his rank alone. That was a good quality in a leader, as far as she was concerned.

They talked for a few minutes more about inconsequential things. She was glad Xavier had arranged this meeting. It was good to know the rest of the team and at least a small part of the chain of command.

Xavier watched Sarah as she talked with Sykes, impressed all over again by her presence and composure. She was a consummate professional and gorgeous to boot.

"What's up with you two?" Sam sidled up beside him, following the direction of his gaze to where Sarah stood with Sykes across the room. "If you don't mind me asking."

"Nothing I want to talk about with you right now, Sam." Xavier gave him the stink eye, hoping his friend would get the message. But Sam Archer was made of sterner, more stubborn stuff than that. He wouldn't let it go. Damn the man.

"It's pretty obvious you're involved. You might just be in over your head with this one. She's nothing like the women you usually date."

"I said I don't want to talk about this."

"Damn, buddy. You've got it bad. Can't say I blame you. She seems like one hell of a woman. I just hope you know what you're getting yourself into. Things aren't exactly stable in either of your lives right now."

"I'm well aware of that. But it's still none of your business."

"Just trying to look out for a friend, Xav."

A long look passed between them. Sam wasn't backing down, but then Xavier hadn't expected him to. They'd been friends a long time, having come up through the ranks together. They owed each other their lives several times over, which gave Sam more than a little latitude. That went both ways. They had each other's backs. Always had.

Working together on the same team was a recent development. Sam and he had trained and studied together, but they'd always been assigned to different units. When Xavier's unit had been decimated in the zombie fiasco, he'd been reassigned and given the opportunity to form his own small task force. The first person he'd picked had been Sam.

They'd worked well together, but sometimes—like right now—the lines between their longstanding friendship and their commander-subordinate relationship blurred. So far it hadn't been a problem. Xavier wondered if this thing with Sarah would be the straw that broke the camel's back. He hoped not. For the sake of the mission, their friendship and his blossoming relationship with Sarah.

"Leave it alone, Sam. I appreciate the concern, but we'll just have to see how it goes."

"Don't say I didn't warn you, brother."

Chapter Ten

Matt Sykes dialed the admiral's number as he drove himself to the airport. A small plane was fueled up and waiting to take him back to Fort Bragg, but he had to make his report first. The admiral had demanded a call as soon as the meeting ended, and Matt knew it was never wise to keep an admiral waiting.

The phone was answered on the second ring.

"Sir, this is Matt Sykes. I'm on my way back to Bragg. The meeting with Beauvoir's team just broke up."

"Good. I'll want you to coordinate reports between the two areas of operation. Give me daily status updates on both groups at 0900 and 1800 each day until further notice."

"Yes, sir." Twice-daily updates? Matt was curious about the admiral's sudden interest but glad he was taking the situation more seriously. Matt gave his report on the meeting as he drove, filling the admiral in on what he'd learned from the New York investigation.

"What is your opinion of Officer Petit?" the admiral asked bluntly.

"She is a capable officer and from all accounts lives up to the picture painted in her file. She's faced the creatures several times and, according to Beauvoir, reacts well in combat situations." Matt decided to stick to the facts.

"Call me a dinosaur, but I don't think I'll ever be comfortable sending female personnel into situations where hand-to-hand combat is likely."

The admiral's personal observation made him more human to Matt. He didn't really know this admiral. He'd never worked with him or for him before, though he'd certainly heard of him and his reputation as a harsh but fair taskmaster. The more Matt saw of him, the more he respected the man.

"I can understand your reasoning, sir." Matt wouldn't go so far as to share his own views, which marched along the same lines as the admiral's. He wasn't quite that comfortable with the man yet. "Sarah Petit seems able to handle herself. She and Captain Beauvoir found video someone had taken of the attack that left her immune. It's worth watching. The woman was seriously concussed, yet she managed to fight free from two of the creatures."

"I saw it." The admiral's voice was grim.

Matt was impressed the man had already viewed the digital file he'd forwarded only an hour before.

"She got lucky. If her head had hit the concrete any harder, those things would have damaged her irreparably before anyone could have found her."

Matt knew the truth of the older man's statement. Sarah had saved herself that day, there was no doubt in anyone's mind about that. The video only proved how very courageous she'd been in the face of dire circumstances. Even though she had later proved to be immune from the contagion, those zombies could still have killed her by slicing, dicing, clawing and biting her to death by slow degrees. Blood loss would have been the kindest way to have died but not the most likely. She would have suffered terribly before finally succumbing.

"How's her commitment to the mission, Commander?" the admiral demanded.

"She's in for the duration, sir. She understands how much we need her and is willing to go the distance."

"Thank heaven for that," the admiral muttered. "And what do you think of her personally, Commander?"

"She is what she seems. A dedicated, skilled officer, willing to protect and serve. Those were the words she used. She seems to see this mission as an extension of her oath as a police officer."

"That's good, but what were your impressions of her? You talked to her. Give me a feel for her character."

Sam was surprised by the request but willing to try. "She's smaller than I expected. Very petite. She's also fierce and has a lively sense of humor, even under the circumstances. She saw right through my poor attempts to ingratiate myself and called me on it." The admiral chuckled on the other end of the line, but Matt didn't pause. "She seems to like plain talk and honesty, which is something I respect. All in all, I think she's a good addition to the team."

"The fact that she's female isn't going to be a problem?"

"The men seemed to accept her as a member of the team. They all seemed to respect her and I think Beauvoir has taken her under his wing. She told me he'd been teaching her how to work in the field and she'd been sharing her investigative knowledge with him. They've already turned up more evidence than the military personnel has at Bragg. I think having her on the team will cause more good than harm in the long run."

"She looks like a pretty young girl in her file photo. No hormone issues among the men?"

Matt had to stifle a laugh at the way the admiral phrased his question.

"As I said, sir, I think Captain Beauvoir has taken her under his wing, so to speak."

"Do you think they're involved?"

He could hear the admiral's frown in his voice. Matt wasn't prepared to cause trouble over something that might or might not be going on. He didn't really care what his people got up to in their private time, but he knew there were a lot of older officers especially who weren't so lenient.

"It doesn't appear so, sir. Captain Beauvoir has a reputation for protecting underdogs. In Ranger School, he helped another candidate who had fallen ill with a twenty-four-hour virus until he was over the hump and able to compete again. Beauvoir's been known to give extra training on off-hours to those in his command who don't perform up to his standards. The men flock to him. He seems to inspire loyalty and the desire to perform at peak ability in his men. From the conversation I had with Sarah Petit tonight, he's had the same effect on her." Matt privately thought there probably was something romantic going on between Sarah and Xavier, but nobody would hear about it from him.

"What did she say to lead you to this conclusion?"

The admiral sounded skeptical to Matt's ears.

"She told me she thought she'd performed poorly in her first two encounters with the creatures but that, with Beauvoir's help, she was doing better. Her tone was clearly one of admiration when she spoke of the captain and his skills in the field. He's definitely had an effect on her." Matt had seen the way Sarah and Xavier had looked at each other. He'd also noticed the way Beauvoir protected her without being too obvious about it. The man was probably already halfway in love with the pretty policewoman.

Matt almost envied him. Sarah was a fine-looking woman and had a big heart. She also understood duty and honor. Such a woman would be a good match for a man in Xavier's line of work. Matt's line of work, too, for that matter. Too bad he hadn't met Sarah first. Maybe if he had, he'd have had a chance with her. As it was, she'd only had eyes for Xavier.

"All right." The admiral regained Matt's attention with his decisive tone. "Now, what can you tell me about the situation at Bragg? Any new developments come out of your meeting in New York?"

Matt made a face, glad the admiral couldn't see him. Frankly, he was disgusted by their lack of progress in identifying the source of the outbreak. Luckily, the number of zombies at Fort Bragg was minimal compared with what had been unleashed so far on Long Island.

"We still haven't been able to locate the source of the contagion at Fort Bragg, sir. I've downloaded a lot of information from the New York investigation to my people in North Carolina and we're scheduled for a group debrief tomorrow at 0600. You'll have the results of that session in your 0900 report."

"How about the creature count at Bragg? Any increase?"

"No, sir." That was the one small blessing in this whole messed-up situation. "After the initial creature that spread the infection before I came on scene, the instance of new cases has been minimal."

"I'm concerned that we haven't been able to locate the source of that initial creature. Where there's one, there's bound to be more. If someone is experimenting with the contagion in North Carolina, we need to find them and stop them."

"Yes, sir." Matt couldn't agree more. It was how he was supposed to accomplish that feat with not a single clue to work with that had him stymied.

The admiral sighed audibly. "All right. Keep me advised. I'll expect your next report tomorrow at 0900. If anything big happens in the meantime, call me directly. I don't care what time it is."

Matt was impressed by the instruction. Very few admirals would welcome being awakened in the middle of the night by a ringing phone. For that matter, very few admirals would have asked Matt to call after a dinner meeting. Matt knew this number was the admiral's private encrypted cell phone, which he kept with him at all times. Most likely, the man was at home right now, after having put in a long day at the office.

After a short good-bye, Matt disconnected the call. The admiral's dedication to the mission was inspiring. It gave Matt hope that Uncle Sam wasn't trying to sweep this problem under the rug. When this was all over, Matt might still have a career left.

That question had been running through his mind for a while now. He knew where all the bodies were buried, after all. That could either work out to be a very good thing for him career-wise, or a very bad thing. Which it would ultimately prove to be was still up for grabs.

This early in the autumn, the night air wasn't all that cold. The campus was hopping with life in the main areas as Xavier and Sarah drove through in her patrol car. They made a quick stop at the security office to let the campus cops know they planned to conduct a search on the premises. They had a little trouble with a supervisor until Xavier placed a call and had the rent-a-cop set straight.

"Lot of people around here," Xavier commented as they rolled slowly around the loop road that ringed the perimeter of the main areas of the big campus. There was a network of smaller roads passing through the center of the grounds surrounded by wooded areas beyond the loop road.

"It's well-lit, too. Even at night. Chances are the zombies won't want to get caught in the lights near the center of campus."

"They'll be in the woods."

"Yeah, but where? Nearly the whole campus has pockets of dense trees."

"Well, they need someplace to hide during the day. Are there any dorms or empty buildings near one of the larger thickets of trees?"

Sarah thought for a moment. "Over near the train station." She swung the car around. "It's a spur of the Long Island Railroad that doesn't get much activity compared to the rest of the system."

The tracks were dark. Only the small station was lit by a few lonely light posts when they arrived. Sarah parked her patrol car near the edge of the big commuter lot. There were a number of cars still parked, waiting for their owners. The school offered night classes for those who worked during the day and Sarah knew more than a few students would be either walking to their cars or catching a late train in a few hours' time as the night classes ended.

The tracks themselves were kept free of debris. Only scrubby weeds grew here and there—those that had escaped the conscientious LIRR trimming crews this time. The trees were well back from the tracks, but dense.

"Over there." Xavier spoke in low tones. "If I were a zombie, I'd go for a spot like that."

She saw what he meant. The gloom was intense. And to top it all off, a light layer of fog was beginning to form low to the ground. Fog wasn't too unusual in certain areas of Long Island, especially at this time of year, but it still creeped Sarah out.

"Will that fog get any thicker?" Xavier asked.

"Not likely. Fog isn't too prevalent out here. Just in certain spots and under certain weather conditions. Of course, I could be wrong."

"Great." He shot her a look filled with concern despite his sarcastic tone. "Just stay close."

He surprised her by grabbing her hand. Startled, she sought his gaze and found him struggling for words. The emotion on his face floored her. He was genuinely worried for her, and not in a casual way. The man looked like he was in agony. She squeezed his hand.

"It'll be all right." She knew darn well she was walking into a potential lion's den, but she had no other choice. "We're armed to the teeth and immune. What could go wrong?"

They had restocked their ammo and added extra clips in addition to what they'd already been carrying. It was bulky but worth it, considering how many darts it took to end those infected with this particular strain of the contagion.

"Everything could go wrong, Sarah." Vulnerability showed on his face for a stark moment. "I don't want to lose you, *mon ange*. You're clear on the use of the headset?"

He tapped the side of her face where a small microphone now rested. Sam had outfitted her with one of the unit's miniature radios for short-range communication. She and Xavier could talk to each other as long as they stayed within about a half mile.

"Clear, Captain." She tried to cheer him with a smile, but it wasn't working. Xavier was as serious as she'd ever seen him. She tried a different tack. "You know there's no other way. Our first priority has to be protecting the kids on this campus from the contagion. If Sellars or his people make a grab for me, I'll fight like hell, but for now I have no other choice but to go in there and get the creatures before they have a chance to ravage this campus. You know I'm right."

"I know, dammit." He looked pained. "If there were any other way . . ."

"You know there's not." She squeezed his hand once more. "It'll be okay. No matter what happens."

"*Dieu.*" He pulled her in for a quick hug, tight, almost bone crushing, and heartfelt. "Promise me you'll be careful, Sarah." He let her go but didn't go far.

"I promise."

Xavier seemed to pull it together right in front of her eyes. His spine straightened, though there was still an echo of softness in his gaze as he looked at her. The commander was back, but he was tempered with the lover she'd come to know over the past hours. Nothing would ever make him seem a stranger to her again.

"All right. Let's do this. Back-to-back, if we get cornered. Otherwise, stay in my line of sight at all times. I'll do the same. We need to stay together in there, no matter what they throw at us. We can't help each other if we get separated."

"Roger that, Captain." She sent him a soft smile that said she understood his worry and shared it. He nodded and off they went, side by side, into almost certain danger.

"Could this get any creepier? The fog, the trees and brambles, the lonely train tracks off to one side, rising on an embankment as the ground dipped. Damn," Xavier mused aloud as they made their way into the unknown.

Sarah's soft chuckle at his side warmed him. Her presence also scared the shit out of him. She was the target, and he was escorting her right into the maw of a ravenous beast intent on capturing her and taking her away. He had to be insane to allow this, but she was right. They had no alternative.

To his knowledge, there were only four people on Earth at the moment who were proven immune to the contagion. Xavier, Sarah and the two operatives working back at Fort Bragg. He knew one of them. A SEAL he'd worked with once before named Simon. He didn't know who the other was. Whoever he was, he'd been brought in after Xavier and his team had been sent to Long Island.

There just wasn't anyone else they could safely send against these things. Sellars had devised the perfect setup for a trap, and they all knew it. He'd be a fool to pass up an opportunity like this. Sellars might appear to be apeshit crazy, but he'd already proven he wasn't a fool.

One good thing in this craptastic situation was that Sellars wanted Sarah alive. Even if he did manage to get past Xavier and take her, he wouldn't harm her. He needed her alive so he could figure out what had happened in her body when exposed to the contagion to produce her results.

Sellars needed to know why Sarah was immune. For whatever reason, Sellars didn't seem to realize, or didn't care, that Xavier was also immune. The rogue scientist's target was Sarah, not Xavier. From the video, Sellars seemed to assume her so-called "military escort" was some nameless, faceless soldier who was just along for the ride.

Xavier would be only too happy to show Sellars how very wrong he was. No doubt the scientist expected him to fight, and to fall. Sellars had no idea Xavier wouldn't go down that easily. That was the only ace in the hole Xavier and Sarah had going for them at the moment.

"I have movement to my left," Sarah said softly. "About ten yards in."

Xavier immediately went to high alert. "I see it. Let's keep the railroad tracks to our left or our backs. I don't think they'll cross the open area where the tracks are to come in behind us." The tracks were a good five feet above where they stood.

A small hill covered with grass rose from the edge of the trees and the tracks rode its ridge.

About fifty yards into the trees, they had to halt. "They're in front of us now and to our right," Sarah breathed into the foggy silence.

The zombies were arranged like an offensive line. It looked like the most gruesome football team of all time. Even worse, each guy was bigger than the next—bloody, ragged and disturbing as hell. This was not going to be fun.

"As soon as you see a clear target, start shooting. We don't have time to waste." Xavier raised his weapon, waiting for the distant signs of movement to take form in the fog. Damn the weather. These were not ideal circumstances for this kind of mission, but they had to play the hand they were dealt. "You take the ones in front, I've got the right flank."

They positioned themselves, their backs at a ninety-degree angle to each other, ready for action. It came sooner than expected as the zombies did something Xavier had never seen another of their kind do. They rushed forward, like an offensive line, faster than he would have credited.

They were male. Young and big. College students, no doubt. Poor kids. Scratch that. They were a fearsome line of undead muscle making a killer play for him and Sarah.

"Retreat!" he urged, already moving backward, firing as he went. Sarah was right beside him, getting off a few shots as well, but there were too many of them.

"I think the whole freaking football team was infected."

Sarah's voice came to him, low, urgent and filled with both resolve and fear. It was the fear that nearly killed him, but they had to muscle through.

"Oh, God," she breathed.

Xavier followed Sarah's gaze to the line of zombies that were moving faster than any he'd ever seen. They weren't running, exactly. It was more like a fast shuffle. Still, it was intimidating when paired with the size and quantity of the creatures closing in on them.

Then he saw her. A young woman. Maybe eighteen or nineteen years old. She wasn't a zombie yet, but she was in the clutches of one. She was beating at his chest and screaming a name. Tony. Maybe the zombie holding her had once been someone the girl knew.

"We've got to help her." Sarah kept firing, just as he did.

He'd hit each one of the creatures once. There were at least eight of them in his sights. He popped an empty ammo clip and reloaded on the fly, sending another round of darts home. He noticed Sarah doing the same, though she was a little slower on the reload than he was. That was to be expected. She wasn't used to this weapon and hadn't practiced with it as much as he'd have liked.

"I've got eight targets with two darts in each. How about you?"

"Seven. I'm working on the second rounds now."

"Let's get four in each and then we can do something about the girl."

"They're moving too fast. I don't think we'll make it." She kept firing, even as doubt entered her voice.

"We'll make it. We can retreat up the embankment to the railroad tracks if we have to."

"For the record, I don't like this."

Her grim humor hit him head-on and he realized something important. He was falling in love with Sarah Petit. The gutsy woman at his side was the perfect partner for him in any situation, including the most unlikely comrade-in-arms he'd ever considered. She was beautiful, smart, funny and courageous, not to mention the way they lit each other on fire in bed. She could very well be the one.

Hell of a time to realize it. Xavier shook his head and kept firing.

"I don't like it, either, but it's what we've got." He wanted to say something profound but there wasn't any time. The enemy was closing in and already they were inching their way up the embankment.

The tracks above curved to the west, toward Manhattan, and there was a grassy field beyond. No lights. It wouldn't stop the zombies. The whole area was dark and foggy, just the way they liked it.

A quick glance at Sarah told him she was reloading, working on putting her third round in each target. He'd just finished his third round and was on to the fourth. He'd be able to help her finish off her targets as soon as he'd completed his. Then they'd see about the girl. She was being dragged along with the zombie she kept calling Tony, but it didn't look like the creature that had once been a man cared about the girl beating at his chest. He was intent on Sarah and Xavier, working with his nightmare team to box them in against the embankment, forcing them to climb it.

Xavier didn't understand the tactic, but then he'd never really understood what motivated any of the creatures he'd faced. This new variety was even more perplexing. The girl's wailing was grating on his nerves, but he and Sarah had to focus on their jobs. Rescuing the girl would have to come later.

Four darts in each target, Xavier turned to help Sarah with her group. They worked well together, in synch without having to say a word.

"Now what?" Sarah asked when every one of the zombies had been darted four times. Even the one that still held the screaming girl. Shooting that one had taken some tricky aiming, but it had been done all the same.

"Now we wait for them to crumble." Xavier took hold of Sarah's elbow as they walked backward up the steep incline toward the railroad tracks. They kept their eyes on the zombies who had slowed now that they were closing in on their quarry.

"They're taking an awfully long time to dissolve."

An eternity, Xavier thought privately. As soon as this was over, Xavier was going to put a call in to Commander Sykes and see if he could get the science team to pep up the toxic darts. These weren't cutting it, especially when faced with large numbers of these new-and-improved zombies.

Sarah was behind him, a little farther up the hill, when the first of the creatures started to wobble, then crumple into nothing. One by one, they all went down.

"About time," Sarah muttered. She was a few paces away, closer to the tracks, and as the creatures fell her face lit with triumph.

"I'll get the girl. Stay close." Xavier moved forward, confident Sarah would follow right behind.

As the zombie holding her disintegrated, the girl was freed. Xavier ran to her, rolling her onto her back, away from the gooey mess that had been the man she'd called Tony.

She was badly scratched, and her shoulder was a bleeding mess of teeth marks and missing flesh. Chances were good she was already dead.

"What's your name, sweetheart?"

She was sobbing as her life slipped away. The least he could do was find out who she was before she succumbed, so that her family could be notified.

"Donna. Donna Sullivan. Tony Bosco was my boyfriend." She cried harder. "What happened to him?" She was hysterical now, losing energy with every sob.

She was fading fast, but Xavier couldn't be absolutely sure whether it was just unconsciousness or contagion-induced death coming to call. He'd bet on the latter, but he'd give her a chance to prove him wrong before he darted her. Leaving her on the ground, he did a quick survey to find Sarah. She should have been right next to him.

"Sarah?" A knot of dread formed in the pit of his stomach. He started up the embankment toward where he'd seen her last.

And there she was, struggling in the clutches of three big men. One had her caught in a bear hug from behind, trapping her arms, while the others each had one of her legs. They were zombies, but they didn't seem to want to bite her.

Then Xavier caught sight of a shadowy figure, a man standing about ten yards behind them. He stood next to a white cargo van, and suddenly his intent became clear to Xavier. The zombies were doing Sellars's dirty work for him. They'd captured Sarah and were shuffling back to their master with her in their clutches.

Not for long, Xavier vowed. Taking aim, he fired on the run, hitting the two who had hold of her legs. But neither one flinched. He fired again. He had to be careful not to hit Sarah. Panic was driving him. He had to get to her in time. But they were too far apart, and the creatures were moving faster than ever before.

He kept firing. He'd shot the two at her feet with four darts each. The one behind her had one sticking out of his neck and one in his arm, but he was holding Sarah in a way that prevented Xavier from taking any other shots. It wasn't intentional but it was damned effective. He couldn't chance hitting her with the deadly toxin. He paused to aim—this time it would be a shot to the head.

Xavier pulled the trigger, grotesquely pleased when the dart sank into its ruined face and lodged in the back of its throat. That was three.

Sarah saw him and screamed. "Xavier!"

He looked up to see a train bearing down on him as he neared the tracks. Sarah and her attackers were on the other side. The train rounded the curve that had hidden it from view until that very moment, and its bright headlights pinned him in place, slicing through the fog. There was no time to get across. Even as he started forward, he felt the *whoosh* of compressed air against his whole body as the train tore through the night.

"Xavier!" he heard her scream again as the train roared past.

He dug his phone out of his pants pocket and hit one of his speed dial buttons. Nobody could hear him above the roar, but they'd know for damn sure that something was up. They'd be put on alert.

He leapt from side to side, waiting for an opening, but the train was too damn long. Car after car sped past. He tried to see through the breaks in the cars, but everything was a blur.

He could just make out the large white rectangle of the cargo van. He couldn't see much else. And then the blurry white rectangle was gone.

Xavier spat out every curse he could think of, knowing he had failed. His chances of rescuing Sarah diminished with each train car that passed. How the fuck long were these things, anyway? He'd already counted nine cars, and more rounded the bend with each shouted curse from his lips.

Finally, all twelve cars had passed and the tracks were once again clear. Xavier didn't wait for the dust to settle. He ran across the tracks, only to step in a pile of goo. At least one of the bastards that had taken her had already disintegrated. He didn't pause to look for the other one. More than likely, the two that had grabbed her feet were now gone. That left the third one—the one he'd managed to shoot only three times. He could still be around, or he could've gone with Sellars and Sarah in the van.

Xavier punched the speed dial on his phone one more time.

"Go," came the immediate reply. It was Sam.

"They got Sarah. She's in a white cargo van leaving campus from a grassy field about a hundred yards north of the train station. Scramble."

"On it, sir."

Sam would send the chopper and any other resources he had ready and waiting. Although the B Team had been scheduled for downtime tonight, Xavier knew Sam well enough to know he'd be ready for anything. Hell, he'd probably been waiting by the phone ready to play cavalry. Xavier would take all the help he could get at this point.

They'd taken out the zombies. Now they needed to get Sarah back. He'd move heaven and earth to make it happen.

"I'm coming for you, *mon ange*," he whispered after shutting his phone. He pulled the flashlight from his belt. He didn't want to trample any possible tracks, but he also didn't intend to wait around. Sarah needed him and he wouldn't let her down.

Chapter Eleven

Xavier was frantic, but he couldn't let it show. His men knew, of course. Especially Sam. None of his guys were stupid. After the meeting the night before, they had to know that he and Sarah were involved.

With Sarah abducted right from under his nose, all bets were off. Xavier found it impossible to keep his detached professional air. He was pissed, heading toward all-out fury, and those around him knew it.

Sam had the chopper at the site in less than five minutes. By that time, the cargo van was long gone. Xavier had made quick rounds, dropping off transmitters on each pile of goo. The girl was missing. She had either woken up immune or risen from the dead. He would have to figure it out later.

Xavier had hopped into the chopper as it hovered a few feet off the ground, and they'd spent a fruitless half hour in the air, looking for a damn needle in a haystack. That van had disappeared.

"I want you to bring in Dr. McCormick for questioning. No, wait. Let's go get her right now. We don't have time to waste," Xavier said over the headset they used so he could communicate over the noise of the helicopter's blades. Reno was piloting. "Reroute to Cold Spring Harbor," he ordered.

"Get on the radio and arrange for local police to meet us there. See if they can lend us a vehicle. Sam, do you have the doctor's address?"

"Yes, sir." Sam pulled a PDA from his belt and tapped the screen a few times.

Xavier saw Reno keying his mic. He was on the radio, setting up things for when they landed. They were both good men. They'd get the job done. But it wasn't fast enough. Nothing was fast enough to suit him right now, with Sarah in the hands of that unethical son of a bitch, Sellars.

"The county cops will have a tactical unit waiting for us. We're landing at one of their stations. They're loaning us a SWAT team and their gear," Reno reported over Xavier's headset as they hugged the northern coastline of the island on their way west, toward Cold Spring Harbor.

"You told them why we need it?" Xavier didn't want the local cops—good as they were—getting in the way of his team. He also didn't want a lot of targets scattered around the site, ready to become zombie fodder. He was the only one who could do this extraction. He and he alone.

"They wanted to talk to Officer Petit and I had to tell them. Sorry, sir."

"Don't be. They'll throw everything they have our way when they know one of their own is in danger. Your job will be to keep everyone secure, away from the target zone while I do the extraction. Clear?"

Reno grinned. "I'm always up for a little misdirection, Captain. We'll babysit the locals if we have to, while you get your woman. And if you need backup, you know that we have your back, despite the danger."

Two things struck Xavier. First, his men were willing to face the horrific threat of the zombie contagion for him. Now, that was some serious loyalty, especially when they'd seen firsthand what had become of the others who'd tried and died. They were brave men and Xavier was touched by their willingness to face such a threat for him.

Second, though perhaps this was more important, Xavier felt a strange warmth spreading through him at Reno's words about Sarah. He'd called her Xavier's *woman*. Damn if that didn't feel right.

This was about more than retrieving a colleague. This was personal.

"Landing in five," Reno updated the team.

They set down on a small helipad a few minutes later. Xavier was glad to see a welcoming party ready and waiting for them at the pad behind the police station. There were two big trucks that he knew belonged to the SWAT team.

He hit the ground running, making his way to the man in charge. They shook hands and shouted to be heard above the roar of the blades winding down. Reno would park the chopper and be ready to depart before Xavier had straightened out the logistics of who would be in which vehicle.

He wanted one vehicle just for his team. One with no locals hitching a ride.

"Captain Beauvoir," the SWAT commander shouted over the noise. "I'm Sergeant Luke Tomlinson, Emergency Services Section. I've been ordered to assist in whatever way possible."

The rotors on the chopper were slowly winding down. With them went the roar of the wind and the noise from the engine. Xavier was able to speak in a more normal tone as he walked toward the waiting vehicles with the SWAT commander.

"Sergeant Tomlinson, we'd like one of your rides."

The man stopped walking and turned to regard Xavier, taking his measure. "I don't know why the army is involved in this—whatever it is. All I've been told is that an officer has been abducted and you're our best bet for getting her back. Personally, I take offense at that, but then it's been some years since I left the 82nd Airborne. I recognize your beret and your insignia, Captain, but I don't like being left out of the loop."

The cop had been Airborne. That counted for something. Xavier decided to tread as lightly as possible while still making his point.

"I appreciate that, Sergeant. Truly, I do. Unfortunately, I don't have time—and you don't have clearance—to know the details of our mission here. All I can tell you is that it has to do with national security and the missing officer is working as a liaison with my unit. She's been read into the mission and her life is in imminent danger. I intend to get her back with all possible haste. After that, maybe we'll be able to talk more."

Tomlinson stared him down, but Xavier sensed the man understood. Finally, the sergeant nodded, throwing a set of keys toward him. Xavier caught them, his reflexes sharp.

"Take the SUV. It's loaded with standard SWAT gear. We'll act in a support capacity, as ordered."

Xavier spared a moment to thank the man, then heard his unit jogging up behind. He tossed the keys to Sam as he and Kauffman passed. Reno was still a few lengths behind but catching up fast. "We're going to do recon. We'll meet you back here at the station once we have a plan of action."

"You do that," Tomlinson shot back.

Getting rid of the locals had been easier than Xavier expected. It had helped to have a man like Tomlinson in charge. He'd been military. He'd know that a small spec ops team like Xavier's would likely operate more efficiently without a parade of cops tagging along.

They parked the SUV around the corner from Dr. McCormick's home. They were in a fairly middle-class area with small houses every quarter acre or so, in the less fashionable part of town. Xavier waved Sam, Reno and Kauffman to watch each side of the simple house in case the woman tried to flee out a window or through the backyard. Xavier took the direct approach, ringing her front doorbell.

An elfin face moved the curtain over the window in the door and peered out at him. Her eyes squinted a moment before she planted wire-framed glasses on her freckled nose. Her eyes widened as she took in his attire.

"Dr. McCormick? I'm Captain Beauvoir, U.S. Army. I need

to speak with you about one of your former colleagues. Will you come with us?"

The woman looked startled but opened the door a crack. "Us?" she asked, looking around.

"My men are around back. We have a situation and we really need you to come with us."

"You were afraid I'd try to run." Knowing eyes tilted in his direction. "As you can see, I won't. Where do you want to take me?"

She was cagey, this one, and much younger-looking than he'd expected. Her file said she was in her late thirties, but her pixie looks made her appear much younger. She was pretty in a sort of ethereal way.

"The police are letting us use some of their facilities since one of their officers has been abducted."

She seemed upset at the news, but she was hard to read.

"Are you arresting me? You want to put me in a cell?"

"Only if you're guilty of something, Doctor. Right now we need to pick your brain for anything you might know about your former colleague Dr. Sellars."

Her brows swept downward in an angry frown. "I want nothing to do with that man."

"That may be, but we know he's been in contact with you." Xavier sighed heavily. It didn't look like she would come willingly, and time was wasting.

"Why don't you signal your team and come inside?" She opened the door wide. "You can question me here and I'll give you what little I have on Dr. Sellars. I never liked that man."

That last bit was almost muttered under her breath, but Xavier heard it. She didn't look happy, but from what he could tell, she was willing to help.

Xavier considered his options. They weren't many and they weren't good. He pursed his lips and gave a short whistle. That signal would bring his men in. One by one, they appeared from behind the house.

Dr. McCormick stepped back from the door and ushered

them inside the small house. Xavier looked around as he sent his men off to clear each room. Oddly, she didn't object.

She must've sensed his surprise, for she explained. "I worked for the navy on top-secret projects for more than a few years, Captain. I'm familiar with the need for security and the way you soldiers go about assuring it." She sat on a flowered chair that had a matching sofa.

When the guys returned, reporting the house was clear, they took up protective positions around the room. Only the woman sat.

Xavier started with a question. "You know why I'm here?"

"I can guess. I know Dr. Sellars got a job in Stony Brook. He tried to get me to meet him for dinner, but I've declined. He always gave me the creeps. What's he been doing to get your attention?"

Xavier did his best to read her. So far, she seemed on the level.

"He's up to his old tricks. Doing experiments on coeds." He was satisfied when she went pale. Nobody could fake that kind of shock. She truly hadn't known. "So far we've had over a dozen killed. No bodies to show to their parents or loved ones, if you understand my meaning."

She nodded tightly. "I do." The small woman started to shake, but Xavier had no mercy. Sarah was missing and he needed to find her. Every moment lost was a moment when she could be undergoing torture. A moment when she might be killed.

"Then you understand my urgency. One of the first to be attacked was a Suffolk County cop. She survived. About an hour ago, Sellars abducted her. We know he wanted to run tests on her to figure out why she was immune. Dr. McCormick, he's going to sell the technology to the highest bidder."

"Dear Lord." The woman looked stricken.

"I need to know anything you know about Sellars and where he might have taken Sarah." Xavier had slipped and used her name.

"Sarah," McCormick repeated. "Is that the police officer's name?"

"Yes. Sarah's in grave danger, Dr. McCormick. Do you have any idea where Sellars might have taken her?"

"No." She seemed to rethink her answer. "Not really. Maybe." She stood and reached for a black bag that had been propped up next to the armchair. It was a computer bag. She quickly unzipped it and pulled out a slim laptop, opening it and powering it up. She looked up at Xavier as the machine whirred to life. "He invited me to dinner. I accepted at first and he sent me directions to a place nearby. I looked it up online and realized it was a private residence in a very exclusive neighborhood. I thought he was trying to impress me." She rolled her eyes in a mocking expression. "I didn't want to be alone with him, so I cancelled and haven't rescheduled. I thought a nice public place like a restaurant would be ideal to tell him I want nothing to do with him. I didn't want to be stuck someplace alone with him." She placed the computer on the coffee table and began to open software and connect to her files.

"I don't blame you at all." Xavier crouched nearby. She had an advanced system but one he was very familiar with. He was almost vibrating with the need to get to Sarah. He watched impatiently as Dr. McCormick opened one last file and sent it to the wireless printer across the room.

Reno grabbed the paper before it even had time to hit the tray. He nodded to Xavier, who interpreted that to mean it had an address printed on it that Reno could find.

"Thank you, Doctor. Now, I need you to come with us. Sellars could come after you." He stood, expecting her to follow.

"Where do you propose I go?"

Damn, she was going to balk. He could feel it. Xavier didn't have time for this crap.

Sam came over, clandestinely pushing Xavier aside and extending a hand to the woman in the chair. She took it hesitantly but stood, looking up into Sam's smiling face. The man could turn on the charm when he had to, and Xavier was never more thankful for that than now. He didn't have the time or patience to deal with the doctor's fears. Thank goodness Sam had his back, as usual.

"We're going to take you to the local police station. We have some friends there who will keep you safe until we have the situation under control." Sam spoke in even tones. "Maybe you should pack a few things, just in case."

McCormick eyed him suspiciously for a moment, then relented. She disappeared into another room for a few minutes and returned with an overnight bag. Sam took it from her as he led the doctor toward the door.

But she stopped short of their goal. "Am I under arrest?"

"No, ma'am," Sam said, trying to placate her. "More like protective custody until we're sure the situation with Sellars is under control. He might target you because of your past association."

"So you're going up against him and his creations?" She looked around the room, pinning each man with her glance. "Are any of you immune?"

Xavier was surprised by the question, but then he realized she knew exactly what this experiment was all about. She'd been in on the initial experiment. She knew firsthand what the contagion could do. He wasn't certain which side she was on, though her aversion to getting involved with Sellars and willingness to give them his address had to count in her favor.

"I am." Xavier stepped forward and her gaze met his. He could see concern in her eyes as she looked back at the others.

"I have something you might need, then." She lowered the laptop she'd been clutching to her chest and handed it to Sam.

Xavier jerked his chin at Kauffman and Reno to keep an eye on the doctor, who was well on her way toward another room in the small house. They followed behind like well-trained puppies while Sam stowed her computer in the bag she'd taken it from and slung the strap over his shoulder.

"What do you think?" Xavier asked his friend and XO.

"I think she's beautiful." Sam surprised him with the all-too-serious comment. "I'm also pretty sure she's innocent since she didn't want anything to do with Sellars."

"That's my read, too."

She bustled back into the room, holding a small, flat black case that zippered all the way around. It was about an inch thick and roughly five-by-seven inches. She opened it as she moved, and Xavier went instantly on guard when he saw the vials inside.

"What is it?" he asked, suspicion in every bone of his body. For all he knew, this harmless-looking pixie could go all mad scientist on their asses without a moment's hesitation.

"Not an antidote, unfortunately, but the next best thing. If I'm right, it will provoke the immune response in some people after exposure to the contagion. I've been working on it on my own time. I know that puts me in violation of the agreement I made with the navy when they dumped me, but it had to be done. I was afraid some of the other members of the team wouldn't let the work rest, and I feared something like this would happen. I made this"—she held up the small holder full of vials—"to help when the time came. It appears that time is now."

"So if one of us gets bit and we take that stuff, we'll end up like the captain?" Reno asked. "We'll be immune?"

"It should redirect the contagion to act as it was supposed to, but only for some people. It's not perfect yet. I haven't had the time—or the desire—to really test it. Think of this as a last resort. Do everything you can *not* to get bitten. But if you do get bitten, this is something you can try before dying. I wish it was more."

"It's more than we could have expected, Doctor." Sam stepped in and took the case from her with gentle hands. "Thank you."

"Okay, I'm ready." She headed toward the front door without further urging.

Kauffman drove them all back to the police station with Reno and Sam sitting in back, flanking the doctor. Sam had given her the laptop case and she clutched it on her lap.

Reno had engaged her in a somewhat scientific discussion of

how the immune boosting compound she'd developed worked. It wasn't Xavier's field, but he found her talk interesting, to say the least.

"So why would it work for some people and not others?" Reno asked.

Xavier wanted to know, too.

"It has to do with certain antigens. If they are present, the serum seems to work. If not, it has no effect. I haven't nailed down all the factors yet, but I believe the serum will work if the right combination of antigens is present in the person already."

Reno thought out loud. "Tricky. There's no real way to know if the person you want to treat has the right antigens before you administer the serum. Not in an emergency situation." He knew more about science and medicine than the rest of them combined.

"And it doesn't work to create a cocktail of antigens and administer them first," McCormick said. "The substances have to be an integral part of the patient's body before administering the serum, and there wouldn't be enough time for the antigen cocktail to get around enough in someone's system for the serum to work. In fact, the results might be disastrous: a half-turned creature capable of thought and still very, very deadly." She shuddered.

"Could that be part of what Sellars has been doing?" Xavier asked quickly. "His new strain of zombies are capable of some limited speech and following his directions."

McCormick paled. "I don't know what line of research he's been following, but that sounds very bad, Captain. One of the reasons I don't like him is that he once talked about making an army of the creatures, back when we first discovered what had happened to the cadavers they'd decided to use for testing."

"The ones that got up and walked out of the lab in the middle of the night?" Reno asked with a hint of dark humor. "We heard about that. When the trouble started up on our base, the navy guys filled us in."

"It's happening elsewhere?" Dread filled her expression.

"Back at our base," Xavier confirmed. "And here on Long Island. They sent us up to take care of this problem while others are dealing with the one back home."

"That is truly awful." She looked thoughtful and very concerned. "Some of our team struck me as unethical. I was going to request a transfer right before that final, terrible experiment. Then all hell broke loose and we were sequestered for weeks on end. Eventually we were cut loose from our military contracts with all kinds of dire warnings. I suspected a few of my colleagues wouldn't go quietly. I'm sad to say I'm not surprised that Dr. Sellars did this. The man is a snake. I hope you catch him before he kills anyone else and I'll help in any way I can."

"You've already helped a great deal, Doctor. The best thing you can do to help us right now is to remain with the police while we go get Sarah." Xavier was focused on his mission. He was already formulating plans in his mind. They'd take the chopper to the house and he'd rappel in from above.

"Once we've nipped this in the bud, I'm pretty sure our superiors will want to talk to you about that serum you're developing," Sam put in. "We've already had two flare-ups and I think they're afraid there will be more before all is said and done. You and your serum could come in mighty useful."

"I'll be glad to help," she assured them all.

Kauffman pulled into the police station lot, having broken every speed limit along the way.

Impatience was riding Xavier. He wanted to be off. "Sam, settle things with the locals. I'm going to gear up at the chopper. Have the team meet me there ASAP."

"Yes, sir." Sam escorted the scientist toward the police station.

The SWAT vehicle was parked, ready and waiting, right next to them. No doubt the officers from that emergency services division were also ready and waiting, but Xavier wouldn't be using their expertise today if he could help it.

Xavier jogged the short distance to the helipad. It was behind the station, in a clearing. The chopper was equipped with special biometric locks, so nobody could get in it without one of the team members present. Xavier opened it up and went straight for the weapons cache. Loading his gear with the toxic darts he'd need against the zombies, he tried to calm himself. He needed to get into a bright head space to accomplish his mission and save Sarah. Going in half-cocked would be the worst mistake of his life. He counted on his training to kick him in the right direction as he deliberately slowed his breathing and focused on the task at hand.

Sam, Reno and Kauffman were back just as he began to get impatient. He was ready. His mind was set on the mission like an Olympic athlete focused on his few seconds of glory. Nothing would stop him now. It was free Sarah or die trying.

Sarah woke by slow degrees. She was in the dark, in a damp place, probably a basement, and she was strapped down to a hard surface. Probably a gurney or operating table, knowing who had her.

Those last frightening moments came back to her. She'd been struggling with three zombies. Two had her legs and one had her torso in a bear hug from behind. She couldn't move. The bastard who'd grabbed her from behind effectively pinned her arms, and the other two made sure she couldn't kick her way out of their grasp.

Xavier had plugged the creatures full of toxin in a display of incredible marksmanship, but they'd taken so long to dissolve. The moment the two at her feet turned to mush, she felt a needle pierce her throat. She'd been injected in the jugular, and none too gently. Whatever they'd hit her with acted fast. She remembered being lifted by human arms as the zombie behind her disintegrated and dropped on the cold metal floor of the waiting van. Bumpy motion as they drove fast out of the grassy field, and then . . . nothing.

Nothing until a few minutes ago when she woke up here. Wherever *here* was.

She found she could make out faint outlines of things if she used her peripheral vision. There was a line of light around the seam of a door, and she could see a tray at eye level to her right. Yeah, she was in trouble all right. Those were medical instruments on that tray.

All sorts of scary ideas entered her head. Would Sellars dissect her while she was still alive? Would he torture her? Or did he have something else in mind?

Her blouse had been unbuttoned, and she could feel the coldness of gel, plastic and metal. Some kind of sensors had been attached to her skin. Probably a heart monitor and some others. She could feel them on her legs, too. Her shoes and socks had been removed, and it felt like her uniform pants had been either cut or ripped up the sides to give them access for their sensors. She'd been hooked up to all kinds of machines and she hadn't even known it.

The door opened and an overhead light switched on. Brightness flooded the room, assaulting her eyes. She shut them quickly, trying not to scrunch them up against the sudden glare. If she could play possum for a bit, maybe they'd talk amongst themselves and she could learn something about where she was being held.

"Come now, Sarah." A *tsking* sound reached her ears. "I know full well you're awake. I saw it on the monitors."

"The light hurts my eyes," she groused. No way was she going to be a good little prisoner for this son of a bitch.

"Ah, yes. I suppose that would be true. No matter."

She felt him fussing at her side, and she was almost afraid to open her eyes and see what he was up to. A moment later, she felt him swab her inner elbow with something cold. Her eyes popped open.

Sure enough, he had a needle in his hand. It was Sellars, but not. He'd changed his appearance from the last time she'd seen him, as he'd said on his video. His hair had been cut short and dyed an unlikely shade of auburn. He had colored contacts that turned his dark brown eyes to hazel, and it looked like he'd had a spray tan treatment or two. The changes weren't anything earth shattering, but taken all together, he certainly didn't look like the man in his personnel photo.

"I see you've decided to take an interest in your own welfare. How nice."

The sadistic bastard smiled at her.

"I'm just hooking you up so I can tap your veins at will. I can foresee I'll need a number of blood samples from you as my testing proceeds."

"Testing?"

"Of course. Why else do you think I'd go through the trouble of capturing you? I need to know what makes you immune, Sarah. With that final piece of the puzzle, I can finally sell this technology and retire a rich man. Filthy rich, in fact."

He grinned like a fool, making her stomach turn. Sellars was clearly a greedy bastard. He stuck an IV in her arm with no regard to delicacy. She tried not to flinch at the pain.

"You'd let someone unleash that horror on an unsuspecting world?" He met her gaze and she saw no remorse, no conscience there. "And here I thought the zombies were the monsters."

"Touché, Sarah. I'm wounded by your wit." His insulting tone told her he was anything but. "Personally, I don't care what the highest bidder does with my work as long as I'm immune and rich. They could kill off the whole damn species as far as I'm concerned. In fact, that might be for the best. Cleanse the planet and start over with just a few immune souls as seed stock. The more I think of it, the more I like that idea."

"You're nuts."

"Compliments, my dear. You'll turn my head."

He shot her a sly smile that turned her stomach. Nothing seemed to bother this guy. He really was one for the record books. Sarah had never encountered such a strange but strong personality before. She'd have to work to find his Achilles' heel. If he had one. Of course, it looked like she'd have nothing but time to work on her little project.

She knew Xavier and his guys would move heaven and earth trying to find her, but she also knew it would be like searching for a needle in a haystack. While they searched for her she had to do what she could to both stay alive and try to escape.

Chapter Twelve

"What's the plan, Captain?" Sam asked as they took to the air, Reno behind the controls of the big military helicopter.

Bred for speed and stealth, this chopper was a little quieter than its civilian counterparts and more maneuverable. Nothing could cancel the noise of the engines and blades entirely, of course.

"I'm going to rappel down and find Sarah. I want you three to be ready to evac us and provide air support if needed."

Sam tried to offer assistance. "I'm more than willing to go in with you, Xav, to better your odds."

But Xavier wouldn't send his best friend into this kind of danger. "And worsen yours, my friend. Thanks, but the answer is still no. Even with the serum McCormick thinks *might* work on *some* people." He emphasized the shakiness of the argument he knew would be coming. "Go dark," he ordered Reno.

The chopper was black, and full night had fallen. Without lights they wouldn't be seen, and there was enough ambient light in the area that they could easily see features of the land. Luckily, there was no fog on this part of the coastline.

They were on the famed North Shore of Long Island, where million-dollar mansions on the beach abounded. This particular neighborhood was one of the more expensive, boasting multimillion dollar houses on acres of land.

The address they sought was a beachfront property. To get to the beach from the house far above, it looked like one would have to use a set of wooden stairs that led from a small cove upward toward a wooded area. From above, they could see a large villa hidden among the trees. It was a perfect spot for zombies. A lot of cover and a lot of land. The nearest neighboring house was quite some distance away. Far enough away that Xavier didn't worry about the neighbors getting involved.

"Hover by the edge of the cove. I'll work my way up from the beach. Then I want you to go high and watch from above. Use the infrared to follow my progress and let me know over the com if there are any hot targets coming my way." Xavier inserted a small tactical radio into his ear, adjusting the small mic that lay along his cheek. He'd have two-way communication with his team. The infrared would pick up live bodies, but it wouldn't register the zombies well. The longer they were outside, the more their bodies acclimated to the temperature. They would be hard to distinguish from the trees and growth everywhere on the property. Still, it was something. Sellars might have some living accomplices with him.

Sam asked the question Xavier dreaded. "What if she's not there?"

"She has to be." All of Xavier's instincts told him this was the place.

They'd gotten lucky with McCormick. She could have just as easily turned out to be playing for the wrong team. Xavier had looked into her eyes and his gut told him she was genuine. Her information was good, but would Sellars have taken Sarah to this location? He just didn't know.

He prayed as he had never prayed before. Sarah had to be here. It was as simple as that. He didn't have any other leads and he couldn't stand the idea of her staying under Sellars's control for one second longer than necessary.

"Son of a bitch," Reno swore. "Captain, do you see what I see?"

Everyone looked out of the chopper at the beach far below. Xavier could make out the figures walking with oddly staggered steps through the one open area at the rear of the villa.

Zombies.

They looked like they were running patrols. The damn things must be capable of following someone's directions to organize something like that. These had to be the new-and-improved versions.

"Sellars is here. His trained pets are running security," Sam said, summing up the situation.

"Edge of the cove, now, Reno!" Xavier ordered. He grabbed his gear and checked the lines as he prepared to leave the comparative safety of the helicopter's interior. "Hold it steady. I'll signal when I'm on the ground. Stay sharp." Xavier backed out of the chopper, only a thin rope between him and the ground far below.

It wasn't the longest descent he'd ever made, but it was close. He signaled his team through his headset the moment his feet touched the hard-packed beach. The strip of sand wasn't wide, and there was a residue of seaweed and the occasional jellyfish gleaming in the dim light of the moon as he made his way toward the wooden stairs.

Weapon at the ready, he mounted the winding staircase as quickly as possible. The higher ground that the house was built on wasn't too far above. Forty steps and he was ducking into the cover of the trees and bushes that lined the path leading to the house.

Sellars had taken a few vials of blood, then left. He'd turned off the light again, so Sarah was in the dark. It took a while for her eyes to adjust, but her body was busy working on a way out of the straps holding her down.

The table had been designed for a larger person, which worked to her favor. There was a bit of slack in the strap that covered her waist and forearms. There was another strap around her shoulders and one on her forehead, plus a few that laddered down her legs, holding her in place. All the straps went around her from one edge of the table to the other and disappeared beneath the hard surface of the table. No doubt they were secured somewhere below the platform she was lying on.

There was enough play in the forearms' strap that maybe if she twisted a little, she could work her hands free one at a time. It would hurt like hell and probably strain most of the muscles in her arms and middle, but she didn't see any other way. She set to work, grinding her teeth to keep from moaning at the pain she inflicted on herself.

She tried wiggling out the arm that didn't have the IV stuck in it. It hurt like a bitch, but by the time her eyes were used to the dark again, she had worked her hand free of that middle strap. She used that hand to help her get the one with the IV out of the binding next. It was looser now, so it was a little easier. She was tempted to yank the IV out of her arm but didn't want to do it in the dark, in case she started bleeding too much.

With her hands relatively free, she concentrated on her next step. Her shoulders and upper arms were still pinned, but she could move from her elbows and wiggle a bit. It would have to be enough.

She looked around and saw the instrument tray. If she could just . . . reach . . .

The back of her right hand made contact with something metallic. Twisting her wrist at an unnatural angle, she tried to pick up one of the instruments she could feel under her hand. She was careful, in case she came in contact with the business end of a scalpel or something.

In fact, that's just what happened. She sucked in a breath as something sliced the side of her finger. It was a shallow cut, like a paper cut. It hurt and it told her what to concentrate on. She wanted that blade.

She ended up slicing up her fingers some more after a few more tries. But finally, she worked the damn thing around to where she could grasp it awkwardly between her third and fourth fingers. Bending her elbow like a crane, she brought the instrument to her waist and dropped it on her abdomen. Repositioning her fingers, she picked it up in a much firmer grip. At last.

Sarah immediately went to work on the strap holding her hips in place. The sharp blade sawed through the thick strap a little at a time. It took some doing, but she finally was able to move her hips. Next came the strap at her knees, which she could just reach. Once that was gone, she bent her knees and forced her ankles out from under the straps at the lower end of the table.

Free from the waist down, she was able to scoot downward on the table and wiggle out from under the upper straps. A few minutes later, she was free.

She didn't dare flip the lights on in case anybody was monitoring the room. She did pull the IV from her arm now that she could stand. There were packets of sterile gauze on the tray, which she made use of after yanking the sinister tube from her arm. She waited to disengage the heart and pulse-point monitors in case the readings were available somewhere else besides the machines that recorded her vitals inside the room. She'd take them off at the last possible moment. No doubt they were already registering her elevated heart rate and pulse, but she hoped if anyone was reading the stats, they'd assume she was panicking about being tied up and helpless.

Sarah was anything but helpless and she was about to prove it. She buttoned her shirt and looked around for her shoes. They'd been thrown in one corner along with her socks. She slipped them on quickly, knowing it would be easier to escape if she was properly outfitted. She'd been lucky so far. Her utility belt and weapons were nowhere to be found, however She couldn't be *that* lucky.

So she armed herself as best she could from the instrument tray. It wasn't much. A few blades and a couple other pointy things. It would have to do. She also pulled the wire leads off her body, leaving only the suction cups they'd been connected to.

Sarah headed for the door, watching the gap at the bottom for a few moments to see if there were any changes in the light patterns. That might give her some indication about whether people were moving about on the other side, but she couldn't tell anything. There wasn't enough light, for one thing, and for another, anyone moving would have to be right near the door for her to see their motion this way.

"Screw it," she said under her breath as she reached for the knob on the door. It wasn't locked. Sellars had been too confident, assuming she couldn't get free.

She opened the door and found herself in a cluttered lab area. It was dimly lit and empty of people, like it was shut down for the night. Stalking silently forward, she finally plucked the suction cups off her skin. If someone was watching the monitors, they'd know she was up and around. But it couldn't be helped.

There were no windows anywhere, which led her to believe she was probably underground. She moved as quietly as she could. Hanging out with Xavier the past few days and watching the way he moved so stealthily had apparently rubbed off. She didn't make much sound as she went through the empty lab toward the brighter light she saw near a door at one end. She was going under the hope that where there was light, there might be a way out.

Sarah was at the door when she heard a voice drifting down the corridor. It was a one-sided conversation, as if the man was on the telephone. She recognized the voice. It was Sellars. She peeked around the edge of the door to find a corridor. There were a few doors along the hall. One was open with light spilling out, and at the end of the hall there was a stair case leading upward.

Listening carefully for a moment, she realized the volume of the conversation remained constant. Sellars was stationary. Probably inside that well-lit room, which was most likely his office. She had to get past him to get to the stairway.

She weighed her options. He might leave for the floor above if she waited until his call was over. Or he might decide to check in on her again in the room she'd just left. It was late at night. Chances were he'd go to bed soon . . . unless he was on the same schedule as his creations were. Damn. That was a very real possibility she had to consider.

Looking around the lab area, she picked up a few more objects she could use as weapons but nothing really good. Nothing that would work against the zombies. Of course, right now, Sellars was the real danger.

". . . should be fine for now. I've got twenty of them on the grounds right now. Well, at least until they start chewing on the neighbors."

Sellars laughed. Actually laughed. It made Sarah sick to her stomach that he talked so casually about the flesh-eating zombies he had created.

But this was good intel. She'd have to run the gauntlet of creatures if and when she got out of this building. Without the special toxic ammunition or even a decent weapon.

"No way, Jennings." Sellars sounded miffed for some reason. "I've got it under control. I've got her blood and access to more anytime I want it. I'll crack the puzzle and we'll have something to sell Zhao inside of a few days. See if you can get in touch with Rodriguez. I'm still working on McCormick. She cancelled on me for lunch. If she doesn't come around soon, I may snatch her and force her to work with us."

The bastard. Talking about kidnapping another woman like it was no big deal. The more she heard him talk, the more she hated this guy.

"No, I like the house. Krychek came through with a good location. There's even a boat I could use for a quick getaway and plenty of woods for my little army of ghouls." He snickered again but cut it short when an alarm sounded inside his office. "Fuck. No, there's someone on the grounds. The proximity alarm just went off. No, I'm not taking any chances. I have her blood. She can rot for all I care."

Nice. Sarah knew he was talking about her. There wasn't anyone else in the building that she could detect. At least not on this floor. And he definitely had her blood. The bastard wouldn't leave that behind after the difficulties he'd had in acquiring it. The good news was that it sounded like he was leaving. Sarah felt her pulse leap at the idea.

Sellars's voice increased in volume, speed and pitch. He was nervous. She heard him end the phone call, and then she heard cursing and rustling sounds from within the office.

A few minutes later, he was jogging down the hall, a big satchel slung over one shoulder, a large handgun in one hand and a cooler bag in the other. No doubt that was where he'd stored her blood. She couldn't let him get away, but she also didn't have a weapon. If she tried to stop him now, he'd shoot her at point-blank range.

Better to bide her time, follow him out of the house and hope to hell it was Xavier who'd breached the defenses. She knew he would be coming for her. It was only a matter of time. Hopefully, he would find her and they could work together to bring Sellars down.

She crept along the corridor as Sellars ran up the stairs. The lights went off as she hit the bottom step and she heard a door slam shut above. She was in the dark, but she knew where she needed to go—up.

Sarah took the stairs as quickly and quietly as she could. She encountered a light switch at the top of the stairs, but she left the light off. When she opened the door, she didn't want the light betraying her in case Sellars or anyone else waited above. Suddenly she had a bad moment: Had Sellars taken the time to lock the door from the other side? She hoped he'd been in too much of a hurry.

Only one way to find out. She turned the knob. Much to her relief, the door opened. The room beyond was dark, but there were windows, and some ambient light came through them from outside. She was on the first floor, in the kitchen of a very well-appointed house. Of course, she had no idea where the house was. With a sinking feeling, she realized she might not even be on Long Island anymore. Sellars could have taken her anywhere. She didn't know how long she'd been unconscious.

Before she could start to panic about that, a shadow passed

in front of the kitchen window. She crossed the room to peer out cautiously and came face-to-face with a hideous apparition. It was a zombie and half its face had been chewed off. A single eye stared at her blankly, and she had to swallow the yelp of fear that threatened to erupt from her throat.

Too late. It saw her. She jumped back as its fist crashed through the window, its clawed hands reaching for her.

Xavier started shooting the moment he saw the first zombie in the woods. He had no idea how many of them were on this property, but one thing he did know—there wouldn't be any when he was through. He systematically plugged four shots into each target before moving on to the next, counting as he went.

He'd taken care of four zombies by the time he reached the small clearing that surrounded the house. They hadn't started to disintegrate yet, but the first would go any time now. Xavier did his best to ignore the four who followed him from the woods while he plowed his way through the clearing, shooting four darts into each of two patrolling creatures. Six down, who knew how many more to go.

"Alpha One. Two more targets coming around the north side of the house," Reno reported from his vantage point in the sky far above. "We've also got two heat signatures. One in the house and one heading down to the beach."

"How'd that one get past me?" Xavier wanted to know.

He lined up his shots and fired at the two zombies as they rounded the north corner of the house. As he finished darting the second of the pair, the first of the previous batch began to implode. Behind him, he heard the hideous moaning come to an abrupt halt, time and time again as the creatures dissolved.

"Must've been a tunnel from the house," Reno told him. "The heat signature popped up on the infrared near the top of the stairs to the beach. Before that, we saw it in the house for a quick second before it disappeared. I figure it went below-ground or into a shielded area."

"Son of a bitch. But there's another one still in the house?"

"Yeah, and it's on the move. Movements are erratic. It ap-

224 / Bianca D'Arc

peared in the same spot as the first one, about one minute after. Now it's moving around the rooms inside the house."

"Current position?"

"Northeast face, three windows down. It's in that room right now."

Xavier was already on the move. Of the eight zombies he'd shot, six had dissolved. The other two were in his way, and he detoured in a sprint, passing wide around them. These creatures moved a little faster than the previous versions he'd dealt with, but most of them were still hampered by uneven gaits. They couldn't run like Xavier could.

They tried to grab him as he passed, but he was too quick. He counted down to the third window on that side of the house and saw another of the creatures doing his best to break down the window and force his way inside. Xavier took aim and fired on the run.

That made nine. How many of them were there?

Entering through the window wasn't an option until the tenacious number nine disintegrated, so Xavier kept running until he found a sliding glass door several yards away. Using his rifle butt to smash the glass, he jumped inside a moment later, ready for action.

"Xavier?"

He heard Sarah's voice calling his name. Relief washed through him like a fresh spring rain. Thank heaven he'd found her.

"Where are you, Sarah?"

"Kitchen," came the terse reply. "I could use some help and a weapon. There are three of them in here and one trying to get in the window. I'm cornered." Her voice rose as she talked fast, panic entering her tone.

He stalked through the house. The kitchen was right next door. He stormed the room, firing as soon as he had a clear shot. Sarah was standing on the center island in the big gourmet kitchen, flinging pots off the overhead pot rack at the creatures who blocked three sides of the rectangular table.

It was a good position for someone who was otherwise unarmed. The heavy pots and pans kept the creatures at bay some-what, and the width of the table kept her out of their reach as long as they remained on the floor and she on the island.

"Don't move your legs," Xavier ordered. He sent four darts into each zombie with deliberate thoroughness. The creatures didn't seem to notice. They kept trying to get to Sarah, and she kept them at bay with broad swings of a long-handled frying pan.

"Can I move now?" She spared a moment to look at him, and the zombie on the right took the opportunity to swipe at her legs. The claws connected, and Sarah's face showed her shock and pain. Blood welled and she nearly lost her footing from the force of the blow.

"Come here, Sarah," Xavier yelled over the inhuman moan-ing of the creatures. The top end of the table closest to him was clear for the moment. "Jump. I'll catch you."

He held out his arms and caught her. There was no time for the hug they both needed. The creatures followed as they left the kitchen and headed for the room next door where Xavier had busted in. He gave her a pistol from his belt, plus an extra clip of darts, as they moved through the hall.

"Bravo One, I have Alpha Two," he reported over his head-set. "We're heading out of the house now. Stand by for evac."

"Roger that, Alpha One. We're ready and waiting," Sam said. He was the leader of the B Team, hence the Bravo One designation.

Xavier could hear the triumph in Sam's voice even though he kept his talk professional and calm over the radio.

Xavier turned to Sarah as they came to the broken glass door. There were more zombies out there, gathering in the clear space between the house and the woods. That was the space they'd need to use for the helicopter extraction. Damn.

"Can you run?" he asked her.

"I can run," she assured him.

"Good." Because they couldn't stay there. Hot on their heels were three zombies from the kitchen, taking their damn time to disintegrate. Xavier and Sarah would have a better chance of avoiding the creatures out in the open. "Let's go."

"Alpha One, eight more targets entering visual range," Reno told Xavier as he heard the chopper lower closer to the ground in preparation for extraction.

"Roger that. We've got three behind us, already dosed but not going down. Total of twelve already dosed."

"Sellars said there were twenty on the grounds," Sarah reported as she ran, having heard his side of the conversation.

"Alpha Two reports total of twenty."

"Roger that, Captain. We see eight more from above, so that sounds about right."

"Sarah, do you know where Sellars is?"

"He made a run for it, I think. He was the only person I saw in the house. He kept me in a lab in the basement. He used the phone, but aside from the zombies, I don't think there was anyone else here."

Xavier reported the information back to his men. "Clear for you to drop down," Xavier tacked on to his radio message. "We could use some air support, but under no circumstances do I want to see any of you on the ground. Standing orders are still in effect."

Xavier was firing at the zombies coming into view from the edge of the woods as he relayed messages. He saw eight of them and reported that there was too little space to maneuver.

A half minute after his last transmission, the helo dropped into view. The roar of the blades was loud as both Kauffman and Sam leaned out either side of the bird and began to dart the remaining creatures. Sarah and Xavier did the same, but they were surrounded. The zombies from the house had closed in from behind. The stubborn bastards had been shot but still hadn't dissolved. The other eight fresh zombies had fanned out and formed a circle around Sarah and Xavier that drew ever tighter.

Not good.

One by one the fresh zombies were slowly but surely getting their four doses each, but it was taking too long. They were too close. Kauffman sent down the rope ladder, but Sarah was having a hard time negotiating the swaying rungs. She hadn't even cleared enough room for Xavier to grab on and secure a foot- and arm-hold.

Then a blond blur rappelled downward and Xavier saw Sam clinging to a rope in midair, taking the final shots needed to give each zombie four darts.

"Dammit, Sam," Xavier muttered under his breath.

The son of a gun had disobeyed orders—though not technically. His feet weren't touching the ground. He was suspended on a rope from the helicopter.

The zombies were too close. In what felt like slow motion, Xavier saw one reach for Sam from behind. Xavier screamed at Sam, trying to warn him but it was already too late.

Sam jerked as the zombie bit into his leg. Using the butt of his rifle, Sam beat the creature off. It was one of the kitchen zombies. Even as Sam pushed it back, it disintegrated. But it was too late for Sam.

Xavier had had enough. He launched himself onto the rope ladder, caging Sarah in his arms and reaching around her to grab relatively secure handholds.

"Take us up, Reno!"

"You're not secure, sir."

"Don't argue, just get us away from this group. Set us down on the other side of the house and we'll do it right."

"Roger that, Captain."

A second later, they were soaring over the roof of the mansion. Reno lowered over the small clearing in front of the house, hovering. Sam was working his way back up the rope into the copter while Xavier jumped down to the ground and held the rope ladder taut for Sarah to climb. She made steadier progress this time, and Kauffman leaned over and pulled her into the chopper even as Xavier made the quick climb up himself.

When everyone was aboard and the doors shut, Reno sped upward.

"Where to, sir?" Reno asked, but he already seemed to know what Xavier would say. It was obvious from the direction he'd sent the bird in.

"Police station. I want McCormick to look at Sam. Meanwhile . . ." Xavier unzipped the bag holding McCormick's precious serum. The pouch included some serious-looking needles, and she'd given Xavier instructions on how and how much to administer. He hadn't thought he'd need to try it—at least not so soon—but it was the only hope for Sam. Already, Sam was going into shock. Death from the contagion was fast.

Xavier prepared the dose and stuck Sam in the heart muscle with the long needle McCormick had packed. It was nasty and caused Sam a huge amount of pain, but it was better than dying and rising to become a fucking zombie.

"Come on, buddy. Make this work," Xavier prayed under his breath.

Sam's heart distributed the serum fast, sending it throughout his system, where it combined with the contagion. They'd know in the next few minutes whether Sam had the right antigens and whatever other voodoo he'd need to stay alive.

He started to convulse when they were setting down on the helipad behind the police station. Reno had radioed ahead and Dr. McCormick was waiting for them, escorted by the SWAT commander and a few of his men. She ran up to the chopper as the blades slowed, and Kauffman pulled her inside to help Sam while Xavier let Sarah out the other side to make room.

Sarah balked at the idea of leaving before they knew Sam's fate. Xavier stood beside her, looking into the chopper as Dr. McCormick examined Sam. The roar of the engines lowered as Reno shut down the chopper and they were able to talk and be heard without the use of headsets.

"Will he be okay? What was that shot about? And who is she?" Sarah asked, leaning against his side as they watched Sam settle down on the floor of the chopper. He'd stopped convulsing, at least.

"She's a scientist who was part of the original navy team. Sellars was courting her, trying to get her to work with him. She gave us the location of that house where he was keeping you. The shot was something she cooked up. It might counteract the contagion and save Sam's life. Or not. It's experimental." Xavier's words were clipped as he watched his best friend fight for his life.

He put one arm around Sarah's waist, supporting her against his side. It was good to have her back safe. She was a little banged up and her uniform was a mess, but she was alive. Thank heaven. He kissed the crown of her head, not caring who might be looking. The time for hiding his affection for Sarah was over.

McCormick looked up from her patient and sought Xavier's eyes.

"What's the verdict, Doc?" Xavier asked. Sam looked better, but Xavier wasn't a doctor. He didn't know for sure.

"I think he's one of the lucky ones." McCormick sat back on her heels, hands on her thighs as she crouched inside the helicopter. "He's started to stabilize and I think he's out of danger, but I'd like to keep an eye on him. Is there any way we can get him back to my lab? I can rig suitable facilities to make him comfortable, and if he takes a turn for the worse, I have the toxin on hand to deal with it." Her expression was grim. "I don't think it'll be necessary, but I wanted you to know that I'm equipped to handle any contingency. Your friend won't suffer if he does turn into one of those creatures."

Xavier weighed his options. They still had a lot of work to do before they could call it a night. He looked over toward the SWAT team and realized he could use their help after all.

"Wait here a minute." Xavier walked over to the man in charge, Sergeant Luke Tomlinson.

"You got our officer back, I see." Tomlinson's raised eyebrow said he realized Xavier and Sarah were more than just coworkers.

"Safe and sound," Xavier agreed. "I could use your help, Sergeant. I have an injured man who needs to go with the lady you've been looking after for me, back to Cold Spring Harbor Laboratory. She's a scientist there and has agreed to watch over my man until he's recovered."

"Is he contagious?" Tomlinson looked skeptical.

"Not at the moment, and if Dr. McCormick has anything

to say about it, he'll remain that way. I can't tell you the exact nature of the threat, but it's something we have a reasonable handle on. It's also been offered for sale to terrorists, which makes it a threat to national security."

"So not anthrax or sarin. Something new." The man's face paled, but his expression said he was ready for anything.

"Definitely something new," Xavier agreed. "Something we can't let get out. It's worse than anything that's come before."

"And your man was exposed tonight?"

"He was." Xavier nodded grimly. "But McCormick can take care of him. What I need is to get her and him to Cold Spring Harbor. Can you help with that?"

"I'll take them myself." There was no hesitation in his voice, only a willingness to help avert disaster.

Xavier sent Lewis Kauffman along with Sam and Dr. McCormick. Tomlinson was acting as chauffeur. In short order, they were in one of the SWAT vehicles and on their way.

Chapter Thirteen

"What now?" Sarah turned to Xavier. She'd taken a few minutes to go into the police station and call her chief, assuring everyone that she was safe and fit for duty, and then left some instructions for campus security.

"We have to go back to the beach house and make sure we got them all. We also have to tag the remains for the cleanup crew." He looked tired and worried, which was understandable under the circumstances.

She knew enough not to mention Sam. They both knew he was in trouble, but they were powerless to help. Xavier had already done what he could by administering the serum. The best thing they could do for Sam now was to catch the bastard that had caused all this. She wanted Sellars with a vengeance. The man had kidnapped her and his intentions had been horrific. He'd told her flat out he intended to torture her. The man was truly a monster. Never mind the monsters he created. The real contagion was in his mind, and as far as she was concerned, it had to be stopped by whatever means necessary. If the doctor didn't walk away from this, she wouldn't shed a tear.

"I'd like to search the office where I heard Sellars on the phone. He left in a big hurry. He might have left something behind." Sarah tried hard to focus on the case. They needed a lead to tell them where Sellars had gone.

"Let's go. We'll decide where we go next based on what we find at the beach house." Xavier signaled to the pilot as they got back into the helicopter. Reno fired up the engines as all three donned headsets so they could talk over the noise of the blades. "Reno, I want you to do a sweep and see if you can find Sellars's trail while Sarah and I take care of the house."

"Sellars said he had a boat waiting if he needed to get away fast," Sarah put in. Xavier turned to her, clearly surprised. "I told you he was on the phone. He was talking to someone named Jennings about his plans. He said Krychek had come through with a good location. I assume this Krychek person was the one who set him up in the beach house. He also told Jennings to get in touch with Rodriguez, and that with my blood in his possession, the technology would soon be ready for sale to Zhao."

Xavier seemed shocked, pleased and worried all at the same time. "We need to get this information back to Commander Sykes and the brass. I bet they'd be interested in those names." Xavier's expression turned grave. "This also means others know you're immune, Sarah. Dammit!" He grit his teeth as he looked away, clearly angry.

"Do you recognize any of the names?" she asked tentatively. She thought she understood the anger in his expression. If others knew about her, she would still be a target, even after they caught Sellars. She'd realized it the moment she heard Sellars discussing her on the phone, but the enormity of the problem came home to her only after seeing Xavier's response. He knew as well as she did that she'd never be free of danger until this problem was solved once and for all.

"There was a Jennings and a Rodriguez on the original science team. It would make sense that he's in touch with them, if they're working with him to sell the technology." Xavier got himself back under control. He unlocked one of the bins holding their weapons and began to restock his supply of ammo. He also passed a spare utility belt to Sarah. It was already loaded with extra clips of darts and a place for her to holster the pistol he'd given her earlier.

If felt good around her waist. She'd been feeling kind of naked without a weapon or the usual weight of extra ammo and tools settled around her hips.

Xavier had rescued her and she'd nearly wept when he'd come into that kitchen where she'd been surrounded. She'd wanted more than anything to fling her arms around Xavier and never let go, but circumstances had prevented her from doing any such thing. Even now, they both knew they had to see to their duty before they could revel in the fact that they were both safe for the moment.

She wondered if Xavier felt as strongly about her safety as it seemed. He'd certainly put a public claim on her when they were standing next to the chopper before. She hadn't expected the way his arm around her waist had made her feel. For a moment, she'd simply accepted the echoes of caring and tenderness that threatened to make her cry like a baby in front of his men, the cops and the doctor. She'd swallowed the emotion and simply leaned against Xavier's tall form. His warmth had seeped into her, heating the cold places inside with his gentle strength. He was her rock. Her safe harbor. In that moment, he'd said more with that single hand at her waist than she would have believed had she not experienced it herself.

Was she fooling herself? Did he really feel those same momentous emotions? She wasn't sure, and they didn't have time or space to sort it out now. The mission was still on. They had to finish the job before they could even begin to address anything personal.

Whether Xavier would want to explore anything bordering on emotional was another question. He hadn't made her any promises. They were together for now. That had to be enough. But yet . . . her foolish heart yearned.

He'd come after her when she'd been kidnapped. That was his job. But she hoped he'd come after her for more than just the job. She hoped there was some element of feeling for her as a person behind his mad rush to save her from Sellars. She knew if the roles had somehow been reversed, her heart would have been fully engaged in saving Xavier's life.

In all too short a period, he'd become important to her in ways that defied logic.

She felt the helicopter begin to descend. Xavier distracted her by taking a more traditional handgun from another locker and passing it to her.

"It's loaded with armor-piercing rounds, just in case," he told her over the headset.

Armor-piercing bullets. Also known as *cop killers*. Highly illegal for civilian use, but she was with the army now. If anyone had the authority to use this kind of weaponry, it was Xavier and his team. Anyone who would pursue and hope to sell zombie technology didn't deserve to get away. If she shot anyone with this kind of ammo, they'd go down and stay down. Which is probably why Xavier used it.

Reno landed the chopper, dropping into the small clear space between the mansion—in what she now realized was one of the more exclusive parts of Lloyd Neck—and the tree line. Xavier jumped out, then turned to help her out of the chopper. She didn't really want to go back in there, but she knew they had to tidy up and make sure none of those monsters were left—either the human or the zombie kind.

Xavier started dropping transmitters, counting as he went. She followed, guarding his back and scouting the grounds as best she could in the darkness before dawn. It had been one hell of a night.

". . . eighteen, nineteen and twenty," Xavier counted off as he dropped the last transmitter near the house.

"Negative contact on the boat, sir," Reno said over the radio. "There are a few small pleasure craft out here. I saw something a lot bigger and faster leaving earlier. It took off down the coast at a rapid pace a little while ago. I marked the coordinates as far as I could."

Xavier had given Sarah one of the small tactical headsets in the chopper, so she heard Reno's report.

"Come back and land for now, Reno," Xavier ordered. "You can do a wider sweep as soon as we're through clearing the house." He switched off the mic and turned to her. "Ready?"

Sarah took a deep breath and nodded. "As I'll ever be."

Together, they entered through the broken glass door. Xavier paused to flip on the lights as they went through the rooms. He'd put on thin latex gloves, as she had, before they set foot in the house. It was now a crime scene.

They went through the place room by room. Though there were signs of life on the ground level, the rooms upstairs were completely empty and looked like nobody had lived in them for a long time. They went back downstairs to the great room, where Xavier took a few minutes to go through papers that had been left lying on a coffee table while Sarah looked at a small collection of entertainment DVDs near the floor-to-ceiling television screen. Nothing jumped out at her as being important.

Xavier finished with the papers, leaving them just where he'd found them. There was nothing of use there, either. "When I found you, you were in the kitchen. Where was Sellars keeping you before you got free?"

"The basement. He's got a laboratory down there, plus an office." She jerked her chin toward the stairs. "The door locks from the outside. Sellars didn't take time to secure it as he was leaving. He had a duffel bag over one shoulder, a handgun in his left hand and a cooler bag in his right. I believe he had my blood samples in that bag."

"So he was traveling light," Xavier mused. He popped the hinges off the door leading to the basement and set it aside. "This way nobody can lock us down there," he explained. "Reno, we're going below," he said over the radio. They'd both heard the helicopter come in for a landing outside the house. "Stay in the cockpit and stay sharp. Alert us to any problems you might see coming our way."

"Roger that, Captain," came the pilot's ready reply.

He started down the stairs, Sarah on his heels. He flicked the lights on and the basement was fully illuminated.

"He was on the phone in here," she said as they neared the door to the office.

"Looks like he left some of his paperwork behind."

There were open notebooks on the desk and printouts that

looked like they might've come from the monitors that had been attached to Sarah earlier. Other than the odd bits of scientific data Sellars had left in his rush to get away, there wasn't anything else of interest in the small room. They moved on down the hall.

There was another small office. This one was completely empty. The third door led to a walk-in closet filled with scientific instruments, supplies and protective gear. They closed that door after a cursory search and headed for the large laboratory. Xavier whistled through his teeth when he got his first good look at the large space.

"He kept you in here?" Xavier seemed to be looking around for a likely spot, but couldn't locate one.

"In back." She had to clear her throat before she could continue. "There's a room in back. He had me in there."

Xavier made his way toward the back of the huge lab and stopped short. She stopped as well when she saw what was in front of him. It was a bank of windows that looked in on the room where she'd been tied down. Now that the lights were on she realized the room was more than just an examination room. It was a full-fledged operating suite. Complete with the observation area in which they now stood.

"Son of a bitch." Xavier strode forward, stopping in the doorway to the room where she'd been held. "He had you strapped down to the table?"

The answer seemed important to him. In fact, his response was filled with anger and dismay. If she didn't know better, she'd say he was taking her capture and subsequent treatment to heart.

"I couldn't move when I first woke up. It was dark. Then he came in and put an IV in my arm. He drew a lot of blood, then left, leaving me in the dark again. I managed to get my arms free and I was able to reach the tray over there." Her gaze went to the tray that she could now see was filled with lethal-looking medical instruments. "I found a scalpel the hard way and used that to cut the straps below my waist, then wriggled out of the top half of the restraints."

"Let me see your hands, baby."

The tone of his voice touched her deeply. It was filled with a mix of concern and regret. She held out the hand that had been cut.

"It's okay, Xavier." She was quick to reassure him as he removed her glove and examined her hand. "It healed fast." Her hand still sported a smear of blood but was otherwise fine. Not even a faint line was left to indicate the slice that had been delivered to her fingers when she'd grabbed the business end of the scalpel by mistake.

"Damn." His expression was filled with remorse. "I'm so sorry, Sarah. I didn't mean for any of this to happen. I blame myself for everything you've been through tonight."

She took a step closer to him. "Don't, Xavier. It's all right. I got out of it and you came to get me. It all worked out."

"But you shouldn't have had to go through any of it."

"Blame Sellars. Not yourself. All you've done since I first met you was try to help me." She placed a palm over his heart and he covered her hand with one of his.

They stood there for a long moment, looking deep into each other's eyes. Finally, Xavier broke the spell.

"You're too lenient with me, Sarah." He leaned in and placed a peck on her cheek before stepping back.

The small grin he gave her was like sunshine coming out after a long rain.

"Let's finish up here," he said. "We both still have a lot of work to do before we can call it a day."

In full agreement, she helped him go through the laboratory for anything that might be of use to them. They found nothing other than Sarah's weapon and personal items—including her wallet and keys, which they retrieved from a drawer—and then left the more intense search to the technical crew that would follow after. They headed back upstairs to do a final sweep of the grounds before rejoining Reno at the helicopter.

When they had searched the grounds to Xavier's satisfaction, they circled back and climbed into the chopper. She wasn't surprised when Xavier told his man to head for the campus.

"What happened to the girl?" Sarah asked him.

"Her name was Donna." His tone was filled with regret. "I don't know if she made it. She'd been bitten and had fallen unconscious when I realized you weren't behind me. In the excitement I . . . I left her. Damn."

"It's okay." She reached for his hand, squeezing his fingers in reassurance. "We'll find her. Maybe she was one of the lucky ones."

But when they got to the scene, the girl was nowhere to be found. They marked the dead on both sides of the tracks with transmitters and did a cursory search for the girl, but she was a tiny thing, and the small patch of woods was bordered by concrete roads and walkways on three sides. Where she went after she hit the sidewalk, they had no idea.

"If she's turned, she'll show up tomorrow night. If she hasn't, maybe she went back to her dorm or the hospital," Sarah thought aloud.

"Good point. I'll make some calls and put campus security on alert for her. If they can find her during the day, all the better. Otherwise, we'll check back for her tomorrow night." Xavier was already on the phone as they made their way back to the chopper.

Reno had found a nice empty parking lot to land in, which had been cordoned off by campus security at Sarah's request. When she'd run interference with the campus guys they'd been more than willing to help. She took a moment to call and thank them before hopping in the chopper.

Reno headed for the coast to the laboratory at Cold Spring Harbor without even being asked. It went without saying Xavier would want to check on Sam at the earliest opportunity. They'd completed their duties as quickly as possible and now it was time to see to their wounded.

The lab at Cold Spring Harbor was world-renowned. In the prelight of dawn, they spotted the SWAT vehicle near a quaint little cottage decked out with gingerbread trim. One of the surprising features about this laboratory was that the exterior was just the way it had been when people lived there. The outside of many of the buildings on the sprawling campus hid some very high-tech equipment within. A Tudor house could contain giant silver isolation labs.

There were a few buildings that were more modern. The main building nearest the road housed a cafeteria for employees as well as state-of-the-art conference and meeting rooms. The individual labs followed a winding pathway of small roads and walkways all along one side of the cove. From the opposite shore, one would never know there was a world-class laboratory just across the way.

The helipad was on the roof of the main building. It was so early that not many people were about. Still, they drew the attention of laboratory security. Reno interfaced with them, and they were granted permission to land.

"Looks like our SWAT friend smoothed the way for us," Reno reported. "He told security to expect us and give you an escort directly to Dr. McCormick's lab."

"Good man," Xavier commented. He seemed impatient to get on the ground. Sarah understood the feeling. His best friend and executive officer had been in bad shape the last time they saw him.

Xavier had taken the toxic ammo and weapons, storing them in one of the lockers onboard the helicopter. All Sarah had at her disposal now was the handgun he'd given her. She tried not to remember the kind of ammunition it carried. She still wore her police uniform—dirty and tattered as it was—so the security officers who met them on the roof didn't question her right to carry a weapon.

Likewise, Xavier was in uniform, and they had both been vouched for by the leader of the local SWAT team. Tomlinson had definitely coordinated things on their behalf, for which she was grateful. Lab security had a golf cart waiting for them.

Reno stayed with the helicopter. No doubt there was too much sensitive equipment onboard to leave it unattended. Sarah and Xavier climbed into the golf cart and they were off. She was surprised to find lights burning in a few of the buildings they passed. Apparently, there were a few people who either had got up way too early or had stayed much too late last night working on their experiments.

"Some of our people keep odd hours when they have experiments running," the kindly older security officer said as he drove them toward the far end of the laboratory grounds. "They tell me that science waits for no man." He laughed with the slight wheeze of a longtime smoker. "When their experiments are incubating, they have to be here to perform the next step no matter what time it is, so we keep round-the-clock security. The neighborhood isn't dangerous compared to some others, but we still get a few calls to walk people to their cars at odd hours. Women can't be too careful in this day and age."

Sarah agreed but didn't say anything. The older man seemed more interested in talking to Xavier, anyway. She didn't care why. The long hours and the stressful activity of the night were beginning to catch up with her. She was as tired as she'd ever been, dirty and hungry, too. Now that the adrenaline rush had dissipated, she was crashing fast.

The golf cart stopped and Xavier climbed out first, offering a hand to help steady her. It was obvious he knew what kind of state she was in. The small, encouraging smile he sent her way helped to revive her a little. They'd go see how Sam was doing, and then, finally, she could maybe get some rest.

Xavier didn't let go of her hand once she was on the ground. He turned to thank the security man, then headed up the walkway to the front door of the cottage. He didn't bother knocking. He just opened the door and went inside.

What met them on the inside was like something out of a science fiction novel. Three silver bubble isolation labs were spaced around the open interior. The pretty little cottage housed a state-of-the-art high tech facility complete with three private offices in addition to the trailer-sized bubble labs and a separate room where they could see a bed through the open door.

Sam was in the bed and Dr. McCormick was at his side, as were Sergeant Tomlinson and Private Kauffman.

The men had both looked up when the outer door opened.

They came forward, out of the bedroom and into the lab area over to Xavier and Sarah. Tomlinson spoke first, in hushed tones.

"He just fell asleep," the SWAT commander reported. "He had a rough time of it, but the doctor had him well in hand."

"What happened?" Xavier asked in a clipped tone.

"Sam went into convulsions twice more," Kauffman reported. "Each time was less severe. The doctor thinks the worst is passed. She just said he'll probably sleep it off now and will likely be okay when he wakes."

"Thank heaven for that," Sarah muttered.

Tomlinson's eyes narrowed. "The doc won't even hint at what your friend was exposed to and I'm not going to ask. I understand the concept of top secret. As I've already told you, I don't like being kept out of the loop, but I'll accept it for now. The minute this stops being a federal matter and starts affecting the local population, I expect to be called."

It was a bold statement. Sarah respected the other officer's willingness to get involved in something that was clearly more dangerous than even his normal activities on the police force.

Xavier shook Tomlinson's outstretched hand. "I won't forget your help tonight. If things get out of our control here, you'll be the first to know. Let's all pray it doesn't come to that."

"Amen," Tomlinson agreed. "Do you need me to stay? I could loan you a few officers to make sure Dr. McCormick remains safe."

"Thanks, but no. I'll make provisions for her with my people." He glanced toward Kauffman, who nodded. "You've already been more help than I ever expected, Sergeant."

"Just doing my job." He tipped an imaginary hat in their direction as he headed for the door leading to the outside. He was gone a moment later.

Sarah followed Xavier into the small bedroom where Sam lay sleeping. The normally robust soldier looked pale and sweaty. After all, Sarah realized, he'd been in a molecular fight for his life unlike anything he'd ever experienced before. Dr. McCormick got up from the chair at Sam's bedside and motioned them outside the room so they could talk. Kauffman reclaimed his spot, keeping vigil at Sam's side.

"He's resting, finally. I think he's done with the convulsions, although I will continue to monitor him until he wakes up again. I don't know what I'm going to do when Dr. Caruthers gets here. He's my new boss. A Nobel laureate. I'm his research assistant along with one other, Dr. Roberto. He's off today, but Caruthers expects me to help him begin a new experiment today."

"Don't worry." Xavier pulled his phone from the holster at his waist. "I'll get you some help. I hope you don't mind losing this job. After the miracle you just worked for Sam, I think our Uncle Sam will want to put you back on the payroll."

McCormick smiled, and Sarah could see her expression was filled with relief. "I don't mind. I actually prefer to be running my own experiments. Being knocked down to research assistant was a blow to my ego, if I'm being brutally honest. I'd like the opportunity to pursue the antidote to this contagion. It's worked once, but I'm sure it could be improved upon. We were lucky with Sam. He had the right antigens and the strength to live through the ordeal. Given time to devote myself to this project full time, I'm sure I could come up with something much better."

"All right, then. I'm going to make a few calls. What time do you expect Caruthers?"

"He never gets here before nine thirty."

"Good. That should give us just enough time."

Dawn broke while Xavier made his calls. Dr. McCormick had shown Sarah where the small bathroom was located and left her with a set of clean scrubs she could change into. There was even a shower and plenty of hot water. Sarah took full advantage of it, washing from head to toe twice over. She put on the shapeless scrubs, grateful just to be clean for the first time in many hours.

She rejoined Xavier a half hour later. By that time, he had everything lined up. Commander Sykes was on his way and would take over from Kauffman where Dr. McCormick was concerned.

Xavier seemed reluctant to leave, but fatigue was also riding him hard. They walked slowly back to the main building and the waiting helicopter, enjoying the beautiful surroundings and manicured landscape. Swans and Canada geese crossed their path on their way to the reedy shore, and Sarah even spied a small white egret standing in the shallows.

"These grounds are really beautiful." She had a plastic bag filled with her dirty clothes and weapons in one hand, the other hand was held securely in Xavier's. He was still in uniform, so he was still visibly armed. She'd thought it wise to keep her weapon hidden, considering her nonregulation state of dress.

"I never knew this place was here before our mission started. Who knew a world-class biomedical research facility was hidden up here in this upscale neighborhood?"

"I'd heard about it, but I never had reason to come here before. I've been down Northern Boulevard a time or two, and the big landmark across the road is the fish hatchery. Other than that, I've passed right by this place any number of times without even realizing it. The town is fun, too. They have a lot of little touristy shops."

"Maybe someday I'll have reason to return under better circumstances." He squeezed her hand.

The way he looked at her made her breath catch. Did he mean to imply some future visit with *her*? She wasn't sure, but the promise in his eyes made her hope. She settled for a non-committal answer, just to be on the safe side. She didn't want to look like a fool, after all, just in case they weren't on the same page here.

"That would be nice."

"What would be even nicer right now"—he drew her closer, facing him, bending his head so his forehead touched hers in an intimate caress—"would be if we were back at your place, in that big bed of yours."

"I vote for that." Her voice was breathless as his head

dipped lower. His mouth caught hers in a tender caress that made her knees quake. His arms came around her, steadying her and pulling her against his hard body.

In the idyllic setting of the dawn-lit cove with nature all around, he kissed her. For this moment they could comfort each other with hugs, kisses and caresses after the horrors of the night.

"I thought I'd lost you, baby."

Xavier's voice came to her as a rough whisper when he broke the kiss and crushed her to his chest in a warm, wonderful, welcoming hug.

"I'm not that easy to get rid of." She stroked his back, feeling the emotion he tried hard to suppress in the rigidity of his muscles.

"Thank heaven for that." He eased off, letting her go by slow degrees. "This has been one hell of a night."

"You can say that again. I'm just glad Sam survived."

"Yeah, me, too." He tucked her under his arm and they began walking again. "Between you and him, I think I lost a couple of years of my life just in worry."

"You were worried about little old me?"

"Silly, I know." He bussed the crown of her head as they walked along, in no particular hurry to get to the chopper. "Damn, baby. You cut yourself out of a harness; that's going to give me nightmares for the rest of my life."

"Really? Why?" She heard real fear in his voice.

He slowed his steps. "You had to have felt so helpless."

His voice dropped so that she could just barely hear his words.

"I can't even imagine being so totally immobilized and at the mercy of a madman in a fucking operating room. That's a scenario I don't even want to contemplate. It's like something out of a horror movie."

"Xavier, this entire situation is like something out of a horror movie." She tried to cheer him up and it seemed to work.

He gave her a little lift of his mouth that was almost a

smile. "I guess you're right." He began walking a little faster. "Let's get Reno to drop us at your station so your chief can see you're okay. Reno can secure the chopper at Brookhaven for the day, and you and I can head back to your place."

"I like the sound of that. So you've been hiding that black helicopter at Brookhaven National Labs? Convenient."

"They've got adequate security for it." He shrugged. "I can't make the boy sleep in the chopper."

Sarah giggled at his ironic tone, as he'd probably expected. His arm tightened around her shoulder for a small moment as they neared the main building. The black helicopter sat on its roof.

"Let's go home."

Matt Sykes had awoken at dawn to a ringing phone. He'd been catching a quick combat nap while he waited to learn the status of his operatives. Like the admiral had admitted to him days ago, Matt wasn't entirely comfortable having sent a woman into a combat situation. Not one where it was more than likely she'd have to go hand to hand with a bunch of face-eating zombies.

Then Sarah had been abducted and now Sam Archer was in critical condition. Or so Matt had learned from his early-morning phone call. The situation kept escalating and he feared it would only get worse before it got better. Worst-case scenario, the whole thing could spiral out of control. Which was why Matt was getting very little sleep lately. The threat of the contagion being sold to enemy powers or terrorists—or re-leased on a wider scale from whatever source—was something that kept him up nights.

As a result, Matt was now in his car, headed for the airstrip before full light. He took to the air less than forty-five minutes later, speeding toward New York.

Beauvoir had managed to pull a rabbit out of his ass, dig-ging up Dr. McCormick and her magic serum. This could be a big break for them . . . if it worked. Unfortunately, Sam Archer had become their first guinea pig. They claimed he was stable for now. Further testing would be necessary to see if he'd stay that way.

Matt had liked the tall lieutenant. He was gruff, but his loyalty to Beauvoir was clear and unequivocal. If Archer survived this new treatment and turned out to be immune, Matt had just gained another highly skilled operative to send out against the zombies that continued to turn up at Fort Bragg no matter what he did.

They'd vaporized another one last night. By dribs and drabs, the casualties were starting to add up. And as yet, nobody could seem to pinpoint the source of the problem. It was enough to make him want to scream in frustration—or beat the shit out of someone.

Since he couldn't very well do that, Matt resigned himself to working steadily on the problem until they found a solution. The situation at Fort Bragg was under control for the moment. Unfortunately, the investigation was going nowhere fast. Matt hoped the action in New York would provide them with some solid leads.

Dr. McCormick could be key, which was another reason Matt had decided to make another excursion northward. He planned to take control of Sam Archer's recovery and the good doctor as well. By tonight, they'd both be ensconced in a secure hospital lab area at Fort Bragg.

Matt had entertained the idea of sending them both to Quantico, but Matt spent more time at Fort Bragg nowadays and his current problem was centered there. No more zombies had been sighted at Quantico since they'd dealt with the initial infestation months ago.

The scientists who'd been on the original research team had scattered. He found it interesting that not a single one had stayed in the Virginia area. They'd given various forwarding addresses, all of which were being checked out now.

More than one of them was tinkering with their old research. Sellars wasn't alone. Sarah had heard four names. Beauvoir had relayed the information to Matt and they both recognized at least two of them. More than anything, Matt wanted to track down the bastards that would prey on innocent people like this. They were worse than wild animals. They had no regard for human life whatsoever.

He also needed to get a handle on Dr. McCormick. She'd disobeyed orders and continued to work on the zombie technology—developing her serum even after she'd taken a new job. That was probably a good thing in retrospect. However, it was also a big problem. For her.

Matt could easily have her arrested on charges of endangering national security by continuing the research she'd been specifically forbidden by the highest possible authority to pursue. Such actions amounted to treason. If the good doctor wouldn't play along with Matt's plans, he'd pull that out of his pocket and give it a spin. He'd be interested to see what she'd say then.

For now, he'd try the soft approach. If her serum proved viable, it could be a great help to them. It could save a lot of lives. And if Sam Archer made a full recovery, he would want to continue the fight. Matt had no doubt of that whatsoever. Sam had been eager to face the zombies even before he was immune, and Matt couldn't imagine that gung-ho attitude changing now.

Having Sam on the team wouldn't solve the zombie problem at its root, but it would help mitigate the damage the zombies caused. That was a damn good start.

By the time Matt's plane landed on Long Island, a helo had been arranged and was waiting to ferry him to Cold Spring Harbor. They landed on the roof of the main building a few minutes later, and lab security was waiting to escort him. He found himself at the most unlikely laboratory building he'd ever seen. It looked like a gingerbread house from the outside, but inside it was pure twenty-first-century tech. He wouldn't have believed it if he hadn't seen it himself.

Private Lewis Kauffman snapped to attention when Matt entered the building and gave him a quick sitrep.

"Sir, the lieutenant woke up about twenty minutes ago and

seemed coherent but weak. He fell back asleep after a few minutes and Dr. McCormick has been with him ever since."

Matt could just see a feminine form wearing a white lab coat through the door to an inner room. She was bending over a bed, taking someone's blood pressure. He couldn't see the occupant of the bed—only his arm—but he assumed it was Sam Archer.

"At ease, Private." Matt kept his voice down, as had the private. The lab had an air of stillness that he was loath to disrupt. "I'd like to see your lieutenant and meet the doctor."

"Yes, sir. Right this way."

Private Kauffman led Matt toward the small room. The woman straightened upon hearing their approach and turned to face Matt.

Matt was utterly charmed by the look of her. He had to take a few seconds to get his head together. She was a beauty, and totally not what he'd been expecting. He'd seen her file photo, but the Coke-bottle glasses were gone and her hair was loose. The girl who had looked like a cute young geek in her photo was in truth a beautiful woman with a wholesome kind of elegance about her.

She stepped back, allowing Matt to view the man in the bed. Matt had to give himself a little shake to get his mind back where it should be—on business. Not on the unexpectedly lovely doctor.

"Ma'am," he acknowledged her in a soft voice, mindful of the sleeping soldier in the bed. "I'm Commander Matt Sykes, U.S. Navy." He held out his hand, unaccountably eager to touch her, even if it was only just a handshake. She had a surprisingly firm grip, though he could feel the fine bones of her much smaller hand in his.

"I'm Sandra McCormick. But you probably already know that." A slight flush touched her features, though she didn't smile.

She seemed nervous and maybe a little indignant. It was an interesting response Matt filed away for further study.

"How is he?" Matt shifted focus to the man in the bed.

Sam Archer looked like hell. He had deep, dark circles under his eyes and his face was pale under his tan. He looked utterly wrung out.

"His vitals are strong and when he woke, he seemed coherent, though he wasn't awake long. He survived several rounds of convulsions and a period of very high temperature readings. I won't call it a fever, because it wasn't a typical infection. I believe it was a biochemical reaction taking place as the two foreign agents warred within his bloodstream for dominance. I need to do more testing, but I believe the serum I developed, along with his own body chemistry, won the war. He is beginning to stabilize. The next twenty-four hours should tell us a great deal more."

"Is he stable enough to be moved?"

The doctor bit her lip, in the most endearing way, as she thought through Matt's question.

"I believe so. As long as we take certain precautions and the end result is a bed in a hospital or secure lab facility."

Matt decided to test the waters and see how she'd react to his plans. "I'd hoped to move him—and you, Doctor—to Fort Bragg. I have a chopper waiting to take you to the airport and a plane ready to take you both down to North Carolina. How does that sound?"

Her gaze clashed with his in a subtle test of power. "I'd have to make preparations to move him and pack the necessary instruments and supplies should we encounter problems en route. I'd also like to get my clothes and other things from my place."

So then. She was willing to follow his lead. To a point. "That can be arranged."

"If I get a vote, I'd rather go back to Bragg, sir." Sam's weak voice came from the bed, surprising them all.

"Sam." Matt rushed to his bedside. "How are you doing, Lieutenant?"

"I'm all right, sir."

"Tell the truth, soldier. You look like hell."

That startled a cough out of him that turned to a chuckle as

Dr. McCormick poured a glass of water on the nightstand at the other side of the twin bed.

"Yes, sir. I feel about as good as I look, I guess."

"Can you be more specific?" McCormick asked gently, flicking a button that raised the head of Sam's bed.

"Sorry, Doc. It's an all-over kind of ache. Nothing hurts worse than anything else. It just all hurts."

"I'm sorry, Lieutenant." The doctor had a suspicious wet sparkle in her eyes as she offered the glass of water, complete with a flexible straw in it, to her patient.

"Not your fault. In fact, from what Lew told me the last time I woke up, your research saved my life. You have my thanks, ma'am."

"You're welcome, Lieutenant."

She turned away after Sam had downed half the glass of water and stopped drinking. Only Matt saw her surreptitiously wipe her cheek and the tear that had fallen down its soft curve.

Matt thought about her reaction. She probably felt guilty. That was good. Matt could capitalize on her feelings of guilt if she began to give him trouble.

He'd prefer that she go along with him quietly, of course, but he wasn't above manipulating her—or anyone, for that matter—to get what he needed. This mission was too important. Too many lives were on the line. Matt had to be ruthless in his pursuit of the bastards that had unleashed this contagion on unsuspecting populations of innocent civilians.

"No trouble remembering anything, Sam?" Matt asked, trying to gauge for himself the man's mental acuity. He'd leave the real testing to the scientists, but he wanted to get a read on Sam before they went any further. "Do you know what day it is?"

Sam dutifully recited the date, much to Matt's relief. He could see relief on the doctor's face, too. She'd be a terrible poker player, he thought. He could see every emotion in those lovely eyes of hers.

Sam fell back asleep a short while later. They left Lew Kauffman watching him while Matt asked Dr. McCormick to accompany him into the outer lab so they could talk.

"Please prepare what you need for travel, Doctor," Matt said crisply when they'd stepped out of the small bedroom. "I'd like to leave within the hour, if possible."

"It may take longer to get everything I need." He liked the fire in her eyes as she challenged him.

"Make whatever preparations you need, ma'am, but be quick about it. Dr. Sellars may know where to find you."

Her face paled as his words sank in. "You think we're in danger here?"

Matt refused to pull any punches or sugarcoat the truth. "You could be. He's already abducted one woman. Sellars is dangerous, and I'd prefer to have both you and Sam someplace where we can protect you."

"I'll be ready as soon as possible."

The harsh truth seemed to ease some of her resistance. Good, Matt thought, she was a sensible woman at heart. He could work with that.

"Private Kauffman and I can help you. It's been a while, but I think I still remember how to follow orders. Tell us what to pack and we'll give you a hand."

Finally, she seemed to thaw. A tiny smile quirked just one corner of her mouth. She soon put Matt and Lew to work packing supplies and a few small instruments. They were ready within forty-five minutes, and meanwhile Sam had woken again and was able to get into a wheelchair with their help. He stayed awake longer this time and conversed with them as they wheeled him to the helo with an escort of lab security guards.

Matt didn't breathe easy until they were all on the plane, in the air, headed for Fort Bragg.

Chapter Fourteen

After a brief stop at the police station in Stony Brook to assure Sarah's chief she was all right, one of her fellow officers dropped Sarah and Xavier back at her house. It seemed
like ages since she'd left the house the night before.

"It's good to be home." Sarah dragged herself through her
front door and paused in the entry.

Xavier came up behind her, closing and locking the door
behind them. He wrapped his arms around her waist and drew
her into his embrace. Her back was warmed by his muscular
chest, making her feel safe and cocooned in his strength.

One of his hands slid down over her abdomen and into the
loose waist of the scrubs.

"Oh, baby, if I'd known you were going commando under
there . . ." He trailed off as his fingers combed through her
curls and slid into her warm heat.

"What? What would you have done, Xavier?" Her voice
was breathless as he rubbed her clit.

He leaned closer, nibbling gently on the shell of her ear. "I
wouldn't have been able to control myself, *chère*. I probably
would've fucked you in the back of that police car, given half a
chance. I know I wouldn't have been able to keep my hands
off you. You're irresistible."

She liked the sound of that. Being irresistible to a man like

254 / Bianca D'Arc

Xavier was something she'd never expected in her life, but she was grabbing on with both hands. She'd ride this roller coaster to its final destination. Where it stopped, only time would tell.

"You're wet for me already."

His teeth closed over her earlobe gently. It didn't hurt. He bit just hard enough to fire her already flaming senses.

"I love the way you respond to me, *mon ange*. I love how you're always ready for me."

The husky timbre of his voice sent shivers down her spine. His hot breath against the side of her neck did the same until she was putty in his hands. His use of the *L* word made her want to hear it in another, much more serious context.

Sarah had realized something important in all the tumult of the past hours. Her life would be empty without Xavier in it. She loved him. Honest-to-goodness, scary, love.

She should have known it before. She wouldn't have given herself so completely to him without deep feelings on her side of the equation. She just wasn't built that way. She'd never had a one-night stand in her life.

Did Xavier feel the same way about her? She wasn't certain, but she knew he cared, at least in some way. He'd come after her. He'd been angered by the sight of where she'd been held by Sellars. Of course, that could just be guilt over not sparing her from being abducted. He was a natural-born protector, a defender of the innocent. It wasn't surprising he'd be disappointed that something had happened to her on his watch.

It had seemed like more, though. When they'd stood in front of that operating room window, it had felt like something that ran much deeper.

"Xavier . . ." She didn't know how to say what was in her heart or if she should. A declaration might not be welcome. She didn't want to ruin the moment or pressure him into saying something he didn't feel.

"Anything you want, baby. Tell me and it's yours."

Now that was tempting. What she wanted most—well, that was a pie-in-the-sky dream. She wanted his love.

She'd settle for his body.

"I want you, Xavier." She turned in his arms, dislodging his hand as she wrapped her fingers around his neck and dragged his head downward toward her lips. "Don't make me wait."

Their kiss was tempestuous, filled with the roiling emotions of the past hours. Sarah nearly climbed up his body, wrapping her leg around his hip and rubbing against him like a cat in heat. Oh, boy, was she in heat. Xavier was burning her up.

"Wait, *chère*." He tried to slow her down, but she wanted none of it. "Let me take you to the bedroom."

"No. I can't wait. Now, Xavier. Do me now. Here."

He didn't question her again, merely pushed the loose waistband of the scrubs pants down over her hips. They fell to the floor with little resistance. Sarah kicked them out of the way while Xavier lifted the loose top off over her head. By the time she had her arms back around his neck, he'd already dealt with his belt and fly, pushing his camo pants down just far enough to free his hard cock.

Then he paused.

"Don't stop," she pleaded with him.

"I'm sorry, baby. I have to. No condom." Xavier spoke from between gritted teeth as he tried to visibly rein in his rampant desire.

Sarah would not be denied. "You're clean, right? They tested you for everything when you got bit. They had to." She was breathless and her words came in panting gasps. "I'm clean and I'm on the pill. I want you, Xavier."

"Are you sure?" His gaze held hers. It felt like something momentous passed between them as she nodded agreement.

He leaned forward and kissed her. This kiss was different from all the others. It was a kiss that spoke of care and . . . love?

"Hang on, *mon ange*." Xavier lifted her, his hands under her ass as he placed her back against the wall. He was so strong, she felt delicate, like a rag doll he could toss around as he pleased. No other man had ever made her feel so petite and feminine—or so wanted.

Xavier aligned their bodies and rubbed. Just rubbed for a

couple of minutes, staring into her eyes and letting her feel the hard length of his cock against her most sensitive places.

"Are you ready, *chère*?"

"Please, Xavier. I need you so much."

He slid into her in one long stroke as she gasped. He was thick and long, filling her completely. Perfectly.

"That's what I'm talking about," he whispered into her ear, bracketing her against the wall with his entire body. She put her arms along his for support, using his broad shoulders to help hold herself up as he pressed into her from below.

All she could do was moan as he began to move. It was a little awkward at first, trying to keep her back glued to the wall as he thrust into her, but they soon got the rhythm. He felt so incredibly good inside her. She wrapped her legs around him, anchoring herself to him as best she could while he thrust into her over and over.

He grunted on each powerful thrust, the muscles in his shoulders and arms standing out as he strained to keep them both upright.

"Xavier." She moaned his name as his frenetic pace increased. All she could do was hold on for dear life as he pumped into her, sending her nearly into orbit with the mad rush of pleasure they produced every time they were together.

Feeling him inside her, without the thin barrier of a condom, was new and exciting. She couldn't wait for the rush of warmth, the flood of completion she knew was coming. Just the thought of it sent her over the edge.

Her fingers dug into his shoulders with the force of her orgasm as Xavier moved in harsh, fast motions inside her. She screamed as she came and felt his body seize under her hands. He was coming, too. She felt the warm jets of his come inside her and with it a sense of belonging, of caring, of peace. Strange as it was, she felt the rightness of the moment and wanted to hold on to it forever.

But time always slipped away. Xavier held her plastered to the wall for long moments. Both of them were breathing harshly as their shared euphoria began to recede. It had been glorious while it lasted.

"You okay?" Xavier pulled out and let her legs down one at a time.

"More than just okay." She gave him what she hoped was a sultry smile.

"That's my girl." He lifted her into his arms and strode down the hall. His shirt buttons were undone, the shirt mussed from her questing fingers. His pants hung below his waist, but it didn't slow him down one bit. He shouldered his way into her bedroom, being careful not to bump her toes on the doorframe.

When he reached the bed, he stood for a moment, just holding her. Xavier looked into her eyes and the emotion in his gaze made her heart clench.

"We've been through a lot in just a few days, you and I."

Sarah wasn't sure what he was getting at, but he was very serious all of a sudden.

"We've seen more horror than most people see in a lifetime. It's been hell, but it's been worth it. It's been worth it all just to be here with you, *chère*. I wanted you to know how . . ." He seemed to hesitate, then regrouped. "How special you are to me."

She cupped his cheek as he lowered her legs slowly to the floor. They stood at the side of her bed. She swayed toward him, unable to control her body and its need for his touch. There didn't seem to be any answer to his words except the stark, honest truth.

"I love you, Xavier."

He held her gaze for a long, tense, delicious moment, during which she thought she read something in the answering flame in his eyes. He cared. Maybe he wasn't ready to use the *L* word straight out in the open yet, but he definitely cared.

Xavier pulled her close and sealed his lips to hers, taking her down with him onto the soft mattress. His kiss was slow and filled with a sensual kind of heat that took her breath

away. This was more than it had been before. This was . . .
somehow . . . momentous.

When he let her up for air, she freed him from his shirt and
ran her fingers over his tanned, muscular torso. She pushed at
his pants, but he still had his damn boots on.

"You take care of those while I make a quick pit stop," she
said playfully as she jumped up from the bed. He caught one
of her wrists as she headed for the attached bathroom.

"Hurry back."

"I wouldn't miss this for the world." She leaned in and
bussed his cheek. He let go of her wrist and she wiggled her
ass, teasing him as she sought the bathroom. She hadn't wanted
to leave him but she was uncomfortably sticky.

She washed up quickly while Xavier shucked his boots and
the rest of his clothes. When she emerged from the bathroom
moments later, he was gloriously naked, waiting for her in all
his masculine perfection. Damn, he had a hot bod. And she
knew that killer physique hadn't been perfected in a cushy, air-
conditioned gym. He worked hard in the field and it showed.

"Come here, sweetheart."

She'd never actually received a come-hither look before,
but if that wasn't one, she didn't know what was. Maybe it
was more like a command than a request, she reflected as she
sauntered toward him. But it was just fine with her. This particular hot, naked, gorgeous man could order her around any
old time.

He reclined on her bed, waiting for her as she stalked forward. She was feeling playful and inclined to tease. A little
sensual play that would heighten both of their senses.

"My, my. Look at that." She shook her head at him, batting
her eyelashes as she nibbled on one finger and glanced pointedly at his cock. She'd never played the vixen before but found
she enjoyed it. "Do you want Nurse Sarah to make it feel better?" She stopped next to the bed, just out of reach as his eyelids drooped and his whiskey-colored eyes sparkled.

"*Chère*, if I'd had a nurse like you back at the base hospital,
I'd have never wanted to leave."

"We aim to please, soldier." She winked at him. "Now tell me where it hurts and I'll kiss it better." She knelt on the side of the bed, crawling on all fours over him.

He growled when she lowered her head so the loose ends of her hair stroked over his thighs and up over his reawakening cock. She liked the sound that issued from his throat, so she retraced her steps and did it again.

"Vixen," he accused with good humor.

"Only for you, Xavier," she promised, pausing by his side. She lowered herself over his abdomen and placed a kiss on every well-defined muscle in his six-pack, working her way lower. She held his gaze when she could, looking up at him between nibbles and licks over his sensitive skin. She liked the way his muscles rippled under her mouth. She could feel his excitement growing as she continued her downward path.

When she finally reached her inevitable destination, he groaned as she took him in her mouth. Using her tongue and the suction of her mouth, she hollowed her cheeks and sucked, giving him everything she could. She wanted to return some of the incredible pleasure he'd given her. Judging by the faint tremor in his legs and the renewed hardness of his cock, she was succeeding.

She looked up the length of his torso to meet his eyes and flames leapt between them. She felt his passion and it matched her own.

Xavier reached down to grasp her arms, lifting her away from his needy cock and upward to meet his kiss. He sat up, meeting her in the middle, claiming her lips with his in a moment of silent communication. She felt his raw, earthy need for her and reveled in it. She also felt his desire to please her in return, and his care touched her heart.

He kissed her, lying back, taking her with him. She was draped over his body like a blanket. Then he rolled.

He held most of his weight off her, all the while kissing her breathless. She spread her legs eagerly for him and he found his place in the hollow of her thighs. There was no reason to wait any longer. She wanted to feel him, skin on skin, skin *in* skin. She wrapped her legs around his hips, urging him inward with her feet.

Xavier complied with her wishes, pushing his way inward with a smooth stroke. His tongue continued to plunder her mouth as his cock plundered her pussy, laying claim to her body in the most basic way of all. He set up a primal rhythm as he claimed her with slow, deep strokes.

It was a languorous sort of loving she hadn't yet experienced with him. She could easily get addicted to this man and all his moods. This slow lover was intoxicating. The hard-and-fast lover had claimed her heart, but this slow hand claimed her soul.

When he finally released her lips, it was only for a quick gasp of air before he quickened his pace. The long strokes gave way to more forceful digs into her body, each pulse of his cock hitting the spot deep inside that sent her senses into orbit. She came without warning while he was watching her expression. He held her gaze throughout the small climax, his lips widening into a grin.

"One," he counted. "That was only the first, *mon ange*. I intend to push your limits this time."

She couldn't say anything to that. She was still dazed by the little climax, and her body was pushing harder, making her climb higher. Xavier sat up between her thighs, stroking his hands down her body. He paused at her breasts to play with her nipples and the soft mounds that yearned for his touch. Then he dipped lower, his fingers toying with her clit, rubbing expertly.

Just like that, she came again.

"Two."

The smug bastard grinned as she lay helpless beneath him, but she wasn't complaining. Oh, no. Quite the contrary. Xavier didn't give her a chance to catch her breath before he pulled out to flip her over, positioning her on all fours. He slid into her from behind, his strokes even deeper in this position, as well as slightly harder. He was going to kill her, but at this rate, she'd die a very happy woman.

The angle made her whimper in need on every stroke as her body responded to his commanding presence. She hadn't known she was capable of this kind of response before Xavier. It was all his fault. His superior technique. His hot body.

Who was she kidding? It was all those things, but ultimately, it was love that made the difference. She'd never felt this way about anyone before. This was the real deal as far as she was concerned. She would die for him. She would give him anything. She had willingly given her heart to him without any strings attached. It was a small step to give him complete dominance over her pleasure. She realized now, she'd done that almost from the very first time they'd been together. That's why each time with him was so amazingly special.

She hit another peak as he pushed into her. He bent over her, pulling her hair back gently as his lips reached for the sensitive shell of her ear.

"Three," he whispered as she bit back a moan.

He flipped her over and drove into her. Xavier hooked his arms under hers and cupped her shoulders in his big palms for leverage as he thrust home. His movements were more ragged now. He was closer to the edge. Thank goodness. She didn't know how much more she could have taken of his sensuous experiment.

"I meant to make this last longer, *mon ange*, but you're too damn tempting," he whispered as he held her gaze, his face tight with strain.

"I don't want to wait, Xavier." She could barely speak above a gasping whisper as he powered into her. The desire was back and higher than ever before. She would splinter into a million pieces on this next climax, she was sure of it.

"Then come with me, *mon coeur*. Come now." He thrust sharply into her one final time as her body seized in the biggest completion yet. She felt his cock spurt within her, warming her from the inside out with his thick come. The feeling, so rare in her cautious life, made her climax draw out even longer.

She was panting for breath and close to losing consciousness when Xavier withdrew. He flopped to the bed beside her, breathing hard for a moment before reaching out and dragging her back into his arms. She reached up to stroke his chest. Words were beyond her at the moment. Coherent ones, at least.

He cuddled her close and they drifted to sleep wrapped in each other's embrace.

Sarah woke hungry and realized they hadn't eaten anything in far too long. Xavier looked so relaxed in sleep, she couldn't disturb him. She threw on a short nightgown and stepped into her favorite slippers, then headed for the kitchen. She had the vague idea of surprising Xavier with breakfast in bed. Of course, it was already a little past dinnertime. So it would be more like a picnic supper in her bedroom.

She set to work, pulling ingredients from the fridge and cabinets. She'd barely begun setting up things to cook when warm arms surrounded her from behind.

"What are you doing out of bed, *chère*? I woke and you weren't there. Imagine my disappointment." The teasing tone of his voice made her smile as she turned in his arms.

"Poor baby. What does it look like I'm doing? I was going to cook something and serve you breakfast in bed."

"What if all I really want to eat is you?" He nibbled on her earlobe as he spoke, backing her up against the kitchen counter.

"Oh, that sounds good as an appetizer."

She was breathless when he hoisted her up onto the counter, spreading her thighs and pushing up the short hem of her nightgown. His fingers zeroed in on her clit, which was already seeking his attention. Just a few short days and she was already thoroughly addicted to his touch.

"You're so responsive, *mon ange*. You spoil me. I barely have to work at all to get you ready for me." His fingers slid in the slickness between her thighs.

He was right. She was shamefully easy where Xavier was concerned.

"I hope you're not complaining." She took a nibble out of his chin in gentle reprimand.

"Bite your tongue. I love the way you cream for me."

The explicit language made her squirm. Everything about Xavier made her squirm. He was a masterful lover who knew what he wanted and how to go about bringing her the most exquisite pleasure. He made her want to be daring.

"How about if I bite you instead?" Her lips rode over the rough, masculine skin of his lower jaw. She loved the way he felt against her tongue, the way he tasted. The salt of his skin made her thirst for more of him.

"Anytime, *chère*. Just say the word." His voice turned to a growl as he slid his finger inside her. "But how about for now, we just get right to it. It's been hours since I was inside you."

"Mmm. You're inside me now," she teased, squirming on his hand as he added another finger to the first.

"You know what I mean, temptress. I need you."

"I like the sound of that." And she truly did. She liked the way his voice had dipped from light amusement to harsh need in the space of seconds. It echoed the way she felt. "I need you too, Xavier. Don't make me wait."

He slipped his fingers out of her eager sheath and paused only a moment to lower the drawstring of the sweats he'd donned. Pushing them down just far enough to free his hard cock, he lined himself up to slide inside her waiting body. She helped by moving downward on the counter until her ass nearly hung off the edge. Xavier helped by supporting her legs, lifting them up and out, spreading her wide as he took aim and pushed inward.

"Oh, Xavier. Yeah, just like that," she whispered encouragement as he slid into her and started pumping in long, hot strokes.

Before long, his thrusts quickened and deepened. He grabbed her hips, drawing her into each one of his motions as she sighed her pleasure against the strong column of his neck. The man was one in a million. A law unto himself. He could bring her pleasure so extreme, she wasn't always sure she'd be able to live through it.

This was one of those urgent, intense times that seemed to

be typical for them. Maybe in a few hundred years they'd be able to take it slow again, but not now. Not when she needed him so desperately. Like he evidently needed her.

He pulsed into her in shorter, faster digs as she tried hard to bite back the keening cry that wanted to rip from her throat. His hands pressed her into his thrusts. She might have bruises on her ass tomorrow from his grasping fingers, but it'd be worth every last little black and blue.

She let loose with a high-pitched groan as she came. It was a compromise between the scream she ruthlessly tamped down and the growl of pure animal delight at the way he took her. It seemed to spur him on. Xavier came with a gasping groan that echoed in her ears, a complement to the sound she'd made, only much deeper.

As he was much deeper. So deep inside her she didn't quite know where she left off and he began. She felt the warmth of his come and gasped as the new sensations heightened her pleasure.

"Mon Dieu." Xavier's breathing went from ragged to under control a little faster than hers as he continued to stand between her thighs, his spent cock still held tight within her quaking body. "Baby, you're going to be the death of me." His eyes twinkled as she met his gaze.

A sudden, harsh movement behind Xavier caught her attention.

She tried to scream, but nothing made it past her paralyzed vocal cords before the butt end of a revolver smashed into Xavier's temple from behind. He crumpled to the ground, pulling her off the counter as she scrambled to hold him upright. The floaty skirt of her short nightgown fluttered over her thighs as she stood, allowing her some modesty at least. She did her best to ignore the rivulets of come dripping down her inner thigh as she faced the threat in her kitchen.

"Leave him!" Sellars barked the order, waving his weapon in her direction. "You're coming with me, Sarah. We're going to take a little walk."

Weighing her options, she realized she had none. She was

the next thing to naked, and unarmed. Sellars kept a close watch on her movements. Anything she could have used for a weapon was well out of her reach.

"Stop dithering, woman! Out the back door. Do as I say."

Sarah saw no alternative at the moment. She prayed silently that Xavier would wake up in time to help her. Or maybe outside she would find some opportunity to help herself. She'd been doing some gardening last week. Maybe she'd left a rake or shovel near enough to grab. She headed for the back door as slowly as she could. She had to buy time for Xavier to come around.

"Why are you doing this? You got the samples of my blood. You don't need me anymore."

"Au contraire, Sarah." Sellars stuck the barrel of the gun into her ribs, prodding her down the steps and into her backyard. "You're the prize sow I plan to show off to my buyers. The guinea pig they can cut and watch heal over and over again. You're the proof in the pudding. I wasn't about to leave you behind."

Great. The plans Sellars had for her were even more disturbing than she'd imagined. She didn't like this at all. Casting her eyes around furtively, she cursed herself for putting away all the gardening equipment. There wasn't even a stray spade she could grab to try to defend herself.

Her property backed up to a small strip of pine trees, and the shape of the cul-de-sac she lived on prevented her neighbors from seeing into her backyard. When she'd bought the house, she'd thought it was a good feature. She valued her privacy. But right now, she'd kill for a nosy neighbor.

A fine mist hung in the air and crept along the ground. The unusual fog had been around the past several nights, giving every bush and tree branch a creepy aspect. Something moved in the woods ahead of her and she paused midstep. Had Sellars brought along more of his undead friends?

"Move, bitch." Sellars prodded her again with the gun barrel and she dragged her fuzzy pink slippers off the concrete stairs and into the grass.

She shivered as the damp wisps of white drifted over her bare legs and under the high hem of her nightgown. She really wasn't dressed for this, but then, what did one wear to an abduction at gunpoint, anyway? She stifled a laugh that was just this side of hysteria as Sellars walked her toward the small strip of woods at the rear of her property.

Across that small expanse of gloomy pine trees there was a road. It was a back road, and Sellars no doubt had a car stashed there, ready to take her wherever he wanted. The bastard.

"You should let me go, you know. I'm really more trouble than I'm worth," she said, trying some psychology on him in a vain attempt at distracting him.

"You really are, but then, I plan to kill you when your usefulness is over. Don't wish your life away so easily, Officer Petit."

"Xavier will come after you. He won't rest until you're stopped."

"He can try, but we'll be long gone before he wakes up."

That's what he thought. Sellars was missing one vital piece of information. Xavier was immune. He healed fast. Maybe fast enough to regain consciousness from a whack to the head and be coherent enough to do something about it.

The fog thickened as she entered the dark space beneath the pines bordering her backyard. Sudden motion off to her right. She ducked out of the way as a clawed hand came slashing through the darkness. It hit Sellars's gun, sending it skittering away into the underbrush. Sarah crouched, taking stock of the situation. The zombie wasn't after her. It seemed to have turned on Sellars and was stalking him as he tried to bring the creature under control.

"I command you to stop! I am your master!" Sellars was shouting, but the creature kept advancing on him. It lashed out with its claws, catching Sellars under the chin. He went down hard, hitting the loamy ground with a hard thud.

The zombie was on him in seconds, using its teeth to grab on to anything it could. Blood welled as Sellars screamed. Sarah

watched in horror as the zombie turned on its creator, sav-
aging him.

As the zombie sank his blood-stained teeth into Sellars's
shoulder, she scrambled to get away, but the loamy earth wasn't
stable, given the soles of her slippers. She was deathly afraid
that once the zombie was through with Sellars, he would turn
on her, and she had precious little protection. No darts, no
bullets, not even a knife. Perhaps worst of all, no clothes to
speak of, and not even a decent pair of shoes on her feet. What
she wouldn't give for a good pair of boots right now. If that
zombie felt like taking a bite out of her, there was little she
could do to prevent it. She couldn't even run very fast in the
slippers, and ditching them could be hazardous considering
the sharp bits of debris strewn across the uneven ground. If
she stabbed herself in the foot with a tree branch, she wouldn't
be able to outmaneuver the undead bastard at all.

Sellars's screams died to whimpers, but he still managed to
evade the zombie's teeth when they aimed for his nose, ears
and other bits of his face. So far, the damage was to his torso
only. A small blessing, though he was just as likely to die. The
contagion worked fast. It didn't care what route it took into
the human body. Once there, it did its deadly work silently
and efficiently, taking over the host and turning its body into
something out of a nightmare.

Sellars was down for the count. He still fought, but the
zombie had clearly won. It left him and turned its attention on
Sarah. She'd gotten to her feet and managed to move several
yards away, toward the edge of the trees bordering her backyard. She kept her eye on the creature. The last thing she
wanted was for it to sneak up on her. She'd had enough of that
to last a lifetime. She'd learned her lesson from previous encounters.

The creature advanced as she inched backward, her feet
slipping on the thick layer of loose pine needles and other leafy
debris made slick by the dewy fog that lay over the ground like
a blanket. If she could just get to the grass. Out from under the

trees, the grass in her backyard enabled reasonably sure footing, even in slippers. She edged back. She didn't dare take her eyes from the creature. He was moving steadily now, faster than any zombie she'd seen to date.

His eyes looked almost menacing. He was just as dead as all the others she'd faced, but this one seemed more aware somehow. His eyes held a spark of anger, a glimmer of rage. At the moment, it was directed at her, and she felt a tingle of fear race down her spine.

"Look, buddy," she said, trying to reason with the creature. "I didn't do anything to you. No harm, no foul. You go your way, I go mine. All right?"

"Kill . . ."

Carried on the misty night wind, that one word drew out for several heartbeats, scaring the life out of her. The zombie had spoken and it didn't sound good. Its voice was a gravely rasp, a low, pulsing rumble of sound.

"Not me." Her voice, by contrast, was almost a squeak. The pitch went higher as her fear grew and her throat tightened. "You don't want to kill me. I taste bad. I can't ever become like you. They tried. It didn't take. So you're wasting your time."

Still the creature advanced.

"Kill . . ." it repeated.

And she would have peed her pants if she'd been wearing any. She was that scared. Its next utterance only deepened the terror.

"Eat . . ."

"Oh, God." Holding on to her wits, Sarah didn't give way to panic. Instead, she nearly cried with relief as her feet finally came in contact with her neatly mown grass. She was out of the woods.

She took her attention off the creature for just a second to gauge her distance to the small shed where she kept her garden tools. Too far, but she had to try for it. She had sharp things in there. Sharp things on sticks. It was better than nothing.

She looked back, and though she'd kept moving, the zombie had gained on her. It was making those inhuman moaning sounds now. She didn't think she could be any more afraid, but when it started wailing in that low, animal-like, pain-filled sound, she learned different.

Making a break for it, she ran as fast as she could for the shed. She ditched her slippers. There was little in her manicured lawn to hurt her and even with the fog-slicked grass, she could make better time barefoot here than in the flimsy slippers. They'd only trip her up.

She reached the little shed and yanked it open. There was a pitchfork and a heavy, old-fashioned, iron rake. The pitchfork was more deadly, but the rake was at least two feet longer. Since the tines of the pitchfork couldn't kill what was already dead, she went for the rake. It would keep her a little farther away from the creature if she had to engage it mano a mano.

She whirled to find the zombie had gained on her again. Quickly, she left the area of the shed. She didn't want to get pinned down against one of its sides. She'd briefly debated the idea of hiding inside, but the old shed wouldn't stand a chance against the creature's strength.

She faced the thing, her back to the false safety of her house, a heavy rake her only weapon. She kept backing up as the creature advanced. If she could get to the house, maybe she could get to a weapon. Preferably one loaded with toxic darts. It would be hard to do, but she had to try.

She waved the rake at the zombie, but it didn't slow. In fact, it seemed to speed up, moving in much closer than before.

"Kill . . ." it repeated like an undead mantra.

The almost subvocalization was creeping the hell out of her.

It came closer. She swung the rake, knocking it back a step. The next time she hit it—on the side of the head—it stood its ground and moved closer still. She wanted to run, but she was too close to the house now. She couldn't take her eyes off the monster. The back steps were near. Too near.

As the zombie advanced to within three feet, her foot hit the back step awkwardly. She went down hard, her ass hitting the steps as her feet went out from under her. She was trapped between the handrails that framed the stairs, the zombie crouching over her.

And then a dart lodged in his ruined face. Another bloomed in his shoulder and abdomen in quick succession. A fourth hit his right thigh and a fifth landed in his left leg for good measure.

Sarah crab-walked backward as fast as she could up the steps, out of range—but only just barely. Strong hands reached under her armpits to lift her to her feet.

"Xavier! Thank God!"

She wanted to turn and cling to him, but the zombie was still coming. They both knew from bitter experience it would take a minute or two for the toxin to take hold and during that time the creature could still do a hell of a lot of damage.

The steps led down from a tiny porch with a long safety rail. Xavier lifted her over the rail and let go as she jumped the few feet down into a small flowerbed. She saw the zombie hesitate before it backed down the steps and came after her. Xavier followed close on its heels. The object now was to stay away from the zombie long enough for the toxin to do its job.

"Stay in the open, Sarah. Don't let it box you in."

"Why does this thing want me so bad?" She was thinking out loud. The zombie hadn't gone after Xavier. It seemed to want her.

"Mas-ter say . . ." the zombie said, almost as if answering her question.

The very idea freaked her out. The creature could talk— nothing too grand, mind you—but it could say a few words. And now, apparently, it could answer questions as well.

Xavier picked up on it, too. He moved closer.

"What did master say?" he demanded.

The zombie turned to look at him, and she noted again the difference in this one's eyes. It seemed more aware than the previous ones.

"What did master say?" Xavier shouted again when the creature didn't answer right away.

Then the zombie smiled. "Kill . . ."

That was its last word. A second later, the creature dissolved into a pile of goo and old clothes, right there in her backyard. Sarah's weak knees almost gave out on her, but there was still one thing left unattended.

"Where's Sellars?" Xavier asked. They were both thinking on the same wavelength.

"In the trees. The zombie got him pretty bad."

Xavier followed where she led. She made a slight detour in her yard to retrieve her slippers, now thoroughly saturated from the fog and her movement through the grass and trees. They had a sole, though, that's what counted. It might be flimsy plastic, but it was better than her tender skin against the rough ground under the trees.

She saw that Xavier had his utility belt on. He wasn't wearing much else, but at least he'd taken the time to get his weapons and tools before he'd rushed to her rescue. That belt also held the serum.

"Are you going to try to save him?" she asked as she picked her way through the trees to where she'd left Sellars.

"Yeah. I have to try. We need to know who he was working with on this." He opened the case where the serum lay and took out what he'd need as he walked. "It might not work, but we have to give it a shot."

She understood, though she would've just as happily seen Sellars die. She wasn't bloodthirsty as a general rule, but this particular scumbag had caused all kinds of mayhem. He'd caused the deaths of so many innocent people. He'd terrorized her personally and changed her life for all time. The slime. He didn't deserve to live. But she understood why Xavier had to try to save him.

They found him cowering not far from where the zombie had left him. He was hurt badly.

Chapter Fifteen

"What are you doing? I'm as good as dead already." Sellars's eyes widened in fear and he reared back as Xavier knelt next to him.

"Maybe not." Xavier measured the dose expertly before he positioned the long needle and stuck Sellars through the chest, straight into his heart. Xavier depressed the plunger as Sellars screamed.

"Don't torture me. It's over," Sellars whined as Xavier pulled out the needle.

"There's a slim chance this stuff will save your life. One of your colleagues came up with it, but it only works if you have the right antigens in your blood already."

"McCormick! I knew that bitch was holding out on me. I thought she was playing hard to get."

"Impossible for you to get," Sarah muttered, her weapon trained on Sellars.

"It might not work." Xavier sat back and looked at Sellars. "If you have anything to say, now's your chance. You very well might not get another."

Sellars glared silently, clutching his extensive wounds. Then his eyes rolled back in his head and he went through a series of convulsions. When they ended, he leaned to the side and vomited into the grass. He didn't look the way Sam had. Sellars wasn't reacting as well to the antidote as Sam had. It wasn't going to work for him.

"Looks like you struck out, Sellars. The antidote isn't working," Xavier observed coolly. "It was a long shot from the beginning, but we had to try. So why did you do it? Why would you try to sell this kind of technology? Why would you even continue to pursue it?"

"Why else? For the money. You're a fool." Sellars spit on the ground and glared. "This isn't over. There's more—" He broke off as his body went into another round of convulsions, these much worse than the first. Judging by the way Sam had gotten better with each episode, Sellars's body was definitely rejecting the serum.

"More?" Xavier pushed him. They had one chance to get information out of Sellars. If he was going to talk, it had to be now.

"More of us," he eeked out, panting when he finally stopped seizing. "More working on this than you realize. They may have killed me but others will fill the void. Not as well, of course, but they'll try. And they'll succeed. And then you'll all die."

"That's crazy talk, pal." Xavier's tone was designed to annoy Sellars into saying more. He was clearly unstable and babbling, but they were learning a lot here. None of it was good, but they needed to know whatever Sellars would give up before he died. "I bet Zhao sent the zombie to get rid of you because you're nuts."

"Bin Zhao didn't send it. He doesn't have that kind of access. He's strictly the money man. I think it was Rodriguez. He's always been jealous of my genius." Sellars was frothing at the mouth now, his body twitching uncontrollably as he entered another round of seizures. He likely wouldn't survive this time.

"Names," Xavier demanded. "Give me names and I'll make sure you get your revenge from beyond the grave. I'll kill them all for you."

"Jenn . . . ings. Bal . . . es . . . tar . . . do. Sug . . . den . . . Ger . . . ar . . ." He trailed off before he could finish the last name, but it was enough. Xavier recognized some of the names from the list of doctors who had been on the original team. Gerardi was one of them. Some of the others were new names. Damn! He needed more information.

But it was already too late.

"I think he'd dead." Sarah's voice came to him from a few feet away.

Xavier sighed heavily and checked the body. "Yeah. He is."

"Why would the zombie attack him? I thought Sellars had these things under his control."

"It's not one of his."

"How do you know?"

"I got a look at him," Xavier sighed heavily, remembering the creature he'd had to end. "Did you notice the uniform? He was a soldier. My former commanding officer, Major Patrick Lafferty. He went missing after the last wave of attacks on base before Commander Sykes arrived and took over."

"How in the world did he get from North Carolina to New York in that state?"

"I have no idea. Could be that he was captured and brought here, then turned later. Or maybe he was infected at Fort Bragg and transported here by whoever sent him after Sellars. Either way, the implications aren't good." Xavier realized that the presence of the army major here raised even more questions.

"At least now you know what happened to him," Sarah offered quietly.

"He was a good man. A good soldier. And a good friend."

Sarah put a hand on his arm and he looked up to meet her sympathetic gaze. "He killed Sellars. In the end, no matter how it came about, he served his country and saved lives."

"You know, you're right." Xavier felt his spirits lift, though the sensation was bittersweet.

"He died a hero."

They called in the cavalry and watched over Sellars's body until help arrived. Sarah dashed into her house to throw on some clothes while Xavier waited, guarding the scene.

Upon reflection, Xavier realized they weren't sure what would happen to Sellars now that McCormick's serum had been administered and rejected. They needed to know if he'd rise like the others and turn into a zombie.

For that reason, he held off darting Sellars and turned his body over to the science team. They were equipped to destroy him should the worst happen. If he rose to terrorize anyone within biting distance, they'd take care of him. To avoid the possibility of his infecting anyone else, Xavier supervised while the science guys locked Sellars's remains in the rear of one of their reinforced vans. Xavier saw there was a wire mesh cage separating the front seating compartment from the rear, like in cop cars. If Sellars rose from the dead, they could dart him through the grate before he could hurt anyone.

"It's over." Commander Sykes had come out personally to see the scene of Sellars's demise.

"For now," Xavier agreed cautiously. "Sellars named names before he died. There are more people involved than we'd assumed."

Sykes's expression darkened. "We need to debrief. Can we use your house, Sarah?"

"No problem." She led the way around to the front of the house to avoid the crime scene techs working near her back door.

Xavier and Sarah closeted themselves with Sykes only after guards had been posted to assure complete privacy. When Sykes was ready with paper and pen—to take notes the old-fashioned way—Sarah began. She outlined the sequence of events, starting with Xavier getting bashed over the head. She skirted around what they'd been doing directly before, Xavier noted with an inward grin. Sykes didn't need to know, though Xavier would bet he could guess from the way Sarah blushed and stuttered until she'd gotten past that part.

Sykes listened, asking questions here and there as they laid out the timeline and series of hellish events they'd been through that night. Xavier didn't make any effort to hide how close he'd become to Sarah. He sat beside her and held her hand when she related some of the tougher parts of the action they'd just been in. Sykes didn't even raise an eyebrow, leading Xavier to believe Sykes was well aware of their growing relationship. Good, Xavier thought, it would come as no surprise when he wanted to keep her close.

"All right. The rest can wait until later. You both need some downtime." Sykes put away his pen, looking from Xavier to Sarah and back again. "Grab a few hours. We'll pick this up later, once I've had a chance to get these names to the people who can help track them down. I'm posting a security detail around the house—both visible and invisible. There will be one of the county patrol cars out front and a team of my men deployed around the perimeter. I intend to keep you both safe, although I believe the immediate danger is past, now that Sellars is gone."

"Roger that, Commander."

Xavier realized the rest break was likely more for Sykes's benefit than for theirs. He looked as if he'd been through the ringer trying to get back to New York as fast as possible. It was late for him, considering he'd been strictly on day shift since this whole operation started. He would no doubt ask better questions when his mind was sharp and able to assimilate their information. Xavier had a powerful need to hold his woman. He wanted to hug her tight and make promises he'd never expected to make in his life.

"Officer Petit, I've got your chief's agreement to keep you on our team a little while longer. In fact, I want you to start thinking about a career change. I've been authorized to offer you a job as a civilian contractor. We can talk more about this later, but I wanted to give you a heads-up so you can start considering it."

"Thank you, Commander." Sarah looked uncomfortable. "I'll definitely give it some thought."

"If it's any incentive, you'd be working with Xavier. You two make a good team and there are very few people who can operate safely around these creatures. We need you, Sarah. Your country needs you."

Sarah swallowed hard and nodded. "I'll consider it, Commander, and I'll be interested to hear more about the position next time I see you. For right now, you'll have to forgive me. I need to spend a little time figuring out where my career and my life are headed."

"I understand. Probably better than you think. My own career path went careening off the rails onto a whole new set of tracks when this problem first started. I still don't know exactly where it's going to lead." Sykes offered his hand and she took it, shaking affably. "You did good work tonight, Officer Petit. Thanks for your help."

Xavier went outside with Sykes, ostensibly to see him off. He also wanted to eyeball the team that would be watching the house and grounds. Xavier didn't recognize the men but knew with a certainty they were spec ops. Probably SEALs, considering Sykes was navy. Xavier got a glimpse of the team dressed all in black before they faded away into the shadows around the house. They had let themselves be seen on purpose, and the leader had nodded to Xavier before disappearing like a ninja.

"Damn showoff SEALs," Xavier muttered as he reentered the house, shutting and locking the door behind him. Sarah was waiting for him, a look of concern on her beautiful face.

"Something wrong?"

Xavier walked over to her and enfolded her in his arms. "Not a thing now, *chère*. I was just griping about the team Sykes has got watching your house. Navy spec ops. Looks like a whole SEAL team out there."

"Really?" She craned her neck to look out the front window.

"What? You like them navy boys better than us Green Berets? If so, we're going to have to have a long talk, sugar." He squeezed her as she grinned.

"Oh, I like Green Berets just fine. One in particular, as a matter of fact." She reached up and kissed him, just about knocking his socks off. But he had a question he wanted settled first. He drew back and set her away, heartened by the look of concern on her face.

"Sarah, you did such a great job on this mission. I failed you more than once, but you rallied from every setback. You're a good operative. Hell, you're better than good. You're a natural, and I don't say that lightly."

"Xavier, you never failed me," she started, interrupting his speech. But he made a gesture with his hands, asking without words for her to let him finish what he had to say. She subsided, taking a seat on the couch as he paced in front of it.

"I want you to consider Sykes's offer. I mean, really consider it. We could work together from now on. I'll teach you covert ops stuff and you can help me learn investigative techniques. I think we're a partnership made in heaven." He didn't state his intention to take care of them both until she got up to speed. He would really enjoy teaching her how to operate in his world, should she decide to take the job. "What do you think about working with me full time, Sarah?"

"I don't honestly know."

She looked a little lost, sitting alone on the big overstuffed couch. He could see he'd taken her by surprise, and she hadn't yet had time to assimilate all the changes in her life. He knew he was rushing her, but he needed to know. Everything hinged on her decision.

"I thought I'd live and die a county cop. But the idea of going federal is tempting, I'll admit."

Tempting, she'd said. He could work with that.

"Sarah." He sat on the couch, turning to face her. "This mission changed things for me, too. Meeting you . . . being with you . . . This has been like something out of a dream. Okay, sure, parts of it were pure nightmare, but the good parts—the parts where we were together—those were some of the best moments of my life."

Her gaze lit with something he prayed was hope.

"What I'm trying to say is that I don't want this to end. I want to be with you, Sarah. If you take the job with Sykes, you can make that a condition. That we stay together as a team. We've already proven we work well together. Sykes won't mess that up. He'll let us be a team and we can spend our time together, both on duty and off duty. Like we've been doing here. Only this would be long-term."

"How long-term?"

Her tone was challenging, but her eyes held a glimmer of joy that gave him hope.

"Forever, if we can manage it." He took her hand and slid off the couch, dropping to one knee in front of her. "Sarah, *mon ange*, will you marry me?"

"You want to marry me?" Disbelief warred with bubbling happiness in her tone.

"You know I love you, don't you?"

"You do?"

"I guess I'll have to work on my communication skills," Xavier joked as she launched herself into his arms. They tangled on the floor in front of the couch, both on their knees. "Sarah, I love you with all my heart."

They didn't make it to the bedroom until much later. After a session on the floor, where Xavier's knees got bruised up and Sarah suffered some minor rug burn that quickly healed, they finally collapsed together onto Sarah's bed.

"I can't believe we're going to get married."

The smile on her face lit his world.

"I'm relieved you agreed. Believe it or not, some women find me a little overbearing." He tried to look earnest. Teasing her was fast becoming one of his most enjoyable occupations.

"No." She overacted her mocking surprise. "You don't say."

"I'm afraid so." He leaned against the headboard, stretching his legs out in front of him as Sarah settled at his side. "But you're stuck with me now. You said yes and I'm never letting you out of it."

She looped one arm around his middle. "I'm not letting you out of it, either, Xavier. You're mine."

"I like the sound of that, sugar." He scooted downward on the bed, settling next to her as they turned toward each other. He cupped her cheek in his hand, his thoughts turning serious. "You should probably know that if you turn down Sykes's job offer, I'll do my best to find a way to stay by your side. You're still in danger as long as the bad guys know you're immune to the contagion. Sykes managed to keep the identities of all immune military personnel under wraps. There aren't many of us. But Sellars told his buddies about you. They could still come after you."

"I know," she said softly, her expression serious. "I've been trying not to think about it, but I've been aware of the possibility since I heard Sellars on the phone in that basement lab. Don't think I haven't factored that into my decision."

"So what is your decision? Have you reached it yet?"

He desperately wanted her to take Sykes's offer. It was the easiest way for him to remain close enough to protect her. He'd find another way if she truly didn't want to join the team, but if they were working together, it would solve a lot of difficulties. He wouldn't pressure her. It had to be her decision. It was, after all, her career they were playing with.

"I'm going to take the job." She held his gaze. "I know it's what you want me to do. It's also what I want to do. I've never been more challenged, more afraid and more alive than I've been these past days working with you and your team. I don't want that to end, Xavier. I want to work with you. I want to be with you. And I want to contribute. I can make a real difference on the team. I can help stop the spread of this contagion. I'm one of the few who can do it in relative safety. I can't waste that kind of opportunity."

"You are one hell of a woman, Sarah."

She blushed prettily as he swooped down for a lingering kiss.

She pushed at his shoulders until he rolled to his back, then she took control. She straddled his thighs, sitting up to smile at him.

"For the record, I think you're one hell of a man, Xavier." She ran her hands down his chest, loving the play of his muscles under her fingertips. "I don't know how I got so lucky."

He caught her hands and laced his fingers with hers. "How *we* got so lucky," he corrected her gently. "In all this mess, somehow we managed to find each other. Somebody up there is definitely looking out for us. What are the odds that we'd both survive being bitten by zombies, only to work together and fall in love?"

"Astronomical." She bent over him, resting her head against his chest. "You know, if Sellars had succeeded, we'd be like Adam and Eve."

"Come again?" His hands stilled.

"He started talking crazy about how he didn't care if the people he sold the technology to wiped out everyone on the planet. He thought it would be good to start over with only a handful of immune people to recreate the human race." Remembering Sellars and how he'd held her prisoner while he told her those things made her feel weak. Xavier's presence gave her strength and helped her come to terms with the horrors of the past days. "We'd be one of those couples he talked about. Both immune. Survivors of a plague that could destroy humanity as we know it."

"It's not going to happen, *mon amour*. We'll see to it." He withdrew his fingers from hers and wrapped one arm around her back, the other cupping the top of her head as she pressed into his chest.

It felt so good, so protective. With Xavier holding her, nothing bad could possibly happen. Even if such thinking was only a pipe dream, it felt real at the moment. He comforted her by his mere presence.

"That, more than anything, is why I'm taking the job Sykes offered. I want to prevent that twisted vision of the future from having even the faintest hope of coming true." She clutched at his shoulders, seeking his strength. "As long as the people Sellars was working with are out there, the threat of this technology spreading remains viable. We may have taken care of one lunatic today, but there are at least a few more out there, willing to wipe out millions of people for their own profit."

"You forget, sweetheart, there's more than just us on this team. There are others like us and still others working on the technology and intelligence angles. Working together, we'll stop the crazies. I promise you. It may take a while, but we'll get them all." He raised her chin and placed a gentle kiss of promise on her lips. When he drew away, she smiled at him.

"Let's help each other forget all our troubles for a little while. What do you say?"

"What do you have in mind, *mon ange*? You know I'm game for almost anything." He gave her his most devilish smile.

"Nothing too dramatic." She sat up again, straddling him as she worked her way down his hard body. "A long, slow lovemaking session might be just the ticket. I know you're always game for that. You Cajun boys don't ever seem to turn down a little lovin'."

"A man would be a fool to turn down a gorgeous little sex kitten like you, Sarah." His eyelids stood at half mast, making his every word ooze with sex appeal.

The look he gave her as she touched him could have set fire to ice and sent her pulses skyrocketing.

"Sex kitten?" She pretended to consider the phrase. "Nobody's ever called me that before. I think I like it." She purred in the back of her throat as she leaned in to lick the length of his hardening cock.

He made a growling sound as she met his eyes. "Do that again, sugar."

She complied, loving the way he responded. He let her have her way for a good long while, and she enjoyed learning his body and how to make him quiver and moan. He was a solidly built behemoth of a man compared with her smaller frame. Having him at her mercy was a novel and extremely sensual experience.

"Do you like this?" she experimented, massaging his sac gently as she took him in her mouth. His groan of pleasure was her reward.

"Too much, *chère*." He lifted her by the shoulders, bringing her mouth to meet his.

His kiss turned her upside down and inside out. Or maybe it felt that way because he was lifting and turning her as he drugged her senses with his long, slow, deep kisses. When she opened her eyes and he ended the kiss, she was on her back with him over her.

"Turnabout is fair play, or so they say, n'est-ce pas?"

"*Mmm*. You can turn me about any time, Captain." She reached up to tangle one hand in the short hairs at the nape of his neck. Her other hand went south, searching for the object of her desire. He was thick and long. Hard and ready. She didn't want to wait.

"I'll take you up on that, Officer." Xavier licked his way down her body, starting at the hollow behind her ear, down over her throat, and then pausing for a good long while at her breasts. She loved the way he touched her, teasing her with gentle pinches while his mouth did wild things to excite her response.

He nipped her gently, causing a moan to rise from her throat. Then he followed up with tender, nibbling kisses over the sensitized skin, soothing and enflaming at the same time. He was a master at bringing her to the point of oblivion, then backing away to let her slide slowly down the slope. He did it to her three times before she growled in frustration. He only laughed.

"Anticipation makes the final moment better, *mon amour*. Don't be greedy. I'll give you all you can take and then some." He punctuated each sentence with a gently biting kiss over her midsection, nibbling on the sides of her breasts and her quivering tummy. "We do this on my terms, love. My terms." A harder bite to her nipple made her moan in ecstasy as he pinched the other peak between his talented fingers. "Who's in charge here, Sarah?" He drew on her breast with a long, sucking motion. The engorged nipple popped out of his mouth with a nearly audible sound.

"You are," she whispered.

"What did you say? I didn't hear you." The fingers of one hand roved downward to toy in the folds of her sex. He rubbed her clit, driving her need higher.

"You are." She managed to say it louder this time, though she was gasping with near desperation.

"Louder." His voice purred over her senses, a sensual rumble in the haze of her growing desire.

"You are, Xavier!" she cried out as she bucked against him, her climax washing over her in a tidal wave of pleasure.

He held her down, his big body pinning her to the bed as she rode the wave to its conclusion and began to drift. But he wouldn't let her go far. He reeled her back in, moving those talented fingers lower, to slide within her sheath.

She gasped at the new sensation. Xavier moved, seating himself between her splayed thighs. He had an unobstructed view of her most intimate places, but she didn't care. He was the master of her pleasure, the man who knew her like no other—body, heart and soul.

"Now for the turnabout," he muttered, sliding downward until his mouth was level with her pussy. He licked out, touching her clit briefly as his fingers began to move within her. "You like that, kitten?"

"Oh, yeah," she moaned as he did it again. A quick little lick that set her senses reeling.

"I can see you do. Probably as much as I liked you licking me."

Realization dawned. That's what he meant by "turnabout" this time. Given her scattered wits, she'd been a little slow to realize what he was getting at. The man had a powerful effect on her. It was hard to think straight when he made love to her. And she loved the way he gave as good as he got each and every time.

"I see you figured out my game." Satisfaction lit his handsome face. "What do you think of my tactics?"

"Very clever, Captain." She reached downward to stroke his cheek as he hovered over her midsection. "I never thought I could love anyone as much as I love you." The words slipped out before she could censor the sappy thought. She wasn't normally given to such outbursts, but Xavier had changed all the rules where her heart was concerned.

To her relief, he grinned. "I couldn't agree more, *mon ange*. Now let me show you just how much I love you."

He pinned her in place with his gaze as he took his place between her thighs. He pushed inward, making them one as her breath sighed out on a soft moan. He felt so good. She'd never tire of the sensations he brought her.

He increased his pace as he held her gaze and she saw the love in his eyes. She knew it was reflected in her own. She'd never felt so connected to another person—physically, emotionally, even spiritually. She'd faced death with this man at her side. She'd found the courage to face the future with him as well. And he with her.

"I love you, Xavier," she whispered as he brought her higher. The passion seemed to flare between them as he moved more urgently within her.

"You and me, babe," he whispered as he lowered his chest over hers, surrounding her completely with his presence. He was close now to the climax that chased her as well.

She wanted to come with him, completing the circle between them.

"Say you're mine, Sarah. I'll never tire of hearing it."

His mouth rubbed over her cheek and neck in a hot slide that made her insides quiver as he brought her higher.

"I'm yours," she readily admitted. She felt the truth of those words in her heart and her soul. "And you're mine."

He pulled back slightly to meet her gaze. A slow grin spread across his face as they both approached the peak at the same time.

"I'm yours, *chère*," he breathed as his muscles tightened in preparation for ecstasy. "Now and forever."

His words, spoken like a vow, triggered the maelstrom between them. She cried out, her jaw working in tight spasms as her abdomen clenched and her core tightened around him, gripping him as he pushed her to the stars.

She felt his body seize under her palms as his muscles tightened and his cock pressed deep inside, holding there as he emptied his tribute into her greedy body. She wanted everything he had to offer. Everything he was. She'd take it all and give back everything she had inside her. Everything they could be together. For him. All for him.

She'd never felt more complete or more fulfilled, both as a woman and as a person, than when she was with him. They shared a perfect moment of shared bliss that was over all too soon. He held her in the aftermath, cuddling her close and placing soft kisses on her face and hair.

"I love you more than life, *chère*." His rough whisper filled her heart to overflowing.

"Me, too, Xavier. You're the best thing that ever happened to me."

He chuckled. "Right after the worst thing that ever happened to you, right? If you hadn't been attacked by zombies, we never would have met."

"I can't bring myself to do it, but in a weird way, I have to thank those mad scientists for bringing us together." She stroked his arm, loving the play of his hard muscles under her fingers.

"Fate brought us together, *mon amour*. I believe in destiny. You and me? We were meant to be."

Epilogue

In the bowels of the Pentagon, a very secret meeting took place. Matt Sykes was the guest of honor, so to speak. He was slated to give a report on the recent action on Long Island and the status of the other issues at hand. The directors of the CDC, the NIH and the CIA were on hand. The CIA man was attending for the first time, now that the foreign-espionage aspect of the case was becoming a reality. Also present were Matt's current, select chain of command all the way up the ladder.

He'd had a private meeting with the CIA director the day before, to bring the man up to speed on the zombie problem. Reacting at first with scoffing disbelief, the director had been convinced by the time Matt had left his office. The director looked grim now as he sat next to the military brass listening to Matt's report.

"The situation on Long Island appears to be contained. There were approximately forty-seven civilian casualties. We also gained a highly skilled immune operative in Sarah Petit. She's agreed to come onboard with our mission as a civilian contractor. One of the Green Berets was also exposed and lived to tell the tale. Lt. Sam Archer will make a full recovery and shows all the signs of being immune despite the way he was infected and treated. Dr. McCormick has agreed to come back to work for the navy, devoting her time to a two-fold project. First, we want her to work on the toxin we use in the darts. It isn't as effective against the new version of the contagion. Second, she will continue her work on the serum. It worked on Lt. Archer but had no effect on Dr. Sellars. We believe, given time and resources, Dr. McCormick may be able to improve her results."

At this point, the medical guys had a few questions, which Matt answered to the best of his ability. They wanted to know where McCormick would be working. Matt sensed a bit of a turf war developing. He was able to counter it by saying the navy had reinstated McCormick's contract and she would be working directly for them. The civilian medical guys didn't seem too happy, but they'd have to deal with it. McCormick had a preexisting obligation to finish the work she'd signed on to do for the navy. Until this situation was resolved, she'd be kept under wraps by Uncle Sam.

"We also have one other new development. A girl by the name of Donna Sullivan was exposed and proved naturally immune." At this point, Matt distributed the girl's short dossier. "She's a senior at the university, scheduled to graduate at the end of the month with a degree in chemical engineering."

"How was she exposed?" asked the CDC man.

"Her boyfriend was part of the football team that was infected by Sellars and sent after our operatives. They used the girl as a distraction in order to separate Officer Petit from Captain Beauvoir. The ruse worked and Officer Petit was abducted from the scene, and later recovered by Captain Beauvoir. The girl was still alive when Captain Beauvoir left her to go after Officer Petit. She survived and checked herself into the university clinic the next day, where we picked her up before she could start spreading tales about her boyfriend becoming a zombie."

"What do you propose to do with her?" The CDC director seemed disturbed by the story. "She doesn't appear to have the skills necessary to combat these creatures. What is she, twenty-one or twenty-two?"

"Just turned twenty-five, actually. She was in a master's

program," Matt explained calmly. "She's older than many of the young soldiers we sent to die fighting the creatures before we knew better." The medical man looked duly chastised. "She's agreed to keep silent about her boyfriend and what happened to him and his friends, but I would prefer to bring her into the program and give her a chance to work with us to solve this problem. She's seen what the contagion does firsthand. She's lost someone to it and nearly lost her own life in the process. I believe she could be an asset, though I'll be honest and say I'm not sure where a shiny-new chemical engineer will fit in our operation."

"Her science background could be an asset," the CIA director said. "We could offer her a post at Langley. Since being brought up to speed on this yesterday, I've been considering who to utilize. I have a man I plan to assign to follow the money trail and he could probably use someone with a scientific background. It would also keep her out of the line of fire while she learns how to operate in the real world. My man could take her on as an apprentice of sorts. It's not our usual way, of course, but nothing about this situation is normal."

"After what happened with the original science team, I'd rather keep this information away from anyone else with the expertise to produce the contagion," the CDC director said. "Donna Sullivan is a chemical engineer. While she is familiar with the concepts, I doubt she currently has the skill to recreate or improve upon the research. She's a good choice to work with the CIA operative." He backtracked. "Not that I don't have confidence in your people, but too many people know about this already. We need to limit spread of this knowledge as much as possible. Since the girl already knows, it makes sense to utilize her."

"Agreed." The CIA man gave the other director a steely look. "Which is why I'm assigning John Petit to this case. He's been in from the field for a few weeks after completing a mission, and I wanted to send him home for some R&R between jobs, but he's too smart not to realize something's going on with his sister. Utilizing him for this makes sense."

Matt Sykes inwardly beamed. The CIA director had given him what he wanted without even realizing it. Matt had grown to like Sarah Petit and knew she and Xavier were an item. Bringing her brother in on this just made sense. Matt was glad to see the CIA director was proving to be sensible.

"If I might make a suggestion?" the NIH director spoke up. "It occurs to me that since Sarah Petit is immune, chances are that her brother might have the right kind of chemistry as well. Someone should run tests on his blood and make comparisons with his sister. This kind of study could help us nail down what makes one person immune and another not."

Matt made a note of it. "I'll have Dr. McCormick do the testing, if that's agreeable." Nods all around confirmed the plan.

Matt was pleased, they'd brought in someone who they probably wouldn't have been able to keep out of it anyway and paired him with Donna. That girl had been traumatized by the death of her boyfriend and his attack on her. She needed a desk job for now, but she also needed to know that she was doing something to avenge her boyfriend's senseless death.

He had interviewed the girl at length. She was young but she was a fighter. She had a desire for justice they could build upon, and good technical skills. He'd talked to her faculty advisor and discovered she was in the top ten percent of her class in a university that turned out some of the best engineers in the state. She could definitely be an asset if cultivated correctly. Matt didn't know Sarah's brother personally, but if Sarah was anything to go by, he'd be hell on wheels.

Just what the doctor ordered.

"Our objective, as I see it, is two-fold," said one of the military brass gathered around the conference table. "First, we need to deal with the immediate threats as we find them. Long Island has been taken care of, but we still need to deal with Fort Bragg. Commander Sykes, the field operations are your bailiwick. That encompasses the science and investigative teams working on antidotes and cures. Second, we need to stop the potential sale of this technology. That'll be in the hands of the CIA, if you're agreeable, Director."

The CIA man nodded. His expression was grave. "John Petit will be our man for that. I'm going to give him full authority to utilize our systems and intelligence on this problem. I assume you'll do the same?"

Again there was general agreement all around the table, but the chairman of the Joint Chiefs held out.

"I think we should meet the man," he said cautiously. "Can you get him here to meet with us?"

The CIA director grinned like a Cheshire cat. "He's waiting outside. Shall I invite him in?" Various expressions of shock and amusement met the old man's knowing grin.

About ten minutes later there was a discrete knock on the conference room door.

John Petit had a lot in common with his sister as far as coloring, but he was easily twice her size and had the hardened look of a field operative. His eyes were cold and calculating, his stance wary but comfortable. This was a man to be reckoned with. He walked in and took a quick look around the room. Not by even a flicker of an eyelash did he betray any sort of reaction at seeing such a large number of top people gathered in one place. He simply nodded to the director of his own agency.

"Mr. Petit, we have a job for you."

Things are getting dangerous in TAMING THE MOON, the
latest from Sherrill Quinn, out now from Brava!

"Look at me." She raised heavy lids and stared into dark eyes glinting with the knowledge that she'd gotten the message. He dropped his hand and strutted away from her, confident that she'd stay put.

She watched him, loathing him with each shaky breath she drew. When the bastard had moved in next door, fate had dealt her a dead man's hand. He'd seen her, had wanted her, so he'd taken her, turning her into a monster. Six weeks ago he'd told her he had a special job for her, a job that could elevate her from Omega to something . . . well, something more than the bottom of the pack.

She'd perked up, as he'd known she would. But when he'd told her the job was to murder someone, she'd refused. She was a middle school phys ed teacher, for crying out loud. Not an assassin.

But then he'd taken Zoe, threatened to kill her if Olivia didn't do as she was told. She'd seen him act with swift ruthlessness where disobedience and defiance were concerned. Just a few months ago he'd broken the neck of another pack member's son as casually as if he were flicking lint off his sleeve. So she had no doubt that, even though he might love Zoe in his own twisted way, he *would* carry through on the threat. So this time when he'd told her to go, she'd gone. Thankfully she had enough tenure and foresight to ask for a leave of absence from work.

Eddy turned to face her. "Go kill Sullivan. You have one week."

She opened her mouth then closed it. He'd not given her permission to speak yet.

A slight smile tilted one edge of his mouth. "Very good, pet." He gave an approving nod. "You may respond."

"A week?"

He lifted his brows. "I've given you six weeks already, two of which you squandered by being stubborn. I hardly think you need more than another week."

She clamped her lips together and gave an abrupt nod. Arguing with him would accomplish nothing except to have him shorten the deadline even further.

He sighed and shoved his hands into the pockets of his trousers. "I'm not such a bad guy, Livvie." He shrugged. "I just know what I want, and I'm willing to do whatever it takes to get it—and that includes killing everyone who gets in my way. Some women find that kind of confidence appealing. Attractive, even."

What kind of women? The ones with a death wish?

She licked her lips. "May I ask what it is you want? Why is it so important that Rory Sullivan be killed? What did he do to you?"

Olivia thought for a moment he wasn't going to answer her, feared that she may have gone too far when his face darkened. But it was remembered rage that colored his features, not anger directed toward her.

"Let's just say there's a man I want to destroy, and I'm beginning by removing everyone who's important to him. Starting with his friends." His lips parted in a grin. "I hear he's fallen in love, so very soon I'll be ready to take that away from him, too. Although"—he tapped his chin—"if she's fetching enough, I may have to use her before I kill her."

"*You'll* kill her?" The words left her mouth before she

could stop them. She bit her lip, preparing to be smacked because of the incredulity in her tone.

The smile faded from his face, and his eyes narrowed, though he didn't lift his hand to her. "Yes. The male friends are peripheral, not enough for me to bother with personally. But a wife?" The grin returned, this time so full of malicious glee it wrapped ice around her gut. "To watch his face, the agony in his eyes as I fuck her and then kill her, with him powerless to stop me?" He nodded. "That is something I must do myself."

Well, if he was going to use Olivia to do some of the dirty work, she damn well deserved to know why. "Who is this man? Why do you hate him so much?"

Eddy turned away from her. "Merr . . ." He broke off and shook his head. "He had everything—a loving family, wealth, power, and the poor sod couldn't stand that he wasn't normal." With his heightened emotions, Eddy's New York accent slipped a bit and took on a British flavor. He shook his head again. "It should have all been mine. If his father had just done what I'd asked—*begged!*—things might have been different."

He trailed off, seeming to be lost in his thoughts. After a moment he shrugged. "Never mind. It's not something you need to know." He glanced over his shoulder at her, eyes hard. "All you need to know is that for your daughter to remain safe you have a job to do."

Eyeing the distance between them, Olivia wondered if she could catch him off guard long enough to kill him. She could morph her fingers into claws now, just like he did. She might be able to do it.

It would only take one quick slash across the throat.

But then what about Zoe? There was at least one bodyguard standing outside her door, his bulk casting a shadow onto the floor of the hallway.

Olivia briefly closed her eyes. She'd never be able to do it. She couldn't kill Eddy and go for the bodyguard before he could get to Zoe.

She had no other choice. She must finish the job she'd been given.

Thinking back over the last few days, she remembered her first impression of Rory Sullivan. Tall, dark and dangerous.

An earnest protector.

Sexy as hell. But . . .

He had to die.

And don't miss LEAVE ME BREATHLESS, the latest from HelenKay Dimon, in stores now . . .

"You call that a clinch?"

Whatever it was it made Callie's head explode. "Sure."

"Tell me something."

No way was she agreeing to that without more information. Hand this man an opening and he'd steer a submarine through it.

He kept talking anyway. Looked pretty relaxed in his slouch as his smile inched up on his lips. "Do you have a boyfriend?"

If he wanted to shock her . . . well, he did. "How is that relevant?"

"Call me curious."

"Are you allowed to ask me about that?"

"You think there's a law against it?"

"There should be."

"So, you're not going to answer?"

Not until she knew where this was going. "What does the state of my love life have to do with anything?"

"You know all about me. Only seems fair I get some background on you."

"I need to know about your life in order to do my job." At least that was the excuse she used when she ventured outside the file Mark gave her. She'd lost her clearance when she walked away from her job at the FBI, but she still had friends of the

304 / HelenKay Dimon

computer-hacker variety. In just a few hours she had all the paperwork that existed on Ben.

She had to admit her little search mission turned out to be a huge disappointment. His background was so clean it squeaked. If he hadn't passed through screening committees and all sorts of interviews to get his current judicial position she would have thought someone manufactured his past. No arrests. No trouble. Great grades. Always within the law. For some reason she expected to find a smart guy with a bad boy past. That sounded good in the fantasy she created in her head but looked as if it wasn't true.

"So, you're not poking around in my life just because you're nosy?" he asked.

No way could he know about her travels through his personal history. She'd been careful and cleaned up behind her. "I don't poke."

"Tell me what you want to know."

She smelled a con. "Anything?"

"You get one question."

She thought about his decision to leave the military and about the scarce information on his parents. She skipped all that and went with the issue at the front of her mind. "What's going on between you and Emma?"

"I've already answered that. We're friends."

Callie snorted just to let him know what she thought of his fake deals. "I don't climb all over my friends when the door shuts."

"Really? When do you climb on them then?"

"Huh?"

He closed in. One minute he shot her a lazy smile. The next he stood up straight and hovered over her with his cheek right next to hers. "What do you do with your friends?"

Heat thrummed off him, surrounding her and filling her with a tingly sensation from shoulders to toes. "I don't—"

"Do you touch them?" Ben trailed the back of his hand down her cheek. Dragged his thumb across her lips.

"I . . ."

"Smell them?" He leaned down and nuzzled her ear. "Do they smell as good as you?"

His mouth traveled down her neck, nipping and kissing. Hot breath tickled her skin as his fingers caressed her waist. The double whammy of touching slammed her breath to a halt in her chest. Her body strained to get closer to him as her palms skimmed up his back.

Holy crap. "This isn't a good idea," she said.

"Probably not but I've been wanting to do it all day."

"I thought you were mad at me."

"Be quiet for a second."

Then his mouth covered hers. His lips pressed deep and strong and his tongue brushed against hers. There was nothing teasing about this kiss. It shot through her hot and wet, electrifying every cell inside her. She fell into the sensation of being overpowered and claimed. Her stomach tumbled and her knees dipped. Muscles relaxed as her brain shifted into neutral.

"God, yes," he mumbled when their mouths lifted on gasps of harsh breaths.

He dove back in. His lips met hers over and over again in a kiss that had her winding her arms around his neck and pulling him close.

Him. Her. Touching. Nothing else mattered. Pleasure crashed over her, drowning out everything around them. Fingers searched and sculpted. Her hands swept into his hair while his pushed against her lower back, easing her closer to the juncture between his thighs. She heard the grumbling moan in his chest and the deep breaths from her own.

She lifted her head in an attempt to get some air. "Ben . . . that . . ."

"You taste so good."

His mouth found that sensitive spot right at the slope of her chin. Her kryptonite. A few nibbling kisses and she wanted to strip that conservative shirt and tie right off him.

She dropped her head back to give him greater access. "Right there."

When his mouth found hers again, lights exploded in her

brain. He kissed like he worked, with an intensity that sent her common sense screaming in wild defeat. The touch of his lips was all she dreamed about and everything she feared.

But her mind shouted out a red light warning through the sensual haze. She had a job and he had a girlfriend.

Callie pulled her mouth away, letting her forehead rest against his cheek as she struggled to breathe without wheezing. "We have to stop."

"God, why?" He mumbled the question against her hair.

"Emma." Callie now hated that name.

With the gentle touch of his palms, he lifted her head and stared down at her. The gaze from deep brown eyes searched her face. The rapid beating in his chest thumped against her as his eyes grew soft.

"I don't cheat," he said in a husky whisper. "If I were with Emma I wouldn't be kissing you."

Callie knew she should pull back, but she rubbed her hands up his back instead. "But, I saw—"

"Evidence of a lifelong friendship." He traced her cheekbones with his thumbs. "That's it."

"You're not—"

"No."

"Does Emma know that?"

His chuckle vibrated against her from everywhere their bodies touched. "Definitely."

Relief washed through Callie. She balanced her head on his chin as she tried to figure out what it all meant. "Now what?"

"You invite me to your house."

Here's a sneak peek at Jill Shalvis's INSTANT TEMPTATION, coming next month!

"I didn't invite you in, T.J."

He just smiled.

He was built as solid as the mountains that had shaped his life, and frankly had the attitude to go with it, the one that said he could take on whoever and whatever, and you could kiss his perfect ass while he did so. She'd seen him do it too, back in his hell-raising, misspent youth.

Not that she was going there, to the time when he could have given her a single look and she'd have melted into a puddle at his feet.

Had melted into a puddle at his feet. Not going there . . .

Unfortunately for Harley's senses, he smelled like the wild Sierras; pine and fresh air, and something even better, something so innately male that her nose twitched for more, seeking out the heat and raw male energy that surrounded him and always had. Since it made her want to lean into him, she shoved in another bite of ice cream instead.

He smiled. "I saw on Oprah once that women use ice cream as a substitute for sex."

She choked again, and he resumed gliding his big, warm hand up and down her back. "You watch Oprah?"

"No. Annie was, and I overheard her yelling at the TV that women should have plenty of both sex *and* ice cream."

That sounded exactly like his Aunt Annie. "Well, I don't need the substitute."

"No?" he murmured, looking amused at her again.

"No!"

He hadn't taken his hands off her, she couldn't help but notice. He still had one rubbing up and down her back, the other low on her belly, holding her upright, which was ridiculous, so she smacked it away, doing her best to ignore the fluttering he'd caused and the odd need she had to grab him by the shirt, haul him close and have her merry way with him.

This was what happened to a woman whose last orgasm had come from a battery operated device instead of a man, a fact she'd admit, oh *never*. "I was expecting your brother."

"Stone's working on Emma's 'honey do' list at the new medical clinic, so he sent me instead. Said to give you these." He pulled some maps from his back pocket, maps she needed for a field expedition for her research. When she took them out of his hands, he hooked his thumbs in the front pockets of his Levi's. He wore a T-shirt layered with an opened button-down that said *Wilder Adventures* on the pec. His jeans were faded nearly white in the stress spots, of which there were many, nicely encasing his long, powerful legs and lovingly cupping a rather impressive package that was emphasized by the way his fingers dangled on his thighs.

Not that she was looking.

Okay, she was looking, but she couldn't help it. The man oozed sexuality. Apparently some men were issued a handbook at birth on how to make a woman stupid with lust. And he'd had a lot of practice over the years.

She'd watched him do it.

Each of the three Wilder brothers had barely survived their youth, thanks in part to no mom and a mean, son-of-a-bitch father. But by some miracle, the three of them had come out of it alive and now channeled their energy into Wilder Adventures, where they guided clients on just about any outdoor adventure that could be imagined; heli-skiing, extreme mountain biking, kayaking, climbing, *anything*.

Though T.J. had matured and found success, he still gave off a don't-mess-with-me vibe. Even now, at four in the afternoon, he looked big and bad and tousled enough that he might have just gotten out of bed and wouldn't be averse to going back.

It irritated her. It confused her. And it turned her on, a fact that drove her bat-shit crazy because she was no longer interested in T.J. Wilder.

Nope.

It'd be suicide to still be interested. No one could sustain a crush for fifteen years.

No one.

Except, apparently, her. Because deep down, the unsettling truth was that if he so much as directed one of his sleepy, sexy looks her way, her clothes would fall right off.

Again.

And wasn't that just her problem, the fact that once upon a time, a very long time ago, at the tail end of T.J.'s out-of-control youth, the two of them had spent a single night together being just about as intimate as a man and woman could get. Her first night with a guy. Definiitely not his first. Neither of them had been exactly legal at the time, and only she'd been sober.

Which meant only she remembered.